Seeds of Murder

Seeds of Murder

Rosie Sandler

First published in Great Britain in 2023 by

Bonnier Books UK Limited
4th Floor, Victoria House, Bloomsbury Square, London, WC1B 4DA
Owned by Bonnier Books
Sveavägen 56, Stockholm, Sweden

A CIP catalogue record for this book is available from the British Library.

ISBN: 9781471415722

This book is typeset using Atomik ePublisher

Embla Books is an imprint of Bonnier Books UK
www.bonnierbooks.co.uk

For my mother, Maureen: with love and thanks for all your support

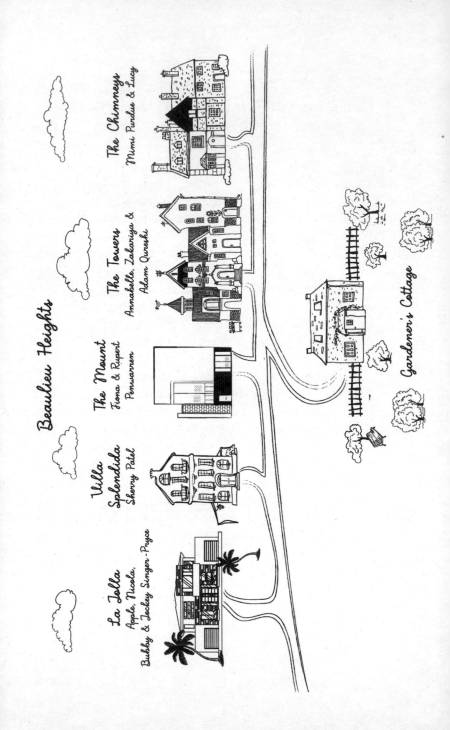

Beaulieu Heights

La Jolla
Apple, Nicola,
Bubby & Jacksy Singer-Pryce

Villa
Splendida
Sherry Patel

The Mount
Fiona & Rupert
Penwarren

The Towers
Annabelle, Zakariya &
Adam Qureshi

The Chimneys
Mimi Purdue & Lucy

Gardener's Cottage

Prologue

It is cold in the paddock. The two Shetland ponies have taken shelter in their shed. The small and expensively dressed group of mourners huddles together against the wind as the coffin is lowered into the grave. One of the group, a woman, is sobbing hard. Now and then, she looks towards a man who is standing slightly apart, his face closed and inscrutable. He has his arm around a girl of about ten, who stares at the coffin with big eyes. When the priest finishes the service, the man takes the girl by her gloved hand and they walk quickly away, across the rough grass towards the far gate.

The woman collapses to the ground, sobs racking her body and a wail wrenched from her throat. The others look on, their faces a tight mix of sympathy and distaste. Then a small woman in high heels steps out from among them, approaches the wailing woman and crouches down to pull her into her arms, her heels sinking deep into the earth. The onlookers shift, uncomfortable voyeurs, then reach a silent consensus: they pick their way back through the field, stumbling in the rabbit-pocked earth, grateful to leave the raw scene behind them.

The two women remain in the paddock until the keening finally eases and the friend supports the bereft woman for the short walk home.

1

Mouse is whining quietly on the passenger seat. He likes to go for drives, but this has been a lengthy one, with only a couple of stops for him to exercise his long legs. A large black dog, he is quite shaggy – and very opinionated.

'It's OK, boy,' I tell him. 'We're there; you can get out soon.'

I swing the van off the main road and on to the private lane, slowing my speed to obey the fifteen-miles-per-hour signs. I whistle under my breath at the smoothness of the tarmac beneath my old vehicle's wheels. There are immaculately trimmed standard bays in planters all the way along the lane, and at the end, there's a pair of those giant gates they have only on really exclusive housing developments. These bear a sign, BEAULIEU HEIGHTS. I was surprised to hear during my online interview that this is pronounced 'Bewley' rather than 'Bowlyer' – more East London than French Riviera. There's a buzzer to press for access. A man's voice issues tinnily from the speaker, asking for my name.

I lean out of the van window, 'Steph Williams.'

There's a pause, then the voice says, 'And whom are you visiting, ma'am?'

I like being addressed as *ma'am*. 'I'm the new gardener,' I say.

There's a satisfying buzz as the gates swing open – and I'm through.

I nearly swerve, staring at the houses as I drive. They're all arranged part-way up a steep slope to my left, to maximise views out to the right, where the land falls away to woodland and farmland, before London raises its metropolitan head.

The first dwelling is so out of place in Old Blighty, I laugh. It's a concrete-and-glass, California-style arrangement – all whitewash and palm trees. The sign on the gate reads: LA JOLLA.

Mouse raises himself to see what's amused me. He's in time to see the next place, which comes into view within another minute or so. It is a pink stucco affair: VILLA SPLENDIDA. 'More like a birthday cake than a house, eh, boy?' I say, and he makes the rumbling sound in his throat that I like to take for agreement.

The van, Mouse and I keep going, and the houses don't stop delivering. From a gleaming, four-storey rectangle that looks like it's built from granite (THE MOUNT) to a building that resembles a miniature castle, complete with crenelations (THE TOWERS), they scream *Money lives here!*

I have been told that there are only five of these big houses, but they take up as much land as a small village. I reckon I drive a quarter of a mile from the start to the end, where I park my van in front of a small one-storey lodge on the right, as per my issued instructions. It has a sign, GARDENER'S COTTAGE, and with its irregular stone walls, blue-painted front door and climbing roses, it's quaint and charming. And, compared to some of the places I've stayed recently, it's a palace.

'Well, we're here, Mouse. What do you think?' He turns a doleful face towards me. I jump down and go round to let him out. But when I open his door, he stays put.

'It's OK, boy. This is our new home.'

Mouse stares straight ahead, as if he's waiting for me to chauffeur him to somewhere more to his liking.

'Suit yourself, but I need to start unpacking.' I leave his door open and walk over to the house. The key's been left in the front door as promised.

I'm reaching in to take the third box from the van when Mouse starts barking and a smallish, stocky woman of around fifty appears. She's dressed in pristine blue jeans with a checked shirt tucked into them, and a thigh-length Barbour jacket; her prematurely white hair is cropped short, giving her a no-nonsense appearance. I recognise her as Mimi Purdue, the chair of the residents' committee, who interviewed me for the job. In person, she bears more than a passing resemblance to my strict English teacher from school, and I have to swallow back the urge to say, 'Good morning, Miss Turner.'

'Hello, Steph,' says Ms Purdue. 'Welcome to Beaulieu Heights.'

I perch the box on the tailgate and hold out a hand. It's only then

I realise how grimy my palms are, from the dust and dirt in the van. I snatch my hand back before she can touch it. 'Sorry! I'm filthy,' I tell her.

'Well, no one expects a gardener to have clean hands, do they?' she says, with a smile. 'As you know, I'm Mimi Purdue. I live at The Chimneys – the end house you see there.' She points to a rooftop dotted with chimneys, a little way along from the cottage and just visible above a line of trees. It's the last house in the road.

'Ms Purdue – thank you for hiring me,' I say.

'Well, as you know, I'm only the chair of the residents' committee. We sifted through the applications together.' She looks me in the eye. It's a direct appraisal, and I stand my ground: I'm not easily intimidated. 'It's nice to get a woman gardener,' she says at last. 'I think you said early thirties when we spoke?'

I nod, 'Thirty-one.'

'So . . . according to all this new-fangled liberal nonsense, I'm not allowed to ask if you're going to start a family and leave us in the lurch, am I?'

I smile politely. 'No, you're not.' There's an awkward pause, which I break: 'I remember you said I could call in support staff as and when. Looking at the scale of the grounds, I'm sure I will need some back-up.'

She nods. 'Just give us notice before you call anyone in – the committee will need to approve any expenditure. A day should be enough. Of course, as I said at your video interview, you won't have to maintain everything – there are tennis courts, a swimming pool, various paddocks, which you won't need to trouble yourself with. The ponies are in the top paddock . . .' She falters and breaks eye contact, and I wait.

'Do the other paddocks not need mowing?' I ask at last, when it's clear she isn't going to finish her sentence.

She looks back at me, and I can see the effort it takes her to refocus. Then she shakes her head. 'No – there are also a couple of horses; and the ponies get moved between the others, so that keeps the grass in check.'

Mouse chooses that moment to stop sulking. He jumps out of the van and leaps at Mimi before I can stop him. Mimi simply stands her ground and says, 'Down!' in such a firm voice that Mouse lies down and whimpers. 'Nothing was said about a dog,' she continues, turning to look at me.

I pull an apologetic face. 'Ohhh. Mouse always comes to work with me. He's very well behaved.' I cross my fingers and hope he doesn't choose that moment to leap up at her again.

She studies him. 'What is it anyway?' she asks.

'He's a cross,' I tell her.

'A cross between what? A giraffe and a sheep?' She snorts. Luckily, Mouse is too good-natured to realise she's mocking his long, skinny legs and unruly fluff. There's definitely some poodle in the mix, and I've always wondered if his legs owe their length to a sighthound of some kind. His tail – the only part of him that dares move – twitches in eager greeting.

I think I'm extra sensitive about Mouse's gene pool, as I've recently discovered I'm something of a mixture myself – Eastern European Jewish on one side and Scottish Presbyterian on the other. There was an African great-grandmother on my father's side, and I don't know if my mass of black curls is down to the Jewish or the African heritage. Either way, I'm tall; at five foot ten, I tower over Mimi, though she seems undaunted. She's still studying Mouse, who is looking up at her meekly. At last, she nods.

'We'll see about the dog,' she says, somewhat ominously. 'Now, do you need a hand?'

'No, we've got this, thanks. Haven't we, boy?'

Mouse barks once, and Mimi says, 'Right, I'll leave you to get settled in. Come to The Chimneys at eight tomorrow morning and I'll show you the ropes.' I watch her stride away – and look back just in time to see that Mouse has jumped into the back of the van, and is nudging the next box towards the tailgate.

'Good boy!' I say, grabbing it before it crashes to the ground. I read the label: CROCKERY. 'That would have made a very fine mess,' I tell Mouse, who makes his rumble of agreement.

For some reason, I'd expected the cottage to smell damp, but the only scent is of cleaning products. It's spotless, with a slate floor in the kitchen and beautiful wooden floors elsewhere. It's also freezing cold, and I have to go around shutting all the windows. Mouse has already discovered the garden and he's learning its nooks and crannies scent by scent. I can see him through the kitchen window as I unpack the utensils and crockery. He stops at every step, smelling the ground, the plants, the air, and examining the trees for new birds to bark at and squirrels to torment. The garden ends at woodland, and he soon vanishes from sight. He'll be back when he's done exploring.

Home, I think, looking around the pretty interior with its beamed ceilings, whitewashed walls, and paintings of woodland scenes and country paths. There's even a large TV set in the living room, which Mouse is going to love.

Things could be a whole lot worse. The involuntary thought brings a shiver.

At that exact moment, my phone beeps. Generally, I keep my mobile turned off or on mute, but I used it to navigate my way to Beaulieu. I take it from my pocket and check the screen. It's from Ben:

Thinking of you and hope your journey went well.

There was a time when a message from Ben would have lit up my world. Right now, I don't want to think about him at all. I turn off my phone and leave it on the worktop before going back out for another box.

It's gone seven by the time I carry in the last box. I have so few possessions, I can't understand how it's taken me over an hour to get them inside.

For dinner, I heat some beans in the microwave and pour them over toast made from a loaf of bread someone's left in the fridge for me. There's a dishwasher – luxury! – so I place my used plate, glass and cutlery inside it.

I can hear Mouse start up barking outside. He's probably found a hedgehog – or, worse, a fox or badger. He's earned himself some pretty bad injuries through run-ins with wildlife, so I open the door and call him, but he doesn't come.

With a groan, I pull on my wellies, grab a torch that's been left beside the back door, and go out to look for him. I find him standing at the end of the garden, where it borders the trees, barking into the darkness.

'What is it, boy?' He glances up at me, but continues barking. He runs toward the trees, then back to my ankles. From his tense stance and upright ears, I'd say he's scared.

I murmur to him reassuringly, but there's something unnerving about standing in that unfamiliar spot, not knowing if the threat is animal or human. I weigh the torch in my fist, glad of its heft.

And then, Mouse stops barking. He emits a last, low growl, before looking up at me.

'Is it gone?' I ask. His body eases and he lets me pet him, his tail swishing gently.

'Well done, boy. You saw them off.' I have no idea what spooked Mouse, but I feel uneasy as we walk back inside the house, and I double-check all the doors and windows before bidding him goodnight.

I leave him guzzling his meal, clean my teeth and head into the bedroom. The lovely carved oak bed has been made up with a pretty patchwork quilt in shades of blue and purple; I instantly decide my old checked duvet can remain in the boot tonight. I slide beneath the covers and lie on my back, relishing the contrast between this cottage and the grotty bedsit I've been renting. My thoughts stray to Mimi Purdue. She'd seemed so in control, and then she'd lost her train of thought entirely over . . . what was it? The paddocks?

I'm too fatigued to wonder for long, and soon I'm asleep, dreaming that I'm mowing a giant lawn while Mimi barks orders:

'*You need to mow the swimming pool after this. And don't forget to feed the giraffes in the paddocks. But watch out for the man in the woods.*'

2

I'm an early riser. It's something in the way I'm programmed. As soon as the sun hits the window, I'm awake and raring to go.

The next morning is no exception. Despite the exhaustion of the long journey yesterday, I'm up and dressed for my jog by 6 a.m. When I reach the kitchen, Mouse leaps to greet me as if he hasn't seen me in months.

'Whoa, boy!' I say, laughing and pushing him off. I give him his breakfast, which he wolfs down as if it's his first meal in months.

'Ready for our run?' I ask him. I'm looking forward to exploring our new patch, and I know he is, too. He brings me his lead, which I clip to his collar and we head out. In daylight, it's hard to remember why I felt so unnerved the night before. Surely Mouse was just barking at a fox or badger.

As we enter the woods, though, I slow and have a good look around, just to be sure. It's a native wood, with lots of oak, plus some birch, lime and hornbeam. There's a smell of bark and rotting leaves but I can't see anything untoward, so we carry on walking, with Mouse sniffing at every tree until we both spot something on the ground. It's one of those disposable gloves that clinicians use. I reach it and stuff it into my pocket before Mouse can chew and potentially swallow it.

'Some people have no respect for the countryside,' I tell him. But he's gone back to his olfactory inspection. There are some wonderful fungi growing out of the leaf mulch, and I stop to examine a particularly fine Collared Earthstar, its five 'rays' giving the impression of a strange land-dwelling starfish.

And then, in a muddy spot beside the fungus, I see a set of footprints, their imprint so clear in the mud that I could take an impression. These are fresh. Someone was definitely here, and I would bet they were Mouse's source of consternation the night before. Why would anyone be in the woods in the night? And did that person drop the glove? There's something unnerving about the idea of a stranger loitering in the dark so close to the house.

I shake my head. My imagination is running away with me. I can't help it: I've never been able to resist a puzzle. An unbidden memory of the detective club my friend Hannah and I set up in school makes me smile. As passionate as we were about following clues and solving crimes, we never had much to investigate besides lost pencil cases and PE bags.

I tell myself it's unlikely the visitor even realised there was anyone in the cottage, until they heard Mouse barking. But still . . . what would anyone be doing in the woods that late at night?

Mouse, meanwhile, has grown impatient to get going. There's no one here now so we set off, picking up speed as we exit the woods and get into a rhythm with our run. We soon find ourselves among fields full of sheep. It's hard to believe we're just on the outskirts of North London. I keep Mouse close to heel – he's a sheep chaser, and we've been in trouble over it in the past. The light is beautiful here, and the air smells of grass, soil and new shoots. Most of all, it smells like spring, the most promising time of year for any gardener – light rains and sun-warmed soil converging to produce those perfect new beginnings. I'm so glad my appointment has coincided with the rising sap of March. I check my watch and eagerly turn back towards the house and my new job.

'Can't make a bad impression by being late on our first day,' I tell Mouse. He tugs briefly on the lead and whines at this curtailment to his morning exercise, but he's soon jogging alongside me again. We pass back through the woods to the cottage, where I fry myself a couple of eggs to have on toast, with a cup of tea. I just have time for a quick wash and to cobble together a packed lunch before I'm due at Mimi Purdue's.

Approximately twenty minutes later, and right on schedule, I'm encouraging my poor old van up the drive to The Chimneys, which is straight and very steep. The gears groan as I shift down to first and accelerate towards the top. Part-way up, there's another gate, but it's been propped open and I head straight through and up the last stage of the driveway. I can almost hear my van's relief as the ground starts to level off. At the top, I park in front of the rambling old redbrick house. Mimi's already there, waiting for me. She's wearing her Barbour jacket again, but this time over a white shirt and jodhpurs. Her calf-length brown boots are highly polished. She's every bit the lady of the manor.

'Good morning,' she says, as I get down from the van.

'Hi . . .' But she's already striding off along the path towards the back of her house, and I have to scramble down with Mouse, swiftly clipping on his lead so we can follow her. Mimi gives a running commentary as she strides, not once looking behind to check I'm there.

'So, this is my place. It's just the one acre of garden. This is the main lawn.' She waves her hand towards a desolate area in front of us, so shaded by overgrown rhododendrons and encroaching trees, that barely any grass has survived. In its place, there's a fair amount of moss, interspersed with patches of bare earth. The entrance to the 'lawn' is marked by two mossy yet still imposing stone urns – promising something far grander than this scruffy affair.

'Ms Purdue, if you could just stop for a moment . . . ?' She wheels around, barely attempting to hide her irritation. I smile brightly. 'It might be helpful, when you have more time, if we could go through the garden, area by area,' I say. 'That way, I can suggest what improvements we might introduce.'

She sighs with obvious impatience. 'You're the gardener. So garden.'

I raise an eyebrow. 'Well, so long as you're happy with an Astroturf lawn, a giant lobster sculpture, and some ugly cherubs spouting water . . .'

The corners of her mouth twitch. 'That sounds idyllic.' She stares at me for a moment. 'Unless you're serious?' I start to laugh, and she joins in. 'OK. I think you'll do just fine.'

'And my predecessor?'

'Simon?' she says sharply. 'What about him?'

'Well, what did he do here?'

'Not a lot, as you can see. Let's just say he seemed to have certain ideas as to which gardens were deserving of his attention.'

'I see. And he hasn't left notes?'

'Not that I'm aware of. Right, here's your timetable.' She hands me an A4 piece of paper, bearing an Excel spreadsheet. 'You can see your time allocation across the five houses.'

A young woman comes out from the house. She's wearing an ankle-length, high-neck floral dress. With her long, light-brown curly hair and glasses, she looks like she's time-travelled from the 1970s.

She calls over to Mimi, 'Mum . . . aren't you taking me to rehearsal?'

Her mother calls back, 'Just coming.' She checks her watch and tells me, 'I have to run Lucy now, or she'll be late. But you've got your schedule. So, you're due at the Penwarrens' place today – it's two over from here, The Mount.'

'Should I take the van?'

'It's probably best. I want to lock up here.'

Mouse is reluctant to get straight back in the van, but I coax him in, aware of Mimi Purdue and her daughter waiting in their Land Rover.

At the bottom of the drive, I turn right and drive past The Towers – where the gateposts are topped by stone lions – before reaching The Mount. It's the four-storey granite structure. There's the obligatory gate with buzzer, so I roll down my window and press the button, but no one answers. I leave it a moment, then try again. At last, a tired female voice comes through the speaker:

'Yes? Who is it?'

'It's Steph Williams . . . The new gardener.'

'Oh . . . is it Tuesday already?'

I'm not sure how to answer this, but I don't have to – the buzzer sounds and the gate swings open. Unlike The Chimneys' approach, which went straight up, this one snakes first to the left and then to the right, winding all the way to the top. At last, I reach the house, where I park alongside a much smarter van than mine; I hope my little Ford doesn't get a complex next to the gleaming silver Mercedes Tourer. Mouse and I climb out and walk over to meet the lady of the house, who's standing waiting.

Fiona Penwarren is the only woman I've ever seen to perfectly fit the description 'faded beauty'. She looks as though she's been washed too many times. Everything about her is pale, from her near-translucent skin to her ash-blonde hair and her trailing, floaty clothes in watercolour shades.

She pats Mouse on the head absent-mindedly, and offers me a hot drink. Her voice is soft, with a Scottish lilt.

'A black coffee would be lovely,' I tell her. She nods, then looks around, as if only just remembering where she is. 'So, this is the front garden,' she says. 'I need it to stay as is for now, if you don't mind. I'm working on a still life, and this is the backdrop.'

'You're an artist?'

She peers at me through eyes that are a watery blue, and I wonder if she needs glasses. 'Oh, you didn't know . . . ? Yes, I paint.'

I do a quick recce. Someone has planned and planted this plot with loving care. A mature, well-tended shrubbery has been underplanted with Pachysandra, an evergreen ground cover that's good for suppressing weeds.

There is a discrepancy, though, between the age of the building and the style of the garden: stone steps lead down to a sunken pond where I can see large koi carp rippling the surface. At the centre, a giant, gilded statue of a goldfish spurts water from its mouth. The garden is old and charming, whilst the house is modern and, to my mind, shocking in its hard lines and reflective surface. It's like buying a vintage Bentley and painting go-faster stripes down the sides.

'How about the back garden?' I ask. 'Can I work on that today?'

She nods. 'I'll take you there; then I'll get you that coffee.'

'It's OK – Mouse and I can find our way,' I tell her. 'Then maybe we can go round the garden together when you get back?'

The path to the back garden actually runs through the centre of the house as a dark tunnel. I shiver at the coolness of the corridor, a cave-like pathway through the granite. However, when I reach the exit, I catch my breath: the rectangle of the opening frames the view of a large fig tree, not yet in leaf. The tree forms a sculptural focal point in the middle of an immaculate knot garden. It's a beautiful scene.

'Look at that, Mouse,' I whisper in awe. I know I should wait for Mrs Penwarren, but I can't help myself: the garden lures me in. I keep Mouse on the lead as we begin our tour. The garden is broken up into what are known in the gardening trade as 'rooms' – separate areas, each with their own theme and planting scheme. The rooms are divided with ancient yew and box hedging, some of which has been clipped into shapes. There are balls and obelisks, peacocks and elephants, all sculpted from the evergreen shrubs and trees. Each level holds more surprises – more hidden areas and secret entrances.

'There you are!' Mrs Penwarren is out of breath from climbing the garden after me.

'I'm sorry! The grounds are so beautiful – I forgot you'd be looking for me.'

She smiles. 'I'm so glad you like it. I'm afraid the last gardener thought it rather a chore to look after.'

'Did he do all the topiary?'

She shakes her head. 'Oh, no, Rupert – that's Mr Penwarren, my husband – does that. He doesn't allow anyone else to touch it. It is lovely though, isn't it?'

'It really is,' I say. 'But I'm confused: the house . . .'

'Oh, isn't it a monstrosity? Apparently the original old manor house had fallen into such disrepair, Rupert had no choice but to tear it down when he acquired it. That was more than ten years ago, before we met. For some reason, he and his architect decided a granite monolith would work perfectly in the setting.'

'What a shame. But it does explain why the garden seems so much older than the house.'

She nods and hands me a mug of dark, steaming coffee. 'I can't quite fathom how a fan of such modern architecture can love a traditional garden. But Rupert has some theory that the dark backdrop of the house provides the perfect foil to all the foliage. Anyway, please just take today to acquaint yourself with the grounds. You can start work next week, when you've had time to settle in.'

'That's kind. Thank you. Is there anything about the garden you would like to discuss with me?'

'I think this is more of a maintenance job than anything.'

'I agree: it's in a wonderful state. It just needs a bit of weeding and tidying.'

She nods. 'Now, if you'll excuse me, I must get back to work.'

'Of course. Thank you for the coffee.'

'You can let the dog off the lead if you like. He's clearly well-trained.' She gives him another pat and he wags his tail.

She's turning to leave when she looks back and says, 'You won't say anything to Rupert about what I mentioned – the house being ugly?'

I smile. 'Of course not.'

'It's just . . . he thinks it's rather beautiful, in some ultra-modern way.'

'Your secret's safe with me.'

She nods, smiles, and takes her leave.

I let Mouse off his lead and he takes off, chasing imaginary squirrels down pathways until he's out of sight. I spend a couple of hours, making notes on the different parts of the garden and the jobs that need doing in each of them.

When I'm done, I call for Mouse, so we can go home for lunch. He takes longer than usual to appear and, when he finally does, he has something in his mouth. That's nothing new, and my heart sinks at the expectation of a fresh corpse to dispose of. I'm sure there's some retriever in him. I walk towards him, but he turns his head so I can't see what he's got. As I get closer, I can't see any blood, which is a relief.

'What have you got there, boy?' The closer I get to him, the more he turns his head away. I crouch beside him, reach a hand around to his mouth and tug. Mouse growls a little, but I know he'd never hurt me, so I pull harder. When it comes free, I'm surprised to see it's a child's shoe, covered in mud and with what looks like leaf mulch inside. It still has its laces, though they are so filthy, I can't begin to guess their original colour. There's something poignant about this single shoe, which fits neatly in my large palm.

'Just the one shoe, boy?' I ask him. He's grumbling quietly. I think of my seven-year-old niece, Alice, and I reckon her feet must be bigger than this by now. I'd estimate the shoe belongs to a child of around five or six.

Mouse is still grumbling, and I hand it back. He snatches it and runs towards the van. It's only after we're both strapped into our seats and have set off down the drive that I realise the shoe stinks.

The odour ranks somewhere between the sludge at the bottom of a stagnant pond and a smelly sock. I cough pointedly, opening the windows, but Mouse seems oblivious.

Back in the kitchen of our new home, I snatch the shoe and take it to the sink. Mouse sits at my feet, whimpering, but I'm ruthless: I fill the sink with soapy water, grab the washing-up brush and scrub the shoe until it's clean. The water quickly turns muddy, and the leather turns out to be brown, not black as I'd originally thought; the laces are an unexpected yellow.

'There, that's better,' I tell him, holding it up for inspection. I let him take back the dripping article, whereupon – with one last grumble – he heads to his basket in the corner of the room, lying down with the treasure between his front paws. He eyes me with an expression that suggests he ranks me on a level between captor and torturer.

Meanwhile, I take a seat at the kitchen table and google Fiona Penwarren on my laptop. It turns out she's quite a famous painter, mainly of landscapes but also the occasional still life. Her work has been displayed in galleries all over the world. I transfer the notes I've made about her garden to an Excel spreadsheet, then shut down the laptop and warm some more beans to have with toast.

'We'd better find a shop this afternoon, if I don't want to eat beans on toast for the rest of the week,' I tell Mouse, who pretends to be asleep; but one ear twitches, giving him away.

I turn on my phone and locate a grocery shop in a nearby village. There's a voicemail from Ben, which I delete without listening, before turning off my mobile.

'Right: let's go shopping,' I say to Mouse, but he's still ignoring me. I give up and head out to the van with my tote bag.

It takes me nearly twenty minutes to reach the store, as there's no vehicular access at my end of Beaulieu Heights. Instead, I have to drive all the way back past all the houses to the locked entry gates, then along the private access lane, until I reach the main road, where I turn left and head at a much faster pace back in the direction from which I came, until I enter a small village, with a church, a pub and a solitary shop. Here, I pull the van alongside a black Mercedes that's been parked so haphazardly, it's taking up two of the three spaces.

From the outside, the store is low and lounging. It looks like several buildings have been knocked together, and they weren't quite the same height. According to the signs outside, it functions as post office, off-licence and grocery store.

I climb down from the van, open the shop door and step inside. As I glance around, I see there are just two other people here – the shopkeeper and a customer (presumably the owner of the Merc) – and they're both watching me.

'Hi,' I say.

'Good afternoon,' says the man behind the counter. His customer merely nods. Her sheen of brown hair with honey-colour highlights drapes her back like a silk scarf, and her skin has that too-golden glow that can only come from a tanning booth. She's wearing an ankle-length, camel-coloured wool coat teamed with long, high-heeled chestnut-brown boots that gleam. I marvel at the heels, which taper to a point and must be about six inches high.

'Can I help you?' asks the shopkeeper.

I tear my eyes away from the stiletto heels. 'I'm just going to look around, if that's all right.' I'm acutely aware of the customer's gaze skimming me, from my dishevelled ponytail to my dirty jacket, filthy jeans and lace-up, muddy gardening boots.

'Are you the new gardener at the Heights?' she asks in an imperious tone. She has a strong Essex accent. Despite her astonishing heels, I'm still physically looking down on her. Not that this woman could be intimidated by someone of my grubby status: she is the queen, and I her subject.

'That's right,' I say, blushing as I realise I'm staring at her. 'Steph Williams.' She nods but doesn't say anything. 'Do you live at Beaulieu Heights?' I ask.

She seems surprised – as if her identity should be known and celebrated far and wide. 'I'm Mrs Patel,' she says.

'Which house is that?' I ask.

She sighs. 'Villa Splendida.' She pronounces it: *Veeller Splendeeder*.

I nod. 'I think you're on my list for Friday. I'll look forward to meeting you then.'

But Mrs Patel is already losing interest. She turns away, waving a careless hand, saying, 'Oh, I doubt you'll see *me*. Francis will show you what needs doing.'

I don't bother asking who Francis is, or whether it's spelt with an 'i' or an 'e' – the male or female form. No doubt he, she or they will reveal themselves on Friday. Hopefully they'll be less rude than their employer.

If this woman and Mimi Purdue are typical specimens, it seems they favour them small and bossy at Beaulieu.

I catch the shopkeeper's eye. 'Do you have any cheese?' He comes out from behind the counter to show me to the fridges, and Mrs Patel makes her exit.

No one else enters the shop while I'm there. I stock up on all the essentials – most importantly, dog food for Mouse, plus several large bars of dark chocolate and a couple of bottles of Merlot for me. They also have Mouse's favourite brand of biscuits, so I buy him a couple of boxes as treats.

On my drive back, I catch up with the Mercedes. Dropping back slightly, I observe Mrs Patel's driving technique, which can only be described as erratic. Whether she's reading the paper while driving or simply counting how many times she can swerve from one side of the road to the other, I can only guess. After she's passed through the main gates, I watch her turn sharply into her driveway, narrowly missing one of the fence posts. Friday's visit to Villa Splendida is going to be interesting.

3

'It's just not the same if you haven't tried it yourself.'

It's morning and I'm at La Jolla, the first house on Beaulieu Heights. The building's California glamour is somewhat tarnished by the loud presence of the Singer-Pryces' teenage daughter, Apple. She's sitting on the low concrete wall beside the kidney-shape swimming pool, dressed in denim micro-shorts and a denim jacket over a pink bikini top, and talking animatedly into her mobile phone. Her pretty, heart-shaped face is framed by tousled candyfloss-pink hair. She has the lean, long-legged build of a catwalk model.

'I'm telling you, Pobble . . .' (And I'd thought Apple was a ridiculous name . . .) '. . . you have to drink it through a straw, just after you've taken the hit . . .' She shoots me a suspicious glance, but I'm giving studious attention to a weedy flowerbed a couple of metres from her. The sun is out and I've taken off my jacket, enjoying the warmth on my bare arms. Mouse is off in the distance, exploring; I hear him bark from time to time at some passing creature.

Apple shrieks and I turn to look. As she's probably just (over-) reacting to something Pobble has said, I'm not concerned – until I see she's gone pale and is backing away from something.

'What is it?' I call.

'Snake!' She looks horrified.

I shove my fork in the soil and walk over to see. 'Oh, it's only a slow-worm.' I nod towards the golden creature that's wriggling along the path.

'It looks like a snake to me.'

'It's really just a legless lizard. It's harmless.'

'It doesn't look harmless. Look at its tongue, flicking in and out.' She shudders.

'That's how it sniffs the air.'

'Get rid of it. Please.'

I shrug and pick it up gently in my gloved hands. I carry it over to the rockery and release it. As I watch it slither away, its scales shining in the sunlight like burnished sand, I forget all about the frightened girl. It's only when she says, 'Thank you,' in a meek voice that I turn back to her.

'You're welcome.'

'My parents say I have to grow up and stop being scared of everything.'

'Most creatures in this country won't hurt you.'

'I know but they look so . . . horrible.'

I laugh, then feel guilty. 'What else are you afraid of?'

She tilts her head, reeling off a list: 'Spiders, wasps and bees, woodlice, beetles, daddy-long-legs, dragonflies, moths, earwigs . . .' She shudders again.

'That's quite a list.'

She nods. 'I'm due to go off to uni in September if I get the grades, and Mummy says I can't rely on the other students to come running every time there's an ant in my bedroom.'

'Well, maybe just keep your windows closed.'

She smiles. 'I'm going to make some tea. Do you want one?'

'Yes, please.'

By the time she returns with my drink, I've finished the flowerbed I was working on, and weeded two more.

'Sorry it took so long,' she says, as she hands me a mug.

'That's OK. Thanks.' I curl my hand around the mug but can feel very little heat through it.

'Can I tell you a secret?' she asks.

Hoping it's nothing too serious, I keep my voice casual. 'Sure.'

She takes a deep breath, then her words tumble out, like coins from a slot machine. 'I've told Mummy and Daddy I'm going to my friend Pobble's for the weekend, but really we're going to a music festival.'

'Right . . .' I take a sip of my tea. It's lukewarm and stewed.

'Do you think it's really bad?' she asks.

'It's pretty undrinkable,' I say. Then I realise she's talking about her secret. 'Oh! It depends on why you're not telling them the truth.'

'Mummy would just freak. She thinks festivals are full of junkies. I mean, I smoke pot, but I don't do anything serious.' She pulls an anxious face. 'You won't tell Mummy and Daddy?'

I shrug. 'It's nothing to do with me.'

'Sorry about the tea.'

I smile. 'That's all right. It was a kind thought.'

'It's just . . . I start to do one thing and then I get distracted and after that I can't remember what I was meant to be doing in the first place.'

She's so endearing, I feel guilty for wishing she wasn't still standing there, watching as I start to dig up the long tap root of a thistle.

'Do you like your job?' she asks.

'I love it.'

I wait for her to leave, but she stays there, not speaking for a moment, clearly considering something.

'Did you ever get into trouble?' she asks at last. I straighten up to meet her gaze but she's staring over my shoulder in a disconcerting way, as if there's someone coming up behind me. I glance behind me, but there's nobody there.

'You mean, by digging up a prize plant, thinking it was a weed?'

She laughs and shakes her head. 'No, I mean, like, get in real trouble with someone?' She doesn't wait for me to answer. 'It's just, I've got this thing. I mean . . .'

Nope: I am not getting involved. I look back down at the thistle, wiggling the fork until I feel the root start to loosen its grip. 'Maybe you should talk to your parents.'

She shakes her head, looking panic-stricken. 'No! They can't know anything about it.'

I'm fast coming to realise that my love of gardening is largely contingent on my being left to my own devices. 'Well, I'm not sure I'm the person to . . .' I start.

'You seem really nice,' she says. 'You know, like non-judgmental.'

'Still, I'm a comparative stranger to you . . .'

'Helloooo! We're home!'

The Singer-Pryce parents spill out into the garden from a back door, chatting and calling to their daughter. With a sigh of relief, I turn back to my solitary pastime.

But my reprieve doesn't last long: within moments, I'm being approached by the group, led by Apple.

'Mummy, Daddy – this is Steph, our new gardener.'

Her parents nod politely, tell me their names (which sound like 'Bubby' and 'Jockey' but I must have misheard) and ask me how I'm finding it so far.

'Great,' I say. 'Everyone's been very friendly, and I couldn't ask for a more beautiful place to work.'

'Steph saved me from a snake,' says Apple.

Her mother looks alarmed. 'A . . . snake? You mean there was an adder?'

I smile. 'It was only a slow-worm.'

'Ah,' says her dad, 'we do get those here.' He looks me up and down in a creepy way before turning to Apple. 'They're perfectly harmless, darling. I do hope you didn't trouble the gardener.'

Apple looks sheepish, so I say, 'Oh, I was close by, and it was no trouble.'

'Well, that was kind,' he says, with a lupine grin. 'Is there anything you need?'

As he seems to be addressing my chest, I cross my arms and stare at him until he finally meets my eye. 'A list of jobs?' I suggest. 'I've just been getting on with the weeding so far.'

'That should keep you busy for a year or two,' says his wife, laughing.

Jockey nods. 'We'll let you know if we think of *anything else* that needs doing.' His eyebrows are raised in a suggestive manner. I usually like to kid myself that men like him don't exist anymore – which is hard to do when they're standing in front of me. He's like something out of *The Inbetweeners*. I feel an urge to step towards him and knee him in the groin. *Not with his daughter and wife looking on*, I tell myself.

They bid me farewell and walk back to the house, sweeping Apple along with them. Relaxing my fists – which I hadn't even realised I was clenching – I check my watch. How is it only 2 p.m.? I'd give anything to head off right now and scrub off my encounter with Jockey in a hot bath.

I take a fifteen-minute break to eat the cheese sandwiches I made at home. Right on cue, Mouse appears. I pour some water into a tin camping bowl and he laps it up before grabbing Shoe and heading back up the garden to resume his escapades. At least one of us is having a good day.

While I eat, I survey the garden. As far as I can tell from the three houses I've visited so far, they all have plots that continue up the hill behind the buildings. This one has been made into a series of broad terraces, each with ornamental trees, shrubs and flowerbeds. They don't quite match the Californian theme of the house, but a mismatched house and garden seems to be a running theme at Beaulieu. A central set of flagstone steps leads up between the levels. I climb to the very top, where a low hedge allows views out over fields. It's only as I turn to survey the garden from above and see the house far below me, that I realise just how high I am. Mouse comes to join me; he's flagging from all the exercise.

'OK, boy,' I say. 'I reckon a couple more hours and we can call it a day.' I wonder how I'm going to avoid hearing Apple's confession over the coming weeks or months. Whatever she's got herself into, I have no desire to become involved.

4

The next day is Thursday and, according to my timetable, I'm due at Mimi Purdue's. Although The Chimneys is the nearest house to the cottage, Mouse and I still take the van; I'm determined to tackle the overgrown rhododendrons and trees that are depriving the lawn of light, so I'll need my power tools. The gate is propped open, as per my last visit, and I park the van at the front and wheel my barrow through with my tools. Unsure if Mouse is welcome to roam here, I put him on his long lead and tie it around a nearby silver birch, with a bowl of water close by. He runs the short distance allowed, then whines at the restriction to his doggy liberties.

'I'm sorry, boy. It's just for now. I'll take you home at lunchtime and you can stay there, if you like.'

I start by doing a tour of the main lawn, making a note of each of the trees and rhododendron bushes, and what needs to be done. My first big job will be to remove all the rhododendrons, which is the highly invasive *Rhododendron ponticum* – a thuggish shrub that's responsible for crowding out any number of native British plants in the wild and generally taking over. With the infiltrator out of the way, I'll be able to thin out the trees, leaving the three silver birches and a rather lovely ornamental cherry with beautiful copper bark.

I haven't seen Mimi yet. Ideally, I'd like her approval before I start with the chainsaw. Remembering how little Mimi wanted to discuss her garden, I hesitate. But this is too major a decision to make without her, so I go round to the front door and ring the old-fashioned bell push. Mimi's daughter, Lucy, comes to the door, wearing another high-neck, seventies-style floral dress.

'Oh, it's you. Hi.' Not the warmest of welcomes.

'Hello. Is your mum in?' I ask.

She shakes her head. 'She's at a WI committee thing. Is it something I might know?'

I tell her about the rhododendrons and she wrinkles her nose. She's about nineteen, I'd guess – probably just a year or so older than Apple Singer-Pryce, although they're worlds apart in demeanour. Where Apple gives off a flaky air, Lucy seems sensible and serious – older than her years.

'I think Mum just really wants the garden to look nice,' she says at last. 'But I can message her, if you like?' Although the offer is made in a pleasant tone, she looks impatient. I am taking up her Valuable Time.

'That would be great; yes, please.'

She nods and types quickly into her phone. She and Apple do have that in common – their phones seem to be surgically attached to their hands.

A beep comes faster than I would have thought possible. 'Mum says: "Tell her to do whatever she thinks is right, so long as she leaves out the cherubs and the lobster."' She reads this in a bored voice.

I laugh. 'OK, thanks.'

'Anyway, I'm busy learning lines, so . . .'

'Sure, I'll let you get on. Thanks for your help.'

I get my chainsaw and protective gear from the van and head back to the offending rhododendrons. Mouse dozes off in his spot beneath the silver birch, while I immerse myself in my work.

By lunchtime, I've made real inroads into the clearing work. It's extraordinarily satisfying, to see the sunlight now shining as it should on the lawn area. There's still no sign of Mimi, so I risk untying Mouse. He gets to his feet and deposits Shoe with me before racing up the garden, out of sight.

Mid-afternoon, I pour myself a mug of coffee from my thermos and take it to the top of the garden, where I notice a gate in the low drystone wall. Passing through, there's a path off to the left. This must be the way to the paddock Mimi mentioned. I walk for a few minutes. There's an attractive wood on the right – but it's the next garden along from Mimi's that brings me to an abrupt stop. *Wilderness* is the only word that fits what I can see here. There are brambles, nettles, thistles and wild roses, with *Clematis vitalba* ('old man's beard': named for its fluffy seedheads in autumn that look like a giant's beard) and ivy crawling over everything. If the whole garden's in this state, The Towers is going to be a challenge.

Shaking my head, I walk on until I come to a field opposite Fiona Penwarren's garden. So this is the top paddock Mimi mentioned. At least the two Shetland ponies are keeping the grass down, as Mimi promised. I wonder if I could release them into The Towers' grounds when no one's looking. Not that they'd be a match for the brambles and roses. I'll have to worry about the wilderness when I come to it on Monday. Walking back along the path, I head down through Mimi's grounds and take up my chainsaw: those rhododendrons are going down.

Around four-thirty, I pack my kit back into the van and call Mouse. I'm ready for a long-awaited soak in the bath. Once again, he takes a long time to appear and, when he finally does, he has something in his mouth that isn't Shoe. When he gets close, I can see it's just a toy rabbit, though I have no idea where he found it.

At that moment, Lucy steps out of the back door: 'Mum's home and she wants to know if you'd like to join us for a cup of tea? She says you can bring the "giraffe-dog".'

My heart sinks at the prospect of not getting home for a while, but I can't think of a good excuse. 'That's very kind. Thanks.'

Mouse follows me happily into the house, the new treasure dangling from his jaws. Too late, I realise the toy is caked in mud.

Lucy has vanished, but we're greeted at the door by a friendly member of staff with a London accent; he introduces himself as Jordan, the house manager, and holds out a hand for me to shake. I hastily slip off my gardening glove and take his hand, which is warm and smooth. Jordan is tall and slim, with gold-frame glasses and his afro hair worn naturally. He's about my age, I reckon, and has an easy confidence that I find instantly attractive. I realise I've been holding on to his hand for a little too long, and let go abruptly, feeling a blush beginning to heat my cheeks. I remind myself that you should never trust a charming man. After all, Ben was a real charmer, and look where that got me.

Jordan smiles, then bends down to stroke Mouse's head. The dog sighs with pleasure, and Jordan says, 'You're a gorgeous boy, aren't you? Would you like to come with me and we'll find you a treat?' But Mouse has other ideas. Holding his new toy aloft like a trophy, he trots purposefully away from us and into the living room before either of us can stop him.

As I chase after him, I'm surprised to discover the whole place is light and bright, not at all like its rambling, old-brick exterior. The walls are painted white, with colourful rugs and enormous house plants. There's a maid setting out china on a table covered in a white cloth beside a picture window. The cosy scene is marred by a shriek from Mimi, who's sitting at the table with her back to the window and pointing at Mouse.

'I'm so sorry!' I say, running up to grab his collar. 'He sneaked past us in the hall. I'll take him out now.'

But Mimi is shaking her head, still pointing at Mouse. 'Where did he get that?'

'Get what?'

'The rabbit. Where did he get Mr Rabbit?' She has turned a strange shade, pale and mottled.

'I'm not sure,' I say. 'He just appeared with it a few minutes ago. Does it belong to someone?'

But neither of them acknowledges that I've spoken.

Mimi looks at her daughter. 'It's Alfie's,' she says, in an almost pleading tone.

'I know, Mum,' says Lucy gently. 'But Alfie doesn't need it anymore, does he?'

There's a pause, during which she takes Mimi's hand. And then something passes between them – a kind of wordless understanding – and Mimi visibly relaxes, sitting back in her chair and nodding.

'Lucy's right: Mr Rabbit's owner won't miss him. I was silly to make a fuss. Your dog can keep the toy.'

'Well, if you're sure . . .' I say awkwardly. I glance over at him; he's making himself comfortable in a cream armchair. I don't want to think about how dirty he and the toy both are. 'Should I be taking him out of here?' I ask. 'I think Jordan was going to settle him elsewhere?'

'Oh, he looks quite at home in that chair,' says Mimi. 'Leave him be and let's have our tea, shall we?' She holds up a teapot, and I walk over to join them at the table. They're both smiling as if the previous bizarre scene never happened. Mimi and Lucy are seated at right-angles to one another; Mimi gestures for me to take the seat opposite her, facing the garden. I oblige, even though I'd prefer to return to the cottage, where the only eccentric beings are my dog and me. I'm tempted to ask about Alfie, and why he no longer needs his rabbit: is he away at university, or did something happen to him? But I don't want to provoke another outburst, so I smile politely and accept the cup of tea Mimi pours for me.

Looking around the pretty space, my gaze is drawn to the walls, which are hung with large, brightly-coloured paintings. One of these catches my eye for its familiar style – it's an unusually vibrant watercolour, featuring a vase containing the dried seedpods of *Lunaria annua* (honesty) and *Physalis alkekengi var. franchetii* (Chinese lanterns). 'Is that by Fiona Penwarren?' I ask.

Mimi says, 'Well spotted. Yes, that was a present from Fiona. I'd admired it at her house, and she insisted I take it when I was leaving.'

'Really? That's so kind,' I say.

She nods, turning to her daughter. 'She's a wonderful artist, isn't she?'

'She's going to paint me one day soon,' says Lucy.

'I didn't realise she did portraits?' I say. 'I looked her up online after I met her yesterday, and I only saw landscapes and abstract flowers.'

'She only does portraits of people she really likes,' says Lucy.

'Lucy!' says her mother. 'Honestly! You know that I asked Fiona to paint you.'

Lucy shrugs, turning to me. 'Do you do anything creative?'

'You mean, apart from gardening?'

'That's more "honest toil",' chips in Mimi. 'You don't need an imagination to garden.'

I feel like pointing out that, without imagination, I wouldn't have a clue what needed to be done to renovate her raggedy 'main lawn', or indeed the rest of her grounds. In fact, in all my gardening projects, if I couldn't visualise the end results, I'd be pretty stymied. Instead, I say, 'I don't really do anything like that. I've always been more sporty. I run.'

'Lucy's at drama college,' says her mother proudly. 'She's got the lead in the latest production.'

'That's great. What is it?'

'*The Importance of Being Earnest*. Do you know it?'

I nod. 'I love that play. Which part do you have? Cecily? Lady Bracknell?'

'Miss Prism,' says Lucy proudly.

'The governess?' Lucy nods. Though vital to the plot reveal, I wouldn't describe Miss Prism as 'the lead'.

I swallow hard and say, 'Great,' in a bright voice, before biting into a biscuit that practically melts on my tongue: lemon shortbread. 'Oh my god – these are amazing!' Mimi and Lucy smile at my reaction.

'We're very lucky with our cook,' says Mimi. 'She's been with us for years.'

'When can I move in?'

They both laugh, then Mimi says, 'How are you finding us all so far?'

I manage not to say, *Well, apart from whatever weird shit is going on with you two . . .* Instead, I nod noncommittally.

'Are the residents all making themselves available?'

I use a white linen napkin to dab crumbs from my lips. 'Relatively. I've only been to The Mount, La Jolla and here, as you know. But the Singer-Pryces seem happy for me to find my own work. Mrs Penwarren was keen for me just to explore on my first visit there.'

Mimi nods. 'What did you think of the Singer-Pryces?'

'They seem friendly enough.'

'Did you meet their younger daughter?'

'Apple? Yes; we got to know each other a little.'

'Watch out for that one,' she says, setting down her cup.

'In what way?' I ask.

She looks at Lucy, who reaches for a biscuit. 'Leave it, Mum. Apple's all right.'

'You're too soft on everyone,' says her mother. She looks back to me. 'Let's just say Apple Singer-Pryce is a bit like a whirlpool – anyone who stands too close is liable to get dragged down with her.'

For some reason, I feel defensive on Apple's behalf, despite my own worries. 'She seemed sweet,' I say. 'A bit flaky, perhaps, but she's only, what? Eighteen?'

'Seventeen,' says Lucy. 'She's a year younger than me. She doesn't turn eighteen till the end of July.'

I take another biscuit and nibble on the edges, wondering how many I can eat before someone notices. There's a moment's silence, then Lucy says, 'What did you think of *Mr* Singer-Pryce? He's *very* friendly, isn't he?'

'Lucy,' says her mother, in a warning tone.

'What?' says Lucy, all bright-eyed innocence.

'That's enough,' says Mimi.

Unwilling to listen to any more Beaulieu gossip, I set down my drained cup in its saucer and push my chair back. 'Thank you so much for the tea and biscuits.'

'Oh, are you leaving already?' says Mimi.

I nod. 'I'm done in. I'll need to get someone in to clear all the wood from today. Would you mind getting permission from the committee?'

Mimi says, 'Oh, we've all got open fires and log burners – I'm sure we can distribute it among ourselves. I'll get Jordan to arrange for staff to collect from their respective houses.'

'Oh, really? That's great.'

Mimi nods. 'The main lawn area is already looking much better – the light's coming through.'

I wasn't aware she'd seen the space, but then I realise she can probably see it from the house. There's an unpleasant moment when I imagine all the residents standing at their windows, watching me work when I believe I'm alone. But I give myself a mental shake and say, 'One thing I do need is to call in a contractor to lay new turf.'

Mimi nods. 'If you email over the details this evening, I'll clear it.'

I walk over to Mouse, who's typically reluctant to move from his chair. 'Don't get too used to the high life, boy,' I tell him. He licks my hand and I pat him. 'Come on, we have to go now.' He makes a show of groaning and stretching as he gets up, making my hosts laugh.

'He's quite a character, isn't he?' says Mimi.

'He certainly is,' I agree.

Mimi walks me to the door, and says, 'I'm sorry about earlier.'

'That's all right,' I say. 'Although can I ask who Alfie is?' I regret it immediately: it's as if someone has pulled a blind down over her face. She practically shoves Mouse and me outside, shutting the door firmly behind us.

'Well, that told me,' I murmur, and Mouse makes a little rumble of agreement.

At home that night, I think about Mimi's response to seeing Mouse with Mr Rabbit. She was so obviously upset. Who is Alfie and what has happened to him?

I shake my head. I'll have to work harder with both Apple Singer-Pryce and the Purdues, if I'm going to maintain an emotional barrier between them and me. After all I've gone through over the past couple of years, I don't want to get dragged into their respective messes.

With a sigh, I turn on my mobile. I have six missed calls from Ben; he's left three voicemails and sent two texts. They all say pretty much the same thing: *Hope you're doing OK. Call me.* I turn off my phone and settle on the sofa with Mouse.

We both like a show called *The Dog House*, which is set at Wood Green Animal Shelter, and we've got a couple of episodes to catch up on. Mouse gets very excited when the dogs get introduced to their potential new owners; he runs up to the screen and makes encouraging noises. I wonder if the show would consider taking him on as their canine consultant. He could mentor the dogs in how to make the best first impression, to help them get adopted. After *The Dog House*, we watch a David Attenborough programme about sea creatures; it's one we've seen before, but Mouse is a big fan of Attenborough, especially his ocean work.

At bedtime, Mouse settles in his bed and I head to my pretty bedroom. As I close the curtains, I stop to admire a full moon, silhouetting a line of still-naked trees. I smile. This is the life I've been imagining for myself: a fulfilling job in a beautiful setting. Best of all, it's many miles away from my ex-husband Ben.

5

The dog and I arrive at Villa Splendida bang on eight the next morning. I lean out of the van window to press the buzzer, and the gate swings open without anyone asking my identity.

When we eventually reach the top – after much complaining from my van (is this driveway even steeper than the others, or is my poor old vehicle ageing by the day?) – I find the top gate has been propped open, so I drive straight through and park off to one side, near the garages. Mrs Patel strikes me as someone who wouldn't want her view from the house marred by a clapped-out truck.

All is quiet at the Villa: whoever let me in at the gate certainly isn't rushing to greet me. The pink house that reminded me of a birthday cake the first time I saw it offers more than a nod to Spanish architecture, with a beautiful tiled veranda across the front of the house, edged with low pink walls. I decide to give it a couple of minutes before ringing the doorbell; I'd rather avoid an encounter with the lady of the house if possible. I haven't forgotten our meeting in the convenience store, and I'm in no hurry to renew the acquaintance.

Mouse and I stand for a while at the front, admiring the outlook. Raised up as they are, all the houses have views over treetops, towards hills and the roofs of London. My cottage's view is largely obstructed by a group of pine trees planted just below it. This vista is the best I've seen so far, looking out towards a distant lake or reservoir.

'That would make a great hike for the weekend,' I tell Mouse, pointing at the expanse of water. He rumbles and gives his tail a wag, a freshly washed Mr Rabbit swinging from his jaws like an unfortunate victim.

'There you are!' A harassed-looking man of indeterminate age has appeared behind me. Seeing as I've simply driven through the gate, parked, and waited at the front of the house, I haven't exactly been playing hide-and-seek.

'Are you Francis?' I ask.

He nods. 'And you are Ms Williams?'

'That's right: Steph.'

He nods. 'Follow me, please.' He glances down at Mouse. 'And what does our dog friend like for breakfast?'

'Oh, that's kind, but he's already eaten.'

'Well, I'll make sure he has some water to hand, and I'll have a nice lunch prepared.' Francis is wearing a suit but has an incongruous striped apron tied around his waist. His fringe is sticking up and there's a daub of flour on his cheek. I wonder if he has to perform the role of head cook as well as butler. He has dark hair and bright-blue eyes with laughter lines that give him an air of good humour. Mouse and I have taken an instant liking to him.

'You are going to get so spoilt living here!' I tell Mouse. He's trotting at Francis's heel, as if they've known each for years.

'Is it OK if I take him off the lead?' I ask when we reach the back garden.

Francis shoots a look towards the house. 'It should be safe for the morning. If you could put him back on the lead at lunchtime. Shall we say one o'clock?'

'That sounds good.'

'And may I ask if you have any specific dietary requirements, Ms Williams?'

I think about the cheese sandwiches in my backpack, which I made in haste this morning after my jog. 'Are you feeding me, too?'

He nods.

'That's kind. No – I eat just about everything, thank you.'

He nods again. 'Now, Madam has asked that you start at the top of the grounds, adjacent to the boundary hedge. I'll walk you up there.'

'You can just tell me what needs doing if it's easier.'

He looks disproportionately grateful. 'Thank you so much for that. Well, the rose hedge needs pruning.'

'Did the previous gardener not do that?'

He shakes his head. 'No, he got distracted, so I'm afraid there are quite a few jobs left undone.'

'It seems a bit late to be pruning a rose hedge, but I'll take a look.'

'Also, the pond is overrun with green stuff . . .' He frowns, struggling to remember the name. 'Duckweed?' he says at last. 'Is that a thing?'

I nod. 'It is, and I've got tools in my van that will help. And maybe the pond would benefit from a filter. I'll take a look.'

'Shall I leave you to it?'

'Yes, that's fine. I'll see you later.'

'A cup of tea? Coffee?'

'A coffee would be great, but only if you have time.'

He beams at me. 'I'll make time.' He bends down towards Mouse and strokes his ears. The dog immediately rolls on to his back.

'He really likes you,' I say.

'He's a lovely fellow.'

I make sure I stay near the house until Francis has brought out my drink – which is done a lot more efficiently than Apple managed; it's also a far more palatable brew. There's even a plate of homemade chocolate chip cookies. I think Mimi could have persuaded me to work for less money if I'd known about the quality of the refreshments.

Mouse and I spend a pleasant morning in the garden. It's another unseasonably warm day, with just enough breeze to prevent me from overheating. The rose hedge I've been sent to prune is made up entirely of the shrub rose, *Rosa rugosa*. These don't necessarily need pruning – and, if it was going to be done, it should ideally have been in late summer, just after flowering – but I don't want to start off on the wrong foot with *Madam* (if it's not already too late for that), so I remove some of the older stems and shorten some of the longer ones. I hate pruning rugosas, which have so many thorns they're like cacti; my arms are soon covered in sore red scratches that quickly swell into welts. Some gardeners seem to have impervious skin – unfortunately, I'm not one of them. Once I've dealt with the hedge and delivered all the cuttings to a compost area I've located behind a yew hedge, I head down to tackle the pond.

It's larger than I expected and is full of overgrown lilies and the invasive yellow flag, *Iris pseudacorus*. The water's stagnant and stinks of rotting plants and decay. It definitely needs to have a pump and filtration system installed.

Unfortunately, I've been misinformed: instead of surface-based duckweed, which can be scooped out with a net, the pond is dense with the fibrous alga aptly known as 'blanket weed'. I've not had a lot of dealings with the stuff, but I've heard that it reproduces more quickly if you try to remove it manually. I'm just making a note to obtain some specialist bacterial treatment to deal with the green sludge, when I hear Francis calling my name. Checking my watch, I realise it's five past one already.

'Here, Mouse!' I call loudly. He comes running, Mr Rabbit in his mouth. 'Good boy!' I clip on his lead and we head downhill towards the house.

Francis has set a round garden table with a floral cloth and old-fashioned chintz china. He gestures for me to take a seat. I tie Mouse to a boot scraper beside two china bowls that have been set out for him. It looks like he has fresh chicken casserole for lunch.

Francis lifts the cover from a plate containing a quiche with salad and new potatoes. There's even a slice of Victoria sponge for dessert.

'I feel like the lady of the manor,' I tell him. 'I'm going to be too full to work after this.' Seeing his face fall, I add, 'I'm joking! It looks wonderful.'

He brightens up. 'I'll leave you to it. Just leave the dishes on the table when you've finished, and I'll tidy them later.'

'Thank you,' I say. 'Is Mrs Patel around?'

He glances behind him, as if she might be lurking in the doorway. 'I believe Madam is up and about. However, she may not make an appearance this afternoon.'

'Fair enough,' I say, relieved. I wonder if she's horribly hungover today.

After lunch, I take Mouse over to the pond area, where I tie his lead to a nearby tree. He's had enough exercise and food to be happy dozing in the shade, snuggling his toy.

Over my meal, it had occurred to me that a formal pond like this is bound to have been built with an integral pump and filter – especially as it's a fish pond. When I was examining the blanket weed, I caught sight of shadowy shapes, slipping through the depths. I'm surprised fish have survived in such a suffocating environment.

First, I look for the electric socket and turn it off. Next, I work out where I would fit the pump if I were building the pond, and reach an arm down into the cold, murky water. Spot-on: I touch the casing of the pump straight away. So, why has it stopped working? There's nothing for it: I'm going to have to go in. I fetch my waders from the van, pull them on, then lower myself into the water. Despite the protection of my neoprene waders, the cold water feels like ice, and I shiver as I make my way over to the pump. It's possible it just wore out with age, but I want to check there's not an easy fix. Taking hold of the pump with both hands, I bring it up to the surface. After peeling off the enveloping layer of blanket weed, I can see one of the connections has come loose. I wiggle it back into place and examine the filter; there's something stuck in there. I reach my fingers inside and manage to grab hold of the obstruction. Drawing it out through one of the filter holes, I discover it's a piece of thin fabric. I replace the pump carefully in the pond, wade back to the shallows and haul myself out. Back on dry land, I switch on the socket and feel somewhat smug as I hear the pump begin to whirr.

I examine the cloth scrap. There's not much to see – it's about the size of a handkerchief, and green and threadbare from its time in the pond. There might be a faded print on it, but it's hard to make out. I place it in my wheelbarrow and peel off my waterproofs. I sit on a bench for a moment, checking the pump is still doing its job. This is a lovely spot, with the water shimmering beneath the March sunshine.

'Well, it's good to see what I pay you for.' Mrs Patel is striding along the path towards me – no mean feat, given today's heels, which are, if possible, even higher than those on the boots she was wearing the last time we met. 'Tell me, do you intend to do *any* work while you're here?'

I stand up. 'I've just fixed the pond filter, and I was making sure it's working properly.'

'Oh, really?'

I ignore her sarcasm. 'You'll be amazed how quickly it will clear the water, now it's running again. We will need some extra help to clear that thick blanket weed – I'm going to have to get another product for that.'

'I don't suppose you've got to the rose hedge yet?'

'Actually, I did that first,' I say. 'I didn't cut it back much, as it's late in the season for a hard prune, and rugosas don't respond well to that treatment.'

'Roses need pruning,' she says, in a firm voice.

'Some roses need pruning,' I allow. 'Rugosas originate from a wild rose that grows in east Asia, and they prefer to be left alone.'

She says nothing. We face each other for a moment like duellers. But then she just says, 'What's left on your list for today?'

'It won't take me long to finish the tasks you set. I'd like to take a look around and make some notes on what else needs doing.'

She nods. 'I'll walk with you.' I hadn't seen that coming, and my heart sinks. Micromanagers are not my favourite type of boss, and Mrs Patel is already proving more difficult than most.

We walk uphill, passing a high beech hedge on our left. It's still hanging on to some of last year's brown foliage, but once it's in full, green leaf, it will entirely conceal the small, brick shed behind it. I stop and point to the outbuilding.

'Do you keep tools in there?' I ask. 'I do always have a selection with me, but—'

'That shed is out of bounds,' she says.

'Oh, right, I was only wondering because—'

'If I catch you anywhere near it, I'll have the residents' committee fire you on the spot.'

I glance curiously towards the small building.

She gestures to a path off to the right that leads into a small copse and we head along it, with her leading the way.

'Aren't you worried about damaging your shoes?' I ask at last, watching her stepping over tree roots in those skinny heels.

She snorts. 'They're only Manolos. I've got about ten more pairs.'

'Well, I prefer gardening boots but whatever works for you.' To my surprise, Mrs Patel laughs.

'Sunil – my husband – was always telling me off for doing chores in my best clothes.'

I laugh, too. 'I don't blame him.'

'He died ten years ago,' she says. 'Now, I think I wear my finest clothes on purpose – it's as if I might still get a rise out of him,' she laughs again briefly. 'Here,' she says, stopping so abruptly that I nearly fall over her.

I glance around. We're still in the woodland, and I can't see any trees that need tending.

'What needs doing?'

'I have a video camera I'd like you to set up.'

I stare at her but she's no longer smiling. 'A . . . camera?'

She nods. 'I wanted to show you the spot first. It needs to be on this tree here.' She pats the bark of an ancient hornbeam.

The tree is at the edge of a small clearing. Apart from that, this section looks the same as the rest of the wood; there's no obvious reason to place a camera here. I could point out that setting up cameras isn't normally filed under 'gardening jobs'. But my curiosity has been piqued, so I decide to go along with it.

'Where is the camera?'

She points to a large box on the far side of the clearing. 'It's all in there.'

I look around. 'There's no electricity out here.'

'It has a built-in battery.'

'Right. Well, I'll just get on with it then.'

'There are ladders in one of the outbuildings. Ask Francis to show you. But please don't go near that brick shed we discussed.'

'That's all right – I have my own ladder.'

She nods with what might be approval, were she capable of such a sentiment.

I'd been assuming she'd leave me to it, but she's waiting for me when I return from the van with my ladder and toolbox, and she watches the entire operation. I am intrigued to see what footage the camera captures; Mrs Patel doesn't strike me as the badger-watching type.

'Done!' I say, after I've angled it to her specifications. I climb down and collect up the packaging.

But she grabs my arm. 'Listen . . . Could you take it home? I don't want the staff to see it.'

Now I'm confused. 'What? The camera?'

She shakes her head in frustration. 'No! The box it came in. Can you take it back with you and dispose of it?'

I shrug. 'I don't see why not. I'll just put it in the van with my tools.'

She squeezes my arm. 'Thank you.'

'You're welcome.'

'Oh, and please don't mention it to anyone.'

'Discretion is my middle name.'

As Mouse and I head back to the cottage that evening – he half-dozing on the passenger seat, with Mr Rabbit between his front paws, and me craving another hot bath, this time to scrub the stench of pond water from my arms – I reflect on the neighbourhood I find myself in. 'They're all mad as hatters, aren't they?' I say to Mouse. He regards me through half-closed eyes before dozing off again.

6

Saturday morning is drizzly, and it takes me a while to persuade Mouse to venture outside: he hates the rain. Even once I get him out, he is sulky and slow and I have to coax him along; he doesn't even perk up at the sight of the soggy sheep in their field. Instead, he keeps tugging on the lead, trying to steer me home. After about an hour, I give up and take him back to the cottage, where we spend the rest of the day curled up on the sofa, watching all sorts of underwater shenanigans with Attenborough on the giant TV. When that palls, Mouse engages in a *Boohbah* marathon. It's a show that ran for one season many years ago, and is best described as *Teletubbies* on acid. I stumbled upon it once on YouTube, and Mouse was instantly transfixed. While it's on, he walks right up to the television and makes little excited yaps with his head on one side. It's quite entertaining in its own right.

Sunday dawns brighter, and Mouse and I enjoy a hike to the lake and back. Mr Rabbit comes along, tucked into a pocket in my rucksack. Now and then, I have to take the toy out to show Mouse that he's safe. The lake is glorious: we see all kinds of ducks, and even a heron lifting off close by, silent and pale. Mouse and I are mesmerised.

That evening, while the two of us are chilling on the sofa after dinner, I turn on my phone. As well as a plethora of voicemails and texts from Ben, all of which I delete, there's a message from my brother, Danny. I call him back.

'Hi, sis. How's it going?'

'Yeah, not bad, thanks.'

'So, do they all live in mansions?'

'Pretty much – with butlers and maids and automatic gates and everything.'

He whistles. 'I hope they're paying you well.'

'Obscene amounts – though I'm not about to tell them that. I can't imagine why the guy before me upped and left.'

'Haven't you asked?'

'I'm not sure I really want to know. This gig feels too good to be true, and I'm not ready to find out it is.'

'What's your own place like? Better than the last hovel? I bloody hope so.'

I shiver at the memory of the rental bedsit I lived in for nine months prior to coming to Beaulieu. What I'd thought was patterned wallpaper had turned out to be the result of many years of untreated damp.

'It's gorgeous. A lovely old gardener's cottage. I'll send you some pictures. Though there was someone in the woods behind it on our first night here. Mouse went mad.'

'It's probably just a dog walker,' he says. I'm not convinced, but I let it drop. He worries about me at the best of times; I'd rather it was just one of us wondering about potential dangers lurking in the woods.

'So . . . have you spoken to Mum?' he asks.

I sigh. 'I don't know what I'm meant to do. I've emailed, I've called, I've left messages. And don't forget that crappy visit.'

A couple of months back, I tried visiting our parents, but Dad intercepted me on the doorstep, telling me Mum wasn't ready to talk to me. I ended up spending the night on their doorstep, too stubborn to leave. Dad did bring me a pillow and some blankets – and a coffee in the morning – but still . . .

'She's not going to ignore you forever,' says Danny.

'I hope you're right . . .' I hesitate, then ask quietly, 'Wouldn't you want to know where you came from, if you were the one who was adopted?'

He sighs. 'I don't know . . . I mean, they have been pretty decent parents, haven't they? When you look at what some of our mates had to deal with at home . . . Anyway, it's not like you don't know anything about your birth family. Mum and Dad gave you that file, with all the research they'd done.'

I have a knot tightening in my stomach, which has become all too frequent an experience since I added my name to the Adoption Contact Register. That's when the people I think of as my real mum and dad – the ones who raised me – stopped taking my calls. I especially hate these discussions with Danny, who, as their biological child, can never fully understand.

'They won't even tell me what my birth mother did for a living,' I say. 'All it says on my birth certificate is "researcher"; that could cover just about anything.'

'It's just difficult for them,' he says gently. 'They feel like you're rejecting them.'

'I do get that; honestly I do. But I'd never do that.'

'I know, sis. Have you heard anything?' He means from my birth mother.

'Not yet.' I sigh. 'So, what's new in your world?'

'Karen's pregnant!'

'Wow,' I say, thinking about how busy Danny and Karen's lives are already, with my niece and two nephews. 'Are you planning to keep going till you have a whole football team?'

'This is only our fourth! And no – this is going to be our last.'

'Congrats to you all.'

'Thanks, Auntie.'

Danny won't call me 'Steph'. He goes out of his way to call me 'Sis' or 'Auntie' instead – and his kids call me 'Auntie Lou'. I've given up trying to persuade him.

'Have you heard from Dick Face?' He means Ben.

'Yeah: he keeps ringing and messaging. I'm ignoring him.'

'Do you want me to speak to him, tell him to back off?'

'No that's OK. I'll speak to him when I'm ready, thanks.'

'Sure. So, how's my favourite dog?'

'Missing his favourite uncle.'

'Next weekend is looking pretty clear at the moment.'

'Thanks. I'll think about it.'

'I could invite Mum and Dad, too.'

'Not thinking about it anymore!'

'All right: just us.'

'I'll let you know.'

Rosie Sandler

After his call, I consider ringing Mum and Dad; I really do. I go as far as scrolling to their number and pressing the call icon.

But the knot is tight in my stomach, and my heart starts pumping too hard. I end the call before it even rings, focusing on my breathing until my heart slows to its normal rhythm. Maybe I'll try later in the week.

My phone rings again, and Ben's name comes up. I turn it off. After everything he's put me through, he can stew a bit longer.

7

According to my timetable, I'm due at The Towers – the castle-style house – this morning. It's the one with the wilderness, so I'm not looking forward to today's experience. I approach the wrought-iron gate with its stone lions atop pillars, and ring the bell – closing my eyes briefly, to make a wish that tending this garden might not prove a Herculean task.

I'm buzzed through by another wordless gatekeeper, and I shift down to second gear, then first, accelerating up the driveway, which thankfully is not as steep as the one at Villa Splendida. At the top, I park my van beside a stunning Range Rover SV Autobiography in a gleaming royal blue. I've read about this particular model, and I'm pretty sure it starts at around £150,000. Mind you, even this beast pales into significance beside its neighbour: a bright-yellow Ferrari 488 Pista Spider – worth, if I'm not mistaken, at least a quarter of a million. I can't resist snapping a picture on my phone, to send to Danny: the Ferrari was always his favourite when we used to play with our Matchbox cars. At the end of the line-up, there's an Audi R8 – another sporty and expensive car – in a flaming shade of red. If I sold these three vehicles, I reckon I could buy a pretty decent detached house with a large garden (somewhere less pricey than Beaulieu Heights, obviously).

When no one comes to greet me at the grey stone building, I ring the bell beside the enormous wooden front door. After a couple of minutes, it's opened by a startlingly beautiful young man with golden skin, green eyes and fine, sandy-colour hair that flops over his face so that he has to keep pushing it back. I always wonder why people don't put a clip in hair like that – or just have it cut so it doesn't get in the way.

'Yeah?' he says. It's not the most promising start.

'I'm Steph, the new gardener.'

'Oh, right . . .' He looks behind him, but no parental figure arrives to rescue him. 'I'll just er . . . let you into the garden, shall I?'

'Do you know if there's a list of jobs for me?'

He steps out, closing the door behind him. He's wearing a blue striped shirt with beige trousers, a navy jumper knotted over his shoulders, and navy loafers. His ensemble is what the Americans call 'preppy'.

He speaks over his shoulder as he unlocks a door in a wall that leads to the back garden.

'I doubt there's a list, to be honest. Ma and Pa are probably still in bed, I'm afraid. Can't you just find some jobs to do?'

'I'm sure I can.'

Having let me through the door, he turns to leave.

'Just one more thing,' I say.

'Yeah?'

'I have a dog with me . . .'

'Oh, that's fine. You can let it off the lead here. Mitzi and Fritz are around somewhere – they're very good with new dogs.'

'Mitzi and Fritz are . . . ?'

'Ma's Pomeranians.'

'Right. Great. Thanks.'

He raises a hand in a casual farewell and leaves.

I fetch Mouse from the van and take him through to the back, where I release him. He bounds off, Mr Rabbit flopping from side to side in his mouth. A moment later, I hear a chorus of barks and infer he's met the Pomeranians. Mouse is always delighted to make new friends, so I leave them to it.

Contrary to my expectations from the wilderness I spotted from the top path last week, the grounds are immaculate. Unlike at The Chimneys, my predecessor appears to have worked hard here. There's a lush, well-cultivated lawn close to the house (though it could do with a mow), then an arch in a yew hedge leads to a sunken pond, not as large as the one at the Villa, though with far more statuary. Lest one forget one was in the grounds of a mock-castle, we have griffins, more lions, and some sort of curious ostrich-like beast, all carved in stone and spurting water like gargoyles.

On the next level comes a room filled with only low yew hedging and white flowers – tulips and hellebores at present, though from the foliage I can see there will be nicotiana, geraniums and clematis, among others, coming into flower as the season continues. I suspect it's inspired by Vita Sackville-West's famous white garden at her Kent home, Sissinghurst. There's a stone bird bath covered in moss, where a female blackbird is revelling in a wash, seemingly oblivious to my presence.

I walk on and finally, right at the top, come to a walled garden with evergreen *Clematis armandii*, creamy and sweet-smelling, providing the first flowers of the year in what is primarily a rose garden. Tea roses are laid out in neat curves radiating from a central circle, and there are many different clematis varieties trained up the outer walls. Around the inner circle there are stone benches and, at the centre, a tall sculpture, rather like an obelisk. It reminds me of pieces by Barbara Hepworth that I've seen in museums and art galleries. Cast in bronze, it must provide a sleek, modern contrast in high summer to the frilled romance of the rose garden in full bloom.

So, where is the wilderness? Puzzled, I glance around at the enclosing walls. It must be on the far side. I walk along the furthest wall, until I find a small green door in the far-left corner. Trying the handle, I discover it's locked. I will have to ask for the key.

I walk back through the grounds with my notebook, making a note of any shrubs for pruning, dead branches for removing, and flowerbeds for weeding. It really is a lovely garden and, not for the first time, I feel a rush of happiness at having landed this job at Beaulieu. Until now, I've only worked across a number of small private gardens, most of which featured a standard rectangle of lawn surrounded by shrubs: nothing close to the scale or creativity there is here. I take a deep breath, inhaling the spring air with its perfumed undercurrent of Daphne. It's another fine morning, with the sun just now burning off a thin layer of white clouds.

Mouse comes racing towards me, and I brace myself for his leaping up. Close on his heels come two fur-balls, one white and the other honey-coloured – the Pomeranians, both with teddy-bear faces and soft fur. They yap at me, but Mouse places himself firmly between us until they calm down. When they've stopped barking, I bend down and stroke them.

'Mitzi and Fritz, I presume.' The honey one charms me immediately by putting a paw on my knee. I check the name on its collar: Fritz. 'Well, I just might have to take you home,' I tell him.

'I do hope not.' I look around and see a tall woman with the same fair hair and striking green eyes as her son, though with a paler complexion.

I stand up and the dogs race off.

She points after Mouse. 'I take it that one's yours?'

I nod. 'I hope that's OK. Your son said—'

'It's fine. It makes my job easier if they've a playmate. They get bored terribly easily.'

'They're very handsome dogs.'

'Yes, and spoilt.' She smiles wryly. 'My husband didn't even want dogs, but he's the one who can't refuse them anything. Thank goodness for the big garden for them to exercise in, or they'd be hugely overweight by now.'

'Talking of the garden . . .'

'Yes, of course. I'm so sorry I was out riding when you arrived, so you had to deal with Adam. I don't imagine he was terribly . . . forthcoming.' She smiles. 'He's studying law, but he claims he doesn't have lectures on a Monday morning. The amount of time he spends here, I'm starting to wonder if he has any lectures. Oh! I'm prattling on and I haven't even introduced myself: Annabelle Qureshi. You won't see my husband Zakariya today, but you should meet him soon.' She holds out a hand, and I remove a glove to shake it, hoping my nails aren't embedded with dirt.

'Steph Williams.'

'Well, Steph, what do you think?' She gestures to the garden.

'It's beautiful. And extremely well tended.'

'Ah yes,' she laughs. 'The previous gardener, Simon, started to slacken off in his duties at one stage, but Zakariya had words with him. My husband is a mild man but he can be quite persuasive when he needs to be.'

I feign fear. 'Don't worry – I won't need *persuading* to get on with my work.' She laughs again. I continue, 'Tell me, did Simon leave any instructions regarding projects, or work needed in the garden?'

She shakes her head. 'Sadly, no. But then, he did leave in a bit of a hurry. Did you hear about that?'

I shake my head, 'No. What happened?'

'Do you know, I'm not entirely sure of the specifics. But apparently, things didn't quite work out with some of the residents.' She sighs. 'Such a shame.' As if checking herself, she says hastily, 'Not that you won't do a great job, I'm sure.' She leans closer and lowers her voice. 'But I can tell you one thing – whatever the reason for Simon's departure, it had something to do with Mimi.'

That sounds ominous. But I am here to garden, not gossip, so I don't respond.

She stands surveying me for a moment longer. We're a similar height – around five ten – but that's where the similarities end. Whilst my hair is pulled back into a ponytail from which curls are already escaping, her waist-length golden tresses spill forward over one shoulder, sleek as a waterfall. Where I'm lean but muscular, Annabelle Qureshi has a willowy figure and the grace of a model. From her elegantly manicured appearance, I'd guess that's exactly what she does – or did – for a profession.

'So, what do you feel needs doing?' she asks.

I clear my throat: 'Actually, it's mainly just mowing, trimming, tidying and a bit of weeding.' She nods. I hesitate, then say, 'There is one thing, though – the patch of land just outside the walled garden – the gate seems to be locked?'

Do I imagine her taking a step back?

'Oh – we don't use that land. The grounds are quite big enough without that extra plot. Now, if that's all, I'll send someone out with a coffee. Unless you'd prefer tea?'

'I'd love a coffee, if that's all right.'

She nods, then turns towards the house, leaving as abruptly as she arrived.

I stand for a moment, reflecting on her double take when I

mentioned the wilderness – I'm sure I didn't imagine it. What on earth can they be keeping in that jungle? Gorillas?

The more I learn about Beaulieu Heights, the less I know. With a shake of my head, I walk back to the van for my tools and set to work.

In the distance, Mouse's deep voice is punctuated with excited yaps from the little Pomeranians. I take off my gloves and crumble a clump of earth between my fingers, breathing in the fresh-soil scent and listening to a blackbird sing his sweet refrain. If I ignore all the peculiarities of the residents and their secrets, this really is a glorious place.

8

The following morning, I'm back at The Mount – the Penwarrens' hulking, dark-stone monolith. Fiona is seated at her easel in the front garden, and she waves to me as I climb down from the van. I let Mouse out and he bounds towards her.

Terrified he's going to knock over her easel, I try shouting, 'Mouse! Stop! Come!' but when he doesn't respond, I switch to running after him, calling, 'I'm sorry – I can't stop him!' But Fiona's laughing. She opens her arms wide and lets him drop Mr Rabbit into her lap, put his paws up on her knees, and lick excitedly at her face.

'It's a long time since I've had a greeting as enthusiastic as that,' she says, smiling. I notice her eyes are red rimmed as she pushes her hair back beneath its scarf.

'I was terrified he'd ruin your work.'

She laughs, waving a hand dismissively. 'I can always paint another.'

I stare at her. I'd assumed all artists would be fiercely protective of their work. Perhaps the more talented and successful they are, the more relaxed they can afford to be with works-in-progress.

Fiona – as she insists I call her – walks with me through the dark tunnel to the back garden, with Mouse trotting besottedly at her heel. I can't help exclaiming again at the view from the tunnel – the perfectly-framed fig tree, backed by lush greenery.

'You have an artist's eye,' she says, smiling. 'The fig was already quite a large specimen when I bought it, but it's still taken the best part of eight years to get it to this height, to create the scene I was after. Your timing is excellent.' She laughs. 'Right: I was thinking you might start in the herb garden, if that's all right? There are dandelions coming up among the herbs.'

'I'll get right on it.'

'Do you know where it is?'

I nod and point to the right. 'Behind that elephant topiary, near the door.'

'That's right – for easy access by the kitchen staff. Now, tea or coffee?'

'A coffee would be lovely if it's no trouble.'

She brings me the brew herself a short time later, making me wonder if she lacks the bank of staff I've seen at some of the other houses.

'Thank you,' I say, accepting the beautiful blue-glazed mug.

'You're welcome. Is it OK if I join you for a wee while?' She perches on a low drystone wall that runs along a raised herb bed, hugging her own mug to her chest.

I can hardly say no, so I nod and keep working, pushing my long grubber – a tool for removing tap roots – deep into the soil and wiggling it, to loosen the grip of a dandelion. Perhaps if I ignore her, Fiona will return to her painting and leave me to my lone musings. But Mouse is delighted to have the company: he keeps putting his front paws in her lap. She rubs his ears and pats him absent-mindedly. It's chilly this morning; the sun has yet to break through the clouds and there's a cool breeze pushing the clouds across the sky and making the plants ripple. I'm glad I'm wearing a fleece over my T-shirt; I may yet need to fetch my jacket from the van. Fiona is dressed in an ice-blue polo-neck top beneath a long, white, flowy garment – tunic or dress, it's hard to say – over white trousers. If possible, she looks even more colour-washed than usual.

The soil in the herb garden is what we in the trade call 'friable' – soft and crumbly – and the dandelions give up fairly easily, their long tap roots pale, like skinny turnips. I'm so absorbed in my task, enjoying the scent of freshly-dug earth, the sounds of sparrows squabbling nearby and a woodpecker squawking in the distance, that I forget Fiona's presence, and she startles me when she starts talking.

'I found something out . . .' she says, 'about my husband.'

It's obvious she's about to share her discovery, and I wonder how many confidences one person can absorb before they explode, secrets bursting from them like the seeds from Himalayan Balsam. I sigh inwardly and keep my face blank as I attack another dandelion. I make what I hope is a noncommittal 'uh-huh', but she takes it as encouragement.

'He pays prostitutes.' She starts to sob.

I let go of the grubber and sit back on my heels, turning to look at her. 'Your husband?'

She nods. Her face is in her hands, even though she's still holding her mug. I get to my feet and go over to her, gently prising the handle from her fingers. Mouse still has a paw in her lap; he gazes up at her anxiously.

'Are you sure?' I ask, as I set her mug safely off to the side.

She nods again. 'I discovered . . . a separate account. He buys them lingerie and takes them to hotels . . .' She breaks off, fierce sobs racking her slim frame. With her face in her hands, she looks like the painting of a saint I once saw in a church. I kneel down and put my arm around her, and she cries on my shoulder. I can feel her tears soaking through my clothing, cold against my skin. Her hair smells of coconut and vanilla – suitably pale ingredients.

After several minutes the sobbing slows, before quietening altogether. She pulls back, wiping her eyes on a handkerchief and sitting up straight.

'Well, that was unexpected!' She laughs awkwardly.

'It's not an easy thing to share,' I say. 'How long have you known?'

'About two months.'

'Two months? You've been holding this in for all that time?' She nods. 'But . . . don't you have any friends who'd understand?'

She wipes her nose on the handkerchief. 'I used to have friends,' she says wistfully, 'but I left them behind in London when I moved here to join Rupert.'

'I think it might be time to get back in touch with them,' I tell her. 'And you definitely need to talk to your husband, if you haven't already.'

My knees are aching from the hard ground; I stand up and take a seat beside her on the wall. Mouse puts his head in my lap, and I stroke his soft ears.

'Oh dear, this isn't what you signed up for, is it?' says Fiona, laughing again.

'The ad really should have specified: *Qualified therapist with horticultural skills*,' I say.

She looks horrified. 'I'm so sorry!'

'No, no,' I say quickly. 'It's not just you.'

'Well, that's something, I suppose. Can I ask who else . . . ?' Her expression has turned cheeky.

'You can ask, but I won't tell you anything – unless you want your own secret shared around the neighbourhood. Quid pro quo and all that.'

'Erm . . . it does sound less tempting when you put it like that.' She lets out a short laugh before standing up. 'Well, I should probably get back to work and let you do the same . . .' She takes my hand and squeezes it. 'Thank you,' she whispers.

I watch her wander back to the front garden, then I return to my weeding with a sigh of gratitude. The blessed silence of plants – they keep most of their secrets to themselves.

Mouse delivers Mr Rabbit to me before loping off through the garden. Taking pleasure in the growing pile of weeds in my wheelbarrow, I tune in to the birdsong of a nearby robin and the alarm sounds of a squirrel. I don't expect to see Mouse for hours – so it's a surprise when he reappears after a short amount of time and drops something at my feet with a single bark.

I remove a gardening glove and pick up the item. It's a ragged piece of cloth, about twenty centimetres by ten. It bears a faded print of red and green trains and it looks familiar. I rummage beneath the pile of weeds in the barrow, until I unearth the small scrap of fabric from Mrs Patel's pond. Laying them side by side on the paved path, I crouch to inspect them more closely. The pond one is more washed-out and has turned green, but they are still strikingly similar.

'Now, what on earth was the same fabric doing in two places?' I ask Mouse. I pick up the larger piece and hold it out to him. 'Where did you find this?'

He barks again and I follow him up the garden. He keeps turning to make sure I'm following. At the top, he leaps over the drystone wall and waits patiently for me to pass through the gate. Then he squeezes through a gap in the paddock fence.

'I hope you haven't been terrorising the ponies,' I tell him as I open and close the wooden gate to the field.

But he pays no attention to the two ponies, who ignore us likewise, grazing calmly near their shed, as he leads me over uneven terrain to the far end of the paddock.

'Is this where you found the cloth?' I ask, sweeping my eyes over the area. There's an old oak tree still waiting for its spring leaves; brambles and dog roses range along the fence.

My eyes are drawn to a section of ground beneath the oak tree. I crouch to look more closely. The earth has been disturbed here: instead of the mix of grass and common perennial weeds like nettles, thistles and dandelions that permeate the rest of the paddock, the earth in this spot is peppered with the tiny shoots of field poppies, which tend to germinate only when the soil is disturbed – that's why so many appeared in the churned-up soil of the World War I battle sites. But in that case, what has been buried – or unearthed – here? I count my steps along the length of the poppy-filled area, and work out that it measures about eight feet by two.

And then I sit down on the ground with a thump. 'It's a grave,' I murmur to Mouse, who has finished his own inspection and come back to me. He makes a questioning sound, head on one side in an attitude that I would normally find funny – but the fist in my belly has clenched, and this time it has nothing to do with my own circumstances, and everything to do with what might have gone on here at Beaulieu.

And then I see that Mouse has brought me another find: a filthy shoe. I don't have to pick it up to see that it's a child's – and the mate to the original Shoe.

Not just a grave: a child's grave.

My head is full of questions. Who is buried here? Is it Alfie – and, if so, who was he? How did he die? Should I be going to the police with this, or do they know already? Am I making a mystery out of nothing?

After sitting for a while, I reach a decision. Pushing myself up to standing, I place the filthy shoe in one pocket of my fleece, and the cloth pieces in the other. I need to find someone at Beaulieu to answer my questions. But do I know anyone here well enough to be sure they will tell me the truth?

I reach the top of the garden and am about a third of the way down the steps when a soft voice startles me:

'Oh, there you are,' says Fiona. 'I've been looking all over for you; would you like a drink?' She peers at me. 'Are you all right?'

'I'm fine,' I say, with more strength than I feel. 'Though I did find something odd up there – in the paddock.'

'Go on,' she says.

I look her in the eye. Her expression is open and interested. 'It's ...' I can't think of a delicate way to phrase it. 'It's a grave.'

She nods. 'Oh yes – that's a very sad story. Shall we sit down?' She gestures to a bench in a nearby arbour, which is covered in a rampant honeysuckle in need of taming. We take seats side by side, and she clears her throat. 'Mimi and her husband had another child. It was a little boy they'd adopted. I don't think they could have another one naturally after Lucy.' She pauses. 'Anyway, some years ago the little boy died. It was a fall from a pony ... So sad. They got permission to bury him in the paddock, which was his favourite place.'

'That's awful.'

She nods again. 'It all happened before I moved here. In the last year or so, there's been a family of foxes up there, and Mimi mentioned in one of the committee meetings that they keep digging in that area. She's quite upset about it, understandably.'

Mouse's discoveries now make more sense, but something is still nudging at the part of my brain that loves to solve puzzles. 'I need to show you some things,' I say to Fiona. I draw out the shoe, together with the larger piece of cloth, wondering why this action feels somehow illicit.

'What are those?' she asks, surprised.

'Mouse found them in the paddock. Do you think they came out of the grave?'

She pulls a face as she takes the stinking shoe from me and examines it at a distance. 'It's certainly come from somewhere. But wouldn't the little boy have been wearing his shoes, when he was buried? I should think these are things that have simply been lost in the paddock over the years.'

'So you don't think the foxes dug them up from the grave?'

She considers this. 'I suppose, if they were buried on top of the grave, that's a possibility.' I nod. 'I would suggest you show them to Mimi,' she continues, 'but under the circumstances, it might be too unpleasant for her. Perhaps best to just forget about it. I'm sure they're nothing important.' She places the objects on the bench between us and I repocket them.

I still can't help wondering why two scraps of the same fabric have been found in different places – how one came to be in the pond, and why the other would have been buried. I'm slightly surprised by her lack of interest in Mouse's treasures, and decide to keep this question to myself for now.

'Thank you,' I say, getting up. 'You're right. I'll let you get back to your painting. I have plenty to be getting on with!'

'Indeed. Don't stay too late, though – and be sure to come and find me when you're heading off.'

I spend the rest of the day engaged in the pleasant tasks of tying in overgrown climbers and weeding some flowerbeds near the top of the garden. There is extensive yew hedging in this section of the grounds, which provides a lovely sense of separate rooms, with arched 'doorways' between the areas.

At the end of the day, when I call to Mouse, I'm relieved to see that the only thing dangling from his mouth is Mr Rabbit. Just after I've fastened him into his seat and finished putting my tools in the back of the van, Fiona reappears. She's bearing a large plastic bag, which she holds out to me.

'To say thank you,' she says.

I put up my hands in protest. 'But I didn't do anything.'

'You listened. Please, I want you to have it.'

I hesitate. There's a cynical voice in my head, telling me that some gifts come with an unspoken obligation. But her expression is still open and she's smiling, so I make up my mind: 'All right then, thank you.'

'Don't peek until you get home.'

The package is flat and rectangular: almost certainly a painting. I place it carefully in the back of the van, climb into the driver's seat, and wave goodbye to Fiona. Then I drive slowly down the slope back to the road. My clutch isn't going to last long, taking these driveways on a daily basis. At the bottom, I turn left towards the cottage. Not for the first time, I feel absurdly lucky when I pull into the parking area and take in the chocolate-box house with its climbing plants and blue wooden door. Thanks to the few possessions I brought with me – including Mouse's bed, some brightly coloured cushions and a few large houseplants – it already feels like home.

I'm dying to set eyes on the gift from Fiona so, as soon as I get inside, I wash my hands at the sink, then lay the bag down on the kitchen counter and draw out the contents. I was right – it is a painting. I gasp at its beauty; Fiona has perfectly captured the dark-and-light of the view from the granite tunnel, with that glorious fig tree. The texture and detail of both the tree's bark and the foliage in the box hedging are exquisite. I run a careful finger over the surface. This must be oils or possibly acrylics – there's too much texture for a watercolour.

'This is gorgeous,' I tell Mouse. But he ignores me and starts running towards the front door, barking. A few seconds later, there's a knock. He carries on barking until I hold up my palm and say, 'Quiet!' in my gravest voice. Only then do I open the door.

There's a tall young woman on the doorstep. She bears a strong resemblance to Apple Singer-Pryce, but with dark hair in a neat bob, instead of bedhead pink. She's also a few years older and is wearing black-rimmed glasses and a grey pencil skirt with a charcoal silk blouse. She looks like someone playing the part of a secretary in a Hollywood film.

'Hello, sorry to bother you . . . I'm Nicola Singer-Pryce, from La Jolla.' Her intonation goes up at the end of the sentence, as if it's a question.

'You're not bothering me. Come in, won't you?'

She shakes her head. 'Mummy's having me go round all the neighbours, to see if anyone's seen my sister.'

'Apple? Is she missing?'

She nods. 'You've met her, then? When did you see her?'

'I only met her the once – when I was working at La Jolla last Wednesday.'

'Oh.' She shrugs. 'Well, I'm sure she's OK. This isn't the first time she's gone AWOL, but Mummy's doing her nut, as per.'

'So she goes missing a lot?' I ask, wondering whether I should break Apple's confidence.

Nicola nods. 'Well, if you hear anything . . .'

She turns to leave, but I've made my decision. I take a deep breath: 'Actually, she did say one thing.'

She turns back. 'Oh? What was that?'

'She wasn't staying at her friend's . . . Pobble, was it?'

She rolls her eyes. 'Of course she wasn't.' She sighs. 'Where was she staying, then?' Her voice has turned harder, but it's obvious her anger isn't directed towards me.

'She was going to a festival. She didn't say which one. I think Pobble was going, too.'

'A festival? Of all the Apple things to do . . .'

'Was she due home today?'

Nicola pushes her glasses up her nose. 'She was actually due home last night, but she rang and begged to stay an extra night at Pobble's. She said she'd definitely be home by eleven this morning, though – she promised to accompany Mummy and me to lunch with Grandma Phyllis.'

That sounds worrying. 'Is there anything I can do to help?'

She shakes her head. 'I'm sure she'll just turn up as usual, not giving a shit about all the panic she's caused.'

'Well, I'll let you know if I hear anything, but I can't imagine I will.'

I wonder whether to say anything about the drugs – but Apple swore she only did cannabis, which surely can't have got her into much trouble. There was that mention of her being in trouble with someone – but without any more information, what use is that?

Nicola takes her leave and I shut the door and lock it for the night before heading to the bathroom to scrub off the mud before dinner.

The bath has an old but functional shower fitted above it. I stand under the water, rubbing a soapy flannel over my sore shoulders while going over the puzzles so far. When I was growing up, my dad used to say I could find a mystery in a box of corn flakes. Maybe he's right, but there are definitely some strange things going on at Beaulieu, with lurkers in the woods, mysterious cloth scraps, and a child's grave . . . Then there's Apple's disappearance. I barely know the girl but I can't help worrying; she seemed so agitated when I last saw her. I hope she's all right.

Mouse and I spend the rest of the evening in quiet companionship. He settles in to watch *Boohbah*. Meanwhile, I turn on my mobile and discover three more voicemails from Ben, which I delete before turning my phone back off.

I immerse myself in a book about Vita Sackville-West's garden at Sissinghurst Castle. The book has been compiled from her own notes and journals, and is filled with pictures of Harold Nicolson's designs and Vita's photographs, including the original white garden that has been replicated at The Towers.

Once again, I'm reminded how lucky I am to be working in this beautiful place. Three months ago, I couldn't have imagined I'd be living in a chocolate-box cottage, with a well-paid, fulfilling job.

I'd better not screw this up.

9

I remember Nicola's visit as I pull up to La Jolla the next day. What if Apple's still missing? Perhaps I shouldn't be here at all. The residents' committee has given me codes to all the driveway gates, and keys to all the back gardens, but I consider pressing the buzzer on the gate to announce myself, in case it's a bad time. But what if that's a disruption in itself?

After much deliberation, I key in the code and drive through as the gates open. At the top of the steep driveway, I park near the garages, turn off the engine and peer out. There's no one around, so there are no clues as to the state of affairs in the household.

The weather, with typical March unpredictability, has turned even colder than the previous day, and it's raining. Mouse whines and refuses to get down from the van.

'OK, boy – you can stay here. I'll come back to see you in a while.'

He stretches out across the front seats, snuggling Mr Rabbit. They look very cosy. Shivering, I pull up the hood of my jacket and wish I could shelter in the van with them.

I hesitate again before unlocking the garden gate: perhaps I should call at the front door first? I'm still deliberating when a window opens close by. It's Nicola.

'Apple's still not home,' she says, 'but Mummy's had a text from her.'

'Oh – what did it say? Is she OK?'

'Just that she and Pobble had decided to go down to Bristol for a couple of nights. They have a bunch of friends there, so . . .' She shrugs. 'Anyway, they should be back tonight.' She looks pale and there are dark circles visible through the lenses of her black-rim glasses. Her dark hair is pulled back into a severe bun.

'Are you worried?'

She waves a hand. 'Oh, no, it's typical Apple.'

'Have you tried calling her since?'

'She's turned her phone off. Honestly, she drives poor Mummy to despair. She's probably lost her charger again.'

Should I tell her what Apple told me? But there's nothing tangible to go on.

'Look, it's none of my business . . .' I trail off.

'Yes?'

'Well, has your mother informed the police? If she's not answering her phone, there's no proof she's the one sending the texts.'

Nicola stares at me. 'What – you think she's been kidnapped or something?'

'Probably not.' I see a look of horror on her face, and correct myself. 'I mean, no, of course not.'

I close my eyes briefly and make my decision. After all, if the girl turns out to be in trouble, I'd never forgive myself for keeping quiet. 'Look . . . the other day, when I talked to her, she told me she had got into trouble with someone.'

'What do you mean? What kind of trouble? Who with?'

'I have no idea. But she seemed very concerned about it.'

She folds her arms. 'Look, you've been here – what, two weeks?'

'One and a bit,' I say.

'And you're acting like you know my sister – who we've known for seventeen years – better than we do.'

I take a breath, and step back. Apple's sister is quite formidable given she must be barely twenty. 'You're right, Nicola. I just want you to have all the information.'

'Look, I told you yesterday, she does this kind of thing. This is classic Apple – thinking only about herself and not caring about the rest of us stuck at home, worrying.'

'Well, I hope she gets back soon.'

'She's promised to come home tonight.'

'That's great. Good. Well, I'll get on then. Thanks for filling me in.'

She shuts the window abruptly. With a sigh, I fetch my wheelbarrow and tools from the van, where Mouse is watching the rain forlornly through the window. I wave to him before tramping round to the garden.

For the rest of the day I work in the damp, weeding one flowerbed at a time. Raindrops drip down my nose and somehow make it inside my hood and down the back of my neck. My gloves quickly get soaked through, and my hands become freezing and stiff, making them unwieldy, like badly-fitted prosthetics.

The whole time I'm working, I'm thinking back to my one meeting with Apple. What was the big secret she'd wanted to tell me? And is she in danger of some kind? The family obviously aren't too concerned, but she'd seemed so young and . . . guileless. I hope she really is coming home tonight.

The next morning, Mimi is waiting for me when I arrive at The Chimneys. I climb down from the van to greet her, leaving Mouse in his seat for the time being.

She doesn't bother with formalities, but simply says, 'The urns are missing'.

'Urns?'

'Yes,' she says impatiently. 'The pair at the entrance to the main lawn.'

'Oh, those,' I say. 'Are you sure?'

'Come and look if you don't believe me.'

'No, I believe you. Just . . . how? Who could have got in?'

'I think . . . no, I *know* Lucy left the gate to the garden unlocked overnight.' She sighs, then adds, 'She and I both keep forgetting to shut the gate at the bottom of the driveway; we have a tendency to leave it propped open, for easy access.'

'But someone would still have to gain access to the estate.'

'Estate? Oh, you mean the community. Well, the main buzzer sounds in all of our houses, and some of the staff and youngsters just let in anyone, without checking. I've told them over and over again, but they won't listen.'

'So, you think . . .'

'. . . someone must have come from outside. Any number of delivery people would know how easy it is to access Beaulieu.'

'The urns – were they precious?'

She sighs again. 'They didn't have sentimental value, if that's

61

what you mean, but they were antiques, so they were worth several thousand each.'

'Oh, no.'

'I've called the police, but they didn't seem terribly interested. I suppose they're hardly going to consider the theft of a couple of plant pots – as they're bound to see them – an emergency, or even especially worth investigating.'

We walk through to the garden together. There are bare patches of compacted earth where the urns stood. I don't know what to say, so I point to the lawn instead.

'That turf is taking well.'

'Yes,' she says. 'You're doing a good job.'

Praise from the abrasive Mimi Purdue is so unexpected, I feel myself blush. 'All I've done is let in the light. It was the contractors I hired who laid the new turf. Now I just need to set the sprinklers to come on when there's no rain forecast. I'll do that before I leave today.'

'Yes, well, the lawn is coming along nicely, as you say.'

'I'm glad you're pleased. By the way, have you heard if Apple Singer-Pryce is back home?'

'Oh, you heard about that, did you? She's flighty that one, always disappearing and giving Bubby a scare.' So that *is* Mrs Singer-Pryce's real name. 'Thank goodness I don't have to worry about Lucy vanishing every time I turn my back.'

'So, is Apple home?'

Mimi frowns. 'Come to think of it, I haven't heard from Bubby. I'll give her a call.'

'Can I ask, if it's not too much trouble . . . ?'

'Of course, I'll let you know.'

'Thank you.'

'Meanwhile, if you hear anything about the urns or any suspicious vehicles or activity last night, do let me know. I have notified all the residents, of course, but as the gardener, you spend time in all the gardens, so you might see or hear something . . . Hopefully it's a one-off but you can't be too careful. I've made Lucy understand how important it is to lock the garden gate, even if we are shutting the stable door after the horse has bolted, so to speak.'

'Have you checked on the actual horses?' I ask.

'Yes – Annabelle sent the groom up. They're fine, as are the ponies in the top paddock.' Do I imagine it, or does she stop speaking for a second or two after mentioning the top paddock, as if she's given herself away? I'd love to ask about Alfie, and show her the items Mouse found, but it seems intrusive straight after the burglary.

Mimi heads back into the house, and reappears about fifteen minutes later, when I'm planting colchicum (autumn crocus) bulbs beneath the cherry tree and silver birches by the main lawn. The two bare patches of earth where the urns stood are a blight on the otherwise newly lush landscape. Sunlight filters through the branches above, daubing pale shadows across the grass. I've let Mouse out of the van and he's off in the grounds somewhere, exploring.

I sit back on my heels and admire the shadows of the trees, moving in the breeze like long fingers across the sward.

'Well, well,' says Mimi, walking towards me and breaking through my musings. 'I spoke to Nicola – their elder daughter.'

I sit back on my heels. 'And?'

'The wanderer has returned.'

'Oh, thank goodness!' I'm so relieved to hear Apple's safely home, I don't focus for a moment on Mimi's next words. I tune back in as she's saying:

'. . . a bruise on her cheekbone, and when her mother asked how she'd come by it, the child simply said she'd slept on a stone or some such nonsense.'

'A bruise?' I picture Apple's sweet little face and feel unexpectedly protective. 'But she's all right apart from that?'

Mimi looks at me slightly oddly. 'Well, as I said, she is more subdued than normal.'

'Oh, right! Yes, of course.'

Mimi tuts. 'Honestly, teenagers can be such a nightmare, can't they?'

'I know I was.'

She fixes me with a scrutinising gaze. Once again, I feel like I'm back in my English teacher's class, about to be reprimanded for my bad handwriting.

'Did you cause your mother a lot of grief?' she asks.

'A fair amount. To be honest though, I seem to have upset her more since I became an adult. She's currently not talking to me.' I hadn't intended to tell her that, but when I glance at her face, she looks more sympathetic than judgmental.

'Oh, dear: families. They can be so difficult, can't they?'

I'm embarrassed to feel tears welling up. I've been so caught up with all the intrigues at Beaulieu that I'd forgotten about my own difficulties. To some extent, it's been a welcome distraction to focus on someone else's drama. I lean over to scoop out the next hole with my trowel, placing the autumn crocus bulb gently in the soft soil and covering it. When I glance up, Mimi's still there, watching. 'Cup of tea?' she says at last.

'That would be lovely; yes, please.' I'd prefer a coffee, but I'll take what I'm offered.

While Mimi goes to find an underling for the difficult task of pouring boiling water over a teabag, I listen to Mouse barking in the distance, clearly having a wonderful time.

My tea is brought by the same maid who served us in the living room last week. I find out she's called Kate, and has been working for Mimi for two years. Kate turns out to be one of those people who answer questions you had no intention of asking. I get on with the bulb planting while she tells me stories of her last place, where the 'mistress' shouted all the time. The whole set-up seems archaic to me – a hierarchy that I had naively believed long over. This is *Upstairs, Downstairs* or *Downton Abbey* – except that this is reality, and I live here. My place, I presume, is firmly 'downstairs'. Kate's words keep coming, a continuous current of noise until, mercifully, another member of staff appears at the back door and calls her in.

'I'd better go or I'll be in trouble,' she says. 'Catch you later.'

I say goodbye, then sit back on my heels and close my eyes in relief. There are too many puzzles to pick over, and Kate's chatter was getting in the way. I shudder as an image of Apple, her cheek bruised, comes into my mind. Relieved though I am to know she's home, I can't help wondering how she got hurt. My thoughts wander again to the grave in the paddock, and the items that Mouse has 'retrieved'. Perhaps I *should* approach Mimi on the subject after all. There's something to unravel there, I'm sure of it.

By the time I've planted all the bulbs, I've made up my mind and changed it at least twice. But I fix my resolve: I need to speak to Mimi. I remove my gardening gloves and walk round to the front door. Then, glancing down at my filthy appearance, I have second thoughts about presenting myself there. I'm not sure there's any logic to my thinking, but it feels better to knock on the back door when bearing dirty clothing and leading questions.

Kate answers my knock. 'Did you want more tea? Or a coffee maybe?'

'Oh – maybe a coffee in a bit, thanks. I was just wondering if Ms Purdue's available?'

'Let me check. Do you want to come in?'

'No, thanks – I'm way too mucky. I'll just wait here, if that's all right?'

She nods and heads briskly away down the same corridor I walked last week, when I went in for tea. I wonder if Mimi Purdue will feel differently about having me in her home after finding out I've been 'snooping', as it will probably appear from the outside.

After a couple of minutes, Lucy comes to the door. She's wearing a coat, as if she's just heading out. 'Mum's a bit tied up at the moment. Can I help at all? Though I don't know much about gardening stuff.'

I shake my head. 'It can wait, thanks.'

She fixes me with her intense hazel gaze. 'Are you sure?'

'I'm sure.'

'OK, then.' She shrugs and walks off.

Kate reappears almost immediately. 'Are you ready for that drink?'

'I'll take a strong coffee, please.'

She leans forward and whispers, 'I'll throw in a slice of lemon drizzle, if you're interested?'

'I'm very interested,' I assure her.

'Was it important?' she asks. 'Whatever you wanted to talk to the mistress about.'

'It was important but not urgent, if that makes sense?'

She nods, her eyes wide in her thin, freckled face. 'Do you want to talk about it?'

'Not really, thanks. It's not about me. Oh – if you have a bowl you can put out with some water for my dog, that would be great.'

She nods, looking disappointed. 'Well, I'd better get on,' she says, slightly sniffily.

With a sigh, I take a seat on a wall close to the house and survey the grounds. The truth is, Mimi's garden is more than a little overwhelming. I could do with spending five days a week here, at least until I get it under control – but there are four other clients. It's unusual for a single gardener to be expected to tend five such large plots. I remind myself that there is the option to bring in extra help for specific tasks – with the approval of the residents' committee, of course.

The committee has taken on a somewhat mythical form in my imagination. I keep picturing its members dressed in black gowns and some form of esoteric headgear – somewhere between the Masons and a board of university lecturers. Although I know Mimi is the chairperson, I keep seeing a shadowy Rupert Penwarren at the head of the table. I haven't yet met Mr Penwarren, but his wife's revelation about his cheating has made me dislike him intensely. I am like Mr Darcy: *My good opinion, once lost, is lost forever.* Surely the lovely, talented Fiona Penwarren deserves someone better?

I take a break when a subdued Kate brings my coffee and cake, and I call Mouse back for his bowl of water.

'No grand lunch for you today, boy,' I tell him as he sniffs unenthusiastically at his dish. He seems to understand, and sets to drinking his water so speedily and with such little finesse that I'm pretty sure most of it ends up on the ground. He picks up Mr Rabbit and comes over to me, stretching across my feet. I stroke his soft fur and ears until I've finished my coffee, when I fork the last mouthful of delicious, lemony cake into my mouth and stand up.

'Sorry, boy, but I have to get on. You can stay here and sleep if you like.'

I leave him dozing beneath one of the beautiful silver birches, and head up to my next task, cutting back a *Clematis montana* that has made a bid for freedom from its allocated row of trellis along a wall. I'm not thrilled to be cutting it back right before flowering, but it has taken over various nearby shrubs and trees. I've discovered with some relief that most of the grounds here at The Chimneys are overgrown, rather than unplanned; the bones of it are all here, they just need to be revealed. I feel like Mary Lennox in *The Secret Garden*, gently removing the overgrowth to restore the garden to life.

By four o'clock, my shoulders and back are aching, and I'm longing to get home, so I pack my tools and wheelbarrow into the van and call to Mouse, who has woken from his nap and returned to his exploration. He joins me at the vehicle, where I strap him into his seat and we head back to the cottage.

I cook myself an early dinner of boil-in-the-bag fish with new potatoes, while listening to a crime podcast. It's getting close to the big reveal and I'm convinced I've worked out who the killer is.

Mouse has already had his dinner, and he's out in the garden, barking at shadows. I'm keeping an ear out for any alarm in his tone, but so far he is just enjoying himself. Our night visitor hasn't paid a return visit since that first night at Beaulieu – perhaps they were deterred by discovering the cottage had a pair of new residents.

My mobile rings and I see Danny's name come up, so I answer, putting him on speaker.

He dispenses with the preliminaries. 'So, are you coming to visit this weekend?'

I lift the lid on the fish and get a face full of steam.

'Go on, then. It'll be good to see you.'

'Great. Do you want to come on Friday and stay two nights?'

'Sure,' I say. 'Is Karen all right with that?'

My sister-in-law is always welcoming, but I wouldn't blame her if she occasionally resented the close relationship I have with her husband. A lot of the time, he and I are more like best friends than siblings.

'She'll be fine. You know she loves you and Mouse.'

'All right; I'll drive up after work tomorrow.'

'Perfect. I'll tell the kids.'

In the bath, after dinner, I think about the form I filled in a few months ago, hoping to trace my birth mother. It was perhaps naive of me to hope she might already have registered on the database, but the silence is painful. What if she doesn't want to hear from me? That's too awful an idea to contemplate.

I force my brain to change tack, and go over everything that's happened since I arrived at Beaulieu: there's nothing like an unsolved mystery (or two) to cheer me up. First, there was the lurker in the woods on the night we arrived. Then Apple's interrupted confidence, followed by her going missing and returning with a bruise on her face. Perhaps there's an innocent explanation for that, and she and Pobble really did just go to visit friends. I'm forever hurting myself after all – on thorny bushes or overhanging branches. And what about Mrs Patel and her video camera in the woods? Then there's the disturbed grave, with those scraps of cloth and the child's shoes. And on top of all this, Mimi's urns have been stolen . . . I've been working here for less than two weeks. Perhaps my predecessor left because he couldn't cope with all the drama.

Feeling overwhelmed, I close my eyes and breathe deeply. Not for the first time, I decide that I need to draw some boundaries; after all, my role is not to provide emotional support. As Mimi so charmingly phrased it on my first day of work: 'You're the gardener. So garden.'

10

The next morning, Francis comes bustling out of the back door of Villa Splendida as I'm unloading my tools from the wheelbarrow. He isn't wearing his apron today, though he has a tea towel slung over one shoulder. I suspect he's forgotten it's there.

'Ms Williams, I'm so sorry I wasn't there to greet you,' he says. 'I got held up in the kitchen.'

I look at him. 'I'm staff, too, Francis – you don't have to greet me or wait on me. And I wish you'd call me Steph.'

He smiles. 'I don't think I'd be comfortable calling you by your first name.'

'Well, then, what's your surname?'

'Morgan, but don't worry about that. Now, what can I get for you?'

'I've already had breakfast, Sir Francis. However, a black coffee would be brilliant. I only have instant at the cottage, and it's just not the same.'

He bows slightly. 'I'll be on it directly, ma'am.'

'Oh, now, that's even worse!'

Is that a smile on the face of this formal gentleman as he heads back to the house?

When he returns a few minutes later, bringing coffee, together with a plate of home-baked biscuits, I ask him the whereabouts of the mistress of the house.

'I'm afraid Madam's not down yet. Would you like to see her when she's available?'

'Maybe,' I say, thinking about my discovery in her pond. I keep wavering between talking to Mimi and talking to Mrs Patel. 'I'm not sure . . .'

'Well, let me know. In the meantime, Madam left this list of jobs.' He hands me a scrawled note.

'Thank you. And thanks for these.' I hold up the mug and the plate of biscuits.

He nods and grins – actually grins – and I realise he's younger than I'd originally thought: he can't be older than late thirties/early forties. Thanks to his grave demeanour, I'd had him down for at least his fifties.

The note bears a list of chores, from raking fallen leaves beneath the beech hedge (about as futile as vacuuming a beach – there will be just as many leaves there tomorrow) to weeding the vegetable patch near the top of the garden. The head gardeners and designers of older properties tended to place the kitchen garden close to the house, for ease of access to crops. This was clearly not on anyone's agenda when planning the garden at the Villa. I feel sorry for the kitchen staff, having to climb the hill each time they need some broccoli or a sprig of rosemary. I make a note in my gardening notebook to have the kitchen garden moved for easier access. This will be a big job, but I can bring in a team to carry out the bulk of the work in late autumn.

It's dry and mild today, and the sun is attempting to break through a thin layer of clouds. As per my previous visit, I let Mouse off the lead for the morning. At five to one, I call him back and tie him to a tree near the house. I'm just wondering if I should eat my sandwiches, or if Francis is going to appear again with delicious food, when Mrs Patel opens the back door and steps out.

'Steph, hello. I need to speak to you.'

'Sure.'

She comes over, striding as confidently as ever on high, narrow heels. 'I was hoping we might take a look at that video camera together.'

'OK. But you do know that video security isn't my area of expertise? I fixed it to the tree and checked the switch was on, but that's about the extent of my know-how.'

'It's not about that,' she says mysteriously. 'Follow me.'

I find myself once again hurrying after her down the path into the woodland. She walks very quickly for such a tiny woman on the equivalent of skinny stilts.

'There,' she says, pointing up at the spot on the hornbeam where I attached the camera. I follow her finger.

'Oh!' I say. It's the strangest thing: a black bag has been tied over the lens.

'Quite,' she says. 'Though it does somewhat support my theory . . .' I wait for her to spin me a yarn about dexterous squirrels or highly accomplished owls, but she doesn't elaborate. 'Anyway, can you get it off?'

'Of course,' I say. 'Though whoever covered it might just do it again.' She nods. 'Let's see.'

I decide to take advantage of the pause that follows. 'There is something I wanted to talk to you about.'

'Oh? If it's about your schedule or pay, you should really take it up with Mimi and the committee.'

I shake my head. 'It's not. It's about something I found in your pond, when I was mending the pump.'

'It's not my engagement ring, is it? It's the only place we haven't looked.'

'It's not, I'm afraid.' I stashed the smaller of the pieces of fabric in my jacket pocket earlier, and now I draw it out. Her face is blank – I don't think she recognises it. But then, it is just a greened scrap: there's not much to recognise.

'What is that – an old handkerchief?'

'No, it's a torn piece of cloth. It was caught in the pond filter.'

'And you're showing me this because . . . ?'

'A larger section of the same cloth was in the top paddock, along with a pair of child's shoes.'

It's shady in the copse, but I can still see Mrs Patel turn pale under her fake tan. 'Why on earth have you been poking around up there?'

'I haven't. Mouse – my dog – went to explore, and brought things back.'

'Your dog . . . ? You mean you just let it wander around freely?'

It's my turn to change colour, though mine's an angry flush. 'Most people are happy for him to have the run of their grounds.'

She snorts. 'And you're suggesting these items were in the top paddock? An area that is outside your remit – I'm quite sure that Mimi told you so on your first day.'

'She said I wouldn't need to tend it, which isn't the same thing.'

'Nevertheless, you took it upon yourself to go there.'

'My dog,' I say firmly, 'showed me where he'd found the items: by the grave . . .'

She looks hard at me. 'What do you know about the grave?'

Not sure what she's getting at, I say, 'It belongs to Mimi's son, doesn't it?' I remember the name Mimi used and decide to test her reaction: 'Alfie?'

She glares at me – there's no other word for it. 'You are not to mention this to Mimi. Let me explain your role here,' she says very slowly and deliberately, as if I might not otherwise understand. Her Essex accent has become more pronounced. 'You are a gardener. Your job is not to dig around on private property or stick your nose into our private affairs. Your job is to weed and prune and plant. Nothing else.'

'You left off video cameras,' I say, unable to hold my tongue. 'I have to fix those to trees, apparently, and maintain them when someone covers them in black plastic.'

'You're right,' she says without missing a beat. 'You do have to do that as well.'

Determined she won't provoke me further, I focus on setting up my steps and climbing up to remove the plastic covering from the camera lens. There's one piece of the tape that takes a little while to peel off and, when I get back down, Mrs Patel's gone. I feel a mixture of relief and exasperation. Thanks to her technique of responding to queries with accusations, she's managed to avoid answering my questions all together. She should be a politician. Perhaps she is.

I take my ladder back to the van and go to check on Mouse. He's curled up contentedly with Mr Rabbit, an empty china bowl beside him. I wonder what succulent treat he's had for lunch today.

Then I spot some dishes on the table. My stomach rumbling, I lift a large, silver lid and find a plate with a homemade pie, and potato salad. There's also a pot of coffee with a cup and saucer, and a covered milk jug. Another lid turns out to be protecting a bowl of apple crumble, still steaming, plus a second jug, this time containing custard. I could get used to this life, if it weren't for the clients.

I take a seat at the table and tuck in. The meal is delicious but my hand surprises me by trembling each time I raise the fork to my lips. I pause with it in mid-air, as I try to work out what's going on. It takes me a moment to realise that I've been shaken by my conversation with Mrs Patel. Her evasive attitude when I mentioned the grave confirms my suspicions that there is something troubling about it. She appeared . . . I search for the word . . . threatened.

While I eat, I go over the finds – and Mrs Patel's reaction to them. She is definitely hiding something. I sigh and scrape up the last of the crumble. Whatever is going on, I'm determined to get to the bottom of it.

While I take out Mrs Patel's list and start on the next task, my brain buzzes with questions. Who was she hoping to capture with that video camera, and why did they cover the lens? And what, if anything, is she hiding about the child's grave?

I don't see Her Ladyship for the rest of the day, which prevents me from pursuing any of my lines of enquiry.

Raking the beech leaves turns out to be a meditation in its own right. I find it essential to approach tasks like this with an acceptance of the fact that it can never be finished. Instead, I tune out everything except for the birdsong, the crunch of the dead leaves, the sensation of the rake in my hands and the satisfying sweep of its movement. By the end, I have several neat piles of crisp brown leaves. I shovel them into the barrow and take a break for some swigs from my water bottle. I find my eye drawn to the forbidden shed behind the hedge. I wonder what she keeps in there. Perhaps that's what really happened to the last gardener. I laugh at my own morbid imagination.

After wheeling the leaves up to the composting area, I continue to check off jobs on the list. When I've finished Mrs P's chores, I tour the garden, tying in climbers and removing any shrub branches that are heading in the wrong direction and threatening to obstruct paths.

I'm so exhausted by the time four o'clock rolls around, I wish I hadn't told Danny I'd visit. I'd kill for a night in with a bottle of red wine.

Mouse and I take the van back to the cottage, where I shower, don clean jeans and a sweatshirt and eat a toasted sandwich. After Mouse has had his canned dinner (which he sniffs unenthusiastically after the fine food at the Villa), I make the mistake of mentioning Alice and Frankie's names. He immediately starts tearing around the place, bringing me random items to pack. It appears we need the TV remote, some dirty knickers from the wash bin, a cushion from the sofa, and something that looks like a very old boiled sweet, sourced from goodness knows where. I accept his offerings but pack what we actually need into the back of the van. We're on our way by 5.30 p.m. I hadn't reckoned on Friday evening traffic – the M25 is stop-start for miles, and it's gone nine by the time I pull up outside Danny and Karen's pretty 1930s semi on the outskirts of Peterborough. Mouse has fallen asleep en route, and I've established I was right about the identity of the murderer in the crime podcast.

'Auntie Lou!' The kids come running out of the house as soon as I climb down from the van.

'Hello! Isn't it past your bedtime?' I ask them.

'Mummy and Daddy said we could stay up to see you,' says Frankie.

'Well, aren't I lucky?' I give Alice and Frankie big hugs. Luke's still a toddler and Karen appears in the front doorway holding him in her arms. He's pointing at his siblings, and squirming to get down and follow them.

'Where's Mouse?' asks Frankie.

I lift up my little nephew and let him look through the van window. 'Fast asleep, look,' I whisper. 'Phew! You're getting heavy!'

'I want to stroke him.'

I set my nephew back on the ground. 'Well, I'll bring him in and I'm sure he'll want to say hello.'

Danny comes out of the house and holds the kids' hands while I clip on Mouse's lead and let him out. He's sleepy but he starts panting excitedly and straining on the lead the minute he sets eyes on the kids. He drops Mr Rabbit on the pavement and jumps up at them; I have to pull him back before he can slobber all over their faces.

'Calm down, boy, OK?'

The kids are giggling with pleasure at seeing their old friend.

'Can I walk him in?' asks Frankie.

'OK, but you have to keep a tight hold on his lead.' I say this only to make Frankie feel important – Mouse isn't going anywhere. He adores the children.

'Hello and welcome,' says Karen with a big smile, when I reach the front door with my bags.

'Hiya,' I say. 'Thanks for having me.'

'Any time,' she says, and I know she means it. She and Danny have a bond that means they each will do anything to support the other. It makes me feel both loved and very lonely.

After the kids are settled (I have to read the older two a rhyming bedtime story about a bear who likes to travel by a variety of different vehicles. Alice pronounces the book 'babyish', but still seems to enjoy reciting along with my reading), I go down to the living room and accept a glass of red wine held out to me by Danny.

'Thank you,' I say, sinking into the soft sofa. 'Can I just stay here like this, and never get up again?'

'I'm glad you said that,' says Danny with a laugh, 'because that sofa's going to be your bed. We've given Luke the guest bedroom, and we're going to put the baby in Luke's old room. At the moment, it's general storage-cum-laundry room.'

'That's fine. To be honest, I'm so tired, I'd sleep in the shed if you asked me.'

Karen pulls a sympathetic face. 'Is your new job very tough?'

'The work's not too bad in itself, though there's huge amounts to do. You should see the houses – they're all amazing, with beautiful views. But the clients are all kind of entitled.' For some reason, Fiona Penwarren's distraught face flashes into my head, and I feel a stab of guilt.

'Would you like to turn in now?' asks Danny. 'You've had a long drive to get here.'

'Is that OK?'

'Of course, that's fine. We're knackered, too. There's some Chinese takeaway in the fridge if you're hungry – I'm sorry, we couldn't wait.' He brings me bedding and towels, and they each give me a kiss before heading upstairs. I finish my glass of wine and head to the ground-floor toilet to clean my teeth and face. Before settling down, I poke my head inside the utility room, where the kids have set up a nest of cushions for Mouse in one corner, saving my bringing in his bed. He's asleep already, Mr Rabbit tucked under his chin. The dog's legs are twitching as he chases squirrels in his dreams. I make myself comfortable on the sofa, worried I'll spend the night awake, distracted by Beaulieu and its inhabitants. But sleep drags me down, and I'm plunged into darkness and strange dreams.

11

The next morning, I'm awoken even earlier than my internal clock by Frankie leaping on top of me.

'Oof! I'm dead now,' I complain.

He laughs. 'No you're not – you're talking.'

'I've been squashed to death. Call the police.'

'You're silly, Auntie Lou.'

'Am I? Oh dear. Maybe you'd better call the Silly Police instead.'

He shakes his head seriously. 'I don't think you can be arrested for being silly.'

'Well, that's a relief.' I sit up. 'Now, I hear you humans like to eat something called "cereal". Is there such a thing in this house?'

'Yes! Yes! Yes!' He bounces up and down and I groan for real this time, as he lands on my stomach.

'Off! Off!' I lift him down from the sofa and fold my bedding into a neat pile.

I let Mouse out of the utility room and open the back door so he can go outside for a wee. When I glance out of the window I can see him sniffing his way around the small garden. Hopefully I can put off walking him for a while.

Alice joins us in the kitchen while Frankie and I are eating our cereal, so I set out a bowl and spoon for her. Then I hear toddler-shrieks from upstairs and gather Luke is also now awake.

'Shall we give your mum and dad a break and bring Luke down?' I suggest. Alice and Frankie shrug without enthusiasm but I go to fetch him anyway.

Luke loves his Ready Brek. While I'm trying to spoon-feed him, he's busy sticking his fingers in it, smearing it on his highchair tray and rubbing it in his hair. By the time Karen appears, her youngest son looks like the 'before' part of an advert for washing powder.

'I'm so sorry,' I say. 'He's covered in it.'

'Are you kidding? Have you any idea how long it is since I was able to sleep till seven? You're my heroine. I'm going to name our next baby after you.'

Alice looks upset. 'I thought I was going to choose the name!'

'You are, darling; I was only joking.'

'What names are you considering?' I ask my niece.

'I'm thinking maybe "Steph",' she says slowly and deliberately, looking from her mum to me.

There's a long pause. Then Karen says brightly, 'Well, we've got plenty of time to think about it.'

'Don't you like the name?' asks Alice. I can tell she's testing her mother's reaction, but I'm not sure why. She obviously knows it's my name nowadays – but maybe she's trying to work out why no one in her family calls me by it.

'What would you like for breakfast?' I ask Karen.

'Oh, I should clear the table first.'

'I'll do that,' I say, collecting up the kids' bowls and spoons. I try to take Luke's plastic spoon from him, but he has it in a cast-iron grip and he's not relinquishing it.

'Da!' he says, banging it repeatedly on his tray. 'Da! Da!'

'Just leave him,' says Karen. 'It's keeping him occupied.'

'I've made a pot of coffee if you're interested?'

'I love you.'

'Cupboard love,' I say with a grin.

Danny enters, and I make us all scrambled eggs on toast; we sit and chat about our lives as we eat. Frankie and Alice have gone out to the garden; we can hear them kicking a ball around. After breakfast, I stack everything in the dishwasher and wipe down the surfaces before taking a shower and pulling on fresh clothes. In the meantime, Danny has cleaned up Luke, so I take the toddler out to the garden to join his siblings.

Suddenly, there's a happy squeal from Alice and I see her running towards the house. 'Granny! Grandad!' she shouts. Frankie follows and Mouse runs after them both, barking loudly. Luke also toddles off in the direction of all the excitement.

And there they are: my parents. It's only two months since I last saw Dad, but he looks older somehow. Mum (who wouldn't even come to the doorstep to say hello on my last visit to them) looks pretty much the same as the last time I saw her.

It takes them a moment to spot me. First, Mum bends down to give Alice and Frankie a big squeeze; then Dad does the same. Mum scoops up Luke, and together the group walks towards me, with Mouse trotting happily alongside.

'What's Mouse doing here?' Dad asks. 'Is he staying with you?' Then he notices me. 'Oh, Pamela look: it's Louise.'

I can't hear my mum's response and I am suddenly hyper aware of my blood pumping hard in my ears: thud, thud, thud. I can't catch my breath, so I sit down on a bench with my back to my parents and try to slow my breathing.

And then my dad is standing right beside me.

'Hiya, love. How are you?' he asks.

'I'm OK,' I say cautiously. 'How are you two?'

'Oh, we're fine.' He lowers his voice: 'Your mum's missing you though.'

I remember Danny saying they were scared I might reject them, so I stop myself from saying, *Well, whose fault is that*?

He takes a seat beside me on the bench.

'Dad . . .' I begin. 'I'm not looking to replace you and Mum. You know that, right?'

He smiles but he looks sad. I glance around for Mum and see she's sitting on the patio with Alice on her lap. They're laughing together, and I feel a pang to be a part of that closeness.

'We didn't know you'd be here,' says Dad.

'Danny didn't tell me either.'

'It's lovely to see you,' he says. 'You look well.'

'Thanks, Dad. I am well. How about you?'

'Oh . . . all the better for seeing my favourite daughter.'

'Will Mum talk to me?' I ask him.

'She might. Let's see if we can make that happen in the next week or so.' There's a long pause, then he says, 'Where are you up to, with the search?'

'Nowhere.'

He looks surprised. 'Why not?'

'Well, you have to register on the national database – but if the birth parents haven't registered, then you just have to sit and wait, hoping they do at some point.'

'I see. There must be some way of speeding things up?'

I nod. 'There are agencies you can contact. But I'm not there yet. And you and Mum have made it clear how you feel about it all.'

'Look, love, we were upset. But I've been reading up on it all . . .'

I am touched by this. Dad's idea of research is normally reading the sports section of the newspaper. 'And apparently it's important for you to know where you come from.'

'It is.'

He squeezes my hand. 'Well, then, you have to do it. We'll talk to your mum, eh?'

When we get back inside the house, there are delicious smells emanating from the kitchen. Danny has set up a table in the centre of the living room, and we all squeeze around it and tuck into the lasagne he and Karen have made.

Mum doesn't speak directly to me, but I catch her smiling at my description of Mimi as being like my old English teacher. She and Miss Turner had several run-ins over the years. It's a relief to see Mum softening towards me. I suppose, realistically, she was never going to blank me forever if her concern was about losing me. But it's clear from the way she avoids eye contact that she's still wary.

After lunch, I take Danny to one side. 'Look, I really appreciate you getting us all together – but I was a bit blindsided by it.'

'Yeah, sorry about that. I probably should have warned you about them coming but I was worried you wouldn't turn up.'

I consider this. 'I probably wouldn't have.' We both laugh. 'But Dad seems to have come round to the idea of me looking for my biological parents. It's just, I think I need to give Mum a bit longer . . . He's going to talk to her for me.'

'You want to leave, don't you?'

I nod. 'Is that OK?'

He gives me a hug. 'Of course it is.'

Alice is not impressed at my leaving so soon. 'But we were all going to play *Mario Kart*!' she objects when I say my goodbyes.

'Well, you know I'm not very good at *Mario Kart*.'

She nods. 'I know. But we were going to do the easy courses for you.'

'Well, that's kind. Next time?'

She shrugs and allows me to give her a hug. 'I suppose so.'

The journey home is much smoother than the evening before, and Mouse and I make it back to the cottage in under two hours. When I turn my mobile on, there's a text from Ben:

You can't avoid me forever.

I wonder if he realises how much that reads like a threat. I nearly message back, but it's probably better not to get into a slanging match, so I message Danny to let him know I'm safely home, and then turn off my phone.

'*Boohbah* or Attenborough?' I ask Mouse. He makes a strange, howling noise, which I decide means he wants to watch a programme on wolves. I flick the TV to BBC iPlayer and select a series about the Painted Wolf. He is quickly engrossed, sitting very upright in front of the TV set and making little noises in his throat. For myself, I select an album by First Aid Kit, insert my earphones and immerse myself in my reading.

Sunday is grey and drizzly, so Mouse and I cut short our run, and spend most of the day curled up in front of the TV. Mid-afternoon, I turn on my phone to check for messages. I pick up a voicemail from Danny, who's just checking in. There's also another text from Ben:

Lulu sorry if my last text came out wrong but you need to call me. This is not about the other thing. Please, please get in touch.

As I finish reading, a new text comes through from him:

I CAN'T DEAL WITH THIS. I'M COMING TO SEE YOU.

Shit. The last thing I need is Ben turning up at my new place of work. Does he even know where I am?

I text back:

Don't come. I'm free now if you want to call.

I sit with my mobile on my lap, wondering what can be so urgent that he needs to speak to me. The lawyers finished dealing with everything nearly thirteen months ago – surely anything major would have come up then?

I wait twenty minutes, then call Danny.

'Hiya,' he says.

'Hi. Listen, have you heard from Ben at all?'

'Only twice a day for the past week. His last call was Thursday or maybe Friday.'

'What? Why didn't you tell me?'

'I figured you had enough to deal with.'

'What did he say?'

'Only that he had to get hold of you, and could I give him your address? Sadly for him, I couldn't.' He laughs but I don't join in.

'It's just he's sending some seriously stressed-out messages, and now he's threatening to come and see me. How would he have got my address?'

'Beats me. Unless . . .' I hear him call Alice's name, and then her little voice responding. They have a conversation I can't hear, then he comes back on the line: 'Apparently, my helpful little PA gave it to him. I'm so sorry, sis.' Alice says something, and he says, 'Hold on a moment – Alice wants to talk to you.'

My niece comes on the line. 'I'm sorry, Auntie Lou. But Uncle Ben kept saying it was a "life or death" situation and so I thought someone might really die if I didn't tell him your address.'

'Oh, sweetie, it's not your fault at all. Uncle Ben is naughty to have worried you like that.' I silently curse myself for teaching her how to spell Beaulieu.

'Auntie Lou?'

'Yes?'

'When are you coming to see us again?'

'Well, I only got back yesterday.'

'You promised you'd come again soon.'

'You're quite right: I did. I shall consult my diary and get back to you.'

'That's good,' she says. 'Because Grandad's even worse at *Mario Kart* than you are.'

12

By Monday morning, I still haven't heard from Ben, and I'm more than a little anxious about the threat of his imminent arrival. As Mouse and I pass through the woods on our morning run, then hit our stride on the path along the sheep fields, I keep wondering what can be so bad that he has to see me urgently.

We turn at an old elm tree which we often use as a landmark and start back for home. Mouse starts barking the minute we're in the woods behind the cottage. I can tell he's excited to greet someone, and my heart sinks as I let him off the lead and watch him bound towards the house, where Ben must be waiting.

By the time I emerge, Ben is crouching with Mouse, stroking his ears and making a fuss of him. He stands when he spots me and his long, sinewy figure and shock of red hair are so familiar to me that I feel a tug of longing for him before I remember all his crimes – and common sense prevails.

I walk towards the back door where he's waiting, and we're face to face for the first time in months. He has new lines around his mouth and a deep furrow above his nose. But his eyes are as bright blue and intense as ever.

'Hiya,' he says.

I nod and move behind him to unlock the door. 'You coming in?'

'If that's all right?'

'Just for a few minutes, or I'll be late for work.'

'OK. Thank you.'

He follows me into the kitchen, where I put the kettle on. 'Have you still got my cafetière?' I ask.

He pulls a face. 'Shit. Sorry – I think it went in the house clearance. I'll get you a new one.'

I gesture for him to take a seat at the kitchen table. In typical Ben fashion, as soon as he sits down, he pulls my gardening notebook towards him and starts reading.

'Hey,' I say, striding over and closing it firmly, before placing it on the worktop. 'We're not together any more, remember? And I didn't like you reading my stuff when we were.'

He leans back, puts his arms behind his head and smiles. 'It's good to see you, Lulu.'

'It's Steph now,' I say, placing teabags into two mugs and pouring on the steaming water.

'Yeah, Steph. I forgot.'

As I approach with the mugs I notice that, despite his apparent nonchalance, one leg is twitching: always the first sign Ben is stressed or anxious about something. Mouse has clearly picked up on Ben's mood; he's growling quietly – presumably remembering, as I do, that our rows always began when Ben was wired.

'So,' I say, placing the mugs on the table and pulling out the chair opposite him, 'What's going on with you?'

'Oh, nothing . . .'

'Caroline all right?'

'She's fine. She's . . . Caroline, you know?'

From what I've witnessed from the outside, his new girlfriend is high maintenance, both financially and emotionally. They started dating within a couple of months of my leaving him. I think Ben just can't stand to be alone.

I check my watch. I may have to skip my shower before work.

'Well, you didn't come over here just for a chat,' I point out.

'No, it's . . . It's difficult to say.'

'Go on.'

'I need money.'

I burst out laughing. 'And what money exactly would that be? Have you forgotten you bankrupted us?'

He gestures to the cottage. 'You've fallen on your feet with this job. Looks like a cushy number.'

'I'm still in debt, you know. I had to borrow money to do that tree surgery course.'

'Right, right . . .' His leg is twitching more now, shifting up and down until the table starts to shake and I have to grab my mug of tea. 'I was just hoping . . . What about your parents?'

I stand up. 'You need to leave now.'

He looks shocked. 'Come on, Lulu,' he cajoles.

'It's Steph,' I remind him again.

'You'll always be Lulu to me,' he says, in a soft voice that would once have seen me fall into his arms. But charming men are not to be trusted: a hard lesson, which he taught me.

'Just go,' I say.

'Look, Lulu . . . Steph, I'm in trouble.'

I feel anger flame like a struck match. 'What's new, Ben? Really?'

Mouse comes to stand in front of me, still growling at Ben.

Ben gets to his feet. 'So, is that it?' He sounds incredulous.

'What did you expect? I trusted you – and you squandered everything we owned.'

'I'm sorry, Lu . . . Steph, but I didn't mean to. It got out of control.'

'I know: you told me. But it's been over a year since the divorce and you're still turning up as if I owe you something. Look at me: I don't even own this house. And the van outside was the cheapest I could find – and even then, I had to borrow the money from my dad.'

'I'm sorry. But this will be the last time, I promise.'

I shake my head. 'It isn't going to happen. Now, if you can see yourself out, I'm late for work.'

By the time I've changed into my gardening gear, Ben has left. I stroke and pat my lovely loyal dog, and then we head off in the van for The Towers. At least we're going to Mouse's favourite place, where there will be excellent canine pals. He starts straining at his seat belt and making excited little barks as soon as I turn in at the gates.

Once again, there's no sign of anyone when I reach the top of the drive. At least this time I won't have to ring the bell and disturb the Qureshis' ungracious son. I pull in alongside the gleaming Autobiography, unload Mouse and my tools, unlock the back gate and head through to the garden.

It's another fine day, and Mouse and I are greeted enthusiastically by the two little Pomeranians before the three race off together, out of sight. It must be love: Mouse has chosen to leave Mr Rabbit behind. I place the toy in one of the top pockets of my jacket and fasten the Velcro flap to keep it safe.

I wheel my barrow past the paved terrace and the lower lawn, and up to the perennial flower garden on the next level, where the bearded irises have been left to clump together for so long, they're competing each other out of existence. I'm looking forward to forgetting all about Ben's disturbing appearance and immersing myself in this purely physical work. But I've just got my fork under one side of the enormous rhizomatous bulk when I hear voices. One of them is female and evidently upset. The other sounds like a young man's voice, but it is calmer and quieter.

If this were a normal conversation I'd ignore it, but something in the evident distress of the female's high-pitched responses decides me. With a sigh, I leave my fork plunged into the soil and follow the sound of the voices, up through the levels to the top – where, in the walled garden, I come upon two young people, deep in argument – the Qureshis' son and Apple Singer-Pryce. He's gripping her wrists while clearly remonstrating with her. Tempted though I am to stride in and separate them forcibly – nothing would give me greater pleasure at this moment than to put this young man in his place – I'm aware that, if I pull them apart, Apple might get hurt. So, instead, I walk purposefully until I'm directly in his eyeline. It works: he drops her wrists as soon as he sees me, and I step forward.

'Apple, are you OK?' I ask. She starts – she hadn't realised I was here. Her gaze meets mine, then veers off over my shoulder. 'I'm fine.'

'What's going on? Why are you two fighting?'

Adam laughs. 'Oh, we're not fighting,' he says. I'm shocked by the ease with which the lie falls from his tongue.

I fix him in the eye. 'So, why were you holding her by the wrists?'

'We were just mucking about, weren't we, Apps?'

Her eyes now fixed on the ground, she nods miserably.

'Come on, Apple, I'll take you home,' I tell her.

She picks up her bag and almost runs towards me.

'Just remember what we talked about,' he calls after her.

She doesn't answer him. She's wearing platform sandals and cut-off jean shorts with a long-sleeved crop top. Despite the warm day, she's shivering.

'Here,' I say, removing my jacket and draping it around her shoulders as we walk. It's at that moment that she starts to sob. She looks so young and vulnerable that I put an arm around her and say gently, 'Hey, don't cry. It'll be OK.'

'It really won't,' she says.

'Come on, we'll go in my van,' I say as we reach the front of the house. I open the passenger's door for her, then walk round and open the driver's side. She just stands there. 'What's wrong? Why aren't you getting in?'

'The seat's covered in dog hairs.' She sounds disgusted.

I laugh. 'Seriously?' I shrug. 'You can walk home if you prefer.'

She pulls a face but climbs in. As I start the engine and reverse out of the space, she starts sobbing again; it turns into a wail, long and low, a curious, guttural, animal sound.

'Oh, sweetie!' I say, helplessly. Will Alice be like this when she's a teenager? How will Danny and Karen cope?

The sound keeps coming, all the way to the gates of La Jolla, where at last it subsides into quieter sobs.

'Are you OK if I drop you here?' I ask, but she turns panicked eyes towards me. Her mascara has run down her cheeks and she looks even younger than her seventeen years. 'It's fine,' I say quickly, 'I'll drive you up to the house.' I have an almost preternaturally good memory for numbers, and I remember the code to punch in to open the gates. When we reach the glamorous white house at the top of the steep drive, she unstraps her seat belt and hands me my jacket.

'Why did you tell them?' she says.

I frown. 'Tell who what?'

'Mummy, Daddy and Nix – why did you tell them about the festival?'

'I had to tell them. Have you any idea how worried they were – we all were – about you? You might have been kidnapped from the festival or something.' She nods but doesn't speak. There's still a drop of water poised on her cheek like a Pierrot's tear. 'Look, do you want to tell me what was going on back there? What did the Qureshi boy want?'

'He's called Adam,' she says.

'Right, Adam. Why was he gripping you like that?'

'He wants me to do something I don't want to do,' she says, staring ahead through the windscreen.

'That doesn't make it all right for him to hurt you. Apple, please will you look at me?' She turns damp eyes towards me. I can see the bruise on her cheekbone through her tear-smudged foundation.

'You do know that no one has the right to touch you unless you want them to, don't you? And they certainly mustn't threaten or harm you.' She shrugs. I lean across and rummage in the glove compartment until I find one of my business cards. 'Take this,' I say. 'It has my number on it. Call or text if you're in danger or trouble of any kind.' I make a mental note to stop turning off my phone.

'Thank you,' she says again. 'You're really kind.'

'Whatever's going on, you have to believe you're worth looking after.'

'But I'm not. I'm not worth anything.' She opens the door and climbs down before I can respond.

I sit in the van for a moment after she's gone. When she wanted to confide in me, I discouraged her; now that I want to know the truth, she won't tell me. I sigh and turn the van around, heading straight back to The Towers. I'm itching to get back to that iris clump. This time, the butler is out the front as I pull up. I jump down and call out a greeting.

'Hello, Steph,' he says. 'Would you like a bite to eat?' The butler is called James. He has grey hair down to his collar. Instead of a suit and tie like Francis, he wears a black polo-neck jumper under a blazer. I wonder if this counts as alternative style in Butler World.

'I've brought sandwiches with me, but a cup of coffee would be lovely,' I say.

'Are you sure? There are some delicious smells emanating from the kitchen today.'

'Oh, go on, then – you've twisted my arm.'

'And Master Mouse?' I'm touched he's learnt my dog's name.

'I'm sure he'd appreciate a bowl of water – thank you.'

'Fritz and Mitzi will be eating lunch.'

'Oh. He normally just has two meals a day, but I suppose he might feel left out if the others are having.'

'I'll bring some food for him as well, in that case.'

'Thank you.'

'Shall we say twelve thirty?'

'Sounds great.'

James has a different air from Francis. Despite his more casual dress, there's something especially formal about him, almost remote. He's quite a bit older – in his mid-to-late sixties, if I had to guess. I can't imagine James laughing at anything. His formality makes me feel awkward: I want to break out in a dance or start telling knock-knock jokes. I resist the urge and head back to my task.

Nothing interrupts me for the next couple of hours, and I have a lovely time splitting the congested rhizomes and cutting away all the rotten sections with my knife. Now and then, the trio of dogs races past in a blur of fur and excited yaps. By the time I've finished the splitting process and have replanted several healthy sections of rhizome in different parts of the border, I have the glow of satisfaction that comes from a job well done. I check my watch and find I've even managed to forget about Ben for a good couple of hours.

After the irises, I tackle the lawns. Rather like with their cars, the Qureshis own more than one mower, and they're all top-of-the-range. I challenge anyone who has used one of these high-tech beasts to be unmoved; it's like driving a race car: all purring motor and sleek ride. I get the top lawn done, then check my watch; it's one o'clock and my stomach's growling.

My food has been set out for me inside a small, wooden summer house near the main house. It's blissfully warm inside, and I take a seat on a cushioned chair at the little table, sighing with pleasure. It's such a luxury to have my meals prepared for me. The food has been placed on a hot plate heated by candles, so it's still steaming. I cut into a filo pastry shell that has a chicken and mushroom filling; it's amazing, all creamy richness and herbs I can't quite place, though there's definitely some tarragon in there. I pour myself a cup of coffee from a stainless-steel pot and sip it slowly. It's wonderful, too: rich and strong.

As I sip my drink, Annabelle Qureshi appears in the doorway. 'There you are!'

'Have you been looking for me?'

'Yes; I've been up and down. Where were you?'

'I was mowing the top lawn until I came down for lunch.'

'Oh, right . . .' She seems distracted.

'Is there something wrong?'

She takes a seat across from me at the table. Leaning towards me, she says, 'Please don't say anything to Zakariya, but I think we've had a theft.'

'Not another one. What's missing?'

'It's an abstract sculpture that normally stands at the centre of the rose garden.'

'I know the one,' I say.

'Well, I can't say I particularly liked it, but it's by a rather famous artist – Barbara Hepworth. Have you heard of her?'

I do a double take. 'I recognised it as her style, but it never occurred to me it was the real McCoy.' I restrain myself from making a bad joke about a 'real McHepworth'. Now is not the time.

She nods. 'It's worth rather a lot, as you can imagine.'

'Won't your husband notice it's missing?'

'I'm wondering if I can replace it with something similar, before he realises. He rarely visits the top garden before the roses come into bloom. But he inherited the piece from his uncle, and he'll be rather upset if he finds out it's gone.'

'I can imagine. Who do you think has taken it?'

She shakes her head. 'I have no idea. You haven't seen any . . . shady types hanging around the Heights?'

I contemplate asking whether she considers her son a 'shady type', but decide against it. 'I can't say I have. According to Mimi, delivery vans come and go . . .'

'Yes, that's what she said last week, when her urns were taken. We really need better security.'

'But I still don't understand how someone could get through your gate,' I say. 'I mean, they'd need the code, wouldn't they?'

'Well, Adam has been known to just buzz people through without asking who they are. I've spoken to him over and over again about it, but he's far too trusting.'

'So pretty much anyone who got into Beaulieu Heights could have tried buzzers until someone let them through?'

She sighs. 'It's rather distressing, isn't it?'

'It is. I'm sorry, Mrs Qureshi.'

'Annabelle, please. Do you have any thoughts on how we might acquire a replacement?'

'I understand you don't want to upset Mr Qureshi, but that piece is far too valuable not to report to the police. You'll need to make an insurance claim.'

She rubs her forehead. 'You're right, of course: I'm not thinking straight. I'll call them today.'

'I am sorry,' I say. 'It must feel horrible, to know someone's been here.'

'At least they didn't come into the house,' she says. 'Although we do have a state-of-the-art security system, which may have deterred them. I wonder if we could extend it out to the garden.'

'Not a bad idea,' I agree. 'So, first Mimi's urns and now your sculpture. Were there other thefts, before I arrived at Beaulieu?'

She reflects for a moment. 'Not that I can think of. Fiona had problems with a maid who was stealing cutlery, of all things, but apart from that . . .'

I have a moment's paranoia, wondering if Annabelle believes I took their sculpture. But she doesn't seem to be accusing me, so I push the concern away.

She leaves to call the police and I head back to the large flower border, where I spend some time tying in a jasmine that's come away from its arch. With the climber under control, I'm able to access the area beneath, which is filled with straggly plants that couldn't reach the light before, plus a smattering of weeds. I won't get all the tidying up done today, but I can make a start.

Towards the end of my working day, I wheel the waste up to a large composting area sited behind the far-right wall of the rose garden. Then I park the barrow and walk over to try the mysterious door in the left-hand corner again. It's still locked.

'Can I help you?'

I jump at the sound of Adam's voice, close behind me.

'Oh, I just thought I'd inspect the remaining bit of garden and see what needs doing,' I say airily. 'Do you have the key?'

The young man has several inches on me, but he's quite lean, and I eye him up and down, trying to determine whether I could take him in a fight. But when my eyes return to his face, I see he's smiling pleasantly. It's as if the whole incident with Apple never happened.

'Do you not have enough work to get on with?' he asks with a grin. I make an effort to smile in return, though I doubt I'm as convincing: he has that whole beautiful charmer thing going on.

'Oh, I've got plenty! I just don't want any nasty surprises down the line, if there's another area that needs tending.'

'Trust me – you do not want to inspect that particular area of garden.'

'Is it that bad?'

'It's so overgrown, you'd need to raze the whole thing and start again.'

'Oh, my goodness. So Simon just left it, did he?'

He frowns. 'Simon? Oh – is that the other gardener? Yeah, he was happy to leave the door locked and focus his attention elsewhere.'

I shrug. 'Fair enough. I'll concentrate on the manageable sections of garden.'

'Great idea.'

I collect my barrow and wheel it quickly back along one of the paths out of the rose garden, trying to work out why a seemingly casual exchange with him felt like a veiled threat. Was it my imagination? It takes sheer force of will not to glance back to see if he's watching me. Images of Apple sobbing keep flashing through my mind. I hope she's OK.

When I get near the house, I find the three dogs in the summer house, curled up together on a wicker sofa, fast asleep. It's time to go home, and I feel bad having to wake Mouse, who whines piteously. Mitzi joins in the pleading when I lead Mouse out of the little building, to take him home. She and Fritz follow us to the van.

'You'll see each other again next week,' I tell them, as I open the van door and throw Mr Rabbit on to the passenger seat; Mouse climbs in after his toy.

I was fully intending to go straight home, but a last-minute impulse has me driving past the cottage and turning left into The Chimneys' driveway. Perhaps the fabric scraps are one mystery I can clear up. As no one's expecting me, I ring the buzzer by the gate. Lucy's voice answers,

'Yes?'

'It's Steph. I was hoping to have a word with your mother.'

'Oh, Mum's about to take me to rehearsal, so she hasn't got time. Sorry.'

'Oh, right. Thanks anyway.'

'Did you want me to pass on a message?'

'No, it can wait, thanks.' I back out the van and drive across the road to my cosy little home.

While cooking an omelette for dinner that evening, I muse over how badly Simon neglected the garden at The Chimneys. At least Annabelle Qureshi explained why The Towers was so well tended. La Jolla is also immaculate – did Bubby or Jockey also take Simon to task? Maybe I can get his phone number tomorrow and give him a call.

Thanks to my tiring day, I fall asleep quickly – but once again my dreams are restless. This time, they're filled with images of Apple, crying and reaching out to me as Adam carries her off. But it isn't Adam, it's Ben, and he's saying, 'I told you what would happen if you didn't let me have the money.'

13

I'm woken by my phone at 5.30 a.m. My heart is beating hard as I reach for it and read 'Unknown Caller' on the screen. I answer anyway, as it could be Apple.

'Hello?' I say.

'Hello Louise; it's Caroline.' The voice is high, with a slightly nasal quality. My heart sinks: it's too early in the morning to be dealing with Ben's highly strung girlfriend.

'Caroline, hi. How are you?'

'Are you sleeping with my boyfriend?'

I'm so shocked by this question my mouth drops open. 'Er . . . I'm sorry, what?'

'I know you are, so don't bother denying it.'

'With . . . Ben?'

'Of course with Ben.'

I sit up in bed. 'Why would I be sleeping with Ben? Have you forgotten the divorce?'

She tuts loudly. 'No, of course I haven't forgotten the divorce. But he left to see you on Sunday night and he hasn't come back, so I know he's with you.'

I rub my forehead. 'He hasn't come back?'

'No.' She sounds less certain. 'He sent you that text that he was coming?'

'Yeah, but he didn't actually arrive until yesterday morning. We rowed and he left about twenty minutes later.'

There's a long pause, and when she speaks again, her tone is anxious. 'He didn't get to you till yesterday? Where did he go beforehand?'

'I have no idea; I'm sorry.'

'And he really isn't with you now? Are you sure?'

I think about my tiny one-bedroom cottage, where it would be very hard for a tall man with red hair to make himself invisible. 'Very sure.'

'He isn't with you,' she says again, slowly.

'That's right. So, you haven't heard from him since?'

'No. I mean, at first I thought he was just, you know, busy telling you about everything. And then I thought you must have started shagging again.'

I wince at the image this conjures up. 'Definitely not.' I don't add that there is no way in hell I'd ever sleep with Ben again.

'Shiiiit.'

'Look, he isn't in . . . danger or anything, is he?'

'I have to go.'

'But—'

She hangs up before I even finish the sentence. So is Ben missing or has he just left Caroline and not bothered to tell her? That would be pretty Ben-like behaviour. I should have told her to check if his clothes were still there.

Mouse has sneaked on to the end of my bed in the night, and I nudge him with one foot. 'Walkies?' I suggest. He goes from Sleepy Dog to Manic Beast in the blink of an eye. First, he starts barking; then he leaps from the bed and races around the room. Finally, he grabs Mr Rabbit from the bed and shakes the toy like he's trying to shake the life out of it.

'Can you fetch your lead while I pull on some running clothes?'

He drops Mr Rabbit and dashes out of the room, returning a moment later with his favourite lead. It's wearing thin in places and won't be usable for much longer, but I concede, 'OK, boy,' clipping it to his collar and heading towards the back door.

That's when I see a piece of paper on the floor. I bend to pick it up and read:

WATCH YOUR BACK IF YOU KNOW WHAT'S GOOD FOR YOU AND THAT DOG OF YOURS

It's so unexpected, I nearly laugh. But then the reality of the threat sinks in and the cold finger of a shiver traces my spine. Mouse whines at my slowing of pace, but I'm staring at the note.

'What on earth?' It's handwritten, but all in capitals using a black ballpoint pen, so there's not much to go on. I turn it over, but the other side is blank. The edges are ragged, as if it's been torn from a larger sheet, but that also doesn't tell me much. I unlock the door and open it cautiously – even though Mouse would be barking if anyone were still out there. If he hadn't been sleeping in my bedroom, which is at the front of the house, he'd have heard the caller in the night and alerted me. As it is, they must have been pretty stealthy not to disturb him.

I scan the ground outside, as if they might have left me some helpful clue to their identity – a driving licence, perhaps, or their business card. But this isn't *Scooby Doo* so there's nothing, of course. I wonder if this is the same person who was in the woods on our first night at Beaulieu. But what have we done to upset them? It's hard to 'watch my back' if I don't know what I've done to offend them. Threatening messages really should come with explanatory footnotes.

I wonder if this has something to do with Ben. Perhaps he hasn't just upped and left Caroline; maybe he is in actual trouble of some kind. Then I remember how Adam discouraged me from investigating what was behind the locked door at The Towers: maybe the note's from him. I step back inside the cottage – much to Mouse's distress – just to place the note on the kitchen counter. Then I lock the door behind us, check it twice, and go around to the front door, to check that it is also locked.

And only then do we set off for our morning run.

'This was under your door?' Fiona looks at me with concern in her pale-blue eyes. We're in her front garden, where she's seated at her easel. The scarf over her hair is slightly askew, giving her a dishevelled, distracted air.

I nod. 'Whoever wrote it must have put it there this morning, after Mouse came to sleep on my bed. Not that they could have known that – they were taking a risk that he might wake up and start barking, and we'd catch them in the act.' I'm most bothered by this: that our Writer of the Threatening Note was so casual, almost blatant. It suggests an arrogance that makes them more threatening than if they had waited until we were out.

Fiona hands back the note and shakes her head, reaching out to stroke Mouse's soft head as he sits patiently at her feet. 'Who could ever threaten you?' she asks him. He gazes up at her adoringly. 'Are you going to report it to the police?' she asks me.

'Do you think there's any point? What can they do exactly?'

She thinks for a moment, then says, 'Well, at least if you notify them, they can start a file . . .' She notices my expression, and says quickly, 'I'm not saying there will be anything else! I just mean . . .' Her pale skin is flushed.

'I know what you meant; it's fine. And you're right: I should be notifying them.' The truth is that there's a tiny voice in the back of my head, whispering that Ben might have written it. He certainly wasn't very pleased with me when I refused him money and told him to leave. But he wouldn't stoop so low . . . would he? I push away this troubling notion and say, 'I think I'll just keep hold of it for now. Hopefully, this will be a one-off.'

'And you say you don't know what they're talking about?'

I shake my head. 'No idea whatsoever.' I decide to change the subject. 'Did you say you have Simon's phone number?'

'Yes, I've got it stored in my phone.' Fiona picks up her mobile and holds it out to me. 'You'll have to find it yourself – I'm terrible with this thing; Rupert's always telling me off for pressing the wrong buttons and dialling people by mistake.'

I take the phone and locate the previous gardener's number, stored under *Gardener Simon Drake*. I copy it into my mobile, then hand hers back.

As I do so, I am distracted by the current painting on her easel, which depicts the distant view. It's an exquisite piece of work – far-off fields and hills, rendered in blues, reds and purples – colours I'd never have imagined could work, yet somehow they do.

Mouse, clearly feeling it's his turn for some attention from Fiona, drops Mr Rabbit at her feet.

'Oh, here's your rabbit toy again,' she says to him. 'Isn't he fine?'

Mouse barks once in agreement as Fiona picks up the rabbit and pretends to examine it, before leaning over to hand it back to him. 'Thank you for showing me,' she says.

It's easy to see why Mouse adores her – whoever she addresses becomes her entire focus for that moment. I can't understand how her husband could cheat on her. Perhaps he doesn't like feeling singled out by her kindness; some people don't feel deserving of such devoted attention. Still, what a fool.

My mind flicks to Apple Singer-Pryce. I've been worrying about her since our encounter yesterday. I've noticed that people who don't hold themselves in high regard are more likely to do reckless things. After all, if you're not worth anything, why take care of yourself? I wonder if I should be more proactive. I could approach her parents . . . but I can't imagine Bubby and Jockey appreciating the hired help's input into their child's welfare. I sigh.

'Are you worrying about the note?' asks Fiona.

'I was just thinking that it's hard sometimes not to get dragged into clients' personal matters.' I regret this the moment I've said it. She turns abruptly towards the easel and her tone becomes uncharacteristically matter-of-fact:

'Right – well, I'd better get on.'

'OK,' I say, wishing I could rewind and unsay my tactless comment.

'Please start in the knot garden. The box needs trimming.'

'I thought Rupert . . .'

'Oh, he only does the large topiary. He hates trimming the box – says it hurts his back.'

'I'm on it.'

As I head through the gate to the tunnel with Mouse, I glance behind me; she's still facing her easel, but I can see that her shoulders are unnaturally hunched and stiff. I hope she isn't crying.

'What can we do with these people, boy?' I whisper to Mouse. He and Mr Rabbit tear off up the garden, oblivious – or indifferent – to the whims of humans, and I take out my shears and set to work.

Most people I know hate repetitive tasks, but I love them. Just like raking the fallen beech leaves, I enter a kind of trance-like state while I'm cutting hedges, weeding borders or pruning shrubs. Trimming the box hedging is a job that can only be done slowly – if I rush it, the result will be uneven, which will ruin the perfect symmetry of the design. I forget my concerns as I tie strings in place to ensure a level finish, and set to work with my shears and spirit level.

When I break for lunch, perching to eat my sandwiches on the stone wall where Fiona confided in me last week, she appears, bearing a tray with a cafetière and two mugs.

'I'm sorry if I was abrupt before,' she says, setting the tray on the ground.

'No, I'm sorry. I spoke without thinking. I honestly wasn't referring to you.'

She shakes her head. 'But you were right – it isn't fair or appropriate to burden one's staff.'

'Well, maybe it's OK if there's no one else to confide in,' I say with a smile.

'You're too kind – that's why people keep telling you their secrets.'

'So I need to turn mean?'

'Absolutely,' she says, almost seriously. 'If you act as if you don't have time for people, they won't be tempted to share their problems.'

'And how's that working out for you?'

She looks puzzled. 'What do you mean?'

'You're worse than me – you seem to care about everyone.'

'Oh, that's not true. But I decide instantly, based on my instincts. If I hadn't liked you straight away, you would have known it, believe me.'

'I'm scared now,' I say with a laugh.

'No, it's true! You see, Simon and I didn't see eye to eye.'

'Why was that?'

'Well, to be honest, I didn't trust him even from his interview – it was an instinctive thing. But, as I couldn't produce anything concrete against him, the rest of the committee ignored my concerns and hired him. But it turned out he was simply unreliable. He'd start a job and then vanish with his van, without telling a staff member or myself where he was going. I don't mind if someone has an appointment they need to attend, but this was every Tuesday, and sometimes twice in the one day.'

'Where was he going? Did you ever find out?'

She shakes her head. 'At last I told him he had to work the full day and only break for lunch. I'm afraid I really lost my temper.' It's hard to imagine what an angry Fiona might look like; I try, but all I see is her smiling or looking vague. 'He was not at all happy about it,' she says.

'What did he say?'

'It wasn't what he said – it was how he reacted physically. His face looked as if a shadow had come over it. I was quite scared. He stepped very close to me and called me an "interfering bitch" and a few worse names.'

'Did he hurt you?'

'No, but I think he might have done if Rupert hadn't been working from home that day. He saw us talking through the window and came out. Simon just turned away as if nothing had happened and got on with his work. But I couldn't get rid of the memory of his expression – it was so angry and . . . vicious, almost.' She laughs nervously, 'I can still see it now!'

'Did you tell Rupert the things Simon had said to you?'

'I did – and he said if I wanted to fire Simon there and then, he'd back me up with the residents' committee – he's the secretary.' I'm glad to hear that Rupert has redeeming qualities. She continues, 'As it is, he had words with Simon, and the vanishing act stopped, which was a relief, and he really focused on the garden. I did keep out of the man's way after that, though – I didn't fancy another altercation.'

She reaches down to the tray on the ground, plunges the cafetière, then hands me an empty mug to hold while she pours the dark liquid into it. The aroma is so tantalising, it makes my nostrils tingle. They really know their coffee at Beaulieu.

'I'm sorry again for what I said earlier,' I tell her. 'I'm quite worried about Apple Singer-Pryce.'

'She hasn't gone missing again, has she?'

'No, but she seems very unhappy.'

'Oh dear, she's a worry, that one. I'm not sure she gets everything she needs at home. This place seems idyllic but it certainly has its share of problems.' She puts a hand to her forehead. 'Oh! There's something I want you to see. It went completely out of my head when you showed me that nasty note.'

She leads me back through the granite tunnel to the front garden and takes me over to the sunken pond, where giant orange-and-white koi carp plough furrows through the water.

'Look,' she says, pointing towards the centre of the pond.

I look. 'Where's the goldfish fountainhead?'

'It vanished overnight, from Saturday to Sunday. I mean, it's not the end of the world, but it's a concern. We're supposed to be safely locked away in the Beaulieu community – or "compound", as I privately think of it – but someone is getting in and stealing things.'

'Was it worth anything?'

She shrugs. 'According to Rupert, quite a lot. It was imported from China a couple of centuries ago.'

'Oh, dear.'

'Quite.'

The water is trickling in underwhelming fashion from the pipe leading to the missing fountainhead.

'So that's thr—*two* thefts at Beaulieu,' I correct myself, remembering that the abduction of the Qureshis' sculpture may not yet be common knowledge. 'Have you rung the police?'

'Oh, yes. I rang them on Sunday. They didn't come out until this morning. But I suppose it doesn't count as an emergency, so one can't really blame them. And it's not as if they can dust for fingerprints! I was offered victim support, though – can you imagine?'

'Well, some people would be quite traumatised to discover a stranger had trespassed on their property and stolen something.'

'I suppose so.'

'How did they gain access? The thief or thieves, I mean.'

While she considers this question, she reties the pale-blue scarf that holds back her hair. 'Rupert thinks I was forgetful about shutting the gate on Saturday after I came back from the shops – and it is possible. But . . .'

'You don't think it's likely?'

She shakes her head. 'It closes automatically, as you know – I would have had to wedge it open, and I only do that if we're expecting a delivery.'

'Is there any chance . . .' I hesitate.

She turns her watercolour-blue eyes on me. 'What?'

'Well, Simon – he still has all the entry codes, unless they've been changed?'

Her eyes widen. 'I hadn't thought of Simon!' She frowns in concentration. 'I'm trying to remember when we last changed the codes. I'll have to ask Mimi.'

'I'm probably wrong; it was just a thought.'

'No, it makes sense. He's bound to hold a grudge against us, for letting him go. I'll mention it to the committee.'

'Shall we get back to work?' I suggest.

She nods. 'Definitely. This painting's a present for Rupert's parents, for their golden wedding. They love this view.'

'How lovely; I'll leave you to it.' As I turn back to the covered passageway, I see Mouse coming through, his tail wagging. He barks excitedly in greeting.

'Oh, is that my friend?' calls Fiona. She's already in position at her easel. 'Can he stay with me for a bit? I'd love the company.'

'Of course. Just send him back if he gets in the way.'

She pats her legs and calls to him, and Mouse rushes past me as if I'm irrelevant. After all, I've only fed and cared for him since he was a rescue puppy.

At quarter to five, I finish the box hedging and stand back to admire my handiwork. I've trimmed the sides as well as the top, and it's all beautifully level, symmetrical and easy on the eye. My back's aching from all the bending, but it's worth it. Fiona appears with Mouse as I'm packing my tools into the wheelbarrow.

'Oh, that looks lovely!' she says, with a smile. 'Thank you so much.'

I perform a smart salute. 'Just doing my job.'

'Ah yes, but only a true craftsperson takes so much care. Gardening is an art, after all.'

I blush at this praise. I'm glad Fiona doesn't share the Purdues' opinion that gardening is just 'honest toil' without creativity.

As I soak in the bath later, it occurs to me that I haven't rung Simon, to try to establish why he so neglected the garden at The Chimneys, and to see if he'll tell me why they laid him off. Mind you, after talking to Fiona, I'm not so sure I want to speak to him, in case he turns confrontational or defensive. Perhaps I'll leave it a day or so and sound out a few of the other residents, to uncover their impressions of him.

I close my eyes and try to relax, but between my missing ex-husband, the warning note, the grave, the scraps of cloth located in two different places, Apple's troubles, Adam's shady ways, and all the confessions and confidences, it's hopeless: I find myself trying to solve the various puzzles with too few pieces. I give up and pull the plug. Tomorrow, I'm going to focus on gardening and ignore everything – and everyone – else.

14

Despite my decision of the night before, to focus purely on the job, I'm concerned about the spate of thefts. I decide to call on Annabelle first thing, to see how she got on with telling Zakariya the news about his missing sculpture. I'm also hoping she received a more proactive response from the police than either Mimi or Fiona seems to have done.

As she's not expecting me, I lean out of the van window to ring the bell on the gate, rather than input my code. However, after five minutes of tapping my fingers on the steering wheel, I give up and use the code to let myself in. Perhaps she's in the garden. I have to repeat the code to pass through the top gate, and I shudder as I wait for it to open and realise these Beaulieu driveways resemble those prison corridors, where each section of the passage lies between two locked doors.

When I reach the house, I see that all three of the family cars are missing; it looks like they've gone out early and I've wasted my time. But, as I put the van in reverse, I hear a sound from one of the garages. I park, climb down and walk over to take a look. The up-and-over garage door is raised and the little red Audi is inside, with its boot open. There, too, is Adam. Beside him is a stack of transparent plastic bags, filled with a white substance that I'm pretty sure isn't self-raising flour. He's piling the bags into the boot of his car.

I freeze, recalling my encounter with this young man when I asked about the locked gate in the wall. I also remember his hands around Apple's wrists.

I take a few slow, calming breaths and assess the situation. Adam has his back to me and clearly hasn't heard me approach. The wing mirrors are folded in, which means they won't reflect my movement. And then I see he's wearing earbuds. So that's how he didn't hear the van – he's listening to music.

I take slow steps backwards, away from the garage. As soon as I'm out of sight, I run to the van, climb in, close the door as quietly as I can and start the engine. It takes three attempts to fit the key into the ignition slot. At last, it's in. I turn the van and head towards the top gate. As I draw level with the sensor, the gate starts to open, but too slowly: I'm a sitting duck. I keep an eye on the garage through my rear-view mirror; I can see Adam, his back still turned towards me. My hands are slick with sweat; I wipe them on my trousers. I realise I'm counting superstitiously under my breath, as if everything will be all right if the gate lets me through before I reach twenty. I'm dimly aware that Mouse is surveying me with curiosity.

When I reach seventeen, the gate is finally open wide enough for me to pass through. With the engine in first gear, I let the van roll forward. Near-silently I coast down to the bottom, braking at the bottom gate, which opens more swiftly. Then I turn right out of the drive towards La Jolla, where I'm due to be working today. It's only then that I let out the breath I must have been holding all the way down; I gulp in air, feeling light-headed from relief and lack of oxygen. At that moment, a pink Mini Cooper passes, and I see Lucy Purdue at the wheel, clocking me. I didn't even realise she could drive – her mother always seems to take her to rehearsals. I manage to raise a hand as if all's well with the world, and she nods a greeting in response.

And then, two or three minutes later, I'm pulling in at La Jolla. After parking the van at the top, I sit for a moment, eyes closed, focusing on my breathing. Just as I'm feeling my adrenaline subside, Mouse commences barking, which is swiftly followed by a hammering on my window that makes me jump. I open my eyes and see a face that's far too close. It's Apple, grinning and waving. With a final deep breath in, I open my door slowly and she steps back, allowing me to climb down.

'You can let the dog out, too,' she says. I go around to unstrap Mouse and he jumps down and greets her enthusiastically. 'He's a lovely dog,' she says. Mouse, knowing a compliment when he hears one, promptly sits back on his haunches and lifts a paw in greeting.

'Awww! You're adorable, aren't you?' She kneels down and rubs his ears. From the side, I can see that the bruise on her cheek has turned yellow; she isn't wearing make-up today to cover it.

'Did you want to speak to me?' I ask her after a moment. I wonder if it's selfish of me to hope she has nothing major to confide. Two days ago, I wanted to know her secrets. Today, I'm exhausted before even starting my day's work; my close encounter with Adam has drained me.

'Oh, yes!' She stands up and pushes her hands through her pink hair, making it stick up in all directions. 'Lucy messaged, saying she saw you coming out of The Towers just now. What were you doing there?'

I frown, feeling my face go hot. What if Lucy has also told Adam about spotting me?

Apple looks concerned at my reaction. 'It's just, Annabelle's gone out, but you can get her on her mobile.'

'Right. Thanks,' I say shortly.

'Did you go up the driveway?' she asks.

The sweat from my earlier panic has turned cold inside my clothes and I feel chilly. 'Why the third degree?'

She takes a deep breath. 'It's just, since all the thefts, we've been asked to keep an eye on anyone coming and going when we know the houses are empty.'

'Right . . . So you're accusing me of stealing from The Towers?'

She blushes, bending down to stroke Mouse in an attempt to hide her embarrassment. 'No! Of course not! It's just, Mummy said we needed to keep an eye out – Neighbourhood Watch, you know?'

'I didn't even go up the driveway, Apple. But thank you for your trust,' I snap. I head round to the back of the van, where I open the door and lower the tailgate. I climb in and look around at my tools. I'm too angry to focus for a moment, so I count to ten. At last, I'm calm enough to grab my wheelbarrow and tools. Donning my gardening gloves, I step down backwards from the van, lowering the barrow after me.

But Apple has walked over without my realising; she's standing so close to the vehicle, I step on her foot.

'Shit!' I say, stumbling into her and nearly falling over. She steadies me.

'I'm sorry!' she says. 'I didn't mean to get in the way. I just wanted to thank you for being so kind the other day.'

'Right.'

'Please don't be angry.'

I glance at her pleading face. She's like a much younger child – in fact, I reckon my niece Alice might be more mature in some ways than Apple Singer-Pryce.

'I'm just having a bad day,' I say. 'It's nothing to do with you.' With some effort, I manage to smile at her, and I see relief flood her face. I call to Mouse and we head around to the back of the house. I can hear Apple trotting after me: she's wearing flip-flops which make a flapping sound against the ground.

As I near the back door, Mr Singer-Pryce steps out. He blocks my path, forcing me to come to an abrupt stop. I hear Apple say, 'Oh!' as she walks into my back.

'What's going on here?' He looks from his daughter to me and back.

'Nothing, Daddy,' says Apple.

'I hope she's not bothering you, Steph,' says her father. 'The whole community keeps talking about what a great job you're doing – I'd hate it if my daughter here was making your life difficult.'

'Not at all,' I say, crossing my arms to block his gaze, which is scanning my body as if mentally undressing me. 'She was just coming to remind me I've left my van open and unlocked; with the recent spate of thefts, it's a risk.'

I can tell he doesn't believe me, but he can hardly call me a liar. Instead, he nods and says, 'Well, have a good day. I'm off to the office but Bubby's around somewhere with a long list of jobs for you – enough to last you several months, I should think.' He's addressing my crotch, so I lift the handles of the wheelbarrow to block his view, and his gaze returns to my face with obvious amusement.

'Oh, well, I like to be kept busy,' I say coolly.

'Good girl!' I half expect him to try to ruffle my hair, but he nods in a distracted way and takes his leave, giving his daughter a hug and a kiss. 'Now, you stay out of trouble, you hear?'

'Yes, Daddy. I'll stay right here.'

'Just keep out of Ms Williams' way, all right?'

Apple turns and starts walking towards the front of the house.

And then Mr Singer-Pryce passes me again, and I feel the tips of his fingers graze my right buttock.

I have lightning reflexes where gropers are concerned; I grab his wrist and spin to face him, saying quietly, 'If you ever try something like that again, I'll remove your testicles with a pair of rusty shears.'

His surprise morphs into amusement, and I twist his arm slightly. 'Ow!' he protests.

'This is not a joke,' I tell him. 'Do you understand?'

He looks like he's about to protest again, so I twist a bit more. 'Do you understand?'

'I understand,' he says weakly, all bluster gone.

'Good,' I say. I drop his wrist, and leave him rubbing it pitifully. I go in search of Bubby, wondering if she knows her husband is a groping lech.

I find her near the top of the grounds, in the tropical garden. This section comprises a large, boggy bed, punctuated with masses of *Gunnera manicata* – which will grow umbrella-shape leaves like giant rhubarb as the season progresses. In among the gunnera are the glossier leaves of zantedeschia – the white arum lily. Around the outside of the bog, in the drier soil, there are huge tree ferns and *Trachycarpus fortunei* – a palm with large, fan-shaped leaves. I have yet to see the tropical garden when the gunnera is in full leaf, but I can tell it will be glorious.

There's a slight breeze today but it's still quite warm; Bunny is stretched out on a bench wearing a summer dress and cardigan. 'Mrs Singer-Pryce?' I say, as I approach. She's reading a book. I squint and make out it's something to do with the law.

'Are you a lawyer?' I ask, barely hiding my surprise.

'That's right: property law. I'm taking some time off, to brush up on the impact of Brexit: it keeps changing all the time, and there's never enough time to catch up in the office. Are you here for your list?'

'That would be great.'

'I have it right here.' She takes a sheet of paper from inside her book and passes it to me. 'Let me know if you don't understand anything.' She goes back to her reading, so I take it I'm dismissed.

As I walk away, it occurs to me I didn't see where Mouse went. I've never actually checked if the Singer-Pryces mind my dog free-ranging in their grounds, but I decide to leave him be – Bubby can always tell me if it's a problem.

I'm striding down the garden steps, reading the list as I go, so I don't see Nicola coming towards me until we've nearly collided. She jumps back just in time with an 'Oh!', and I come to a stop.

'Sorry!' I say.

'That's OK. I was looking for you; are you free to talk?'

I regard her warily. 'Sure,' I say, after a long pause. I'm remembering the last time we talked – when I expressed concern for Apple, and Nicola pretty much told me to mind my own business.

'Thanks. Shall we go in the wood?'

I nod and follow her into the small wood that borders the estate. This is a very artificial version of woodland – the trees are of many different varieties and spaced quite far apart, so that it's more like an arboretum. Nicola walks between the trees to a bench beneath a beautiful cypress, where she sits and gestures for me to join her. I've just decided that if she starts with, 'Can I tell you a secret?' I'm going to bolt, when she says,

'I think you were right about Apple.'

'Right about what?'

'I don't think she was in Bristol with friends. And I don't think she got that bruise from sleeping with her head on a stone, or whatever she claimed.'

'OK . . . Have you talked to her about it?'

'I've tried . . . But she can be really stubborn. If Apple doesn't want to tell you something, there's no way of getting her to.' There's a pause. At last, she says, 'I was wondering . . . will you talk to her?'

'Me?' I stare at her.

She pulls a face. 'I'm sorry I wasn't very nice to you the other day, when you were just worried about her. But I think she must really like you. She keeps hanging around while you're working, doesn't she? And she did tell you about the festival.'

I shrug. 'I got the impression she was just keen to tell someone.'

'She never tells me anything.' She sounds bitter.

'Did you use to be close?'

She nods. 'She used to come into my bed when we were little. We'd talk for hours, till Mummy or Daddy came and told her to go back to her own room.'

'When did you lose that closeness?'

'When I went off to uni. She acted like I was leaving home to spite her, or something.'

'That's sad.'

Nicola nods again. 'So, will you?'

'Will I what?'

'Will you try and find out what's going on? I'm worried she's in some kind of trouble.'

'I did see her arguing with Adam the other day at The Towers.'

'Adam?' I nod. 'But they're friends; they've always got on really well.'

'Well, they didn't seem to be getting on well when I intervened. He had her by the wrists.'

She stares at me. 'Adam? No way; he wouldn't do that.'

I take a calming breath. 'I saw him, Nicola. Your sister was quite upset afterwards; I had to run her home.'

'He wouldn't hurt Apple,' she says stubbornly.

I sigh. 'Well, I need to get on,' I say. 'You do realise your parents are paying me to do the garden? And, believe me, that's a big job.'

She looks close to tears. 'Please, just, if she comes to you, will you at least listen?'

'OK. But if your dad spots her talking to me, he'll definitely send her away – he gave her strict instructions to let me get on with my work.'

'Daddy's gone for the day now, so you won't have to worry about him. And Mummy's swotting up on some legal stuff, so she'll be occupied for hours.'

'And you?'

'What do you mean?'

'Do you have a job?'

'I run a branch of the family business,' she says. She doesn't offer any more information, and I don't ask.

Before leaving the arboretum, I check my list. Bubby has written that there's a dead tree somewhere here – but she's given me no directions to help locate it. Nicola's still sitting on the bench, so I go back to ask her.

'Oh, it's the robinia,' she says. 'I'll show you.'

Robinia pseudoacacia is one of my favourite trees. Its beautiful, delicate, yellow-green leaves resemble a wisteria's – or those of the acacia, after which it's named.

When we reach it, I'm dismayed to see its glorious foliage stunted and brown. I stroke the bark, as if it's a living creature – I can't help myself.

'Can I leave you to it?' asks Nicola.

'Of course. Thanks.'

After she departs, I assess the tree. I recently qualified as a tree surgeon, and I'm planning on paying off the course loan – and the cost of the equipment – with the first few months of my earnings at Beaulieu.

When I go to fetch my ladders and chainsaw, Apple is sitting on the drive beside the van. She's stroking Mouse, who's lying beside her. At least he's not careening about the grounds, as I'd thought.

I lean into the back of the van and draw out my ladder, plus a harness, a length of rope and my chainsaw, along with thick gloves, goggles, a helmet, chaps and ear defenders.

'What are you going to do?' asks Apple, watching me put on the chaps to avoid chafing from the harness and rope. I fit the helmet and then the harness before answering,

'Chop down a tree.'

'Can I watch?'

'OK. But you must listen to me, and stand where I tell you.'

She nods. Her eyelashes are dark and clumped together as if she's been crying. Perhaps that's why Mouse has stayed with her – he's a sucker for any person in distress.

She gets up and Mouse follows. She relieves me of the goggles, gloves and ear defenders, and I carry the ladder, with the rope slung over my shoulder. I can't manage the chainsaw: I'll have to come back for it. I leave it on the ground and lock up the van.

As we walk, she doesn't speak. At last, I say, 'How's Pobble?'

'Oh, she's great.'

'And the festival? Was it worth all the drama?'

She turns her big, brown eyes on me. 'Are you kidding? It was amazing.'

'Oh, good.' I smile but when I glance at her, I see she's biting her thumbnail. 'Is everything all right?'

'At least, it *started off* amazing,' she says, 'but then it stopped being good.'

'What happened?' We've reached the sick tree and I busy myself with the ladder.

'There were these boys . . . Well, men, really.' She stops. I glance back at her, my ladder partially extended. I don't like where this is headed.

'Did they cause you trouble?'

She shook her head. 'Oh, no. They were really nice.'

I finish opening the ladder, and position it so it's firmly in place. Then I throw up a line with a weight on one end. I get a perfect hit first time – it goes straight over the strong branch I was aiming for, and the weight heads back down the other side. I tie my climbing rope to the line and haul it up into the tree. With the rope in place, I anchor the other end by tying it securely around a neighbouring tree.

'I have to go back for my chainsaw. Do you want to walk with me?' She nods and we head to the van. Mouse has vanished, presumably feeling he's done his bit for Apple and it's up to me now.

I collect the chainsaw. As I start back towards the woodland, Apple grabs my spare arm.

'It wasn't their fault,' she says.

I put down the heavy tool. 'What wasn't?'

'The fire.'

'There was a fire?'

She nods. 'They just wanted a bonfire – we were all cold, and they thought it would be good to warm us up. But there was a no-fires rule at the festival, and they got into trouble.'

'Well, that doesn't sound so bad.'

'The fire had already started spreading,' she says quietly.

'Spreading? You mean it wasn't contained?'

She shakes her head. 'It was on a spare bit of ground – between the tents, you know?'

'So, these young men lit a fire next to flammable tents?' I can't keep the horror from my voice.

'Yes. And then, we couldn't put it out. We couldn't stop it, and it just . . .' She starts to sob.

'Was anyone hurt?' She nods. 'How badly?'

'Two men. They had to go to hospital . . . One of them was really bad I think.'

There is a long silence. Then I say, 'Oh, Apple . . .'

'Those guys didn't mean it,' she says. 'It was an accident. And then the police came, and it was horrible – they wouldn't listen, they just kept trying to arrest our friends. We got between them, but they pushed us out of the way.'

'Is that how you got that bruise on your face?'

She nods miserably. 'They were quite rough.'

I can imagine exactly how Apple and her companions – no doubt all stoned and probably drunk as well – would have appeared to the law enforcers.

'And what about the argument with Adam Qureshi?'

She looks confused for a moment at the sudden change of topic. Then understanding dawns and she looks away, murmuring, 'As I said, he's cross with me because I don't want to do something.'

'Your sister's worried about you.'

'Nix? She's always making a fuss about something. If she cared so much, she wouldn't have gone off and left me alone here. She was only studying in London; she could easily have lived at home and travelled in every day.'

I rub my temple wearily. 'Are your parents not kind to you?'

She shrugs. 'They're kind, I guess. They're just not *interested*, you know?'

I can't decide whether Apple is merely the product of an entitled, affluent upbringing – or whether she is borderline neglected by her parents. There is too much information to absorb and process. 'Are you OK if I get on now?' I ask.

'Can I still stay and watch?'

I show her where to stand so that she's well out of range of any falling branches. Then I attach the clip from the climbing rope to my harness, don my protective goggles and ear defenders, clip the chainsaw to a rope at my hip, and start my climb.

I love tree work. Up in the branches, with my ear defenders on and the saw roaring, nothing can touch me; I'm isolated from the world in the best possible way. When I've severed all the dead branches and there's only the trunk remaining, I sit for a moment at the top, wishing I could stay. No potentially violent, drug-dealing young men; no desperate young women; no missing ex-husbands; no dead children. No secrets to hear or keep.

At least there's still the trunk to cut. I saw it in sections, ensuring each piece falls in the same direction, so there won't be too much rationalising to do afterwards. As I work, I remember Apple's first attempt at a confession to me – telling me that she had got herself into some kind of trouble. I am certainly not ready to hear the rest of that story.

Finally, I climb down and set the saw on the ground, with the safety catch on. Removing my goggles and defenders, I glance around for Apple. With relief, I see she's wandered off. The job has taken me a good two and a half hours, so it's no wonder she got bored.

I take my gear back to the van, then return to the tropical garden, where Mrs Singer-Pryce is still in the same position, studying her law book.

'Sorry to interrupt,' I say, 'but should I leave the wood for the residents to share out?'

'Yes, that's fine,' she says. 'I'll let them know. Is that all you've done so far?'

'It was a big job,' I explain. 'I had to use my harness and safety gear and there's a process to it – you don't just fell a tree with a few strikes of the axe like the foresters you see on TV. There are other trees to protect. I'm a gardener and tree surgeon, not a logger.'

'I get it,' she says, somewhat stiffly. She checks her watch. 'It's a bit early for lunch.'

'Yes; I'll get on.'

She wafts a hand as if to shoo me away as she goes back to her book.

As soon as I'm out of the tropical garden, I consult my list. Some of the jobs are too lengthy (and tiring) to begin now, but I reckon I can start mulching the roses. This is not on Bubby's list, but it's something I've noticed needs doing. Unlike the formal garden at The Towers, where most of the roses are gathered in the walled garden, La Jolla has all manner of climbing roses, shrub roses and tea roses scattered throughout the borders and shrubberies. I've noticed huge vats of well-rotted leaves in the composting area near the top of the garden, so I wheel my barrow up there and shovel in a load.

I'm on my fifth barrowful – and my shoulders are aching – when a flapping sound behind me announces the arrival of Apple in her flip-flops.

I set down the barrow and rub my shoulders, rolling my arms backwards.

'Are you all right?' she asks.

'I'm fine, thanks.'

'Oh . . .' she says vaguely. 'Can we talk about something?'

I'm about to say it will have to wait, but then I remember my promise to Nicola. 'I need to empty the barrow,' I say. 'Will you come with me?'

'Sure.' Although it's only early April and the sun's not especially strong, she's put on dark glasses, and I can't read her expression behind them.

We walk in silence – me wheeling the barrow and she following behind, like my lady-in-waiting. We head down the path, to the next border with roses.

'You can sit here,' I say, parking my wheelbarrow beside an ornate metal seat.

She sits and says nothing. I ease my shovel into the soft mulch and walk across to the back of the border, where I lay the leaves around the base of a shrub rose. I love the scent of the mulch: earthy and fresh.

When I get back to the barrow, I say, 'What did you want to talk about?'

She says nothing. Her silence is so uncharacteristic that I put my shovel down and take a seat next to her. Without warning, she throws herself at me and, for a split second, I think it's an attack and reel away. But then her arms are round my shoulders and she's crying again. I close my eyes. *This is why it's best not to have children*, I think. *They need so much emotional support.*

She sobs for a minute or two, while I watch a robin land on the barrow and start pecking its way through the mulch, tossing aside any leaves that get between it and the grubs. At last, she lets go of me, removes her sunglasses and wipes her eyes on the heel of her hand. She sits up stiffly, looking straight ahead.

'What was all that about?' I ask.

She shakes her head. 'Nothing, really. I'm being silly.' She smiles and gets up.

'It didn't look like nothing.'

'Would you like some tea? Or coffee?' she asks. Her dark glasses are askew and she loops them back over her ears.

I narrow my eyes. 'Will you be making it?'

She puts her hand to her mouth. 'Was it dire?'

'I poured it away,' I say in a stage whisper.

She laughs. 'Sorry! I'll ask Becky to make it.'

'In that case, I'll take a black coffee, please.'

She leaps from the bench. 'I'm on it!' And she's gone.

I'm left feeling uneasy. And as if I've failed both Apple and Nicola. With a sigh, I turn my focus back to my work.

Mouse appears as I'm shovelling more leaf mulch into my wheelbarrow. He seems exhausted. He accompanies me down to the next rose bushes, and stretches out beneath a wooden bench to sleep.

A maid appears, bearing a tray with a cafetière of fresh coffee, a little jug of milk and a plate of sandwiches, which look much better than the ones I've brought from home. I must stop making a packed lunch – it only goes to waste.

I check my watch as I step out of the border to meet her. 'How did it get to two o'clock?' I ask her, accepting the offering gratefully, and she smiles.

'Time goes fast here; there's always so much work in a place this size, inside and out.' She points down the garden. 'There's a table you can use in the wisteria arch, if you'd like,' she says. 'Or you'd be welcome in the kitchen, if it's too cold out here.'

'That's very kind, but a table in the wisteria arch sounds perfect, thank you.'

Mouse follows me drowsily to the pergola, where he stretches out across my feet, keeping them lovely and warm. The maid brings him a bowl of water, which he laps at sleepily before dozing off again, Mr Rabbit between his paws.

As I bite into a Cheddar and chutney sandwich (peach chutney, clearly homemade, and delicious), I consider Apple's sobbing fit. After the terrible fire at the campsite, I had worried she might be about to tell me something else awful. But I was braced to hear it and support her if necessary. Now, I'm wondering what could be so bad that she can't even speak the words.

My mind wanders after lunch, as I return to the jobs on Mrs Singer-Pryce's list, until I'm reliving that moment at The Towers, watching Adam load bags of white powder into his car. Do I tell his parents their son is dealing hard drugs?

Too many secrets are weighing on me.

By five o'clock, I'm exhausted. Mouse and I travel home in the van. Before we enter the house, I check everything is secure: after that threatening note, I'm not taking any chances. But all is as it should be, so I let us inside, where Mouse runs straight to his bed and I spend a good hour soaking in the bath, before doing some gentle stretches to ease my aching back and shoulders. When I finally make it into bed, my dreams are again filled with Apple Singer-Pryce. This time, she's Alice in Wonderland, crying so hard her tears are forming a lake around us.

Nicola is close by, performing doggy paddle as the water rises. 'I told you to look after her,' she says. 'Now we're all going to drown and it's your fault.'

15

As I make the absurdly short drive to The Chimneys the next morning, I muse once again about how to proceed with regard to the scraps of cloth in my pocket. Should I make another attempt to get Mimi on her own, and show them to her?

'What do you think, Mouse?' I ask, as I lean out of the window to punch the code into the gate, before accelerating up the steep driveway.

I glance over to the passenger seat, where the dog is surveying me without emotion, his beloved rabbit between his paws.

'I know, I know,' I say. 'You're a dog – you can't be expected to get involved in the petty concerns of bipeds.' I park the van and unfasten my seat belt, then climb down and go around to let him out.

He jumps down with his toy and follows me to the back of the van, where I lower the tailgate and bring out my wheelbarrow and everyday tools. Then we head for the back gate, which turns out to be unlocked.

'Maybe Mimi or Lucy are around somewhere,' I suggest. Mouse looks up at me with his big eyes. I swear he understands more than he lets on.

We walk through the garden together – Mouse doesn't seem in a hurry to race off for once – but there's no sign of either mother or daughter.

I knock on the back door and Kate the maid answers. 'Hi,' she says. 'How can I help?'

'I noticed the back gate was unlocked . . .'

'Again? Ms Purdue has told Lucy over and over to lock it.'

'So you think it's been left unlocked overnight again?' Kate nods. 'Someone will have to do an inventory – check nothing's missing,' I say.

'Well, I can't do it.' She sounds indignant. 'I mean, I've got the dining table to polish, then all the floors to mop and hoover . . .'

'I didn't mean you,' I interject quickly. 'Is Ms Purdue available?'

'I'll go and look.'

She shuts the door in my face. Did I do or say something to offend her on my last visit? I rack my brain, and at last dredge up a vague memory of having refused to tell her why I wanted to talk to her mistress. Oh well, nothing to be done there.

After a long wait, Lucy appears. She's dressed in another long, high-neck floral dress.

She doesn't smile as she greets me. 'Hi.'

'Hello.'

'Did you want something?'

'How well do you know the garden ornaments and statues?'

She looks surprised. 'I guess I've grown up with them; why?'

'The garden gate was unlocked when I arrived just now, and I need someone to check there's nothing missing.'

She frowns. 'I definitely locked it. I remember, because it was a bit stiff, and I thought I'd better ask someone to oil it today.'

'That's strange. Does anyone else have a key?'

'Only the night staff and they were already inside.'

'Well, that's a mystery. Do you think you could do a check of the garden?'

'Let me see if Mum's around.' She turns back inside, leaving the door ajar. I infer I'm expected to wait here.

At last, Mimi herself appears. 'The gate was unlocked again?' she asks, in her usual perfunctory manner.

'It was, I'm afraid. Yes.'

'For heaven's sake – if I've told that girl once, I've told her a million times . . .'

'Lucy's sure she locked it,' I say. 'She remembers, because it was stiff and needed oiling.'

'So, did she oil it or get one of the staff to do it?'

'I'm not sure . . .'

Mimi sighs and shakes her head. 'She's a good girl – she really is – but she can be such a scatterbrain sometimes.'

I can't fit this description to Lucy, who seems . . . mature and in control, especially if compared to Apple.

'I wonder if one of the staff might have needed to go out through it after Lucy locked it?'

'Highly unlikely. We only have two night staff, and the day staff leave when they get here. Was there anything else?'

'There were two things, actually; have you got a minute?'

She checks her watch. 'I have precisely nine minutes before I have to leave.'

'Nine minutes it is.'

We walk over to a bench out of earshot of the house.

I start with the easier topic: 'I feel that someone needs to go through the whole garden and take stock of the statues and planters and such like. I can't do it, as I'm not familiar enough with them all yet.'

'I'll ask Jordan to do it.' For a second I wonder if that means I'll get to spend some time with the lovely house manager. I make myself focus on the matter in hand.

'The other thing is . . . this,' I say. Slowly, I undo the Velcro on my jacket pocket and draw out the smaller of the pieces of cloth. My hands are shaking. I hold the scrap out to Mimi, but she just leans across and peers at it.

'You're showing me a torn piece of fabric.'

'Yes. It matches this.' I reach into my larger pocket and withdraw the piece that Mouse found in the paddock.

It's clear she doesn't recognise the scraps. 'I really do have to go . . .'

'I'm sorry; this might be important.'

'Could you just get to the point, please?'

I take a deep breath. 'I believe Mouse found the larger piece in the paddock. The smaller one was stuck inside the pond filter in Mrs Patel's garden.' I hold them side by side. 'Even with the fading and the greening from immersion, they're clearly the same cloth. And, if you look closely here,' I point to the tiny area of detail still visible, 'I think that's a car or a train or something.'

Mimi turns a strange colour.

'Are you all right?' I ask with concern.

She places one hand on her forehead and closes her eyes. I wait quietly. After about half a minute, she opens her eyes and says, 'Who have you told?'

'Only Mrs Patel and you. I did show one of the scraps to Fiona, but she doesn't know about the piece from the pond.'

'Can we keep it that way?'

I nod, hoping I'm not becoming an accessory to anything. 'OK ...'

'And can I take those?' She gestures to the fabric pieces and I hesitate before handing them over. 'Thank you.' She tugs nervously at the pieces of fabric in her hands and says, 'My little boy Alfie loved this shirt. We had him buried in a smart suit with black patent shoes. I buried the shirt with his favourite shoes on top of the grave, and the foxes must have dug them up. As for why there was a scrap of his shirt in Sherry's pond, I will explain – I promise. Just not now. Not today.' She sounds exhausted. 'And now, if you'll excuse me, I have a meeting to attend.'

'Of course.'

She stands slowly, like a much older woman; I watch her walking back towards the house. Mouse has been sitting at my feet, observing the exchange. Now, he puts his paws up on my lap. It's unclear whether he's seeking to reassure himself or me, but I stroke his ears and talk softly to him while I process my conversation with Mimi.

The back door flies open just after I've taken Mouse off the lead and he's raced off into the woods. Lucy comes striding out of the house, clearly furious. She's tall – much taller than her mother – and holds herself very upright; when she's angry, her long skirt flying behind, she resembles a righteous queen leading her troops into battle. I tense in anticipation of the onslaught.

She approaches and says, 'Mum says I have to go round the whole bloody garden, checking there's nothing missing.'

'I thought your mother was going to ask Jordan to do it?'

'Apparently his workload's "too great to trouble him".' The sarcasm in her voice is unmistakable.

'Is he not genuinely busy?'

She shrugs. 'Mum always gives him a list about a mile long.'

'So your mum really does need you to do the checking.'

She scowls and says, 'Isn't it curious how things didn't start going missing till you came here?'

I stare at her. 'Are you accusing me of being the thief?'

She shrugs. 'I'm just saying . . .'

I feel my fists clench involuntarily. I take a deep breath in and out, and keep my voice steady: 'Well, please stop saying, and start doing the checks for whatever else might be missing.'

'As if I didn't have anything better to do. Normally, she lets me get on with my music practice. She knows how important it is. And there must be someone else she could ask, like Kate or Ellen in the kitchen. I mean, there are auditions next week, and I need to rehearse.'

'Well, perhaps it won't take long.'

'I wish.'

'Oh, well, the sooner you start . . .' I say brightly.

'By the way, Kate's bringing you out a coffee,' she says unexpectedly.

'Lovely.'

'When you see her, can you make sure she brings me a cup of tea?'

'I'll ask her.'

And then she's gone, striding up the garden in her long dress and UGG boots. I take a moment to enjoy the peace while I look around, assessing the work in progress. With the main lawn looking so much better, it feels like there's more incentive to recover the rest of the grounds. I've allocated today to removing ivy from a large shrubbery sited about halfway up the garden. I've discovered some wonderful specimens there, struggling on beneath their blanket of strangling vines.

I set to work and soon become engrossed in gently disentangling the ivy strands from the shrubs beneath, before digging out the roots wherever I find them. I'm planning on putting down a thick membrane when the job's done, to suppress ivy regrowth. I'll have to cover it with something in keeping – perhaps slate chippings or a reddish material that ties in with the many low brick walls and herringbone paths that run throughout the grounds.

Engrossed as I am in my task, it takes me a little while to realise that I can hear people talking. Perhaps one of the household staff has come outside to talk to Lucy. The voices continue, low and monotonous, and I carry on with my digging. The shrubs I've uncovered so far include a *Magnolia grandiflora*, which should be far taller but has been stunted by the ivy's hold; a glossy-leaved camellia, which clearly hasn't flowered for a long while; a burgundy-leaved (and very thorny) berberis; and *Arbutus unedo*, which bears clusters of fabulous, strawberry-shaped fruits. Whoever designed the planting gave it a lot of thought: all four of these shrubs are evergreen, providing some year-round structure to this part of the garden.

I've got rid of all of the ivy tendrils and most of the roots in one section, and I'm standing back to admire the newly revealed plants, when the voices stop abruptly and Adam Qureshi goes striding past, ignoring me. A minute later, Lucy runs past, clutching her cheek.

'Are you all right?' I call.

She wheels round. 'I'm fine!' she says – but I can see tears in her eyes.

I dig my fork into the earth for safekeeping and go after her. 'Wait, Lucy. Did Adam hurt you?'

She's ahead of me, running down towards the house. She shakes her head, but her shoulders are heaving. Then she slows and stops, allowing me to catch up.

'Show me,' I say, and she removes her hand from her face. She has a bright-red handprint embossed on her cheek.

'What is wrong with that boy?' I say.

'Drugs,' she says. 'Did you know he does cocaine?'

My mind flashes back to the garage scene – all those bags filled with a white substance.

'No, I didn't know that. So, why do you let him come to see you here?'

She avoids my eye. 'Oh . . . He's hard to say no to . . .'

'Well, it's time someone said something. Has anyone spoken to his parents?'

'I don't know . . .'

'Well, talk to your mum when she gets home, and make sure she talks to Annabelle Qureshi.'

She nods, looking so vulnerable I'd like to hug her. But Lucy doesn't give off the same puppy-dog vibe as Apple, and I'm not sure she'd like it. Instead, I say,

'Arnica's good for bruising.'

'I have a drama class tonight,' she says, looking horrified. 'Do you really think it will bruise?'

124

'It might, I'm afraid. Try the arnica. Do you have some?'

'I don't think so.'

'Follow me to the van.'

I lead her down the garden and around to the front drive, where I grab a tube of arnica cream from the glove box, where I keep my first aid kit.

'Here,' I hold it out to her. 'Put some on your fingers and rub it gently into the sore area. It will really help. And you can always apply a thick layer of foundation to hide the redness.'

'I suppose . . .'

'I'm sure Apple will help, if you don't normally wear make-up.'

She nods. 'That's a good idea.'

As she rubs the arnica cream into her face, I muse on the problem that is Adam Qureshi.

'Some people think they can get away with whatever they like,' I say.

'What?'

'I'm thinking about Adam. Did you know he was arguing with Apple a few days ago, gripping her by the wrists?'

Her eyes grow wide. 'Really? She didn't say anything.'

'I hope it's OK that I mentioned it. But if you're both being bullied by the young man, surely your parents will want to step in?'

'Mum will go mad when she sees my face.'

'I should hope so, too. I'm feeling pretty angry myself, and you're not my daughter.'

'Do you know why Adam was doing that to Apple?' she asks.

I shake my head. 'They were having an argument of some sort. You'll have to ask her.'

She nods. 'Will do.'

'What about you? Can I ask why you and Adam were fighting?'

'I wouldn't exactly call it fighting. I said something he didn't like, so he slapped me. He's like that.'

'What was it about?'

'It was only because I said he could do better than his girlfriend.'

'Who's his girlfriend?'

'She's called Trudy. She's very pretty, but she's not very bright.

I simply said he could go out with someone who makes good conversation as well as . . . you know.'

'There's no excuse for him hitting you, but you have to admit, that isn't a very nice thing to say . . .'

She snorts. 'Oh, please! You should hear the way he badmouths her. He calls her "the slut princess" when she's not around to hear.'

'Well, that's unpleasant . . . Do you know, I think your cheek's fading already.'

She peers in the van's wing mirror. 'Maybe it won't be noticeable by tonight.'

'Hopefully not. And now, if you're all right, I'm going to get back to my work.'

'Sure. Thanks for the cream.' She moves to hand the tube back to me.

'Oh, no, you keep it. I've got more at the cottage and you should probably reapply it tonight before bed.'

'That's so kind – thank you.'

It's only when her face lights up with a smile that I realise she's beautiful. Her thick brown hair has been drawn back into a French plait, which lays bare her high cheekbones and creamy complexion.

I smile in return and head back towards the garden. Kate meets me near the house, looking disgruntled.

'I've been looking everywhere for you!'

'Sorry – I had to go back to the van for something.'

'Well, your coffee's on the table in the jungle. But it's probably cold by now.'

'Oh – hold on, Kate.' She turns with a look of . . . what? Disdain? Anger? Resentment? I decide to ignore it. 'Lucy asked if you could please make her a cup of tea.'

'Right.' She disappears back inside the house.

I sigh and start to walk up the garden. Then I realise I have no idea where Kate means by 'the jungle'. I give up on the dream of coffee and get back to clearing the ivy.

At around one o'clock, I stop for a break, taking a seat on one of the old brick walls and tucking into my sandwiches. Mouse comes to find me, and I pour water for him into the tin bowl I keep in my backpack.

Seeds of Murder

While we're keeping a companionable silence, Jordan appears, looking harassed.

'Steph, hi.'

'Hiya. Sorry – mouthful of sandwich!'

He grimaces. 'I'm too late. Ellen in the kitchen wanted to know if you'd like some lunch. She's got a casserole all ready.'

'Oh, no!'

'I'm so sorry. I was going to send Kate to ask you earlier but I got waylaid.'

'Don't worry. I just hope the food doesn't go to waste.'

'Oh, it won't. The family are having it for their dinner. Ellen just made a little extra, in case you were hungry.'

'I'm starting to think I should stop making sandwiches; everyone seems pretty keen to feed me.'

'Yes, I think you might be better off having your lunch from the kitchens. As you might imagine, the standard of catering is pretty high throughout Beaulieu.'

'Yes, I've tasted some of it already. It's all been delicious.'

He smiles; he has one of those smiles that lights up his whole face; it's impossible not to smile back. 'How about dessert?' he asks. 'I've heard rumours there's a choice between an apricot flan or an apple pie with custard.'

'I think I've died and gone to heaven.'

He laughs. 'How about a little of both?'

I manage to bite my lip before I accidentally ask him to marry me. Instead I say, 'Jordan, where's "the jungle"?'

'Er . . . the whole garden? Before you arrived, at least.'

'It's just that Kate said she'd left my coffee in "the jungle".'

'Oh, that's just her little joke. She probably means the area between the woodland and the tennis court.'

'There's a tennis court?'

'The grounds continue to the far side of the woodland – did no one tell you?'

'You mean . . . there's more to tend?'

He sees my look of panic and raises his palms in a calming gesture. 'Not really. There's a tennis court, as I said, and an area

127

that's deliberately left untended, for the wildlife. Would you like me to show you?'

'No, that's all right, thanks. Do you really think Kate would have left my coffee all the way over there?'

He pulls a face. 'Only if you'd done something to upset her. She's very . . . sensitive.'

'I have noticed.'

'I'm sorry; that's very unprofessional of her. It's just so hard to get good maids – and she's a wonderfully thorough cleaner and polisher.'

'You don't need to apologise.'

'I do if she's meant to be providing you with refreshments but she's leaving them somewhere inaccessible. I'm the one who hired her, so she is my responsibility.'

As I watch him speak, a question builds in my mind. 'Jordan . . . I know you have to get on, but I'm curious about something.'

He meets my eye with a pleasant, interested gaze. 'Go on.'

'How does someone like you end up doing a job like this?'

He raises an eyebrow. 'What? Waiting on white people?'

It's my turn to pull a face. 'That's not what I meant. It's just, you're young and intelligent . . .'

He smiles. 'I trained in hospitality and managed a large hotel in central London for three years. Ms Purdue used to stay in the hotel regularly, and we got to know one another fairly well. When she offered me an enormous pay rise to come and work for her, I wasn't going to say no.'

'I see. I'm sorry, I didn't mean to pry.'

He shakes his head. 'You weren't prying. It's not a job I ever imagined myself doing. I mean, no one grows up, thinking: *I hope I can be a house manager one day*, do they? But working for one family and helping their day-to-day lives go as smoothly as possible is surprisingly . . . OK.'

'Good. That's good.'

'What about you? Did you always want to be a gardener?'

'Not always, no. When I was little, I wanted to be a detective. Or a long-distance lorry driver.'

He laughs. 'A lorry driver?'

'What's funny about that?'

'Oh – you were serious.'

'I had some romantic notion of what it would be like to be alone on the road for days on end.'

He considers. 'OK – I can see that.'

'I kind of fell into gardening, when I didn't know what else to do. Luckily, I love it.'

He nods. 'We're the fortunate ones, who find our jobs worthwhile. It's pretty rare, I reckon.' There's a pause, during which we maintain eye contact for slightly longer than is customary. I feel myself begin to blush. He breaks the silence first, saying, 'And now, if you'll excuse me, I must get on. I'll send Kate out with those desserts, and I'll make sure you receive them this time.'

'Great. Thanks. Please don't be hard on her.'

He nods and leaves.

By the time Kate arrives with a tray of dessert, I've already returned to The Great Ivy Challenge. She has to say my name twice before I realise she's standing there.

'Sorry! Sorry! I get pretty engrossed . . .'

'That's OK. I'm sorry I was a bit off with you this morning.'

'Don't worry about it.'

'Did you find your coffee?' I shake my head. 'I'll get you another one.'

'That would be lovely – thank you, Kate.'

She smiles and sets down the tray close to where I'm working. Even before she's out of sight, I've abandoned my tools to grab the bowl and sniff the sweet scent of fruit, before tucking into two of the tastiest desserts I've ever eaten. The flan's pastry is light and flaky, and it's filled with a smooth *crème pâtissière* and sliced apricots, whose sweetness complements the slight tartness of the apples in the crumble. The latter is topped off with a traditional custard – the sort the French refer to as *crème anglaise*.

Kate's only gone for a few minutes, but I've already polished off the desserts by the time she reappears. The mug she hands me is steaming and full of richly scented coffee.

'Those puddings were amazing,' I say.

She nods. 'Ellen's puddings are always fantastic.' She pauses and adds, 'Mind you, her main courses are great, too.'

'I can't wait to try one of those.'

'So . . . did you get to speak to Ms Purdue?'

'I did eventually, thanks.' I'm relieved she doesn't ask what it was about this time. 'I'm sorry I couldn't talk to you about it; it was something private – for her, not me, or I would have told you.'

'I get it. I shouldn't have asked. It just gets a bit boring sometimes – you know, just cleaning and fetching – and a bit of gossip can make the day go that bit faster. Do you not get like that, doing the garden?'

'I suppose some of my tasks can be a bit repetitive,' I concede, not adding that those are my favourites.

'Did you hear about the Qureshis?' she asks suddenly.

'You mean Mr and Mrs?' She nods. 'What about them?'

'They got into a huge row outside the front this morning. Anyone driving by could hear them yelling!'

'Oh, dear.'

She nods with evident satisfaction. 'And then a police car came! I reckon he's going to prison!'

I don't tell her about the stolen sculpture, and that I suspect Annabelle had kept this from her husband and he'd just found out and summoned the police. Instead, I say, 'I hope that's not the case. I'm sorry to hear about the row. Hopefully it's nothing serious.'

She shrugs. 'You can never tell what goes on behind closed doors.'

'That's true.'

She picks up the tray with my empty bowl and says, 'I'd better get back. Mr Samuels has asked me to dust the bedrooms.'

'Mr Samuels?'

'You know – the house manager,' she says.

'Oh – Jordan.'

'Oh, we're on first-name terms with the boss, are we?' she says with a laugh which makes me uncomfortable; I have a bad feeling I might be next on her gossip sheet.

It's a relief to get back to my gardening. I've cleared a good five metres of ground so far today, although the ivy is still growing up the brick wall at the back of the shrubbery. However, I'm tempted to leave some of that as a backdrop – especially as the wall looks fairly brittle, and I don't want to risk bringing it down. While I'm examining the brickwork, I muse on Kate's revelation about the Qureshis' row. It occurs to me that, if Mr Qureshi has only just found out about the stolen sculpture, he might hold me partly accountable for keeping the whole thing hushed up – he might not know that I recommended Annabelle call the police. This is not a pleasant thought. Luckily, as soon as I'm back clearing the ivy, my brain lapses into its meditative state.

I pass the afternoon in pleasing isolation, focusing on my task and keeping my concerns at bay. It's only when I pack up to go home that I remember Adam Qureshi's run-ins with Apple and Lucy. I have a duty to talk to his mother and father. Should I make sure they know about the drugs I saw him handling? Or that he may be using cocaine? Or should I focus purely on his abuse of Apple and Lucy? And what if his parents know about the drugs and are somehow involved? I could put myself in real danger.

I call for Mouse and we walk to the van together. He moves slowly, clearly worn out by another energetic day in the grounds, and I'm looking forward to reaching home and being able to collapse on the sofa with him for a big cuddle.

My phone rings an hour or two after I get home, when Mouse and I have fallen asleep in front of Attenborough. It's Danny. I fill him in on my ethical dilemma over Adam.

'So, this young man keeps assaulting young women and getting away with it?' My brother sounds horrified.

His reaction decides me. 'Not anymore,' I say. 'If Lucy and Apple don't make a stand, I'm going to talk to Annabelle, Adam's mum.'

'But that shouldn't be your job,' he says. 'You're the gardener!'

'It's kind of strange how hazy the boundaries are between what is and isn't my job,' I say. I tell him about installing the camera for Mrs Patel, and becoming Apple's confidante at her sister's request.

'What?' He sounds distracted. 'Hold on a minute, Steph.' His voice grows muffled as he addresses his daughter, 'Alice, why aren't you in bed?' I can't hear my niece's response, but he says, 'Well, go up now, and I'll come up in a few minutes to tuck you in again, all right?' He returns to me. 'Sorry, what were you saying?'

'Nothing – never mind. So, how are my favourite niece, nephews and bump?'

'All pretty good, thanks.'

'And Mum and Dad?' I ask quietly. 'Do you know if Dad's talked to Mum yet?'

'I don't know, sorry. You should ring him and ask. Mum has her Zumba class on Thursday evenings; you could catch him then.'

'I might do that, thanks.'

'So, Alice and Frankie want to know when you're coming again.'

'Look, I know I promised Alice, but things have got a bit complicated here, so give me a week or two, and then we can discuss a date for my next visit. Give them all hugs from me in the meantime, and tell them I miss them. Is Karen keeping well?'

'Yeah, great, although she wants it to be over as soon as possible.'

'Isn't she only about four months' pregnant?'

'Yeah but she's got big really quickly; the midwives say it's because it's her fourth – her body's still slack from the other three or something.'

I grimace. 'Please don't tell Karen her body's slack.'

He laughs. 'She's the one saying it!'

'She's allowed.' I glance at my watch and see it's close to eight. 'Look, it's lovely to hear from you, but I've not had dinner yet . . . I fell asleep when I got home from work.'

'Sorry! I'll let you get on. Speak soon, all right?'

'All right. Hugs to everyone.'

'Big hugs back.'

I cook my dinner of chicken breast with a creamy mushroom sauce from a jar, plus some new potatoes and green beans, and eat it in front of an episode of *Death in Paradise*. After I finish dinner, I turn off the TV just to hear the silence. I'm not sure I've ever lived somewhere as quiet as Beaulieu before. Even as I'm thinking this, a car revs its engine past the cottage, its headlamps shining momentarily like searchlights through my living room window.

I go to the window and look out. I can't make out any details, but the car turns in at The Chimneys, taking the turn at reckless speed. There are lights on the gateposts and these come on at the vehicle's approach, but I still can't see a number plate or make out the colour or model of the car.

Perhaps I'm being nosy; I don't want to become one of those lonely, curtain-twitching people. I back away from the window and draw the curtains. The car could just be Lucy getting home from a rehearsal.

Sitting back on the sofa, I reflect on a saying by my old friend, Hannah: 'Don't get involved in other people's shit. They won't thank you for it and you'll be the one who ends up stinking.' Hannah had a pithy way with words.

But it seems too late for me to disentangle myself. Like it or not, the Beaulieu Heights residents have drawn me into their misfortunes and intrigues. I guess, one way or another, I'm going to end up stinking.

16

'I specifically said not to mention it to Mimi,' says Mrs Patel.

I've just climbed down from the van at Villa Splendida where she was standing waiting for me; she's clearly furious.

'I felt she had a right to know,' I say, walking around to the passenger side, then having second thoughts about letting Mouse out – he's probably better where he is for now.

'You felt? *You* felt?'

'Look, if the pieces of cloth are from Mimi's dead son's shirt, they belong to her.'

'Well, it's too late now, anyway,' she says.

'Yes, it is too late,' I say. 'Anyway, she seemed pleased I'd come to her.'

'Pleased? She called me last night. She was beside herself. She'd only just started to sleep properly through the night after years of insomnia and nightmares.' She glares at me. 'It's on you if she has to go back to taking sleeping tablets.'

'Well, maybe you can explain what's so important about those clothing scraps. Do they have something to do with how Alfie died?'

Mrs Patel glares at me. She purses her glossy lips in an immaculately made-up face. With a tight white dress that shows off her curves and high-maintenance tan, she looks like she's about to take a limousine to a red-carpet event, rather than spend time reprimanding her groundskeeper.

'None of your business,' she says at last. 'I'd appreciate it if you could focus and get on with your work. I don't know if you've noticed, but you're the gardener, not the host of *The Stephanie Kyle Show*.' She smiles, pleased with her wordplay.

'Fine,' I say. 'Where do you want me?'

'Well, you can deal with the camera situation, for a start.'

'The camera situation?'

'You'll see when you get there.' She waves a hand towards the woodland area.

'And after that?'

'The top lawn could use a mowing. Francis will show you where we keep the ride-on, as he says you used your own push mower last time. And after that, it's up to you.'

Up to me? Did she really say that? I realise my mouth is gaping, and close it. 'Right. Great.'

She strides away, and I see her take a seat on a bench overlooking the fabulous views. She has a bottle of red wine beside her, and a large glass. It's not yet nine o'clock. I wonder if it was her car I witnessed driving at high speed to The Chimneys last night.

I head into the woodland and over to the hornbeam. For a moment, I think I've made a mistake: the wrong tree; the wrong garden. But no: this is definitely the right place – and, when I peer up the trunk, the camera is missing.

I glance around, as if it might have removed itself from the bracket and gone for a walk. In the end – and for no reason I can rationalise – I fetch my ladder from the van. When I climb up to the bracket, I find a note taped there, with 'Sherry' written on the front in black cursive script. Removing it carefully and placing it in my pocket, I climb back down and return the steps to the van. Mrs Patel is still on her bench, sipping at her glass of wine, so I walk over.

She doesn't turn as I reach her, but simply says, 'So?' while staring out at the view.

'I found this.' I hold out the note.

She doesn't take the folded paper, but returns to gazing at the view. 'I was hoping there might be a different explanation.'

'Am I meant to know what's going on? Only I haven't a clue.'

'Trust me – you're better off that way.'

'I'm guessing whoever left this note isn't holding the camera to ransom, so they must have some other reason for removing it.' She doesn't answer, but sips her wine. 'I'll just leave it here,' I say at last, placing the note beside her on the bench and weighing it down with a stone. 'I'm going to mow the top lawn.'

She nods, and I walk back to the van, where I release poor Mouse, who's staring out with a woebegone expression. He races off and I let him go. If Mrs Patel objects, I can call him back. I follow slowly, trying to make sense of the whole incident with the video camera. Mrs Patel seemed unsurprised by the various developments. Has she been testing someone?

I realise I've walked all the way to the top lawn without asking Francis about the mower. I sigh and head back – encountering him part-way.

'Ms Williams,' he says, with a nod so formal it could be taken as a slight bow.

I bow back. 'Sir Francis.' He has his striped apron on today, and his black hair is a little untidy, as if he's run his hands through it absent-mindedly.

His mouth twitches. 'I hear you're doing a wonderful job in the gardens.'

'That's good to hear, thanks. Have you been working here a while?'

He nods. 'Coming up to twelve years. And you'll have noticed that, while some of the gardens have been well-maintained, others have been . . . somewhat neglected.'

'Do you know why Simon was so inconsistent?'

His normally professional demeanour turns angry. 'Perhaps the *landscape* of certain properties suited him better than others.' He blushes and says, 'Please can we pretend I didn't say that?' He runs his hands through his hair, making it even more dishevelled.

'I don't know what you're trying to tell me,' I say, hoping he'll expound.

He puts a finger to his lips and shakes his head. 'So . . . lunch,' he says, as if we were just talking about it. 'There's a choice between either a beetroot and feta salad, or a spinach and blue cheese frittata.'

I'm clearly not going to get anything more helpful out of him. 'Frittata, please.'

'And when would Master Mouse like to partake of his refreshment?'

I lower my voice. 'I've let him off his lead . . .'

'That's fine; Mrs Patel will be going out shortly. I'll bring your food out at one o'clock and leave it on the table nearest to the back door. If you call for Mouse when you reach the house, I'll bring his food and water, too.'

'You're a star, Sir Francis,' I tell him, noting with delight that he grins with pleasure. 'Oh, before you go, I need access to the ride-on mower, please.'

'Of course. We can go over there now.'

He leads me past the forbidden shed, which has blinds over the windows, so I can't see in. Not that I'd want Francis to catch me trying to peek inside. There's another outbuilding just past it, half-covered in Russian vine, and here he stops to open a garage-style door.

He points to the mower. 'The key's in the ignition, and there are ear defenders on the seat. Do you need me to show you how to work it?'

'No, thanks; I should be fine.'

'Very well. And can I tempt you with a hot beverage?'

'I'd kill for a coffee.'

'I can assure you that bloodshed won't be necessary.' And he departs.

When he returns about ten minutes later with my mug of coffee, I'm riding the mower across the large expanse of lawn, so we just wave to one another.

I know it's childish, but I love a ride-on. It takes me back to childhood dreams of driving tractors and lorries, and feels like a giant toy. The top lawn is about an acre in all, and it takes me an hour to complete, with occasional breaks to empty the large tank of grass cuttings on to the compost heap. When I'm done, the lawn is immaculate. Simon must have applied a fertiliser in the autumn for it to be so green and healthy now. I return the mower to the outbuilding, but I don't have the key to lock up, so I must remind Francis to do that. Unless I'm mistaken, the little tractor is a £7,000 piece of kit, and I don't want to be responsible for its going missing.

The rest of the morning passes uneventfully. I find plenty of small jobs to pass the time, and enjoy another tasty lunch, set out for me as promised by Francis. Mouse's dish smells strongly of giblets, which he loves.

After lunch, I busy myself with tackling a mass invasion of the wild, yellow-flowered *Geum urbanum* (also known as 'wood avens' or 'herb bennet') – a pretty but pernicious weed, which grows nasty burrs that hook on to everything for easy seed distribution. As I refuse to use weed killer, it's a job that can only be tackled on my knees; a couple of hours in, my back and knees are aching. It's a relief when Mimi Purdue appears, striding towards me as I'm standing up from weeding to tie my hair back for the umpteenth time.

'Mimi – hi. How are you doing?'

'I'm afraid I'm going to have to ask you to come with me.'

'Come with you? Is this about the clothing scraps?'

She grimaces. 'It has nothing to do with that. The residents' committee has requested your presence, and I would very much appreciate your discretion on that topic.'

'OK . . . Sure.' I remove my gloves and stuff them into my pockets. 'Is there something wrong?'

'I can't discuss it, I'm afraid.'

'Right . . . I'll just fetch Mouse on the way.'

The dog is fast asleep beneath a lilac that's in full bloom, delicately scenting the air. It feels almost cruel to wake him, but I don't know how long I'll be, so I stroke him gently, saying his name, until he's conscious enough to stand and shake himself fully awake. I clip on his lead.

'I just need to let Mrs Patel know . . .'

'There won't be any need for that. Sherry is already at the meeting.'

'Right . . .' My stomach is starting to tie itself in a large knot. 'Can you not just tell me what's going on?'

'We'll discuss it when we get there.'

'Where are we going?'

'The Mount. We always hold our meetings there. We'll take the Land Rover.' Mimi's Land Rover is a mud-splattered old Defender – a far less grand, more workhorse model, than the Qureshis' glamorous Range Rover.

'You can put him in the back,' Mimi says, nodding to Mouse. He jumps in obediently when I open the old car's back door, and he settles quietly with Mr Rabbit when I ask him to sit.

'Good boy!'

Getting in beside Mimi, I feel a bit like I'm going voluntarily to my execution. Perhaps I shouldn't have agreed to come. What if they're going to accuse me of carrying out the thefts?

'Look, Ms Purdue, I love this job,' I say, as she takes us down the driveway to the road, where she turns left towards The Mount, which is the next house along. She doesn't answer, so I continue, 'And I need it. I wouldn't intentionally do anything to jeopardise that.' She remains silent – tight-lipped, even.

Perhaps they just want to ask my opinion on something gardening-related? Yeah, right – something so important they have to hold a residents' meeting in the middle of the afternoon on a work day: a plague of flesh-eating locusts, perhaps, or a Triffid invasion . . . I sigh and look behind me, to where Mouse has climbed on to a seat and is peering out of the window with interest, Mr Rabbit swinging from his jaws.

Mimi turns in at The Mount, drives to the top of the long drive in silence and parks alongside a row of cars, all of them high spec. I see Annabelle's Range Rover and Sherry's Merc.

I let Mouse down from the back, put him on his lead, and we follow Mimi through the central passage in the granite tower to the garden, then in through a back door and out again to a courtyard I didn't know existed. At the far side of the courtyard is a black wooden building. Mimi strides over, opens the door and walks in. Part of me wants to turn and run, but I follow meekly with Mouse, stepping inside while Mimi holds the door.

I'm faced with a long table, with residents seated along the far side and at both ends. It's like going to a job interview and discovering the entire board will be interrogating you.

'Is it all right that I've brought the dog?' I ask, hoping for a smile or some reassurance. But the faces stare back blankly. My gaze scans the line-up. When I catch Fiona Penwarren's eye, she looks angry rather than friendly. My stomach tightens still further.

Mimi has taken her seat at the far left – the head of the table, where I'd imagined Rupert Penwarren presiding. Beside her is Fiona; then both Qureshis – I assume the large-framed, bearded man to Annabelle's left is her husband – followed by Bubby Singer-Pryce, Sherry Patel and a tall, thin man who may be Rupert Penwarren.

Jockey Singer-Pryce is at the bottom of the table. At least he can't grope me from there.

I stand, frozen, until Mimi says, 'Please take a seat.'

There is only one seat – opposite the inquisitors, of course. I wonder fleetingly if my predecessor, Simon, also had to face this intimidating panel – perhaps right before losing his job.

As I pull out the chair and sit down, I'm grateful to feel Mouse settle himself across my feet, like an anchor.

'Shall we get started?' Mimi glances around the table, and the attendees all nod. 'Zakariya, would you start us off?'

In a panic, I say, 'Before you say anything, I want you all to know that if I've done something to upset you, I'd really appreciate the chance to put it right . . .'

Mr Qureshi holds up a hand to silence me and clears his throat. 'Ms Williams, we haven't met, but an extremely rare and valuable sculpture was taken from my garden within a short time of your arrival at Beaulieu Heights.'

'I know that,' I say. 'And I can assure you I had nothing to do with the theft – nor any of the stolen items.' I look along the table, but get very little reaction, other than a small nod from Fiona.

'Zakariya, that isn't why we're here,' says Annabelle, quietly.

'May I chip in?' Rupert Penwarren asks.

'Go ahead,' says Mimi.

'I've also not met Ms Williams, but, as you are all aware, I've reason to believe my wife may have confided certain . . . rather personal information to her – information that even my closest friends do not know.'

I rub my temples. 'What exactly is going on here? What are you accusing me of?'

Mimi says, 'The thing is, Ms Williams, several of us at this table have received unpleasant—'

'I'd say "threatening",' breaks in Bubby Singer-Pryce.

Mimi nods. 'Very well: a number of us have received *threatening* messages over the last few days. We have reason to believe you are the only person to whom much of this information has been confided – thus you are, of course, the primary suspect.'

I burst out laughing, but stop abruptly when no one joins in. 'You're joking, right?'

Mimi coughs. 'We are not joking. Indeed, due to the severity of the situation, there is nothing to joke about.'

'Right, well, have you contacted the police?' It's almost entertaining to witness their eyes slide away from mine. 'You haven't, have you? Let me guess: some of the stuff you're being accused of isn't entirely legal.'

'How dare you!' says Rupert, but Fiona raises her soft voice and says, 'Darling, she's right – you know she is. Please let her speak.' It's clear from the others' reaction that it's unusual for her to speak out – they all turn their heads towards her with evident surprise.

Meanwhile, fury is rising like bile in my throat. I push my chair back and stand up, sending Mouse stumbling to his feet. I look along the row of residents. 'Do you seriously think I'd jeopardise my position here by blackmailing you all? I have a house, a good wage, and work I enjoy. Where's my incentive?'

I hear Fiona say to the others, 'I told you,' and I could almost run around the table and kiss her.

Rupert ignores his wife and responds to me: 'Your incentive would be to continue to do your work – and get paid – while raking in a tidy extra income.' A few of the others nod and murmur their assent.

'I'm done here,' I say. 'You should all be ashamed of yourselves.' I turn to leave.

But Mimi says, 'Ms Williams, please take your seat,' in such a commanding tone, I find myself sitting straight back down. 'Now, does anyone have anything to add, or should we proceed as agreed?' she asks.

Fiona Penwarren raises her voice again. 'I have something to add.' When she has their attention, she continues, 'I feel we should give Ms Williams a chance to clear her name. After all, as I already told you, she herself received a threatening note, pushed under her door.'

Her husband snorts. 'Which she happened to show to the most trusting person at Beaulieu. Did it occur to you she may have written the note herself, Fiona?'

Fiona shakes her head. 'She did no such thing, Rupert. You are maligning the poor woman.'

Bubby Singer-Pryce knocks on the wooden table for attention, and everyone's eyes turn to her. 'Did you actually receive one of the letters, Fiona?' she asks.

'I did not. But nonetheless, I am a member of this committee, and feel I have a right to be heard.'

'Hear, hear,' says Annabelle Qureshi, and Fiona flashes her a grateful smile.

'How do you suggest she "clear her name" exactly?' asks Rupert.

'I don't know *exactly*,' his wife says, 'but, as far as I am aware – admittedly having seen only one of these notes myself – there is nothing to tie Ms Williams to the sending of them. I, for one, believe in the concept of innocent until proven guilty.'

'You haven't seen all the notes?' I ask. She shakes her head. 'So . . . who has seen them all?'

'No one,' says Mimi. 'Each of us has seen only the note received by themselves or their family member.'

I grit my teeth. 'So you don't even know if they've all been written by the same person?'

Again, there's shuffling and general gaze avoidance.

'For heaven's sake, if you're going to accuse me of blackmail, at least let me see the threats I've allegedly issued. Or would you like a sample of my handwriting?'

'They're all typed,' says Sherry Patel, 'so that wouldn't help, as you probably know.'

I stare at her. 'So you're one of the people accusing me, I take it?'

She doesn't even blush. 'I am. You've shown far too much curiosity in our affairs for my liking.'

I strike my forehead in frustration. 'You've dragged me into your affairs, whether I liked it or not.'

Sherry says nothing.

Fiona speaks again: 'This is scapegoating,' she says firmly. 'Now, I suggest we give Ms Williams at least a month to clear her name.'

'A month!' object Rupert and Zakariya simultaneously; they both look angry and red-faced.

'Well, how long do you suggest?' asks Fiona pleasantly.

'She should be summarily dismissed,' says Zakariya.

'What does the blackmailer want?' I ask. They fall quiet. 'Well, are they after money or something else?'

I've never seen a room full of people more adept at looking away when put on the spot.

'Mr Penwarren,' I say, deliberately, 'what were your conditions?'

He clears his throat. 'They weren't specified,' he says huskily.

'Anyone?' I look along the table. Mimi becomes very interested in her note-taking; Annabelle is studying a large diamond on her finger; Zakariya stoops to rub an invisible speck off one of his shoes. Nobody responds.

I'm starting to get very hot. 'Are you saying these "blackmail" notes don't contain any demands?' I ask. My voice is louder than I intended.

'I'll answer this,' says Mimi to the group. She turns in her chair to face me. 'It would appear the blackmailer has yet to make his or her requirements known. The notes all say something to the effect of, "I'll be in touch".'

'Right,' I say. 'So, if I've understood correctly: even the alleged blackmail isn't in fact blackmail. In other words, I'm being accused of a non-existent crime – and, as half of you seem to be up to illegal dealings of one sort or another, we can't get the police involved. That's even if there was a case of extortion for them to investigate. I'm not sure sending notes telling someone you know what they're up to counts as an offence.'

'The notes were threatening,' says Sherry Patel. 'It was in the tone . . .'. She looks to the others for confirmation, which she gets, with various nods and murmurs of agreement.

I feel like picking up something heavy and throwing it at the wall. Or perhaps at Sherry. There's a paperweight on the table, and it's probably a good thing it's too far away for me to reach. My fingers are twitching. 'So how on earth can I clear my name, as Mrs Penwarren suggests, if I'm not allowed to involve the police?'

'I'll help you,' says Fiona, looking straight at me.

'How?'

She smiles brightly. 'We'll find the actual blackmailer together.'

I remember what she told me about my predecessor. 'What about

Simon?' I ask the panel. 'Surely, if you believe I had access to this information, then so did he?'

They exchange looks among them that I can't interpret.

'There is something else,' says Mr Singer-Pryce.

'What's that?' I ask.

'It would appear Ms Purdue was a little too hasty in accepting your résumé.'

'What do you mean?'

I stare at him as he speaks the words I've dreaded for the past two years:

'Your real name's actually Louise Peterson, isn't it?'

17

The room is silent apart from the buzzing in my head. Even from inside my internal panic room – even as I count my breaths in and out (slowly, *slowly*) – I am aware that the residents have all now rediscovered their ability to make eye contact. I'm faced with a row of stares.

Mouse licks my fingers, and I stroke his ears. *Breathe in 2 3 4 5 6; breathe out 2 3 4 5 6.*

'Well?' It's Annabelle Qureshi, a woman I'd quite liked until today.

'Well, what?' I say. 'There's no crime attached to changing your name.'

'It's *why* a person would change their name that intrigues us,' she says, watching me with interest.

I take a deep breath but Rupert Penwarren surprises me by intervening, 'Actually, I have a newspaper cutting here, which probably explains the name change,' he says.

Mimi looks sharply at him. 'Why didn't you share this with us sooner?'

'I had a feeling I'd seen something about it. But my pile of newspapers is quite large – I keep them for reference – and I had to go back through a couple of years to find this.'

He passes the clipping along the table, saying as he does so: 'It seems Ms Williams was married to a man called Ben Doughty. Her husband ran up huge debts through gambling and loans, and Ms Williams – or Doughty-Peterson as she was then – found her business suffered as a result.'

'He lost everything I'd spent years building up,' I say. 'Perhaps if I hadn't used our married name for my business, I might have been able to retain at least some of my clients . . .' I look around at them all. 'That's why it's so important for me to keep this job: it's my first salaried position since being forced to close down Doughty-Peterson Horticultural.'

'And you didn't think to tell Mimi this at your interview?' asks Jockey Singer-Pryce, slamming his hand on the table. 'You didn't feel it might be pertinent to the position here to admit to having fallen foul of the law?'

Mouse doesn't like his tone: he leaps to his feet and starts snarling, heading so quickly for the man that I have to grab his collar and forcibly restrain him. I doubt he'd actually bite anyone, but it's best not to take any chances.

'Can't you keep that dog under control?' shouts Jockey, leading to increased growling from Mouse and further tugging on the collar.

Fiona speaks up: 'Honestly, Jockey, you're antagonising the poor dog.'

'The poor dog?' he says. 'What about me, the poor man he's attempting to maul?'

I focus on Mouse and say quietly, 'It's OK, boy; it's OK.' He looks back at me and, with one last growl at Jockey Singer-Pryce, returns to me. He puts his head on my lap, and I stroke his soft ears. 'Good boy.'

I look at Jockey. 'I didn't fall foul of the law,' I say firmly. 'My husband is the one who ran up enormous debts. He did not inform me – either that we were in debt or that he had used our home as collateral for a massive loan. I was cleared of all charges – though, of course, I still suffered through my connection to him. While he had to serve a brief prison sentence, followed by lengthy community service, I remained a free woman – as free as you can be when you've lost virtually everything. That's why I changed my first name as well – I wanted a whole new start.'

There's a silence, broken at last by Bubby. 'Well, it's a bit late now to object to her past life,' she says. 'Far more pressing, in my opinion, is the need to get her to sign a confidentiality agreement. Really, Mimi, I'm surprised you didn't get her to sign one at the start. That was negligent on your part.'

'You're the lawyer,' says Mimi.

'Property law,' says Bubby. 'It's hardly the same thing.'

'I can't be expected to cover everything,' says Mimi. 'You know how busy things are, with the clinic and Lucy's schooling.'

'Oh, yes, the girl who can drive but chooses to have her mother chauffeur her instead,' says Jockey.

'Oh, just stop it!' shouts Fiona. They all turn to look at her. 'This is not why we're here,' she says. 'And poor Steph is still waiting for us to reach a decision.'

Mimi clears her throat. 'Right: well, I have a suggestion. If you're all agreed, I propose that we allow Ms Williams ten days to clear her name and find the culprit, as she so determinedly insists it isn't her.'

'It isn't,' I say.

She ignores me. 'However,' she continues, 'if, after the ten days, she has found nothing to disprove our allegation, she will be dismissed.'

'Without a reference,' adds Jockey.

Mimi nods, 'That's right – without a reference. So, are we all agreed?'

There is a chorus of 'yes' and 'aye'.

'Any objections?' she asks. Everyone shakes their head. Mimi turns to me. 'Do you understand, Ms Williams?' she asks. I nod and she says, 'I'm sorry – we're going to need to hear it.'

'Yes,' I say wearily, 'I understand.'

Fiona insists on driving me home in her Mercedes Tourer. She opens a door in the back for Mouse, but he refuses to jump in.

'Can he stay with me?' I ask.

'Of course.' She slides open a door in the side of the vehicle, where the back seats have been folded flat; she fits them into place, then gestures for me to climb in while her husband stands at the side, muttering, 'Really? We're giving her a lift?'

I get into the van, take a seat, and call for Mouse, who jumps in after me and lets me fasten a seat belt around him.

'We'll have you home in a jiffy,' says Fiona, in her gentle voice.

'Thanks so much,' I say. 'But my van's at the Villa.'

Her husband clears his throat. 'You'd better give me the keys. I'll have someone pick it up for you and drop it at the cottage.'

'They won't be insured.'

'It's such a short distance – I'm sure it won't matter for once.'

I hand over the keys reluctantly. But right now I just want to get home and process what's happened. I remember the unlocked shed, and say, 'The ride-on mower – please can you get a message to Francis at the Villa, that it needs locking up?'

'I'll make sure that gets passed on,' he says.

'Thank you.'

We sit in silence for the rest of the journey, past The Towers and finally to the cottage.

'Thanks for the lift,' I say, as I unfasten the seat belts, slide open the door and climb down with Mouse.

'Wait a moment,' calls Fiona. I stand at the side of the van, and she comes round.

She gives me a big hug. 'I am so, so sorry,' she says. 'This will all work out.'

'I hope you're right,' I say. 'I love this job and, as you just heard, I do really need it.'

She pulls away and looks me in the eye. 'You're going to keep your job: I'll make sure of it.' She smiles; I try – and fail – to smile back.

She insists on walking with Mouse and me into the house and checking everything is as it should be and there are no unpleasant notes awaiting us. Then she stands on tiptoe to plant a kiss on my forehead before heading back out to Rupert. Despite her kindness, a darkness settles over me as soon as I hear her van driving away.

I look down at my dog. 'Can you believe this, Mouse? It's ridiculous.'

He sighs and gives a single bark with his head on one side.

'What would I do without you?' I ask him. He rumbles at me, and I stroke his head and soft ears.

I make a soothing chamomile tea which I carry through to the living room, where I take out my mobile and ring my brother. Mouse stretches out beside me on the sofa and begins to snore softly as I fill in Danny on the afternoon's events; he's gratifyingly indignant on my behalf:

'They're doing *what*?'

I take a deep breath. 'They're giving me ten days to "clear my name", after which they're booting me out, without a reference.'

'But . . . It doesn't make sense. Why don't they just get the police involved?'

'Ah – because whatever I'm allegedly blackmailing them over is highly dodgy.'

He snorts. 'That figures. What fucking arseholes. Do you need me to come over there?'

'That is a lovely offer, Danny, but I think you have enough on your plate.'

'Well, the offer stands if you need me. Honestly, they think they're above the law. What entitled pricks. What are you going to do?'

'I have no idea. Make a list of suspects and interview them, I guess?'

'But it's not your job! You're a gardener, not a bloody detective!'

'I know. I'm starting to wish I'd studied law, like Mum wanted.'

'If you'd studied law, you wouldn't be a gardener for a bunch of wankers – so you wouldn't be in this situation.'

'You're swearing a lot more than usual.'

'Yeah, well I'm a lot angrier than usual. Also, Karen's away at her mum's with the kids overnight, so I don't have to watch my language. I'm trying to get a month's worth of swearing out in one night.'

'Are you going wild while they're away?'

'Of course. I've already watched *The Transporter 1* and *2* – and I'm on my third beer. Oh – and I've ordered an Indian takeaway.'

'Out of control.'

'Don't I know it.'

There's a pause; then he says, 'What did you tell them, when they asked about your name?'

'I didn't need to tell them anything: one of the residents turned out to have a newspaper clipping about Ben's misdoings.'

'Oh – that's my takeaway arriving. Speak soon, sis. Don't let the bastards grind you down.'

'I'll try not to. Love you.'

'Love you, too.'

He hangs up, and I stare at the telly for a minute, tempted to turn it on and lose myself in something mindless. But I have work to do. I gently push Mouse to one side so that I have room to get up. Walking through to the kitchen, I take a seat at the table. Then I pick up my gardening notebook, turn to the back and make a list of the names of all those whom I know have received a note. I include myself, but my mind flashes to Ben. It's still possible that my note was left by him. I go over to the counter and bring back the scrap of paper bearing the message in block capitals. No, it's not him, I'm sure: I can picture his writing and it's tiny. Even when he's trying to form large letters, he can't make them any bigger than classic spider-crawled-across-the-page script. So, where is he? Did he encounter the actual writer of my note and come off badly? This thought makes me uneasy. I wonder if I should be reporting him as missing to the police. But then I remember Caroline. Ben has a girlfriend. He's no longer my responsibility.

Forcing my focus back to the matter in hand, I take up my pen again, turn to a new page and note down everything I know about the recipients. On the following page, I note the potential suspects:

All of the residents, including their offspring.

The staff – each house appears to have numerous staff. Kate at The Chimneys is especially inquisitive and likes to talk – even if she isn't the blackmailer, she could have shared information with the blackmailer (possibly unwittingly).

Simon Drake, the former gardener.

I consider what I know about the adults in the Qureshi and Singer-Pryce families. Bubby is a lawyer. Is Annabelle a model? Mimi said something about a clinic. Perhaps she's a physiotherapist or an osteopath. I have no idea about Zakariya and Jockey's professions.

It's gone six, but I'm too exhausted to cook or eat. Mouse has moved to his bed and is snoring in his corner of the kitchen, Mr Rabbit tucked under his head.

I pick up my phone again and scroll through until I find the number for Simon Drake.

He answers on the third ring. 'Hello?' He sounds wary – but who doesn't when an unknown number flashes up on their phone?

'Hi. Simon Drake? My name's Steph Williams.'

'Who?'

'You don't know me. I'm the current gardener at Beaulieu Heights.'
He laughs; it's a sardonic sound. 'Lucky you.'

'Look, I'm sorry to bother you, but have you got time for a chat?'

'That phone was mine,' he says defensively. 'Just because that dizzy
Singer-Pryce girl had one that looked the same . . .'

'I don't know anything about that. It isn't why I'm ringing.'

'Oh, right.'

'I'm not sure where to start. It's just – some of the residents at
Beaulieu have received threatening notes and I'm hoping you might
have some information for me.'

'You mean they're getting blackmailed?'

'Yes, it looks like it.'

'Well, at least they're getting what they deserve,' he says.

'How do you mean?'

'They're all stuck-up and they treat their staff like something they
stood in. You must have noticed that?'

'OK . . . But do you know anyone who might want to blackmail them?'

'Why do you care?'

'I'm being made to care, because they're accusing me of doing
the blackmailing.'

He whistles. 'Those are some powerful people. I reckon they could
send you down without any evidence if they wanted.'

This thought hadn't even occurred to me. I go cold for a moment,
then I shake myself and say, 'That's why I have to find some evidence
to prove it's not me. If you don't know anyone who might want to
blackmail them, maybe you can suggest a reason why some of them
are being targeted?'

He's quiet for a moment. Then he says: 'I mean, that Sherry Patel's
a frigid bitch, but apart from that I don't know anything about her.'

In my experience, a man only describes a woman as 'frigid' when
she's rejected his advances.

'How about Mimi Purdue?' I ask.

'Oh, her . . . She's the one that had me fired. Couldn't stand me.'

'Why not?'

'She claimed I never did any work, even though I spent hours slaving in that garden. It's not my fault it'd been left in such a bad state by the previous gardener.'

I hold my tongue again.

'So, is that why you left?' I ask. 'Because Mimi Purdue claimed you weren't working hard enough?'

'Her and that Penwarren woman,' he says. 'They ganged up on me.'

'And you're sure there's nothing else you can remember?'

'No, sorry. Now, if you'll excuse me, I'm due at a mate's. Good luck.' And he hangs up.

I stare at my list, which I'd been hoping to update with new information from Simon. I put down my pen and close my notebook.

I have a shower and sit on the sofa with my book on Sissinghurst. But I can't focus; I keep having flashbacks to facing the residents' committee – all those suspicious faces fixed on mine. I shiver and take a throw from the back of the sofa, draping it over me. Then I sit and mull until I have come up with a couple of possible culprits.

Adam Qureshi troubles me, for a start. That beautiful boy, with his green eyes, golden hair and cool manner, who I've twice now seen picking on his young female neighbours. I had been intending to talk to his parents, but maybe I should hold off for now, until I've sorted out this mess.

And what about Simon? He didn't tell me much, but he certainly has a grudge against the Beaulieu inhabitants.

My head is aching, so I put the book down and retreat to bed. Tomorrow is Saturday, but I'm determined to begin my investigation. Perhaps I'll pay a visit to The Chimneys.

As I'm climbing into bed, Mouse starts barking and I tense. Should I get up, in case our note-writer is making a return visit? Before I've made up my mind, I hear the familiar sound of an engine, and then my van keys are posted through the letterbox. At least that's one less thing to worry about. But I still lie awake for hours – and, when I finally get to sleep, I have a dream in which I fail an audition for a musical about a gardener.

'*You're just not convincing as a gardener,*' the director tells me. '*Now, a blackmailer – that I could believe.*'

18

'Thanks for seeing me this morning,' I say to Mimi, who's sitting across from me, pouring coffee from a silver pot into china cups. We're in the room where she and her daughter entertained me once before – the one filled with light and paintings. Music and singing drift in from a room close by. Lucy must be rehearsing.

Mimi hands me a cup of coffee, gesturing for me to help myself to cream and sugar, which are laid out on the table in front of us.

'Was there something specific you wanted?' she asks. Her manner is stiff and formal. I suppose she might feel she's entertaining the enemy by allowing me inside her home.

I take a sip of coffee; it's too hot and burns my tongue. Setting down my cup, I take a deep breath and look her in the eye. 'I need a list of everyone who's received one of the notes.'

She sips her drink and eyes me over the rim. 'I'm not sure the others will be too thrilled if I share that information.'

'So, don't tell them.' She raises an eyebrow but doesn't respond, so I press on, 'It's hard enough trying to get to the bottom of this when I can't see the notes themselves and don't know what the alleged misconduct is in each case – but if I don't even know who's being blackmailed, how can I rule people out?'

'It's possible that the blackmailer may have written him- or herself a note, to draw suspicion away from themselves,' she says. I wonder if she's thinking of the note I received.

'That has occurred to me. But it would still be helpful, to see who's implicated, and who isn't. I can then start to work out who might have access to so much private information about other residents.'

'Bubby and Jockey Singer-Pryce,' says Mimi.

I stare at her. 'You think they're the blackmailers?'

She shakes her head. 'I'm giving you the list of names you asked for – the people who've received the notes.'

'Oh! Right! Hold on . . .' I rummage in my jacket pocket for my gardening notebook, but it's not there – there's only my pencil. I try the other pocket, which is also empty.

'Do you need some paper?' asks Mimi.

'Yes, please. I seem to have left my notebook at home.'

She gets up, goes over to a beautiful, walnut, roll-top bureau in a corner and brings back a notepad. 'Here you are.'

'Thank you.'

When I lift the cover of the pad, the paper beneath is cream-coloured and thick. It's more like a luxurious linen than writing paper. I resist the urge to sniff the pad or stroke the pages. Instead, I begin to write notes.

'And next?' I say, after jotting down the first two names.

'Myself.'

'Just you? Not Lucy or your ex-husband?'

'Just me, as far as I know – though I haven't contacted Connell. Technically, we're separated, rather than divorced.'

'There's also Annabelle Qureshi,' she says.

'Not Zakariya?'

'No. Nor their son, Adam. Their other son, Harry, is away at university, but as far as I know, he also hasn't been contacted.'

'Would Harry know enough about everybody to potentially be the blackmailer?'

She shakes her head. 'I don't think so; he's been gone far too long – he's doing a PhD, and he's out of the loop.'

'And Rupert Penwarren,' I say.

She nods. 'And Rupert.'

'What about Fiona?' I ask. 'Was the note also addressed to her, or did she receive a separate one?'

Mimi shakes her head. 'Of course, I haven't seen it, but I didn't get that impression, no. I think it was just Rupert.'

'So that leaves Sherry Patel,' I say.

'Yes, that's right. Sherry also had a note.'

'So has no one been asked for anything by the note sender?' I ask.

She shakes her head. 'As you were told yesterday, the messages all say something to the effect of: "You'll be hearing from me", so I think it's safe to assume the demands will be following in due course.'

'Do you know what anyone's notes are about?' I ask her.

She sets her cup carefully back on its saucer. 'I know the subject of mine, of course; and I have a fair idea about Sherry's – she and I are good friends. But, as for the others . . .'

'I spoke to Simon Drake last night,' I say.

She sits back in her chair. 'And how did you find him?'

'Bitter and resentful' I say.

'We did not part on good terms.'

'I know you all suspect me, but is there a chance he could be the blackmailer?'

She shakes her head. 'I just don't believe he has the nous to organise something like this.'

'But you did hire him, so you must have seen something in him.'

'To be honest, I believe he forged his references. There's no way he had the level of qualifications he claimed – he made far too many mistakes with things like pruning. He was good on lawns, although you wouldn't know it from my place! As time went on, he started to take more and more liberties. He seemed to think he had a right to be paid for doing virtually nothing.'

'Your garden was certainly very neglected when I arrived.'

'It was. Fiona's garden always looked lovely, though. Despite that, she was one of the main proponents for his dismissal.'

'I get the impression he wasn't very nice to her.'

Mimi sighs. 'Fiona's too soft – always has been. She lets people trample all over her. You're lucky she had the guts to speak up for you at the meeting yesterday – that was quite out of character. You must have made an impression.'

'She gave me a painting.'

'Really? Well, well. You're quite the favourite.'

'I think it's Mouse who's the favourite really.'

She smiles. 'For all his curious appearance, he has a sweet little character, that dog of yours.'

'Ms Purdue?'

She looks questioningly at me. 'Yes?'

'Please could I have your husband's contact details?'

She frowns. 'Why on earth do you want Connell's details?'

I take a deep breath. 'I'm going out on a limb here, but I'm guessing the note you received had something to do with Alfie. And possibly . . .' I hesitate, 'Mrs Patel's pond?'

She eyes me with a shrewd gaze. 'You're not just a gardener, are you?' At last, with a nod, she leans across the table, draws the pad towards her and writes on it. 'This is Connell's phone number. Good luck getting him to cooperate.'

'Is he not generally helpful?'

'Oh, he's very helpful – when he wants to be.' Her tone is bitter.

'Thanks for that, anyway. I'll try him.'

'Just do me a favour and don't mention the fabric scraps.'

'Why not?'

'Because there's something that's going to come out sooner or later, but I'd like him to hear it from me.'

'OK . . . That reminds me – you promised to explain what was going on with all of that?'

She sits back. 'You're right; I did. But that was before you were suspected of being behind these notes. If there's any chance you're either the culprit or in league with them, it's not really in my interest to give you any more ammunition, is it? And don't forget, I have no idea what most of the notes were about.'

When it's clear I'm not going to get any more information out of her, I say, 'Would it be possible to talk to Lucy before I go?'

'Lucy? I can't see any reason to involve her.'

'As you're probably aware, she and Adam Qureshi had an argument on Thursday, while I was working in the grounds.'

'An argument? Surely you must be mistaken.'

'Did Lucy not still have a red cheek when you saw her? I gave her some arnica cream, but it's unlikely to have healed that quickly.'

Mimi pauses, reflecting. 'She was wearing a lot of make-up when I took her to evening rehearsal. I remember commenting on it, but she just said it was for her role.'

'I see. I'm not trying to stir . . . Especially if she doesn't know about the notes.'

Mimi holds up a hand. 'No, it's fine. I have told her about the notes. I'll get her for you.' She walks out, returning a moment later. 'She'll be along in a minute.'

Her daughter appears before she's finished speaking. The young woman's curly hair is in a high ponytail. She's dressed in grey joggers and a pink sweatshirt with a sequin outline of Mickey Mouse on the front. It's a far cry from her long, floral dresses, and gives her a younger appearance than usual – more like the teenager she is.

'Mum said you want to talk to me?'

'That would be great.'

'I don't have long.'

'I'll make it quick.'

Lucy remains standing as I ask, 'Do you think it's possible that Adam could be the blackmailer?'

She considers this for a moment. 'What makes you say that?'

'Only the way he's treated both you and Apple. I know very little about him otherwise.' I decide not to mention the drugs I saw him packing into his car, or the fact she told me he takes coke, which must be a costly habit.

'I suppose it's possible,' says Lucy. 'He's got quite a hot temper.'

Mimi interrupts. 'Steph says he hit you?'

Lucy pulls a face. 'I didn't want to make a fuss. He didn't really mean it.'

'That is not acceptable,' says her mother. 'I'll have a word with Annabelle.'

Lucy looks mortified. 'Oh, Mum, don't! Honestly, it's all blown over and I'm sure it won't happen again. If it does, I'll slug him back.'

Mimi glances at me. 'Lucy is a proficient kick-boxer – she was nearly a brown belt.' She turns back to her daughter. 'I don't know why you gave it up.'

Lucy rolls her eyes. 'God, don't start on that again.' She turns to me. 'Can we just get this over with?'

I continue: 'So you think it's possible that Adam is the blackmailer?' I ask.

Mimi interrupts again. 'Before I heard about him hitting my daughter, I would have said that blackmail's not his style . . .'

'I don't know,' says Lucy. 'He does get cross quite easily.'

'That's interesting,' I say. 'I also keep coming back to Simon. He definitely holds a grudge.'

'As I said, Simon isn't clever or thorough enough to carry off something on this scale,' says Mimi. 'When he worked at Beaulieu, he could barely remember what he was meant to be doing from one day to the next.'

'Are we done here?' says Lucy.

'I guess so. Thanks for taking the time . . .' She's already striding away.

'I hope that was helpful,' says Mimi.

'It was,' I say. 'Although part of me was naively hoping Lucy would say, "I've seen Adam writing the notes!" just so I could stop investigating and clear my own name.'

'Is that Peterson, Doughty or Williams?' she asks wryly.

I say nothing. Instead, I tear the page from the notebook, thank her and turn to leave.

I'm already at the door when she says, 'For what it's worth, I don't really think you are the blackmailer.'

I look back. 'If you don't think it's me, then what on earth are we doing?'

She looks helpless. If she hadn't put me in such a shitty situation, I might feel sorry for her. 'As the chair, I have to go with the majority. Don't get me wrong, I did consider it might be you. But you're too . . .'

I wait for a compliment, which doesn't come.

'Too what?'

She surveys me. 'You just don't give off a devious air.'

Not exactly high praise, but at the moment I'll take anything.

At the end of the corridor, Jordan intercepts me by the back door. 'Are you OK?' He looks genuinely concerned.

'I'm not sure. I don't know if you heard, but I nearly got fired yesterday.'

'I did hear something about that; I'm sorry. Let me know if there's anything I can do.'

'Well, you can tell me who might be blackmailing the residents at Beaulieu Heights.'

He raises an eyebrow. 'Blackmail, huh?' He whistles softly. 'That's pretty serious. And where do you come in?'

'I'm their prime suspect.'

'No way!'

'Yep.'

He frowns. 'Why you? You've only been here a few weeks.'

'That's just it – the threatening notes only started appearing after I began working here.'

'So do you think you're being framed – for the thefts as well as the blackmail?'

I stare at him. 'Do you know, that hadn't even occurred to me?'

'Could be,' he says. 'Someone wants to make a quick buck so they come up with a couple of schemes and make it look like the newest incomer is the culprit.'

'Do you have any ideas who it might be?'

He shakes his head. 'No, sorry. I don't really think any of the long-termers would resort to blackmail. There's a new-ish staff member working at The Mount, but from what I've heard he's in training – he's very young and inexperienced, so I don't think he can be your guy. I'll let you know if I hear anything else, though.'

'Thanks. I appreciate it.'

He opens the door and holds it for me, but I have another thought.

'Jordan . . . ?'

'Hmm?'

'What can you tell me about Alfie? About how he died, I mean?'

He looks surprised. 'He fell from a pony. It's not exactly a secret.'

'If you hear anything that might help pinpoint the blackmailer, you'll let me know?'

'Of course.'

'Thank you.' He squeezes my shoulder and I take my leave.

I've left Mouse tied to a silver birch by the main lawn. I've just finished untying him when I hear someone calling my name. I stand up, holding his lead, and see Kate the maid bearing down on me. She's holding my notebook, and the look on her face is reminiscent of a vengeful harpy. Kate's small and thin – but anger makes her appear far larger.

'So, I'm nosy and gossipy,' she says when she reaches me. 'Very nice.'

'It doesn't say that. Anyway, you aren't supposed to be reading it. It's just some notes to help me with working out . . . something.'

'"Even if she isn't the blackmailer, she could have shared information with the blackmailer, possibly unwittingly",' she reads. 'So I guess that means I'm thick as well. I'm just spilling out secrets to anyone who'll listen, is that it?' She glares at me. 'Anyway, who's being blackmailed?'

'I can't talk about it.' I don't point out that there's a list of recipients on an earlier page of the notebook.

'Right. But you can make a list of everyone's faults, though. Mr Penwarren's paying whores, is he? Young Adam Qureshi's dealing drugs and is a cokehead. Where do you get this crap? I've been here years – don't you think I'd know if there was stuff like that going on?'

I take a deep breath. 'There is stuff like that going on.'

She shakes her head. 'You're delusional, you are.'

I swear under my breath. 'I am not delusional.' Making an effort to continue in a calm tone, I say, 'Look, I'm genuinely sorry for upsetting you. I really didn't call you "nosy" or "gossipy" – I'm pretty sure I just said you were "inquisitive" and "liked to talk". There's nothing wrong with either of those things.'

There's a long silence, and then, to my surprise, she deflates.

'You're right: you didn't call me such bad things,' she says. 'I'm sorry I overreacted. My mum always says I fly off the handle at a trifle. And I'm sorry if they're saying you're blackmailing them. I don't believe it.'

'Thank you,' I say. 'I don't believe you're the blackmailer either, by the way. I just have to write down everyone who might be a suspect. I'm trying to save my job.'

She hands me the notebook. 'Here. Sorry I read it.'

'That's all right.' I put it inside the breast pocket of my jacket, making sure the Velcro sticks firmly.

'I'm going to help you,' she says.

'Really?'

'Yep. I'm going to ask around, see what I can find out from the staff at the other houses, and then you can keep your job.'

My eyes fill with tears. 'Thank you.'

'You're very welcome.'

I head back to the van with Mouse, but stop short. 'What the hell?' The passenger window has a jagged hole in it. I unlock the van, open the door, and see a rock on the seat. There's a piece of paper wrapped around it, fastened with an elastic band. I remove the band and open out the crumpled sheet. It's another note, but this time it's typed and reads:

THIS IS YOUR FINAL WARNING! STOP DIGGING NOW OR YOUR DOG GETS HURT!

I crouch down to put my arms around Mouse, who looks at me with big, bewildered eyes. Glancing around, I see no one. I've been at The Chimneys for at least an hour, and there's no way of knowing how long ago this happened. What's more, the top driveway gate has been propped open, and I'm guessing I'll find the same when I get to the bottom: anyone could have come in.

'Come on, boy,' I lead him back around to the rear of the house, where Kate quickly responds to my knock.

'You again?' she says with a grin, before noticing my anxious expression. 'What's wrong?'

'Can you fetch Mimi for me, please, and tell her it's urgent.'

'Sure.' She hurries off down the corridor, and Mimi appears within moments.

'Steph? Kate said it was urgent.' I hold out the note, which she takes and reads. 'My god! Where did you find this?'

'They threw a rock through the van window; the note was attached.'

'Christ. You'd better come back inside while I call someone.'

'Who?' I ask her. 'If I'm not allowed to involve the police, who do you think's going to be of any help?' I can't keep the anger and frustration from my voice.

'Well, we could get someone to repair the window . . .'

I snort. 'Yeah, I thought so: really fucking helpful, thank you. Come on, boy.'

'Steph—' but I raise a hand to cut off her words.

'Don't even bother.' I stride back to the van with Mouse trotting alongside me.

Rummaging in the back of the vehicle, I find an old towel, which I wrap around my hand before knocking all the remaining glass from the window. The glass pieces on the seat have bevelled edges, so they shouldn't cut Mouse, but I don't want to take any risks, so I sweep the majority into my hands, dropping them into the cup holder on the dashboard. Then I grab an old blanket from the back and fold it several times, before laying it on the seat for Mouse. He jumps in readily, snuggling down with Mr Rabbit into the unexpected cushioning.

I climb into the driver's seat and start the engine. But halfway down the drive, I start to shake. My arms and legs are trembling so much, I have trouble steering and braking. I just manage to slow to a stop before reaching the road, where I need to turn right. It's lucky I do: a car screeches along from the right, barely slowing before turning in at the entrance. I see Mrs Patel, wearing huge dark glasses and a large floppy hat. I hope she doesn't think these items disguise her in any way – especially as she's still driving her Merc. She lowers her window when she sees me, and I do the same.

'Why have you stopped there?' she asks. Although she's hit the brake, the engine's revving as if the car itself is impatient to get going.

'I just needed a breather. I'll be on my way now.'

'I hope you haven't been pestering Mimi.'

I don't even grace that with a response. She waits for a moment, glaring at me, then starts up the driveway. There's enough room for her to pass, which she does. I restart my engine and pull slowly out on to the road. The only problem is, I have no idea where I should go next.

I cruise along the road, past my cottage on the left, then past The Towers, The Mount and Villa Splendida on my right, until I reach La Jolla. Without giving myself time to chicken out, I turn in. At the top of the drive, I catch sight of Apple, perched on a boulder of artfully placed sandstone, talking animatedly into her phone.

I climb out of the van and walk towards her, staying far enough back that I don't seem like an eavesdropper. She waves to me and I wait for a while, but as she shows no sign of finishing her call, I walk to the front door and press the bell. While I stand there, I check back to where Mouse has settled on his seat beside the broken window. As long as Apple is out there, I don't think anyone will try to hurt him.

A young woman in an apron answers. She takes in my dishevelled hair and scruffy clothes, and says, 'Good morning. May I ask your business?'

'I'm Steph Williams, the gardener.'

'Oh! We normally ask tradespeople and workmen to use the back door.'

'This isn't a gardening call.' She looks unsure. 'It's OK,' I say. 'I'll take the blame if anyone complains.'

Grudgingly, she asks, 'Who would you like to see?'

'Mr or Mrs Singer-Pryce?'

'Neither of them is free, I'm afraid. Can I take a message?'

'In that case, is Nicola available?'

'If you don't mind waiting in the hall, I'll just see if the young lady's free.'

She allows me access to the lobby, which is like one of those atriums you get in modern office blocks – glass walls all the way up to a glass roof, and giant plants making the whole place resemble a greenhouse. There are armchairs, but I don't want to feel as if I'm waiting at the dentist's, so I remain standing. Who cleans all these windows? And who dusts the plants?

I'm examining the glossy leaves of a *Monstera deliciosa* – aka a cheese plant – when Nicola arrives.

'Are you dusting for clues?' she asks.

'You heard, then?'

'That you're the greatest criminal mastermind since Moriarty? Yes, I've heard. It's ridiculous.'

'Thank you – I appreciate it.' As soon as I've spoken, it occurs to me she might be suggesting I'm not clever enough to be a master criminal. Perhaps I should be offended.

'So . . . What can I do to help?' she asks.

'I was told your parents weren't available, but I was just wondering if you knew the subject of the note they received?'

'I've no idea: they wouldn't let me see it. Do you want me to try and get hold of it?'

I am touched at the offer. 'That's so kind, but no – not if it's something they are keeping from you. I'm sure they have their reasons.'

'I won't read it.'

I don't see how she could possibly determine if something is the threatening note without reading it. 'No – it's all good. I'll try your mum and dad again. Thanks, though.'

'By the way, did Apple open up to you the other day?'

I glance around, but I can see Apple through the windows, still perched on her rock.

'She burst into tears and sobbed for a bit but she wouldn't tell me anything.'

'Thanks for trying. At least she didn't tell you one of her made-up stories. Her favourite's this one about a pair of men getting injured in a campsite fire started by some boys she's just met. She seems to really like that one.'

I don't say anything, but my expression must give me away, because Nicola says, 'You've had that one, haven't you?' She sounds delighted.

'But why would she make it up?'

'Apple has this great imagination, and she learnt when she was little that she could make people like her by confiding in them. So she started sharing secrets. When she didn't have any, she just made them up.'

'All right. But if that awful story about the campsite isn't true, what sort of trouble is she in? Because something's bothering her.'

Nicola's face turns sombre and she shakes her head. 'I don't know. I wish I did, though. Have you seen that bruise on her face?' I nod. 'And she's been acting super secretive. I'm worried about her.'

'Did you get a chance to ask her about that argument with Adam?' I ask.

'She said it was nothing – they were just kidding around.'

'It didn't look that way; she was quite shaken up afterwards.'

'Maybe I'll ask her again. They used to be really good friends; I hope they haven't fallen out.'

'He also slapped Lucy when they disagreed about something.'

She stares at me. 'He slapped her? Are you sure?'

I nod. 'You should have seen her cheek – it was bright red. She was really upset.'

'OK. Leave it with me. I'll try to find out what's going on with Adam. It's really weird.'

'If there's any link with my enquiries, please let me know.'

When I reach the van, I first check Mouse is where I left him – even though I'd have seen anyone approach while Nicola and I were talking by the window. Then I glance over at Apple, who grins and raises a hand in farewell. I wave back, but I don't return her smile; I feel like an idiot. Of course that story wasn't real – why was I so ready to believe her? The answer is painfully simple. It's because Nicola's right: Apple made me feel special, and I liked it.

19

I receive a text from an unknown number at around seven that night. I click on the message with my breath held, hoping the note-writer hasn't got hold of my number. But it reads:

Nicola here. Found the note. Meet me here at 9. Come on foot.

It sounds clandestine, which I suppose it is. I'm reminded of Sherlock Holmes's expression: 'The game is afoot.' But what is the game, I wonder, and who's making the rules? I'm still shaken by the rock through the car window, and haven't let Mouse out of my sight, but I'm determined to work it out. Hopefully this will help me to clear my name and get back to the business of gardening.

The gates are open when I reach La Jolla. It strikes me, not for the first time, that security is far too lax across the whole of Beaulieu.

Despite my best efforts (and judgement), I've left Mouse at home. He was asleep on his bed, and refused to cooperate when it was time to leave. Each time I tried to rouse him, he whined and wriggled further away. In the end, all I could do was make sure I locked up properly and hope no one saw me leave without him.

It's taken me five minutes to jog from the cottage to La Jolla. But the climb to the top of the drive takes me at least another five. The whole landscape looks very different in the dark, lit only by the small beam from my headtorch. By the time I reach the top gate, I feel like Rocky, when he conquers the infamous steps.

I'm just catching my breath when a hand clamps my arm, and I pull back with a jerk.

'Who's there?'

'It's only me.' Nicola is so close, I can feel the warmth of her breath on my cheek; she smells like chocolate and wine. 'Turn off your torch before we're spotted.'

Obediently, I flick the lamp off. 'You gave me a shock,' I say, patting my pounding chest.

'Sorry, but there's always someone around here. Come on – let's go inside the garage.'

She's carrying a remote control. The door rises up as we approach, and we hasten inside. As soon as it's shut, she hits a switch, and I blink at the brightness of the enormous space, which has gleaming white walls and branched ceiling lights. This is the most glamorous garage I've ever set foot in. There's even a pool table at the far end.

'So you found the note?' I ask her.

'Yes. I have it here.' She draws a piece of paper from her pocket and passes it to me.

The message reads:

I KNOW WHAT YOU DID. YOU MAY HAVE FORGOTTEN GARETH BUT OTHERS HAVEN'T. YOU'LL BE HEARING FROM ME.

'Who's Gareth?' I ask.

'Mummy and Daddy used to have friends that Apple and I called "Uncle Gareth and Auntie Sylvia". And I found this.' She pulls up a photo on her mobile phone. It's a snapshot of a page from an address book. 'Look there,' she says, pointing to a single entry. I take the phone from her, and see that the second entry on the page reads: *Sylvia and Gareth Stevens.* There's a local address that's been crossed out, and a new address written in: *Hedges Farm Hall, Lancs.* There's also a phone number.

'Shall I text this to you?' she asks.

'Yes, please. Was that the only Gareth in there?'

'Yes – I went through the whole book.'

'That's so helpful; thank you,' I say as she sends me the picture. 'Hopefully, Sylvia can help, even if Gareth isn't around to answer questions.'

There's a pair of tawny owls nearby; I can hear their 'kewick' and 'hoooo' signifying one's query and the other's response. Other than that, I'm aware only of Nicola's breathing. I want to leave, but it feels like she's waiting to say something.

'Was there anything else?' I ask her.

'Do you think...' She pauses. 'You don't think Mummy and Daddy killed Gareth, do you?'

I stare at her. 'Do your parents seem like the kind of people who might be capable of murder?'

'Not really.'

'Then you have your answer.'

'But they can be quite strange sometimes – secretive, you know? I have no idea who their guests are tonight.'

'I doubt it's anything sinister,' I say. 'But why don't you ask them?'

'I tried: they wouldn't tell me.'

'Right . . . well, sorry but I've left Mouse on his own at home, so I'd better get back. But thanks again for your help – I really appreciate it.'

'That's OK. Let me know what you find out.'

'I will.'

Travelling down the drive on foot turns out to have its own challenges. The slope is so steep in places that a couple of times I have to throw myself into the hedgerow at the side, to slow my pace. I'm covered in scratches by the time I reach the road.

By this point, I can't get home quickly enough. What was I thinking, leaving Mouse alone? What if he's been taken? My heartbeat feels too loud and my blood is pumping hard in my ears. By the time I reach the cottage, my breathing has turned shallow and fast, and even finding the cottage secure does little to reassure me. I let myself in at the back door, and it's only when I've found Mouse snoring in his bed that I start to calm down. I pour myself a glass of red wine and down it like medicine.

His ears twitch as I pass on my way to bed, but he doesn't open his eyes or get up to greet me. Part of me would like to coax him on to my bed overnight, so I can keep an eye on him, but after my failure to budge him earlier, I decide to leave him be – especially as he's more likely to hear a would-be intruder from his spot in the kitchen, and have time to warn me.

Just after I make it into bed, the moon comes out from behind a cloud, shining through a gap in the curtains that I'm too tired to get up and close. My brain won't let me sleep in any case – I lie awake, thoughts and images chasing one another through a fog of tiredness. I'd thought I was stressed after my trial-by-committee, but the threat to Mouse has set me far more on edge. It's made it hard to know who to trust.

One person I am sure of is Fiona Penwarren. Tomorrow, I will call on her and Rupert. It will be Sunday, so hopefully I'll catch them both at home.

20

There are April showers the next morning, so Mouse only steps outside to do his business. He stubbornly refuses to accompany me on my run, so I leave breakfast for him and check both the front and back doors before setting off through the woods towards the fields. I like to think Mouse could defend himself, if it came to it – he's big and quite strong. But what if the person comes with a weapon, or poisoned meat? I shake my head to clear it of nightmarish images, and start to run as I come out of the woods. The rain feels refreshing on my face and I put in my earbuds and run in time to my playlist, my body easing to its rhythm.

I cut across the fields and run along the road to the village, avoiding the mud. Out of nowhere a car passes me, not slowing; its tyres hit a puddle, soaking me. The driver goes by without acknowledgement, and I gaze angrily after the gleaming red backside of Adam Qureshi's Audi R8. I wonder if he's on his way to deliver drugs to the next person in the chain. Drenched and shivering, I turn back, switching my playlist to a faster, more upbeat selection and picking up my pace.

Back home, Mouse has eaten his breakfast and has curled up on the living room sofa with Mr Rabbit between his front paws. I have a quick shower, pull on joggers and a sweatshirt, fix my damp hair in a loose topknot, and make myself some scrambled eggs on toast with a glass of fresh orange juice and a mug of nasty-smelling instant coffee. *You're spoilt*, I tell myself, but I can't help grimacing at the bitter taste; I end up pouring the remainder of the drink down the sink. I'll have to get a new cafetière. After stacking the dishwasher, I sit down with my notebook and pen, plus the sheet of paper Mimi gave me the day before, and dial her ex, Connell.

'Hello?' His voice is deeper than I expected; it has a slight Yorkshire lilt and the sort of gravitas you hear in older Shakespearean actors.

'Mr Purdue?'

There's a moment's hesitation before he says, 'I think there's some mistake.'

'You're not Mr Purdue? Mr Connell Purdue?'

'I'm Connell Fitzgerald. My ex is Miriam Purdue.'

'Oh! I didn't realise you had different surnames – I'm sorry.'

'Who is this?' His voice is cautious.

'My name is Steph Williams. I'm the gardener at Beaulieu Heights. I hope you don't mind, but Ms Purdue gave me your number.'

'Ah, right. So, how can I help you, Ms Williams? I'm afraid I don't know much about the gardening side of things.'

I fill him in about the notes.

'So, you think I might be sending heinous messages to the residents of Beaulieu Heights, is that it?' He sounds amused.

'No, not at all. I was really just wondering if you'd received one of the notes yourself?'

'No, nothing like that. I feel quite left out.'

'Right. And do you have any idea what any of the residents might have done, to be targeted?'

'You mean, do I know if any of my ex-neighbours might have a stash of bodies under the patio?'

'I was thinking more along the lines of skeletons in the cupboard – in the form of tax fraud or insider trading, for instance.'

'As far as I'm aware, my Beaulieu neighbours were all law-abiding citizens.'

'Right . . .'

'I do have an inkling why Mimi might have been targeted, by the way.'

'Does it have anything to do with Alfie?'

'She mentioned him?' He sounds surprised.

'She did,' I say cautiously, not wanting to reveal how little I know.

'Ah, right.'

'The grave has been disturbed,' I say.

'Yes, I am aware of that. Mimi said there'd been a problem with foxes.' There's a long silence, during which I can hear his radio playing something classical in the background. 'Well, if that's all, Ms Williams . . .'

I make a last plea: 'Is there really nothing you can tell me about Beaulieu that might be helpful?'

After another pause, he says, 'Look, it sounds like they've landed you in a mess of their making rather than yours, so I'm going to take pity on you. I have a couple of suggestions that may be of help.'

'That would be great.'

'But,' he says gravely, 'none of this came from me.'

'Got it.'

'Right, well Jockey and Bubby at La Jolla . . . They host parties.'

'You mean kids' parties or . . . ?' I break off, blushing at my slowness. 'You mean sex parties.'

'I do.'

'OK. Can you tell me anything else?'

'Just that you might want to check out that locked gate at the end of the Qureshis' grounds, behind the walled garden. I heard a strange rumour from one of the staff about something that might be going on there.'

'I'll see what I can do.'

'There is one more thing . . . I believe that . . . shall we say, an *escort* has been seen occasionally, around the Penwarren place.'

'Right.' I wonder if this is the prostitute Fiona claims her husband has been hiring.

'And remember: you didn't hear any of this from me.'

'Of course not. I'm just a brilliant amateur sleuth.'

He laughs. It's a warm, genuine sound.

'Thanks so much,' I say.

'Right, well I wish you luck.'

He hangs up before I have a chance to respond.

I sit for a moment, mulling. There's certainly some blackmail material here. But how on earth am I going to get the key to the Qureshis' secret garden?

I look over at Mouse, who's perched on a kitchen chair so he can see out of the window; he's watching the rain fall with a dismal expression.

'You coming investigating with me today, boy? I'm going to see your friend, Fiona,' I coax.

He barks once at her name but refuses to budge. I tug him gently by the collar, but he resists. Next, I attempt to pick him up, but he squirms and wriggles so much in my arms I have to set him back down for his own safety. He immediately lies down on his bed, watching me with one eye as if challenging me to try again. I give up. Perhaps we need to go back to dog-training classes: he certainly seems to think he's in charge.

'OK, well I'll be back around lunchtime, so I'll see you then.' I lock the door on the way out and peer in through the kitchen window. Mouse has already gone to sleep. I test the front door on my way to the van – definitely still locked.

For the sake of the environment, I really ought to jog over to The Mount, but I don't fancy getting wet a second time. Also, taking the van means I can get back to Mouse more quickly. The rain blows in through the gap where the window should be, making my nearside arm wet. I curse myself for not having had the foresight to tape a plastic bag over the opening; I must remember to do that later. I lean out of the van window to press the buzzer. It's answered almost immediately by a voice I recognise as Rupert Penwarren's.

'Ms Williams? Were we expecting you?'

'No, I'm sorry for the intrusion but . . . are you and Mrs Penwarren free to talk?'

I hear him speak to someone in the background, then he says, 'I'm buzzing you in.'

The gate swings open slowly, and I rev the engine ready for the ascent. It seems to take longer than usual, and all I can think is that I'm leaving Mouse further and further behind.

Despite the damp wind, Fiona is at her easel when I reach the top. A small canopy has been erected over her and the canvas. She turns and waves, and I wave back before parking and climbing down.

'Where's my little friend?' she asks, as I approach.

'He decided to stay at home. He doesn't like rain. Or wind.'

'Ah – a fair-weather dog,' she says. 'I miss having a dog.'

'Why don't you get one?'

'Rupert's not keen. He says they make the whole house stink.'

'Some do,' I agree. 'But it's worth it.'

She smiles warmly. 'My thoughts entirely. Now, how's the investigation going?'

'Slowly,' I say.

'And you're wanting to talk to us?'

'Yes, please. I'm trying to find out why each person is being targeted, so I can figure out who might be behind it.'

She nods. 'I'll be right there. If you go round the back and knock, someone will let you in.'

The back door opens as I approach, and I'm admitted by a young man who has the nervous air of a new-starter. This must be the trainee Jordan mentioned.

'Ms Williams?'

'That's right.'

He nods but doesn't smile. I follow him along a wood-panelled corridor to a study, where I find Rupert Penwarren standing in front of a log fire, a glass of whisky in his hand. The servant states my name, then departs.

'Drink?' asks Rupert, walking over to a drinks cabinet.

'I'll just take a soda water, if you have it, thanks.'

He nods and fills a glass from a dispenser.

'Here,' he hands me the glass and pulls a chair close to the fire. 'Please, take a seat.'

'Thank you.' I'm touched by how courteous he's being, but also cautious – he certainly wasn't on my side at the meeting two days ago.

'So, how's the investigation going?' he asks, as I take my seat.

I tell him about the rock and the message. He's frowning by the time I finish. 'That's disgraceful! Who on earth would do such a thing?'

'I don't know. But I need to find the blackmailer as quickly as possible.'

Fiona walks in as I'm talking. 'Yes, we must find them ASAP.' She smiles at her husband. 'You've lit a fire – how lovely.' He pulls two more chairs over to the fire, and she sits in the middle, next to me, while he takes the seat on the far side of her.

'I didn't offer you a drink, my love,' he says.

'That's all right; Henry's bringing me a cup of tea. So, where are we up to?' she asks me.

'I was hoping you could fill me in on the content of the note you received?'

'We cannot,' he says firmly. 'From what I've gleaned from my wife, you already know more than I'm comfortable with.'

It's tempting to suggest he shouldn't have cheated on his wife if he wanted to feel comfortable, but I bite my tongue. I need his cooperation, after all.

'OK . . .' I say. 'Well, do you have any thoughts on who might know enough about you – and the other residents at Beaulieu – to be attempting blackmail?'

'We were actually up late, discussing it,' he says, looking at Fiona. 'I'm afraid I'm still having trouble accepting that it isn't you.'

'And where am I meant to have printed out the notes?'

He waves a hand. 'It's easy enough to get access to a printer if you need one,' he says.

'I suppose so. But I've been kept pretty busy with the gardens – it's a lot for one person, especially doing only one day per week at each property.'

'Hmm.' He looks unconvinced.

I sigh. 'It's very hard to clear my name, if no one will tell me what they're being accused of.'

'I don't see why you would need that information,' he says.

'How can I work out who might know specific facts about each of you, if I don't know what those facts are?'

He seems to be considering this. After a moment, he nods and stretches out his long legs. 'Very well,' he says in a grudging tone. 'What has my wife revealed so far, Ms Williams?'

Fiona cuts in. 'I'm afraid I didn't get my facts right. I told Steph you were paying for prostitutes.'

'Right . . .' he says. He tips his glass and watches the ice knock against the side. 'Look, I'm really not comfortable sharing this . . .' he says.

Fiona looks at me. 'Rupert explained it to me last week. He thought I'd be upset, but honestly I was just relieved.'

'So the prostitutes . . . ?' I ask.

'There are no prostitutes,' says Rupert firmly. 'I have never cheated on my wife.'

'But the hotels?' I ask. 'The . . . purchases?'

His face flushes. 'I would have preferred not to talk about this, but the clothing purchases are for me – I pay for a room at a hotel so that I can dress as a woman.'

I take my time, weighing up the likelihood of his story. At last, I say, 'But someone . . . one of the residents . . . said they'd seen an escort coming and going when Fiona was out?'

As he flushes an even deeper shade of pink, understanding dawns, and I say quickly, 'Well, thank you, Mr Penwarren – I appreciate your openness. It must be a relief to know the blackmailer has nothing on you, now that you've told your wife everything?'

'I am very lucky to have such an open-minded wife,' he says, taking her hand. 'But the rest of the world is unfortunately not as sensible. I simply can't risk any of the residents finding out. If it got back to the firm, I'd be a laughing stock. There's still a very, shall we say, *homogeneous* culture in the City.'

'I won't say a word.' I promise him.

'I appreciate that.' He turns to Fiona. 'Did you want to speak to Ms Williams about anything, darling? I take it you've already heard about the nasty business with her dog?'

'With Mouse?' She looks horrified. 'What's happened to my wee pal?'

'Oh, nothing!' I say quickly. 'But I received a second threat that he would get hurt if I didn't stop investigating – this one was delivered via a rock through my van window.'

'What? No! We can't let anyone hurt him. I just can't imagine who would even threaten something like that.'

'That's what I'm thinking,' says her husband. 'Surely no one at Beaulieu would do that?'

Fiona shakes her head. 'We have to get to the bottom of this. I've been trying to find out what I can from the staff. There's quite a lot of gossip, but most of it seems pretty thin. The only thing I did hear was that there might be something in a locked area at The Towers.'

'I heard that, too,' I say. 'I'm going to look into it. I'll have to see if I can get a key from one of the staff.'

'Good plan. Let me know if you get stuck and maybe we can break in!' she says, looking excited at the prospect.

'Good lord,' says Rupert. 'That's all we need – the two of you getting hauled in front of the police for breaking and entering.'

Fiona's face falls. Then she says, 'Do you not have a key, Rupert? I thought the main committee members had all the keys?'

'Only to the properties themselves and their main gates, not access all areas, as it were.'

'Shame,' says Fiona.

'I'd better get back to Mouse,' I say, standing up.

Rupert nods. 'Of course. I'll call for Henry to show you out.'

He rings a bell and a moment later the young man from earlier reappears.

Fiona stands up. 'Henry, you never did bring my tea . . .'

The young man flushes scarlet and puts a hand to his mouth. 'I'm so sorry, Mrs Penwarren . . .'

'Ma'am,' corrects Rupert.

'Sorry, Mr . . . I mean, sir.'

'Well, don't apologise to me, apologise to my wife,' says Rupert.

'Rupert, it's fine,' says Fiona quietly, laying a hand on his arm.

'It's not fine, my dear. If you must bring in a young boy for training, you must at least allow me to train him.'

Henry looks like he's about to burst into tears. 'I'll get that tea now, ma'am.'

She nods. 'Thank you, Henry. I'm heading back outside; please bring it to me at the front.' She turns to me. 'Come on, I'll show you out.'

I bid Mr Penwarren goodbye and walk back with Fiona along the wood-panelled corridor.

'Fiona, do you know why Mimi Purdue is being blackmailed?'

She shakes her head. 'I have no idea. To be honest, I didn't know there was so much going on at Beaulieu. When I came to live here, I thought it was a quiet, rather dull place.'

'And now?'

'Now, I'm finding myself hoping our neighbours haven't done anything too awful.' She laughs briefly. 'It's not healthy, to start suspecting everyone around you.'

We walk back through the granite passage together, and she pulls a face as we emerge into the rain. 'I hope it's going to stop raining soon – I can't believe it's April already; though I suppose there's a reason they talk about "April showers".'

'Before I forget, do you know where I can get my van window repaired?'

'Just call one of those mobile glass repair services. I'll pay for it, if you pass on the bill.'

'You don't have to do that.'

'I want to. It's bad enough you're being wrongly accused; you shouldn't also be out of pocket from someone threatening you.'

'In that case, I will accept gratefully,' I say, thinking about the next payment for the tree surgery course loan. 'Thank you.'

'It's my pleasure.'

I take the van back down the drive, and five minutes later I'm pulling in at the cottage.

As I walk round to the back of the house, I discover the back door is wide open.

21

'Mouse?' I call, running from room to room, but he's not in his bed in the kitchen, nor on the sofa in the living room, nor in my bedroom . . . 'Mouse?' Stupidly, I search in the bathroom and even the cupboard under the stairs. I go over to his bed again and lift it, even though he's far too big to be hidden beneath it.

But at that moment Mr Rabbit falls out from his blanket, and I know for sure that something awful has happened.

With a shaking hand, I take my phone from my pocket to call the police. But then I realise that they're unlikely to take an interest in a missing dog. Also, if I'm to keep my job here, I need to be the one to work out who's threatening me and blackmailing the residents. If Beaulieu's skeletons get released from their cupboards, they're bound to blame me, and I'll be out on my ear.

I go back to examine the door and find that there's no damage to either the door itself or the lock. Whoever has taken Mouse must have had a key.

I call Mimi on her mobile, breathing deeply to try and stay calm. 'Yes?'

'It's Steph. Mouse is missing.'

'Was he in your van?'

'No; I left him in the cottage.'

'And you're sure he's not there?'

'I'm sure.'

'Did you leave a door or window open?'

'No, nothing like that.'

'So someone has broken in?'

'They've used a key. Who has one?'

She pauses. 'Well, I have one – which I can see hanging here. Then there are three others: Rupert Penwarren, Annabelle Qureshi and

Bubby Singer-Pryce. You'll find all their landline numbers on the document with your timetable. Also, and I know this is the least of your concerns right now, but I'll get a locksmith out to change your locks as soon as possible.'

'Thanks.'

I hang up and grab the document from the kitchen counter. I start with the Penwarrens.

'Hello?' It's a young male voice – I'm guessing Henry.

'Hello. Is Mr Penwarren there, please?'

'Who is it, please?'

'Steph Williams, the gardener. Please tell him it's urgent. Perhaps Mrs Penwarren's available, if you can't find her husband?'

'Let me check.'

While he's gone, I try not to panic. Mouse will be all right. He will be unharmed – it's not in the blackmailer's interest to hurt my dog – unless they want to go to prison for that as well. But then they won't be planning on getting caught . . . I start to pace.

The voice comes back on the line. 'Hello?'

'Is that Henry again?'

'It is. I'm afraid there's no sign of either Mr or Mrs Penwarren.'

'Mrs Penwarren was just out the front, painting . . . Never mind!' I run my hand through my hair, thinking fast. 'Please can you check something for me?'

'Sure . . .'

'Apparently, Mr Penwarren holds a key to Gardener's Cottage. Do you know where he keeps it?'

'All the keys are on hooks in the hallway, ma'am.'

'Please can you see if it's hanging on the hook?'

'The key to the cottage? I'll look now. Shall I take the phone with me?'

'Yes, please. It's really urgent. My dog's been stolen.'

I need Henry to reassure me – to give me a reason to believe that Mouse is fine. But he's too young, too inexperienced or too untrained, and he doesn't say anything. I can hear his shoes on a tiled floor, then a door opening, and more steps on tiles. Finally, I hear the clink of keys.

'The key for the cottage is still here, Ms Williams.'

'Right.'

'Was there anything else I could help you with?'

'No, that's it, thanks.'

I hang up and dial La Jolla. A young woman answers. 'Singer-Pryce residence.'

'Is that Apple?' I ask.

'Yes, who's this?'

'It's Steph.'

'Steph – hi!'

'Apple, someone's taken Mouse from the cottage. They've stolen him and I'm worried they're going to hurt him . . .'

'Shit! I love that dog!' she says.

'Listen, Apple, whoever took him had a key. Your mum has a spare key to the cottage. Do you know where she keeps it?'

'Yeah. It hangs on a hook in a little cupboard in the den.'

'OK. Can you look and see if it's still there?'

'Sure.' She runs with the phone – I can hear her breathing coming fast. 'Yes, it's still there.'

'Thanks, Apple. I've got to go.'

'But Steph . . .'

'What?'

'Well, someone could have used it and put it back, couldn't they?'

'They could but I'm just hoping they won't have had time to.'

'I suppose they'd need time to hide him . . . It's got to be somewhere no one will hear him barking, hasn't it?'

'Unless they've drugged him – or worse.'

'But no one would do that to him, I'm sure!'

'I hope you're right.'

'Steph, I'm sure Mouse will be all right. I bet he's waiting at the cottage now, for you to come home.'

'I am home, Apple.'

'Oh . . . Well, I bet he'll be there soon. He'll be like those dogs you hear about, that run for hundreds of miles to get back to their owners.'

'I have to go.'

'Call me when you find him.'

I hang up without replying and dial the last number, the Qureshis'. A young man answers, 'The Towers.'

'Is that Adam?'

'Yeah, who's this?'

'Steph Williams, the gardener.'

'I'll get Mum.' I pace the kitchen while I wait. Why does anyone need to live in such a big house? It's ridiculous.

At last, Annabelle comes to the phone. 'Steph, hello.'

'Hi. Ms Purdue tells me you keep a key to the cottage.'

'Oh, I did have one, but it went missing about a month ago.'

'Missing?'

'We had a big clear-out and were a bit overenthusiastic: we haven't seen a lot of things since. Are you locked out?'

'No. Someone's taken Mouse – my dog. And they obviously had a key, as there are no signs of a break-in.' My voice sounds far away, and not my own.

'Oh, no, how awful! Have you rung the police?'

'I can't. You see, I . . .' my voice breaks, and I start again, 'I received a threatening note yesterday, saying I had to stop investigating the blackmail or something bad would happen to Mouse. So, if I call the police, I'll have to tell them about the note – but no one at Beaulieu wants the police involved about the blackmailing. And . . .' I try to hold in a sob, 'I really need this job.'

'Goodness! I didn't realise you'd been threatened. Can you just hold on a second?' Her voice becomes muffled, but I can make out the words, 'Fritz and Mitzi', so I know she's panicking about her own dogs. I can't say I blame her.

'Sorry about that, Steph. I'm back now.'

'Well, anyway, I just thought, if I could work out who had a key to the cottage, I could trace Mouse quickly, without involving the police.'

'As I say, I don't know what happened to our key, so I can't help you.'

'Right . . .'

'Where do you think they would have taken him?'

'I don't know.'

'I tell you what: I'll take my two for a walk along the top path, and see if they get excited at any point. If Mouse is being held somewhere, I'm sure Fritz and Mitzi will be able to sniff him out.'

'I'd really appreciate that – thanks so much.'

'Don't worry too much, Steph. I know it may not seem like it at the moment, but I'm sure no one at Beaulieu Heights is wicked enough to hurt a dog, especially one as lovely as Mouse.'

'I hope you're right.'

After we hang up, I take Mr Rabbit and walk outside to look for Mouse. I head into the woodland at the end of our garden and shout his name, but I get no response. Then I climb into the van and drive slowly along the road with my window open, calling him. The wind whips through the two window openings, yanking my hair across my face, so that I have to keep pulling strands out of my mouth. As I drive, the note keeps flashing in front of my eyes – *Stop digging now or your dog gets hurt.* What if they've hurt him? I try to blink away images of Mouse, cowering beneath a whip or a knife blade. By the time I reach the main Beaulieu gates, I can hardly breathe. I turn the van quickly and head straight home.

I've left the back door open in case Mouse should come back in my absence, but he isn't there. That doesn't stop me running through the cottage again, checking for him.

I spend the rest of the afternoon pacing beside the phone, trying to work out who else I can call. I could ring Danny for moral support, but there's nothing he can do from Peterborough.

I'm sitting in the dark when my mobile rings. I have no idea what time it is.

'Hello?'

'Steph, hi. It's Annabelle Qureshi.'

Hope and fear surge inside me. 'Did you find him?'

'I didn't, I'm sorry. The dogs got quite excited at one point, but I think there must have been a fox.'

'Whereabouts was it?'

'We were on the top path, by the entrance to the paddock behind the Penwarrens' garden – the one that Mimi uses for her ponies.'

'Maybe I'll go and take a look.'

'Well, you can do, but it's pretty dark out now. It was already getting dark when we were there. I did take Mitzi and Fritz into the paddock, and they sniffed around a bit, but we didn't find anything.'

'Thanks so much for trying. Maybe Mouse left some smells behind, the last time he was there.'

'That's possible. I just wish I could do more. I hope you get him back by tomorrow.'

'Me, too.' I hang up before my tears get too heavy for speech.

It's impossible to think about food, but I microwave a hot chocolate which I take over to drink at the kitchen table. A few minutes later, when I've just determined to get my coat on and go back out to search, there's a whine at the back door. Afterwards, I have no memory of leaping from my seat, crossing the kitchen and opening the door. What I do recall is that, as I throw it open, I'm nearly knocked down by my beloved dog, hurling himself at me.

'My darling boy!' He's as happy to see me as I him – we spend several minutes hugging before I put the light on to check him over. And then I see what a state he's in: his jaw is bloody, his fur's matted, and one of his eyes is swollen shut. He has a cut on his nose, and he's not putting his full weight on his front right paw. On closer inspection of the paw, I find a small piece of rope, knotted around it and digging into his flesh. I take a knife and gently cut away the fibrous threads.

'What did they do to you, boy?'

There's an odour coming off him, tangy and acrid . . . Wood smoke, I realise. Has he been in someone's home, where they lit a fire? Or, more likely, he's been tied up near a bonfire. It occurs to me that I'd know if one of the residents had been building a fire – I am their gardener, after all. I'll have to worry about that later. For now, my dog needs tending.

I run a bath and clean him with a soft sponge. His paw pad looks tender and a bit swollen, though I can't see anything still embedded in it. His eye, on close examination, has a bit of grass or something in it; I manage to wipe it out slowly and carefully. His gums are bleeding, but they look so sore that I daren't investigate the source of the blood.

'My poor boy,' I say, pulling the plug, heaving him out and wrapping him in a big, soft towel. 'Aren't you clever, to escape and come back home?'

His tail wags so hard at this, it beats like a drumstick against the bath.

22

Monday starts with a visit to the local veterinary clinic, recommended by Annabelle Qureshi, who has insisted the surgery put Mouse's bill on her tab. I'm grateful to her; I'm pretty sure Mouse's treatment would otherwise amount to several months of my salary. I've covered the broken window with a plastic bag, so at least Mouse doesn't have a breeze blowing in on him.

He undergoes a battery of tests and checks before being placed in some kind of hydrotherapy unit. At last, his paw is bandaged and I'm given antibiotic drops for his eye, which still looks sore. He also receives a course of oral antibiotics, which I'm going to have to conceal in his food – he hates taking tablets. The vet says Mouse must have been tied up and his bloody mouth has been caused by his chewing through the rope.

'You have a brave dog there,' she says.

'He's the best,' I tell her.

On our way home in the van, I say, 'I'm not leaving you behind again, Mouse – you'll just have to come with me from now on.'

Only one ear twitches as he lies curled around Mr Rabbit. He must have been so scared, being separated from his toy, his home and his human. I wish I knew where he'd been. I'd like to ask him to take me to the place he escaped from, but I know he's not up to it. I'll just have to do my own detective work.

It's already day three of the ten days I've been allocated. Now that Mouse is safely back with me, I need to make headway with the investigation. Next on my list is the note Nicola showed me, and the entry in her parents' address book.

'Right: let's get you settled and then I need to make a phone call,' I tell Mouse, as I swing the van into the parking area at the cottage. As promised by Mimi, there's already a locksmith working on the front door.

'Morning,' he greets me. 'I've changed the lock on the back and I'm nearly done with the front. Here are the new keys.' He hands me two keys on a ring.

'Please don't give a key to anyone else for now,' I say. 'If you could just let me have any spares, that would be great.'

He looks dubious, but he hands over four more keys, which I pocket. 'Thanks,' I say. At least that's one less thing to worry about.

I get Mouse settled on his bed with Mr Rabbit to cuddle, then I place a cushion on the floor beside him, sit down and call the number Nicola texted me the other day.

'Hello?' It's a woman's voice.

'Is this Sylvia Stevens?'

'Yes, that's right.'

'I'm sorry to bother you. My name is Steph Williams, and I'm the gardener at Beaulieu Heights.'

There's a long pause – so long, I find myself saying, 'Hello?'

'I'm still here.' Her voice has become small and subdued. 'What do you want, exactly?'

'Well, it's quite strange really, but I'll just come out with it. Some of the residents at Beaulieu are being blackmailed at the moment—'

'You're not accusing me, are you?' she cuts in. 'I haven't been near that place for nearly ten years. And god knows, they've had their pound of flesh from this family.'

'God no, nothing like that. They've actually accused *me* of being the blackmailer.'

'I see. And you're trying to clear your name?'

'Clear my name and save my job.'

'So, where do I come in?'

'It's just . . . the blackmail note received by Bubby and Jockey Singer-Pryce is the only one I've managed to see. It mentions someone called "Gareth". Your husband is the only Gareth listed in their address book, so I'm hoping you can shed some light on things.'

There's an even longer pause. This time, I don't check she's still there, but wait, holding my breath and crossing my fingers.

'It's not really my story to tell,' she says at last.

'I understand. But I've only been given ten days to find the blackmailer, and I'm already on day three, so anything you can tell me might help. Please.'

'Are you recording this call?'

'No. Should I be?'

'Absolutely not.'

'Right.'

'If I tell you this, it remains between us. I don't under any circumstances want that chapter of our lives reopened. I am only sharing this with you because I don't want another potentially innocent person framed by those awful people.'

'I won't tell anyone.'

'OK . . .' She takes a deep breath. 'So, we'd go over to La Jolla once or twice a month, for a drink or a swim. I suspect there were less salubrious things going on in that house, but thankfully we were never invited to be part of that. I wasn't a big fan of the couple, but Gareth thought of Jockey as his best friend. They'd known each other since school.'

'So, what changed?'

'It was . . . an accusation.'

'Go on.'

'So, one night, their younger daughter, Penny, came outside while we were sitting by the pool. She was crying because she couldn't sleep.'

'Penny? Their younger daughter is called Apple.'

Sylvia laughs. 'Well, she didn't use to be. She was definitely called Penny.' She laughs again. 'Apple! What nonsense!'

'So, how old was Penny?'

'She'd have been six or seven. Anyway, Gareth hadn't been in the water, so he was still fully dressed, whereas the rest of us were in damp bathing suits. So he offered to take her back to bed and read her a story, which she jumped at – she loved her Uncle Gareth.'

I think I know where this story's going, but I say, 'Go on,' again.

'He was back within fifteen minutes, saying he'd read her a chapter of *Polly and the Wolf*, and now she was sound asleep.

'The next morning, the doorbell rang while Gareth and I were having breakfast at home. It was two police officers. They said that

Jockey and Bubby had made a formal complaint, accusing Gareth of having sexually abused Penny.' Her voice breaks.

'Oh my god! That's awful!'

'Isn't it, though? Gareth never hurt anyone in his life.'

'Did the Singer-Pryces claim to have proof?'

'No, and in the end the police dropped all charges, saying there wasn't enough evidence to support the accusation. There wasn't *any* evidence, in fact. I doubt Penny ever knew anything about it.'

'So, why did Mr and Mrs Singer-Pryce make the accusation?'

'I didn't know until then that Gareth had loaned money to Jockey. Quite a large sum, in fact. Apparently, Jockey had run up all kinds of debts and didn't want Bubby to know, and he'd asked Gareth to keep it quiet at his end, too. We suspect Jockey wanted to discredit Gareth. If Gareth was prosecuted, he wouldn't be chasing Jockey for a repayment of the loan money.'

'I guess that makes sense. Did you see any record of the loan?'

'Yes, I did actually; my husband did not invent the story of a loan to pull the wool over my eyes.' She sounds angry. 'Gareth showed me a statement from one of his accounts, revealing that money had been transferred a couple of months earlier, into an account in Jockey's name.'

'I'm so sorry. I didn't mean to upset you; I just have to make sure I have all the details.'

She sighs. 'It's not you. Everything to do with that time upsets me. The rumours spread and Gareth lost his job. He ended up having to set up his own company, as no one would hire him. It took him a long time to build himself back up. We had to move up north, to get away from people who'd shout things as we passed in the street, or deface our cars. It was truly the worst time in my life – in both our lives.'

'It sounds horrendous. I'm so glad you and Mr Stevens managed to recover your lives after what you went through.'

'Thank you.'

'I can't thank you enough for talking to me today, especially when it must be such a difficult topic for you.'

'In a way, just telling someone who appears to believe me has been a tiny bit cathartic.'

We say our farewells and end the call. I take my notebook and update my notes.

I'm not sure I'm any nearer to pinpointing the blackmailer, but I feel even less likely to trust anything the Singer-Pryces – and particularly Jockey – tell me.

I make myself a cup of chamomile tea, which I drink at the kitchen table while reading through my notes so far. Suddenly, Mouse gets up and limps into the hall, barking at the front door – but his tail is wagging.

'Who is it, boy?'

There's a knock and I open the door to find Apple outside.

'Hi, Steph, I heard Mouse had come home! Is he OK? Can I come in?'

'I'm not sure. Do you have any more stories to tell me?'

She takes a step back, looking hurt. 'What do you mean?'

'Nicola tells me you make a habit of inventing fairy tales to amuse anyone foolish enough to believe them.'

'What are you talking about? I don't make stuff up.'

'So there really was a fire on the campsite at the festival, and your friends started it?'

She hesitates. 'Please can I come in? I can explain.'

I leave the front door open and walk back along the hall to the kitchen. I hear her shut the door and greet Mouse: 'I'm so glad you're all right, boy. We were so worried about you.'

'How is he?' she asks, entering the kitchen with Mouse limping beside her. 'He looks so beaten up.'

'He is. Whoever abducted him tied him up, and he had to escape by chewing through the rope. I don't know how his eye and nose got injured, though.'

'A wire fence?' she says. I look at her questioningly, and she explains, 'All of the gardens have that wire fence to keep the rabbits out. You must have seen?' I think about this and realise she's quite right: the outer walls and fences all have rabbit-proof mesh. She crouches and strokes Mouse on his ears and under his chin. 'Isn't that right, boy?'

'But what makes you think he hurt himself on one?'

'Well, he can't have gone far if he managed to get back the same day, can he?'

I have had the same thought myself, but I'm finding it difficult to imagine who would have done this to poor Mouse.

'I bet whoever took him held him in something underground, like some kind of cave, so his barking wouldn't be heard.'

'Do any of the houses come with caves?' I ask with a laugh.

'All right, not a cave, but like ours has an old air-raid shelter; it's left over from the house that was there before ours.'

'He smelt of wood smoke.'

She shrugs. 'OK – not an air-raid shelter!'

'But an underground structure of some kind would explain why no one heard him barking, if he was hidden somewhere on the estate.'

'By "estate" you mean Beaulieu?'

'Yes. Although, technically, each of the five properties and grounds could probably be called an estate in its own right.'

'I was thinking you made it sound like a council estate.'

God forbid anyone think Apple Singer-Pryce lives on a council estate.

Mouse is lying on his back for her to stroke his tummy; she sits on the floor beside him and obliges. 'I've got something I want to talk to you about, if that's all right?'

'If it's another of your tall tales, you can save your breath.'

Apple stands up. 'I really thought you believed me.'

'So the camp fire gone wrong really happened?'

'Yeah, it did really happen,' she says, sounding less confident.

'But?'

'It just didn't happen to me.'

I slap my forehead. 'Of course it didn't!'

'But I thought if I told you what really happened at the festival, you'd think I was an idiot.'

'Why? What did happen?'

'I got beaten up.'

There's a long silence, during which I look her in the eye. Various expressions cross her face, including fear, shame, anger, hurt and resentment. I don't see a trace of duplicity.

'Let's go in the living room,' I say at last.

Mouse accompanies us to the next room, where Apple takes a seat on the sofa and helps him up to join her. He fills most of the space, but she doesn't seem to mind. I take the armchair and wait for her to explain everything; but she just sits stroking the dog's head.

At last, I say, 'You're going to need to start talking at some point.'

She looks up in surprise, as if she'd forgotten where she was. 'Sorry! Yeah, of course.' She tucks her pink hair behind her ears. 'Well, I went to the stupid festival. But someone – a friend – had asked me to do this thing for them. All I had to do was take in some drugs in one of my bags. This friend said they had the buyers set up. I just had to be in a set place at a set time, wearing a red top, and hand over the package.'

'And this seemed like a good idea?'

She sighs. 'I know – I'm an idiot. But they promised me a favour in return.'

'What kind of favour?'

She blushes. 'They were going to set me up with this friend of theirs, this guy I like.'

'So, what went wrong?'

'I got in all right with the drugs, and I thought we were safe. But then this guy I'd never seen before came over when we were watching one of the bands. He said he knew my name was Apple, and he knew I had "gear" with me.'

I sit forward. 'What did you say?'

She shrugs. 'I said he must have got me confused with someone else and I didn't know what he was talking about.' She pauses and looks down at Mouse. 'That was stupid – I should have just told him he could have the gear.'

'What did he do?'

'I thought he'd gone, but he must have been watching us for the rest of the day. Pobble and I had quite a lot to drink, and when we went back to our tent, the guy came up behind me and put his hand over my mouth. He said I could either give him the drugs without a struggle or he could hurt us both. I tried to shake him off, but he threw me down on the ground and I hit my face on a stone – I didn't make that part up. Then he kicked me.' She lifts the hem of her top, exposing a pinkish-brown area of bruising that was clearly much worse when it happened.

Some people bring out the protective instinct in me; Apple is one of those people. I realise with a jolt that my teeth are gritted, my fists clenched. 'He kicked you?'

She nods. There are tears in her eyes. 'Then he went into our tent behind Pobble and threatened her with the knife. She was terrified. He grabbed the gear from my bag and left without even looking back at us.'

'What a bastard.'

Her eyes are wide in fear as she relives the event. 'It was really, really frightening. I've never met anyone like that before.'

'Was Pobble all right?'

'Not really. I mean, she wasn't hurt but she was really shaken. We zipped our sleeping bags together and slept with our arms round each other.'

'I'm not surprised. What about the person who wanted you to deal the drugs for them?'

'Not deal, just deliver.'

'OK, so what about them? Were you in trouble with them for losing the drugs?'

'Not really. They were more worried about me and Pobble. Apparently, this guy is a rival dealer, and my friend hadn't realised he'd be at the festival.'

'Who is this friend of yours, Apple? Is it Adam?'

Her eyes grow even wider. 'Adam? Why would it be him?'

'OK, so if it's not Adam, who is it?'

She shakes her head. 'It's not anyone you know.'

I think back to her sobbing fit on the bench. 'You know when you were crying the other day . . . ?'

That seems to be the trigger for her to shut down our conversation. She gently pushes Mouse's head off her lap and gets to her feet. 'I'd better go; you've still got to save your job.'

With a sigh, I lock the front door behind her and make myself a quick sandwich, which I eat in the living room to keep Mouse company. Then I stack my plate in the dishwasher and walk back to him.

'Well, boy, I can't sit around here all day. I have three more households to interview. Come on – it's time to go in the van.' He looks up at me with his best woebegone expression. In the end, I have to scoop him up and carry him – no mean feat, given his size and weight, but at least this time the poor boy is in no state to struggle. On the flip side, he's a bit of a dead weight, and I stumble more than once. But we reach the van safely, and I manage to deposit both him and Mr Rabbit on top of the blanket nest on the passenger seat.

I drive over to Villa Splendida, where Francis answers the buzzer on the gate. 'Mrs P's not here, I'm afraid.'

'Is it all right if I come in anyway? I wanted to check out something in the garden.'

'Of course.' He buzzes me through. I had been considering using the entry code if he'd said no, but I'm glad it hasn't come to that.

I lift Mouse down from the van, and he takes his toy from me in his sore mouth. He limps alongside until we reach the garden, where I settle him beneath a beech tree. I want to attempt to get into the locked shed, but first I go for a roam. I'm not sure what I'm looking for, but I'm hoping something will strike me as I walk around.

First, I visit the large hornbeam tree in the woodland – site of the Great Camera Disappearance – and sit on a tree stump, trying to work out who Mrs Patel could have been attempting to spot. Does she have children? It occurs to me that I know very little about her.

While I'm sitting, I hear footsteps close by. A twig snaps, some dried leaves crunch. Perhaps Francis has tracked me down and wants to feed me.

But the man who appears isn't Francis. He's of average height, in his forties I'd guess, with dark skin and brown eyes. He stops when he sees me, makes a panicked noise, and bolts further into the trees. It's like startling a deer. If it weren't for the wood pigeons flying off in a panic, I might feel as if I'd imagined the interloper.

I head back to the garden, to check on Mouse. In my rush to get to him I keep seeing the man's face. Why did he seem so scared to see me? Who is he? Is this the person Mrs Patel was trying to spot with the camera?

Mouse is curled up asleep with Mr Rabbit, so I risk another walk around. This time, I head up to the top lawn and over to the outbuilding where the mower's kept. I try the door, which is locked, and peer through the window, but there's nothing to see apart from the mower and a few tools. The forbidden shed beside it seems to taunt me with its secrets.

Glancing around, I see there's no one in sight. I've brought some wire with me, and I slide it inside the padlock to attempt to trick it into opening. I've never tried this before, and I'm not actually sure how it works. I keep jiggling the wire in the lock, but nothing seems to happen.

'I have the key if you're so desperate to see inside.'

Shit! I remove the wire and turn to see Sherry, watching me. She's wearing dark glasses, and her lipstick's smudged.

'I wasn't planning on stealing anything – I just . . .'

'You wanted to see what's inside. I get it. I don't print my blackmail notes in there, if that's what you're thinking.' Her voice is slightly slurred, and her Essex undertones are pronounced. She stumbles forward, and plunges her hand into the pocket of her capri pants. Up close, I can smell the alcohol on her; the scent is so strong, it's hard to say if it's coming from her breath, or if she's been bathing in the stuff.

Drawing out a bunch of keys, she inserts one into the large padlock, swearing when it won't turn. She tries three more keys before one finally obliges and the lock clicks open. She removes the padlock and pushes open the door, flicking on the light inside. 'Come on, then.'

I follow Sherry reluctantly over the threshold. My overactive imagination has started to conjure bodies frozen in time by a taxidermist; but the shed is warm and dry, and there are no horrors. Despite her drunkenness, Sherry is somehow managing to remain more-or-less upright in her astonishing heels, and she totters over to a large shape covered with a cloth, which she removes with a flourish.

I whistle as she unveils a gleaming red Ducati: the caviar of motorbikes.

'This is yours?' I ask.

She shakes her head. 'It belonged to my husband, Sunil.'

'So, why the secrecy?'

She sighs and runs her hand over the bike's red paintwork. 'As far as the police – and public – are concerned, my husband died ten years ago, when he drove his bike off a cliff. It was ruled a suicide, though his body was never recovered.'

I'm sure my first response should be, *How awful!* but I'm confused. This gleaming beast of a machine is not a vehicle that's been run off a cliff. 'Sorry – his bike? This bike?'

She nods. 'Do you see any number plates?' I hadn't noticed before, but the reg plates are missing. She's leaning on the bike, watching me. 'I'm going to tell you the full story, Miss Marple, and you are going to decide what you want to do about it.'

'OK . . .' I say. 'I'm listening.'

She gestures to the immaculate motorbike. 'Sunil isn't dead.'

I stare at her. 'So, where is he?' Even as I ask, I know the answer: Sunil is the man I saw in the woods.

She continues her story: 'He took the plates off his beloved bike and fitted them to an identical model, which he ran off a cliff – without a rider, that is.'

'But why? For the money or . . . ?'

'So he wouldn't have to go to prison. He'd got involved in a scheme involving the "reallocation" of staff pension funds at Smith & Fryett, where he worked.'

'I take it "reallocation" is just a posh word for "theft".'

She nods. 'I was furious when he told me. Not only had he cheated all those people out of their pensions, but he stood to go to prison. Sunil knew he wouldn't cope in jail. White-collar workers have a particularly bad time of it apparently . . .'

'So . . . what? He faked his own death and ran away?'

She nods. 'He skipped the country. And he promised me,' she sounds fierce now, 'and I mean *swore* to me, he wouldn't return, not ever.'

'You put up the video camera because you suspected he had come back to England, didn't you?' She nods. 'I saw him today,' I tell her.

She grabs my hands and I'm surprised at her strength – even inebriated, this diminutive woman has a forceful grip. 'Where did you see him?'

'In the woods.'

'I knew it!'

'Do you think anyone else knows he's back?' I ask.

'Maybe someone among the staff – I'm not sure. But the question is – why is he back? He knows how much he's risking.'

'Can I ask: how did you know he was back?'

'Oh, just little signs, out in the garden. He'd move something I'd left in one place, or he'd drink a cup of tea I'd left untouched.'

'So, he wanted you to know?'

She nods. 'But what does he want? If he comes back, I'll be an accomplice. We'll lose the house, as well.' She regards me for a moment, then says, 'What are you going to do?'

'Nothing,' I say. I speak without reflecting – it appears my subconscious has made the decision for me. 'None of this has anything to do with me.'

'Thank you,' she says. 'Thank you so much.'

'I do need something from you, though.'

'What's that?'

'I need you to tell me about Alfie. Did he really die in a riding accident?'

She steps back, a look of horror on her face. 'I can't talk about any of that.'

'Why not?'

'Because I promised Mimi . . .'

'Then can you please ask Mimi to talk to me about it?'

She nods. Her eyes are wet and she looks vulnerable. 'I can ask her,' she says. 'She doesn't always do what I ask, mind you.'

'Well, see if you can influence her. It might help me to find the blackmailer, as it seems Mimi's being threatened over something to do with Alfie.'

She looks as if she's about to deny it, but then concedes, 'That's right.'

'What about you? Was your note about Sunil?'

She nods. 'Someone knew – or guessed – he'd faked his death. I've been wondering if they spotted him, the way you did. It would have to be someone who was au fait with the situation – that he'd allegedly killed himself.'

'So the blackmailer really knows you?'

She tries to smile. 'It'd appear they know each of us intimately.'

23

I have mixed feelings as I pull up outside La Jolla the next morning. At least it's a fine day, and Mouse has agreed to come out in the van.

'What do you think, boy? Shall we venture into the den of iniquity?' He picks up Mr Rabbit and looks expectantly at me. 'You want to get down, I take it?'

I climb down and go round to let him out. 'Come here, boy,' I put my arms around him and lift him out. My phone starts to ring, so I set him gently on the ground and answer it.

'Steph speaking.'

'Steph – it's Kate, from The Chimneys.'

'Hi, Kate. Why are you whispering?'

'It's just . . . I've found something you might want to see. I don't want to say it on the phone. Can you come here?'

'I've just arrived at La Jolla. How about I come over afterwards?'

'Yeah, that's fine. Text me when you're on your way.' She rings off abruptly, and I put my phone back in my jacket pocket.

'You OK to walk a bit, buddy?' He limps along determinedly, and we take our time proceeding to the back door nearest to the swimming pool; I don't want to risk making too much fuss by presenting myself at the front of the house.

A male staff member answers my knock. From his bearing, I'd guess he's the house manager. 'Yes? We're not buying today.'

'No – I'm Steph Williams, the gardener.'

'Oh! Are you expected?'

'No. I was hoping to have a quick word with either Mr or Mrs Singer-Pryce.'

His face is cold. Perhaps my reputation as an extortionist has preceded me. 'Follow me, please, and I'll see if the master and mistress are available.'

'Thanks,' I say, but he's already marching away from me. I shut the door behind me and follow him down a short corridor, until we enter a large, white room with huge picture windows on to the pool and garden. I feel like I've entered a Hockney painting.

'Please take a seat,' he says, gesturing to a white chaise longue.

I perch on the end, wondering how they keep it so clean and hoping my trousers haven't got dried mud on their rear. Glancing down, I notice that my jacket's filthy and hastily remove it, folding it and placing it at my feet. Mouse lies down on the floor beside me, his head on my jacket and his bandaged paw sticking straight out in front. He's a sorry spectacle.

After a few minutes, Bubby appears. She's wearing one of those iconic Chanel skirt suits and looks chic in an 'old money' sort of way.

'Steph, hi. I'm sorry – did we know you were coming?'

I stand up. 'No. I was hoping we could talk?'

She shakes her head, checking her watch. 'No can do, I'm afraid. I have a charity committee thing in half an hour, and it's a twenty-minute drive to get there. Is it about a garden problem? Can one of the staff help?'

'It's nothing to do with the garden. Just quickly: Gareth and Sylvia Stevens – do the names mean anything to you?'

Her face flickers for an instant – but with what? Shock? Fear? It passes so quickly, it's hard to pinpoint.

'No – should they?' Her voice is cool.

'Oh . . . It's only that Jockey was at school with Gareth, so I thought maybe you'd know him.'

She shakes her head and her chin-length hair swings, glossy and immaculate. 'No, I can't say I do. Was that all?'

'Sylvia Stevens said you and your husband accused Gareth of assaulting Apple.'

She smiles slightly, raising one eyebrow. 'Whoever this woman is, she has an active imagination.'

'I see.'

'Now, if you'll excuse me . . .'

'Is Mr Singer-Pryce around?'

'No, I'm afraid he's not.'

'Oh, well, I'll call back.'

Her face hardens. 'If you're hoping to unearth more ammunition for your seedy money-making scam, you won't find it here.'

'If you're referring to the blackmail, I'm not the one doing it. All I'm trying to do is find out what the culprit's motivation might be, in the hope of tracking them down and clearing my name. I would have thought you'd like to help unearth the actual perpetrator.'

She regards me haughtily. 'You can cut the sham – we all know it's you. You'll be out of here in what – a week?'

'If you get rid of me, it won't put a stop to the blackmailing.'

'Are you threatening me?'

'On the contrary, I'm stating the facts. There is a blackmailer at large, and it isn't me.'

She presses a button on the wall and the member of staff who showed me in reappears almost instantly.

'Show Ms Williams out,' says Mrs Singer-Pryce.

'Yes, ma'am.'

I'm shaking with anger and frustration. I can't resist one last dig before I follow the man out. 'Do you even know what trouble your younger daughter is involved in, Mrs Singer-Pryce?'

'Just get out!'

'What's going on here?' Jockey Singer-Pryce appears at the bottom of the stairs just as I reach the hall.

'Nothing, darling, it's fine. Ms Williams was just leaving.'

I clear my throat. 'Actually, now you're here, Mr Singer-Pryce, I'd like to ask you some questions, if I may?'

Glancing at his wife, I see that her mask has slipped again. This time, I manage to read her expression: it signals anxiety and possibly even fear.

'You can ask me whatever you like,' says her husband breezily, leading me back into the lounge. 'Though what use it will be to you, I can't imagine: an old dog like me. Shall we . . . ?' He gestures for me to take a seat and I sit back down on the chaise longue. Poor Mouse, having struggled to get up, now struggles to lie back down.

Jockey turns to his wife. 'Darling, will you join us?'

'I can't, Jockey. You know I have my meeting this morning.'

'Of course, of course. Well, you get off, then.' He pecks her on the cheek. She hesitates, clearly unwilling to leave her husband alone with me. Jockey takes a seat beside me, announcing in a stage whisper, 'She's worried I'm going to say something inappropriate. Apparently, that's my forte – my three girls are always telling me off for saying the wrong thing.' He chuckles. 'Go on, Bubby; I promise I'll be very good.'

She smiles but shakes her head, still looking anxious. 'All right. I should be back mid-afternoon.' She shoots me a look that can only be construed as venomous, before leaving, her sensible block heels clopping on the tiled floor.

The house manager clears his throat.

'Oh, I didn't see you there, Matthew,' says my host. 'Fetch us some drinks, would you?' He catches my eye. 'Coffee? Tea?'

'I'm fine, thank you.'

'Oh, I'm having one. Do join me.'

'A coffee then, please,' I say, impatient to get on. I smile at the butler, but he does not smile back; he merely nods to his boss and says,

'Very well, sir. I'll have Becky bring it out.'

So many servants. Once again, I wonder if I'm missing a trick by not interviewing them all. But Jordan has promised to keep an ear to the ground, and it sounds like Kate might have turned something up.

Jockey sits back and stretches out his long legs with the easy confidence of one who is master of his domain. One arm rests along the back of our shared seat, too close for comfort. I suspect he has either forgotten our previous encounter, or seen it as a challenge: he's that type of man. I inch forward, until I'm perched awkwardly on the edge, ready to bolt if necessary.

'So, Ms Williams, how is the investigation going?'

'In stops and starts, unfortunately.'

'Well, let's see if I can help. Fire away.'

I take a deep breath and say, 'Gareth Stevens.'

If the name shocks him, he doesn't show it. 'Old Stevie, eh?' he says nonchalantly. 'How did that name come up, I wonder?'

I continue, 'Mrs Stevens says you accused her husband of sexually assaulting Apple.'

'Sexually assaulting? That's a bit extreme. As far as I can remember, we merely suggested he shouldn't have been on his own with her in her bedroom, late at night.'

'Actually, Mrs Stevens is insistent the police were involved. She says her husband lost his job, and they had to move house over it.'

'Dear, dear. I had no idea. Such a misunderstanding.'

A maid appears, bearing a tray, and Jockey and I fall silent while she places it on a nearby table and pours our drinks.

'I'll sort it from here, Becky, thank you,' says Jockey. After she leaves, he goes to the table and holds up the milk jug.

'Just black, no sugar, please.'

He brings my mug over to me. Then he fixes his own coffee and comes back to his seat. 'I must say, Ms Williams,' he says, as he readjusts his long body, 'I wasn't entirely comfortable with the residents' committee meeting; I felt they were very hard on you, without any actual proof.'

'Thank you. The accusations came out of nowhere, as far as—' I stop talking: he's squeezing my knee. I stand up abruptly, spilling coffee down my sweater in the process. Mouse lets out a low growl.

'Dear, dear. Let me get that for you.' He rises to his feet and draws a hanky from his top pocket.

'I'm fine, thank you,' I say firmly, taking the cloth from him. A slight smile is playing around his lips, his gaze fixed on my breasts. I turn away to mop at my chest, but it's no use: my top is soaked. I take my jacket from the arm of the chaise longue, pull it on and zip it up.

'Shall I top you up, as so much has spilled?' he asks.

I avoid meeting his eye. 'No, thank you,' I say stiffly. If I didn't need information from him, I wouldn't be so polite. I resume my perch as far from him as the piece of furniture will allow. It's like a game of tag, in which he's 'it' and there is no safe place.

'I could see you were very distressed by the discussion,' he says calmly, as if he hasn't just been fondling my leg. He bends to stroke Mouse's head, but the dog growls quietly. 'Loyal dog you've got here.'

'Yes; he'd attack anyone who threatened me.' Jockey's jovial expression doesn't change, so there's no way of knowing if the message has got through. And the state Mouse is in, it's hardly a convincing threat.

'May I ask how the poor chap got in the wars?' he asks.

'He was stolen and tied up.'

'Really? Who on earth would do such a thing?'

'I'm not sure, but I'm pretty certain that identifying the blackmailer will answer that question.'

He sighs and stirs his coffee. 'Such a strange, worrying affair. We've never had anything like this before at the Heights.'

'I was wondering about Simon Drake . . .'

He frowns. 'Simon . . . ?'

'The previous gardener. What do you know about him?'

'Oh, you'd have to ask Bubby, I'm afraid; the garden's her domain. From what little contact I had with him, he seemed a pleasant enough fellow.'

'Can we come back to Gareth Stevens?' I ask.

'If you wish, but I'm quite sure old Dog Breath has nothing to do with these awful notes.'

'"Dog Breath"?'

'That's his nickname, you know; we all had them at school.'

'Is that why you're called Jockey?'

He pauses for a moment. At last, he says slowly, 'Jockey is an old family name. So, how else can I help?'

'I had the impression Mr Stevens had loaned you a substantial amount of money.'

Jockey tuts. 'I'd hardly call it "substantial" – we look out for each other, you know? The ties you make at a school like Pembridge last a lifetime.'

'So, you're still in touch with Mr Stevens – Dog Breath?'

His expression turns forlorn. It's quite convincing. 'No: sadly we lost touch after he and Sylvia moved away. I've no idea what we could have done to offend them.'

This man has the most selective memory I've ever come across. 'So . . . the sexual assault allegations . . . ?'

'As if I could accuse my lifelong friend of something so heinous. Miscommunication, that's what it was. At least this explains why he and Sylvia stopped returning our calls.' He puts down his mug on a table beside him and stands up. 'Now, if you'll excuse me, I'll have Matthew show you out.' He walks to the wall and pulls a cord to summon the servant.

I take a deep breath. 'Did you ever pay back the loan from Gareth Stevens?' I ask.

'Of course; with interest, if I remember rightly.'

'And how much was it?'

He sighs. 'It's been a long time, but if I had to guess, I expect it would have been between two and three.'

'Thousand?'

'Hundred thousand.'

Matthew arrives and Jockey instructs him to show me out. The house manager doesn't speak a word as he escorts me towards the back door. At last, to break the silence, I say, 'Do you know that Jordan at The Chimneys doesn't believe I'm the blackmailer?'

He tuts as he opens the door. 'If you'll forgive me, I don't know what you're talking about. All I know is, you've been here under an hour and you've managed to upset both the mistress and the master.'

He ushers us out and shuts the door firmly in our faces.

'Nice manners they have here,' I say to the dog. 'At least we should get more cooperation from Kate.' I text her: *On my way!* and we make our slow walk back to the van.

I key in the code at The Chimneys' bottom gate; the top one is open, as usual. Kate comes out to meet me at the front. She does some complex gesturing that I can't interpret, so I roll down my window.

'Can you drive into the garage?' she says. 'I don't want anyone to see us talking.'

'OK.'

The minute I've pulled in and turned off the engine, she opens my door.

'Are you in a rush?' I ask.

'I didn't tell Mr Samuels I was going out so I need to be quick.'

I move to climb down, but she says, 'No, you might as well stay in your seat. This won't take long.'

'OK. What have you got for me?'

'It's just this.' She holds out a folded piece of paper, which I take and open.

'The note! How did you get this?'

'It was in a drawer in Ms Purdue's dressing table.'

'You're a star!'

She blushes at the praise.

I skim the note, which is as short as the one received by the Singer-Pryces:

I KNOW WHAT YOU WERE UP TO WHEN ALFIE DIED.

'Do you know what this means?' I ask Kate.

She shakes her head. 'It doesn't make sense, if you ask me. He just fell from a pony. His mum was there with him.'

'Mimi?' She nods. 'Were you there? Did you see him fall?'

She shakes her head again. 'None of the staff saw it happen. We were all off that day.'

'Why were you off?'

'Ms Purdue had given us a day's holiday. She does that from time to time. She says we need time to refuel. She's a good boss like that.'

I fish out my phone and take a photo of the note, before handing it back. 'Thanks so much.'

'You're welcome. I've got to get back and return this. Can you try not to be seen?'

'I'll do my best, though I am driving a van – it's not the most inconspicuous way to make an exit.'

She walks ahead of me, beckoning in a furtive way, and I get out without being spotted, as far as I can tell.

Back at the cottage, Mouse heads straight to his bed with Mr Rabbit. I crush the vet's antibiotic tablets and mix them with peanut butter, which he loves. I've tried many methods of giving him pills over the years, and this is the only one that works. I hold out my fingers to him and he licks off all the paste.

'Now, you have a rest while I do some work,' I tell him.

I sit at the kitchen table and update my notes, after which I make myself a sandwich and consider the options for my next step: accessing the land behind the walled garden at The Towers. Would the formal, unsmiling butler consider helping me? Deciding it's worth a shot, I consult my list of landline numbers and dial The Towers.

A young female voice answers, 'You've reached the Qureshi residence.'

'Hello, my name is Steph Williams; I'm the gardener.'

'Oh! Hello!' She sounds almost . . . excited about speaking to me.

'Er . . . Hi.'

'I heard what they're doing to you – that sucks.'

'Thanks, but who is this?'

'Oh, sorry! I'm Simone. I'm on the house staff.'

'Well, thank you for your support, Simone. And yeah, it pretty much does suck, now you mention it.'

'We're all really disgusted.'

'Does that mean you might be up for helping me?'

'Sure – if there's something I can do?' Her eagerness is touching.

'You could help me gain access to the locked portion of land at the top of the garden – behind the wall.'

'Hold on.' I wait, crossing my fingers. I can hear her walking away across a tiled floor. At last, the footsteps return and she says, quietly, 'I've got the key. When you get here, ask for me,' and she hangs up.

24

Now, I just have to persuade Mouse to come out with me again. The poor dog is curled up, snoring in his bed; he only opens one eye when I crouch down to coax him.

'I'm sorry, boy, but I'm not risking leaving you again.' I scoop him up with his toy and blanket, and stagger out to the van. He makes little whimpering noises and I feel terrible. 'I'm so, so sorry,' I say softly, as I settle him on to the blanket on the passenger seat and strap him in.

At The Towers, I use the code for the gates, and at the top of the drive I park off to the side, where the van can't be seen from the house.

After unlocking the garden gate and propping it open with a large stone, I lift poor Mouse down and stagger with him through to the garden, where I place him carefully beneath a birch tree and cover him with his blanket. He settles as soon as Mr Rabbit is placed beside him. I slip back to the gate, remove the stone and make sure the gate locks after closing.

My knock on the back door is answered by James. 'Steph, good afternoon.'

'Good afternoon, James. May I please speak to Simone?'

His professionalism doesn't allow him to look surprised. He even makes a slight bow. 'Of course. Would you care to wait indoors?'

'No, I'm fine here in the sun, thanks.'

He nods and departs, and I wait – but not for long. The woman who arrives is probably in her early twenties. She is of medium height, with lovely almond-shape eyes and an elaborate coil of cornrows on top of her head. She grins when she sees me.

'Hiya,' she says, stepping outside.

'Simone, hi. Thanks so much for helping me with this.'

She starts walking up the garden and I follow. 'That's OK. He was out for the count.'

'I'm sorry . . . who was?'

'The young master.'

'Do you mean Adam?'

'Yeah.'

'Do you all have to refer to him as "the young master"?'

She shakes her head. 'It's just a joke between us.'

'Why?'

She laughs. 'Because he's a bit spoilt. Nice, but spoilt.'

I decide not to follow up on her estimation of Adam as 'nice'. Instead, I ask, 'Did you have to get the key from his room?'

She nods. 'I figure I'll be able to get it back before he wakes up.'

'That's really kind – thank you.'

'You're welcome.'

By the time we reach the locked door at the top of the garden, she's out of breath from the climb. It makes me realise how accustomed I've grown to the steepness of the gardens. She unlocks the door. 'Can I come, too?' she asks.

'Sure, if you'd like. I don't want to get you into trouble, though.'

'Hey, if they catch me now, I'm already done for. In for a penny and all that . . .'

'Well, OK, then.' We grin at each other.

I have to duck to pass through the low doorway in the wall. On the other side, there's the expected wilderness – nettles, daisies and dandelions competing for space beneath a mix of brambles and other wild shrubs and trees. It looks the same from here as it did from the path to the paddock. Why would anyone need to keep this area locked away?

I'm still looking around when Simone points out a trampled path, going off to the right through the undergrowth.

'Good spot,' I say. 'Come on.' She follows me along the narrow track. After a few metres, it snakes back on itself, before heading in the direction of the boundary. And then we see a set of stone steps, leading down to a small door in an underground building. I stride ahead and take the steps to the bottom, wondering if the door will be locked. In fact, it opens easily when I turn the handle.

'Time out,' says Simone, and I turn to look at her.

'What is it?'

'Well, it's just . . . We don't know what we're going to find in there, do we? There might be skeletons or a torture chamber or anything.'

'Tell you what – you wait here, and I'll go in first. If there's anything nasty, I'll warn you.'

Despite my casual words, her suggestion of death and pain unsettles me. I hesitate for a moment before going inside, and when I do, I step in just far enough to feel along the wall until I locate a switch. The lights take a moment to come on, and I hold my breath in the darkness, only breathing out when they illuminate the space. They're fluorescent strip lights – harsh after the natural daylight; I find myself blinking against their glare.

Glancing around, *cleared out* is the phrase that springs to mind. There are four stainless-steel, laboratory-style benches, set out evenly, with matching steel shelves around the walls. Other than those, and the strong stench of bleach, the room is a blank.

It's at this point I realise that what I'd been expecting to find were drugs – stacks of those transparent bags filled with white powder that I saw Adam piling into his car. I walk around the space, but there are no cupboards, and no doors other than the one by which I entered. Whatever used to be here, there's no trace of it now.

'Is it safe to come in?' I'd forgotten about Simone.

'Yep,' I call. 'Although there's nothing to see.'

She enters, looking almost disappointed at the anticlimactic scene. 'So, no bodies?'

'Afraid not.'

'It's like a crime scene that's been wiped down,' she says, looking around.

And I realise that's precisely what it is. Simone is crouching to look under the shelving. When she stands up, I say, 'Simone, is it meth they make in labs?'

She looks offended. 'How would I know?'

'Sorry, I just mean . . . I was hoping between us we might have some idea. I think it's meth that's made in chemistry labs, but I'm not sure.'

She wrinkles up her nose as she reflects. 'It might be. I'm trying to remember from *Breaking Bad* but I only watched one episode.'

She looks at me with wide eyes. 'You think the family have been cooking up drugs in here?'

'Not the family; just Adam.'

She laughs and I frown at her. 'What?'

'He doesn't even get out of bed before noon most days. I don't know how he'd find the time to run a drug empire.'

'I saw him. He had a stash of drugs, and he was loading it into the car.'

'Seriously? Did you tell anyone?'

'Not so far. I didn't have any proof. And this emptied-out lab means I still don't.'

She checks her watch. 'Shit, I have to get back . . .'

'Right.' We leave, shutting the door carefully, and make our way back along the track to the door in the wall.

Simone talks as we walk: 'I was kind of hoping we'd find something major, and I'd be able to say, "I helped expose that massive crime syndicate or money laundering operation or underground sex trade or whatever".'

I smile apologetically. 'Sorry to disappoint you.'

She locks the door in the wall after us and pockets the key. 'Back to the day job, I guess.'

'Were you hoping the exposure would get you a more exciting job?'

'Nothing ever happens here,' she confides, as we walk back down the slope towards the house. 'I mean, seriously, this is the dullest house I've worked at – and I used to be an au pair, so I've worked at a lot of houses.'

'Listen,' I say when we reach the back door of the house, 'I want to thank you for risking your job to help me, when you don't even know me.'

'Hey – we workers have to stick together, right? Can't let the management grind us down.' She holds out her fist for me to bump, and I oblige.

It strikes me that her politics don't chime very well with the almost-feudal system I've seen in play at Beaulieu.

'Did you study politics?' I ask her.

'Modern History and Politics at Southampton.'

'And you're a . . . what – maid?' As soon as I say the words, I regret them. After all, I've been at great pains to ensure the residents of Beaulieu Heights don't pigeonhole me according to my job title.

But she smiles wryly. 'I think my official job title is "She who wipes arse", but I'll take "maid".'

'Well, if I manage to keep my job here, and they give me the funds to hire an undergardener . . . ?'

'Yes, please!'

'Do you have any gardening experience?'

'None whatsoever.' She pulls a face. 'Should I have pretended I'd been to gardening school?'

'Nope. It would be a lot worse if you claimed to have experience, and then took a chainsaw to a prized azalea because you thought it was *Rhododendron ponticum*.'

'Yes, that would be awful,' she says soberly. 'What's a *Rhododendron ponticum*?'

'We can cover that another time. Of course, I can't promise gardening would be any more interesting than your current job.'

'But I could get on with it, and not spend all day fetching slippers and polishing decanters?'

I promise her that there would not be a single decanter or slipper involved, and she nods approvingly before opening the door to go inside.

'Oh, Simone,' I say quickly. 'Please will you see if Mr or Mrs Qureshi is free to talk to me?'

'I'll ask.'

While I wait, I check on Mouse. He's still dozing beneath the tree, his sore paw stretched out at an awkward angle. The poor dog could do with a day or two at home to recuperate, but I can't leave him alone until all this is resolved, and I can't clear my name by staying at home.

I jump as Mr Qureshi's voice comes from behind me: 'You were looking for me?'

I turn around and he says, 'I'm sorry – I didn't mean to startle you.'

'That's all right. I was hoping you might have time to talk?'

'I'm sure I can spare you a few minutes.' He stands beside me and regards Mouse. 'Is your poor dog healing all right? I heard what happened.'

'He'll get there, thanks. Where are Fritz and Mitzi today?'

'Annabelle's taken them to the groomer's. They both needed a trim.'

I nod and we look at one another for a while. He's tall and broad-shouldered with a beard; his handsome face is kinder than I remember from our previous encounter. At last, he says, 'Ms Williams, we didn't get off on the right foot at the meeting last week, for which I take full responsibility. Can I offer you a drink?'

'Do you know, that would be lovely – yes, please.'

'Tea? Coffee? Something stronger?'

'A coffee would be great.'

'If you take a seat in the summer house, I'll have one of the staff bring out a tray.' He gestures politely for me to go ahead, which I fully intend to do – however, I'm distracted by a broken branch on a dwarf lilac, so that when he returns a moment later, he finds me snipping off the damage with the secateurs I always have in my jacket.

I smile sheepishly at him. 'I've been neglecting the gardens. The lawn needs mowing as well.'

'Don't worry – I'll have one of the staff do it. You have quite enough on your plate at the moment. I feel bad that we're not involving the police, meaning all the onus is on you to exonerate yourself.'

We walk together into the summer house, where we take seats at the little table inside. I find myself appreciating Mr Qureshi's formality all the more after my meeting with Jockey.

'As I no longer believe you are guilty, Ms Williams, I'm going to talk to you about our family situation.' He goes quiet as a maid comes in with a tray; she sets out a cafetière with mugs, milk, sugar and a plate of biscuits. 'Thank you, Muriel. That will be all.' She nods and smiles, glancing curiously at me, then leaves. He continues, 'I'd very much appreciate it, if what I tell you remains between us. Obviously, I have no authority over you – but I'm appealing to your compassion and understanding.'

I nod. 'Please go on. I won't tell anyone, unless there are lives at stake.'

'There aren't. This isn't easy for me to talk about, though.' He looks out of the window. I follow his gaze and see daffodils in clumps of sunshine-yellow, drifts of dark-pink hellebores and swathes of violets. I feel an urge to walk out of this wooden shed, grab my tools and set to work, among the smells and colours of the garden's rising sap. But my curiosity is too strong – that and the need to clear my name and keep my job.

My companion depresses the plunger in the cafetière and pours the dark, steaming liquid into a mug, gesturing for me to help myself to milk and sugar. I shake my head, then pick up my cup, just to inhale the intoxicating aroma of the coffee.

'This smells amazing,' I say.

He nods, pleased, as he pours some into his own mug. 'I tried a lot of different blends before settling on this one. I have a different coffee for after dinner, but this is my favourite morning brew. Did you know I'm an importer?' I shake my head, and he says, 'Coffee is my main product, though I do also import some fabric and leather goods.'

'None of that sounds like a blackmailable offence.'

He laughs, but it's a short burst and he looks sad afterwards. 'Have you met our son Adam, Ms Williams?'

'Yes.'

'And what did you make of him?'

I don't want to say, *He's a toxic male drug dealer*, so I hesitate. 'I haven't had a proper chat with him, so I haven't formed a full impression.'

'Did you know he got all A stars at A level?'

'No, I didn't know that.'

'He's meant to be at university now, but I'm not convinced he's attending. He always seems to be in the house, and he claims he has a lot of free periods.'

'I think Mrs Qureshi said he's studying Law?'

'Indeed. It's not exactly a course that's known for its free time. It is Easter holidays at the moment of course, but he must have work to do.' He sighs. 'I sometimes wonder if he thinks he's the parent, and he's trying to keep an eye on us.'

'Was it something to do with Adam, what you wanted to tell me?'

'Oh, no. I just . . . I suppose I'm not in a hurry to share this thing for which I feel so ashamed.'

He's quiet for a moment, then nods as if he's made up his mind. 'All right, here goes: I used to work abroad a lot, in Dubai, where I have another arm to my business. I'd leave Annabelle and Adam for a month, or even two, at a time. I wasn't around to be a good husband and father.' He breaks eye contact and stirs his coffee, looking close to tears. 'What I'm about to tell you . . . I don't want you to judge Annabelle. She was feeling neglected and alone, with too much time on her hands.'

'OK . . .'

'She set up a meth lab at the top of the garden.' He blurts this out. It's so unexpected, it's almost comical.

'Mrs Qureshi did?' I revisit the empty building in my mind, with its strong smell of bleach. It hadn't occurred to me that Annabelle might be responsible. What about Adam? What about all those bags of drugs?

He notes my confusion. 'I know it seems unlikely, but she's always been ambitious. She's a chemist, you know?' I shake my head, remembering how, at my first meeting with Annabelle, I'd assumed she was a model. 'Oh, yes, she has a first from Cambridge.' Despite the confessional nature of his discourse, he's clearly proud of her.

'But why did she do it?' I ask. 'Did she need the money?'

'That was a whole other story.' He sits back and watches me for a moment, as if sizing me up. Then he says, 'Well, I've told you this much, I believe you may as well know the rest.' I sip my coffee and listen as he continues talking. 'Annabelle has a twin brother. Unfortunately, Sebastian struggles with life. He's never found it easy to commit to anything apart from drinking. He came to her after he'd run up debts, asking her to bail him out. She wanted to help, but knew I'd disapprove of her handing over such large sums. The secret meth lab was her solution – a way to generate a stream of income that I wouldn't know about or miss. She hadn't got around to actually selling the stuff, thank god. But she had made quantities, all weighed and bagged, and stacked in her secret laboratory.

'I found out about the lab on one of my short trips home. It was the wake-up call I needed, to stop neglecting my family. I hired a manager for Dubai, and stayed here, to clean things up. I don't know what we'd have done without Adam; he's been wonderful.'

I'm so surprised, I choke on my coffee. 'Adam's been helping you?'

He nods. 'He knew about a rehab charity in London, so he and

I took Annabelle on a visit there. We introduced her to young girls and boys, addicts, who'd been forced into prostitution, to pay for their drugs.' He looks at his hands. 'She'd known how damaging her product was, of course, but actually meeting the young people she would have affected made it real.'

'How did Adam know about this charity?'

'Well, even after we'd confronted Annabelle, she took some persuading to give up her plan. Adam had the bright idea of researching what help was available for young addicts, and this particular charity agreed to let us visit. I gave them a donation, of course.'

There's a long pause while I process all this information. Annabelle seems so benign – it's hard to imagine her cooking up drugs in her own laboratory.

At last, as much to fill the silence as anything, I say, 'What does Annabelle do now, to fill her time?'

'She's been volunteering for a charity, but she's currently looking to get back into research work as a chemist. She still has a few contacts in that industry.'

'Can I ask – was that what her blackmail note was about: the meth lab?'

'Yes. Someone has discovered what Annabelle got up to, and is holding it over her. Of course, the drugs never made it on to the streets, but if the blackmailer has proof they existed . . .'

'How long ago was this? The meth lab, I mean.'

'We closed down the lab around six months ago.'

I run through everything he's told me. It occurs to me that the family might have found out that I witnessed Adam stashing drugs in his car, and this entire story might have been fabricated to put me off the scent.

'What has happened to Annabelle's – Mrs Qureshi's – brother?' I ask, trying to buy time while I work out whether to trust him.

'Prison. His debts became too great and, once Annabelle couldn't help him, he got involved in some shady business and got caught. It will either be the making of him or his undoing. At least he is getting treatment for his alcoholism.' His large, brown eyes are filled with empathy and sorrow.

It's hard to know what to say. I turn away, gazing out of the window at the garden.

After a while, Mr Qureshi says, 'You are very quiet, Ms Williams. Have I shocked you?'

I take a deep breath and say, 'I saw Adam.'

'What do you mean, you saw him?'

'I drove up here a few days ago, and saw him piling bags of drugs into the boot of his car.'

'Ah. I'm sorry you saw that. It must have given you the wrong impression.'

'What wrong impression exactly? What was he doing?'

'He was getting rid of the last of the drugs, so that no one could find them or be harmed by them. The lab is now entirely empty, thanks to our wonderful, brave son. Although I should warn you that there are still some bags buried in the woodland. We will move them away and destroy them soon.'

'Which woodland?' I ask, though I already suspect the answer.

'Behind your cottage.'

So that explains the person in the woods on my first night at Beaulieu.

There's a sincerity in Zakariya Qureshi's manner that makes me inclined to believe him. I look down for a minute, turning my mug of coffee and staring at its dark surface.

'Thank you for sharing this,' I say. 'It will be very helpful as I try and work out who could have had all of the information in the blackmail notes.'

'It has to be a staff member,' he says.

'Why do you say that?'

'Well, all of the residents have something to hide. It's not in their interest to make themselves vulnerable by accusing others.'

'If you're right, I have a lot more work to do – I haven't even met most of the staff at Beaulieu.'

'I can arrange for you to interview my staff, if you like?'

'Thanks. I'll see how things go. I do know some of the butlers – are they still called that? – and some of the maids.'

'A lot of the butlers prefer to be called "house managers" these days.'

I seem to remember that was how Jordan introduced himself. I finish my coffee and Zakariya proffers the plate of biscuits, from which I take a Viennese whirl. I bite into it and savour the soft, buttery sensation as it crumbles on my tongue.

'Good, aren't they?' says Zakariya.

'Amazing.'

He nods with pleasure. 'I hired the best biscuit and pastry chef I could find.' He sighs, and I know we're both thinking that he won't be getting the best biscuits or coffee if he goes to jail for helping to run a drugs business.

'There is one other thing,' I say, remembering what Kate told me about the Qureshis. 'I believe you and Mrs Qureshi had an argument the other day?'

'Oh, yes – you heard about that, did you? Very embarrassing.' He pulls a face. 'Her brother is going to be on day release from prison for a family funeral, and she has invited him to come to our house. In the past, I never dreamt of trying to keep her from seeing him, but the way things turned out . . . She could so easily be in jail herself.'

A thought strikes me. 'How well does Sebastian know the residents of Beaulieu Heights?'

He muses on this, then says, 'He knows far too much about Annabelle – and I wouldn't be surprised if he tried to use that information to his own ends – but I'm almost certain Annabelle herself doesn't know why the other residents are being blackmailed, so it seems unlikely her brother could have found out their dark secrets.' He says 'dark secrets' with a raise of his eyebrows, as if it's a joke. I refrain from telling him that a drowned child and a fraudulent sexual abuse charge are among the skeletons in his neighbours' cupboards.

I down the rest of my coffee and stand up. 'Thank you again, Mr Qureshi, I really appreciate it. And don't worry, I have no desire to expose any of this.'

He stands up and holds out his hand, which I take. His grip is warm and reassuring. 'Thank you so much. I hope you stay, Ms Williams. Anything I find out, I'll be sure to let you know.'

'Thank you. And thanks for the delicious coffee and biscuits.'

'Here – take the rest. You can bring the plate back the next time you visit.' He holds out the plate of biscuits and I accept. I don't stop to examine whether it's a kind gesture or a payoff. If I change my mind about reporting Annabelle, it will take a lot more than a few homemade biscuits to buy me.

'Four days in, and not much the wiser,' I say to Mouse, when we're back at the cottage for a late lunch for me and more healing sleep for him. He's lying on his back in the sunshine that's streaming in through the kitchen window. It's the most relaxed I've seen him since the dognapping, and it warms my heart.

My mobile starts ringing while I'm stirring a pan of tomato soup on the stove. Danny's name flashes up and I flick off the gas to answer.

'Danny, hi. How are you doing?'

'I'm calling with bad news, sis.'

It always amazes me how quickly the human brain can react. Images reel past: Alice, hit by a car; Karen, haemorrhaging and losing the baby; Frankie, tripping and hitting his head on concrete; Luke, climbing a set of shelves and falling, pulling the unit down on top of him.

'It's Dad,' says Danny. 'He's had a heart attack.' I step over to the table and take a seat as the adrenaline leaves my body and my legs start to wobble.

There's a long silence. 'Are you all right?' he asks.

'I'm all right. I was just worrying it was one of the kids, or Karen.' Then I think about my kind, gentle dad. 'How bad is it? Will he be all right?'

'He should be fine, thank god. I think Mum rang the ambulance as soon as he started clutching his chest. And it was a minor one – what they call a "warning".'

'Still scary,' I say.

'So, what do you want to do?' he asks. 'Do you feel up to travelling today, or will you wait till tomorrow?'

'God, Danny – there's so much going on here . . . Mouse got attacked . . .'

'What?'

'I should have told you, I know, but it's been manic here, trying to clear my name and finding out all these secrets . . . And then some bastard took him and hurt him . . .' I start to cry, and Danny doesn't say anything for a little while. Mouse, with that canine instinct for distress, wakes up at the sound of my sobs and limps over to sit beside me and lick my fingers; I stroke his head. 'We're talking about you, boy,' I tell him.

'Is he OK?' says Danny.

'He will be. He's quite banged-up still, and he's got a bandaged paw.'

'OK, look, we can hold down the fort for a couple of days, if that helps? Karen's over at Mum's now, and she's going to stay there overnight. I'll tell Dad about Mouse tomorrow, and that you'll be up as soon as Mouse can travel.'

I make a decision. 'No,' I say. 'We'll come. It'll be a flying visit though, just to see Dad and check how Mum's getting on.'

'OK.'

'By the way, have you heard anything from Ben?'

'Not since my little helper gave him your address. Why do you ask?'

'He turned up here, asking for money.'

'Seriously?'

'Seriously. And then Caroline rang, to ask me if I was sleeping with him.'

'You're not, are you?'

I roll my eyes. 'Not you as well.'

'Sorry – just checking. He did have quite a pull over you.'

'Not any more. Anyway, apparently he didn't return home after visiting me.'

'So he's missing?'

'It would appear so. Unless he's just done a runner.'

'Has he taken his clothes?'

'I forgot to ask her.'

'I'll let you know if I hear anything. See you shortly.'

I run through all the Beaulieu residents and make a decision. 'Yeah. Though I'm not leaving straight away – there's someone I want to speak to.'

25

I'm determined to confront Mimi about how Alfie died. I stagger out to the van carrying Mouse and Mr Rabbit. The poor dog is so tired, he barely objects to this effrontery. I strap him in and cover him with his throw.

I've called ahead and been told Mimi can spare me only twenty minutes. As I park by the garages and climb out of the van, Mimi comes striding towards me. 'Steph, what can I do for you? Do you want to come inside for a minute?'

'Would you mind staying out here? I don't want to leave Mouse.'

She glances in at him. 'How is he doing?'

'He's healing slowly.'

'I see you still haven't got that window repaired.'

'No, and I'm driving to Peterborough after this.'

She tuts but makes no other comment. 'Now, as I said, I don't have long, so please cut to the chase.'

'It's about how Alfie died,' I say softly. 'I don't think he fell from a pony.'

She glares at me. 'You *are* the blackmailer.'

I shake my head. 'No, I'm not. I'm simply following leads, in the hope of finding out who is. Now, who else was present when Alfie died?'

There's a pause, then she says, 'Only Sherry and Lucy,' in a subdued voice.

'Not your husband?'

'Connell was at work.'

I take a deep breath. 'The scrap of fabric in Sherry's pond suggests that he probably died there.' I watch her. It's hard to read her expression. 'So, am I right? Did Alfie drown in the pond?'

She hesitates, then nods. 'You're right.'

'So, why did you tell everyone that Alfie fell from a pony?'

She sighs. 'You've worked this much out, you might as well know the rest. I'm sure you'll just keep digging until you find it out in any case. Sherry and I were in her bed together when he died.' There's a pause while I digest this information. 'Are you shocked?'

I shake my head. 'No. Well, only in so far as I hadn't picked up on it.'

'We were in love. However, Connell had found out a few weeks earlier and given me an ultimatum: him or Sherry.' She sighs. 'I tried to choose Connell,' she says sadly. 'He is such a good man.'

'So, what happened?'

'I couldn't stay away from her. Her husband had . . .' she stops, as if catching herself about to say the wrong thing, then continues, 'killed himself by then, and she was lonely. And she was – still is – so beautiful . . .' She pauses, then continues, 'The day that Alfie died, I'd taken the kids to Sherry's and told them to play in the garden for a while. Sherry and I were inside.' She looks away, coyly. Coy is not a word I would have associated with Mimi Purdue. 'She'd given her servants the day off, as had I – it was the only way to guarantee discretion.' This chimes with what Kate told me, about the staff holiday.

'After a while, we heard screaming, and we ran to see what was going on. Lucy was in the hall, shrieking and hysterical. While Sherry tried to calm her down, I ran outside, to look for Alfie. But I was too late – just the top of his head – his hair – was visible, on the surface of the pond. He must have fallen in. He could swim, but he'd got caught on part of the filtration system, which is how his shirt got torn: hence the scrap you found.' Her eyes are full of tears.

'Ms Purdue, I'm so sorry . . .'

She puts up a hand to stop me. 'No, it was bound to come out sooner or later. It would have been much sooner if Connell hadn't been too distraught to ask to see the death certificate at the time.' She sighs again. 'To be honest, I'm relieved our secret's finally out in the open. I killed our son.'

'Hardly.'

'No, I did. If I hadn't been so obsessed with my lover, I might have realised the garden wasn't a safe place to leave a six-year-old without adult supervision.'

'That's not the same as killing him. How was Lucy afterwards? It must have been traumatic for her.'

'Lucy? She was devastated. Sherry got her to stop screaming, though goodness knows how. That poor girl – she felt responsible for his death, because we'd asked her to keep an eye on him.'

'That is tough.'

She nods. 'And it was the nail in the coffin for my marriage. Connell adored that boy and couldn't get over losing him.'

'It must have been so hard on all of you.'

She grimaces. 'You can't imagine. Trying to reassure Lucy – convince her it wasn't her fault – while feeling cut up inside at my own failure . . .'

'You're very brave.'

'Not really. In fact, I'm such a coward, I didn't even tell my husband how his son died. But I'm going to, now. And that way, the blackmailer will have nothing to hold over me.' There's a long pause, then she says, 'Why are you going to . . . Peterborough, was it?'

'My dad's in hospital.'

'Nothing serious, I hope?'

'A heart attack, but it was a mild one.'

'Goodness! I hope he makes a full recovery.'

'Thank you.' I clear my throat. 'I know this is nosy, but are you and Mrs Patel still together?'

'Oh, no. We're just good friends these days. The decision to end things came from Sherry, you understand. She felt too many bad things had come from our relationship.'

'Did she feel responsible for the drowning?'

'Of course – a child died in her garden. Wouldn't you?'

I think for a moment. 'Probably.'

She smiles sadly at my honesty. There's a pause, then I say, 'Right, I should let you get on, and I need to get on the road myself. Thank you so much for meeting with me, and for trusting me with the truth about Alfie. I hope you get some peace after you've told Mr Fitzgerald.'

'Thank you. I hope so, too.' She walks me to the door. 'You won't say anything to anyone, will you – at least until I've had the chance to explain everything to Connell?'

'Don't worry,' I say. 'I'm very good at keeping secrets.'

26

After I've spent another night on Danny and Karen's sofa, we travel to the hospital in their MPV, collecting Mum and Karen en route. I take it as a good sign that Mum greets me and even lets me escort her to Dad's ward while Karen and Danny follow with the kids.

'He's in nineteen,' she tells me after we've been buzzed on to the ward. We walk along a corridor to room nineteen, where I hold open the door for Mum and follow her through. There are six beds, five of them occupied by men who look considerably older than Dad. He's by the window, sitting up in bed, reading the paper.

Mum comes to give him a kiss and check how he's doing before saying, 'I'll let you two catch up for a minute while I get us a coffee. Do you want anything, Jack?'

He shakes his head. 'I'm good, thanks.'

As soon as she's gone, I take his hand. 'Dad, you do know that you're my dad, don't you? Nothing can ever change that.'

'Aw, I know, love. Oh – I did talk to your mum, by the way. I think she's coming round to, you know – you wanting to trace your birth parents.'

'Thank you. But let's concentrate on getting you well for now, should we?'

His grey eyes crease with concern. 'Daniel said you've been having some trouble at the new place?'

'Again, we don't need to talk about that now.' I smile at him.

'Only it sounds like such a gorgeous spot, and the job's right up your street. Don't let whatever this is get in the way, will you?'

'I'm working on it, Dad. I need this job, and I can't believe I get to work in such a beautiful place.'

He nods. 'You just hold your ground.' He leans in closer and lowers his voice: 'I've reached a decision myself – I'm going to retire.'

'Really?' Dad's a business advisor. I've never been entirely clear what this involves, but he moves from company to company, spending anything from a few weeks to a year at each one. He loves his work, and none of us ever expected him to give it up.

'What will you do with all that spare time?' I ask him.

'I'm going to get an allotment.'

'I see . . . And has the psychiatrist been to see you yet?'

'Cheeky!' he says with a laugh.

'Dad, you've never even tended a dandelion.'

'Well, you can teach me, can't you?'

'Let's talk about this when you're out,' I say, giving him a kiss on the forehead.

He seizes my hand. 'I mean it, love. Don't let the odd naysayer get you down. They're lucky to have you.'

'I won't, Dad, I promise.'

Mum reappears with Danny. As well as hot drinks, they've picked up some puzzle magazines, plus boiled sweets, the requisite grapes and some biscuits, most of which Mum proceeds to stash in Dad's bedside unit. When she's finished, I stand up to give her the chair.

'It's lovely to have all three of you here at the same time,' says Dad, gazing fondly at us. 'Can we do more of this? Maybe a meal once a month or something?'

'I don't see why not,' I say.

'That would be nice,' says Mum. I'm standing beside her chair, and she takes my hand and kisses it. That's when I know we're going to be all right.

I pack up the van as soon as we get back to the house. Alice brings out Mouse's bed while I'm putting my bag in the back.

'Thank you, darling,' I say, taking it from her. 'That's very helpful.'

She doesn't smile but pushes up one sleeve. Her arm is covered in red welts.

'What is that?' When she doesn't meet my eye, I crouch down and say softly, 'Alice, how did that happen?'

'Frankie did it,' she says.

'Your brother hurt you?' She nods. I put my arms around her thin little shoulders and give her a hug. 'You've done really well to show me,' I say. 'That's a very brave thing to do.'

I take her hand and we head back into the house, where she skips off to join my mum in the garden as if nothing has happened.

I find my brother and sister-in-law in the kitchen and tell them what Alice has just shown me. Danny looks startled. He catches Karen's eye but I can't read the expression that passes between them.

'What did she tell you?' he asks.

I pause, looking from one of them to the other. 'So, you knew about this?'

Karen says, 'We were told by Alice's therapist not to make a big deal out of it. She said we should only mention it if Alice brings it up first.'

'Alice has a therapist?'

'She has,' says Danny. 'We felt we were out of our depth, so we sought help.'

I'm confused. 'But surely, if Frankie's the one hurting her . . . ?'

'Frankie isn't hurting her,' says Karen firmly.

I rub my forehead. 'I don't understand . . .'

'She's hurting herself,' says Danny.

I stare at him. 'But . . . why?'

Danny says, 'That's what we're trying to work out. Perhaps going from being an only child to having two siblings . . . although she wasn't even two when Frankie arrived . . . Or maybe she's feeling neglected, or finding the house too noisy or too hectic . . .'

'Maybe we rely on her too much,' says Karen. 'She's always acted older than her years, and it's hard to remember how young she is.'

I'm having trouble absorbing the reality of my niece's self-harming. She's seven years old, and already she's battling internal demons. My skin prickles, remembering those raised, red sores on her thin arm.

I look at the pair of them. 'When all this is over, do you think it might help Alice if she came on her own to spend some time with me?'

'I think she'd love that,' says Karen.

'Are you sure it wouldn't be too much for you?' asks Danny.

'I'm sure. But it can only happen if I have a job.'

I go out to give Mum and the kids a hug goodbye.

And then Mouse and I head off, with Danny and Karen waving from the doorstep. All the way home, as Mouse snores on the passenger seat beside me, I'm haunted by that image of Alice's little arm covered in those angry red welts.

27

Mouse kicks off the moment I get him out of the van back at Beaulieu. He starts growling and barking, limping a few steps towards the cottage and then backing away. There's someone in the house, and Mouse is afraid of them.

The front door is shut, so I reckon they must have gained access at the back. With great difficulty, I persuade Mouse to get back into the van, where I lock him in.

Then I creep around to the back door, which has clearly been kicked in. It's hanging at an angle, attached by just one hinge. I stop on the threshold. There, inside my home, is a figure in a black hoodie. They're leaning over the table, clearly absorbed in something.

My first instinct is to go in and surprise them, but the figure glances up and spots me, so I miss my chance. They give a start, but their face is shadowed by the hood, so I can't tell if they're just surprised or actually scared by the sight of me. Before I have time to process the fact that they're heading straight towards me, the door is slamming into my torso. The force of the impact is enough to knock me to the ground. For good measure, they stamp on my right shoulder as they pass, ensuring I don't leap up to follow them.

'Ow! Shit!' I lie there, winded, and it takes me a moment to get my breath back and manage to move. I just make it to standing before a moped engine starts up and I hear it roaring off. My assailant's gone.

I stagger back to the van, clutching my throbbing shoulder. When I open the door, Mouse is still complaining, though it's more of a low grumble than a growl – he knows they've left.

I stroke his head to calm him. 'Is that the nasty person who took you away and locked you up?' I ask.

He gives what sounds like a rumble of assent.

'I won't let them hurt you again.'

I lead him inside the house, where – ignoring the sharp protests from my injured shoulder – I yank the back door until it's standing upright again in its frame. It won't offer any protection from intruders, but at least it gives the illusion of privacy.

I tell Mouse, 'We need sugar for the shock. Sweet tea for me and a nice biscuit for you.' At the word 'biscuit', his ears prick up and he goes over to the dog-food cupboard, looking up at me hopefully.

I offer him two biscuits, which he takes carefully and carries over to his bed in the corner, placing one in front of Mr Rabbit, and swallowing the other himself. I wonder if he thinks of Mr Rabbit as his pet. Actually, I'm pretty sure that's my position in the hierarchy.

Sitting with my mug of tea at the kitchen table, I pull out my mobile and call Mimi, as the chair of the residents' committee.

She answers on the first ring. 'Steph – how's your father?'

'He's doing really well, thanks.'

'Oh, that's good news.'

'Thank you. But it's not why I'm calling.' I tell her about my one-person welcome committee.

'What a dreadful thing to come back to!' she says. 'Has anything gone?'

'I haven't looked yet. I called you straight away. They were obviously reading something . . .' I glance around, looking for missing objects, and then realise: 'My notebook! That must be what they were looking at, and they've taken it.'

'Is this the book you've been using for your notes about the blackmail situation?'

'Yes.' I smack my forehead. Why didn't I take it to Peterborough, instead of leaving it here, where it was vulnerable?

'Will it be of much use to them, if they are the blackmailer?' she asks.

I think about this. 'I don't suppose it will tell them anything they don't already know. But it might put me at greater risk, if they find out I know something I shouldn't.'

'We need to get you out of that house,' she says at once. 'I'll send Jordan for you.'

I fetch my overnight bag from the van and swap out my dirty

clothes for a few clean things. Mouse is now curled up on his bed, so I can't get it ready to take. I wonder if he could sleep on cushions at Mimi's, the way he did at Danny's.

Mouse starts barking and climbs to his feet, heralding Jordan's arrival in the Land Rover much sooner than I'd expected. When I open the front door, Jordan's face is full of concern.

'Are you OK?' he asks.

I nod, still clutching my shoulder. 'Yeah. Thanks for coming out.'

'Of course.' He steps inside and gives Mouse a pat on the head, before walking through to the kitchen to inspect the broken back door. 'I can't believe this has happened at Beaulieu of all places,' he says, turning back to me. 'You and Mouse both look like you've gone several rounds in the boxing ring. Can you make it out to the car?'

I nod. 'It's only my shoulder that's bad.'

'OK.'

He takes Mouse's bed and my overnight bag, and the dog and I follow him out to the Land Rover.

As he drives the short distance to The Chimneys, Jordan says, 'Kate's fixed up a room for you. Will Mouse be all right in the utility room?'

'That sounds fine – thank you.'

When we reach the old redbrick house, he directs me towards the lovely, bright sitting room. I attempt to take a seat on a sofa, but it hurts too much to sink down on to it, so I choose one of the more upright chairs at the table instead. Through the window, the main lawn is the rich green of new foliage and spring rain.

Mimi enters, and rushes over. 'Steph, are you all right? You look so pale.' I'm touched by her evident concern. 'Let me take a look,' she says, gently removing my hand from my shoulder and putting her own in its place. I groan when she probes along the top of my arm and around to my back, lifting my arm and feeling her way, rather than looking.

'Do you know what you're doing?' I ask, as she prods me in an extra-sore spot, making me cry out.

'I am an orthopaedic surgeon,' she says. She catches my eye. 'Oh! Didn't you know?'

I shake my head. 'How do you get so much free time to run Lucy to classes?'

'Private practice. I make my own hours.' She releases my arm and I sigh in relief. 'Just badly bruised,' she says. 'But I'll fix it up for you; that should relieve some of the pain.' I hadn't noticed the roll of bandage she'd brought with her. Now, she unrolls it and fixes up a sling. I'm astonished by how much better it feels, just for the support.

'And I've brought you some painkillers,' she says, holding out a glass of water and two ibuprofen tablets. 'You're not on any medication?'

I shake my head and take the tablets, chasing them with a slug of water. 'Thank you,' I say, passing back the glass.

She smiles – a rare sight at the moment, I realise. 'You're very welcome. Now, tell me again about this intruder.'

She listens as I run through the short encounter, then says, 'And you're sure it was a moped?'

'I know my engines,' I tell her.

'Right. Hold on a moment.' She stands up and pulls a rope to summon a staff member. Kate appears, and Mimi says, 'Can you fetch Lucy please, Kate?'

'Yes, ma'am.' Kate shoots a curious glance my way, but doesn't ask any questions.

Lucy keeps us waiting. Mimi has looked at her watch twice by the time her daughter trudges in. I feel exhausted; my shoulder is throbbing, and I'm resisting the urge to ask to go to bed.

'Where have you been?' Mimi asks her daughter, rather sharply.

Lucy just says, 'Rehearsing. You know I'm working on that monologue for *The Liars*.' I've never heard of this play or show, but I don't ask.

'Well,' says Mimi. 'You know that I wouldn't call for you when you're rehearsing if it weren't important.' Lucy doesn't respond. 'Who in Beaulieu drives a moped?' asks Mimi. 'Does Adam still have his?'

Her daughter considers this. 'Probably. Why?'

'Steph has just been attacked by someone who drives a moped.'

Lucy frowns. 'If they attacked her, didn't she see them?'

'If she'd been able to identify them, would I be asking you to help?'

It's such a typical mother and teenage daughter exchange, I'm taken back to my own adolescence, and my perpetual reluctance to engage with my mother's questions, which always seemed relentless and pointless.

'I didn't see them,' I tell Lucy. 'They were wearing a deep hood, which covered their face.'

'I don't know if Adam still has his moped,' she tells her mother. 'You'd have to ask him. I know you don't like him, but you don't really think he's going around attacking *gardeners*, do you?' She says the word 'gardeners' as if it's the lowest rank in some predetermined hierarchy – so low, in fact, they don't even merit the effort it would take to assault them.

Mimi sighs. 'All I know is, someone in Beaulieu is up to no good, and it needs to stop before anyone gets seriously hurt.'

Lucy shrugs. 'Can I get back now?'

'Yes, you can get back,' Mimi sounds world-weary. 'Thank you so much for gracing us with your presence.'

If Lucy notices her mother's sarcasm, she doesn't react; she's out of the room almost before Mimi finishes the sentence.

'Right,' says my hostess. 'We'd better visit Annabelle and Zakariya, hadn't we?'

I groan inwardly as my dream of lying down recedes. 'What are we going to say when we get there?'

'We're going to ask them if their son still drives his moped and, if so, whether we might see it. If it's been driven in the past hour or so, it may even still be warm.'

It's the best plan we've got, so I agree to go along with it. I leave Mouse sleeping in the utility room, where Kate promises to keep an eye on him.

We travel over to The Towers in Mimi's Land Rover. Just climbing into the high vehicle proves excruciating. I close my eyes for a moment once I'm safely ensconced, breathing slowly and deeply, focusing outside the pain, outside myself.

At the front door of The Towers, James meets us and shows us through to a living room, which he refers to as the 'Small Parlour'. The cottage's bedroom, kitchen and bathroom would fit easily into this room's footprint. Despite my sore and exhausted state, I'm tempted to ask to be shown the Large Parlour. The room houses six wingback armchairs, plus an enormous sofa. The sofa is heaped with about a hundred small cushions. An unsuspecting person could be swallowed up by soft furnishings and never be seen again. I perch on the edge of an armchair, but Mimi sinks into the soft mass. We sit in silence for several minutes, before Annabelle comes rushing in.

'Sorry to have kept you!' says our hostess, squeezing Mimi's arm and smiling at me. 'Zak will join us in a moment. Can I offer you something to drink? Tea? Coffee?'

'I'm fine, thanks,' says Mimi.

'Steph! What happened to your arm?' asks Annabelle.

'It's a long story,' I tell her.

'We'll fill you in once Zak's here,' says Mimi.

Wistfully remembering Zakariya's hand-selected blend, I wonder if it would be out of line for me to request a coffee. I remind myself that we have come here to accuse their son of blackmail and assault. I will have to forego the coffee.

However, Annabelle puts me out of my misery by saying, 'Well, I'm dying for some caffeine. Can I really not tempt either of you?' I agree readily and she pulls a bell rope to summon a staff member before taking a seat in another armchair.

The person who answers the call is Simone. After Annabelle gives her our order, Simone turns to leave and gestures with concern at my bandaged arm. I just mouth that I'm OK.

The master of the house makes an appearance while we're waiting for the coffee. He greets us, then installs himself in another of the armchairs.

'So,' Annabelle says to Mimi. 'You made it sound important when you called?'

'Does Adam still have his moped?' asks Mimi.

Annabelle considers this. 'Didn't he get rid of that when we got him the Audi?' She looks to her husband for confirmation, and he nods.

'That's right. He said he wouldn't be using the moped, so we passed it on to his cousin Kamila.'

'Is that it?' asks Annabelle, looking from Mimi to me. 'Is that what was so urgent?'

I chime in. 'Someone broke into the cottage today and attacked me when I got back. A person with a moped.'

There's a long pause while this sinks in. Then Annabelle's pale skin flushes. 'So, what . . . ? You came round here to accuse Adam?' I have a sinking feeling I won't be tasting Mr Qureshi's coffee today. 'Our son is not a criminal. Don't you know he's training to be a lawyer?'

Mimi and I quickly murmur appeasing nonsense about having thought someone might have stolen Adam's bike, rather than suspecting the boy himself. When Annabelle has calmed down – thanks in no small part to her husband's gentle reassurances – we make our excuses and slip away. I notice that it takes Mimi three attempts to get up from the pile of cushions.

We pass Simone in the corridor.

'Oh!' she says, carrying a tray laden with cups and saucers. She looks confused at our swift departure.

'Sorry!' I say. 'It turns out we couldn't stay after all.' I could swear the scent from the coffee pot has an undertone of vanilla mixed with rose petals. I nearly cry as I walk away.

'Well, I can cross Adam off my list,' I say, after I've hauled myself painfully back into the Land Rover beside Mimi.

'Don't be too hasty,' says Mimi, setting off down the drive. 'Just because he doesn't own a moped, it doesn't mean he couldn't have hired someone who does.' For about a minute, neither of us speaks. Then she says, 'How big was the attacker?'

I consider. 'Five nine or ten,' I say. 'Smaller than Adam, now I think of it.'

'I still maintain he might have hired someone,' she says.

I'm too tired and achy to answer. My enjoyment at behaving like a detective – hunting for clues and following leads – is tempered today by the pain from my injury.

Back at the rambling old house, I check on Mouse in the utility room. He's still asleep, on his back, tongue lolling, as if he hasn't a care in the world.

Mimi and I have a quiet evening, which would be a relief if I didn't have a little time-bomb ticking away inside my brain, counting down the minutes, hours and days until I'll be out of a job. I've never worked anywhere as beautiful as Beaulieu before.

Lucy has her meal in the music room, and Mimi and I eat together. It's what she terms a 'light supper', but it consists of five courses. The food is brought in by a male staff member I don't recognise, who my host explains is on the night team. She and I stick to bland, safe topics – maintenance of the old brick walls; the removal of some low-yielding fruit trees; what plans I have for her upper gardens. I try to focus but all I can think about is the elephant in the room – that it's now day five, and in another five days, I might not have any grounds to maintain.

At least the meal is delicious. Although each course is minimalist – a cup of consommé, some crackers with pâté, a small plate of mozzarella and tomato salad, a selection of cheeses, a ramekin of gooseberry fool – I am sleepy and full by the time we finish. I'm in bed by nine, but sleep eludes me yet again. I rub my aching shoulder and keep replaying the scene with the intruder. Why didn't I react more swiftly? I should have been the one to floor them, rather than the other way around. My anxious brain keeps inventing ways in which I could have achieved this, but somehow it always ends with the hooded figure standing over me.

28

There's a thudding. With a groan, I open my eyes, dragging myself out of the sleep I'd finally achieved. It's still pitch-dark, and I try to make sense of the noise. The thudding comes again, three in a row, low and persistent.

It's the door. Someone's knocking on the door. Forgetting my injury, I roll on to my side, but the pain in my shoulder has me crying out.

'Steph, are you all right?' It's Mimi.

'Yeah . . . Just my shoulder.'

'Can I come in?' She's whispering, so I lower my own voice.

'Yes, come in.'

The door opens, and she steps inside, closing it behind her.

'I'm so sorry to wake you. Can I turn on the lamp?'

'Yeah.' I close my eyes as she reaches for the switch on the bedside lamp.

'Sorry,' she says again. 'Have you slept OK?'

I open my eyes and see she's not waiting for an answer – instead, she's pacing the room, clearly distracted.

'Is there something wrong?' I ask. 'What time is it?'

'It's 5 a.m.'

I fight the fog in my brain, trying to work out why Mimi would be waking me so early.

She whirls around to face me. 'I'm calling an emergency meeting of the committee, and you need to attend.'

'What? Now?'

She checks her watch. 'In an hour. I've called it for six.'

She places a glass of water and two ibuprofen tablets on the bedside table. 'Here, take these before you get up.'

'Thanks.'

'So, I'll drive us over at ten to six.'

'OK.'

She nods once – then leaves before I can ask any of the questions that are starting to rise through the fog in my sleep-deprived brain.

I give the painkillers twenty minutes to kick in before I get up. I'd love a shower, but I know it will be too difficult with my injury, so I just have a wash down at the basin in my room, where there are towels laid out for me. Getting dressed is a painful and awkward process, but at last I'm in a T-shirt and jogging bottoms. I take the sling downstairs, where I find Mimi – still pacing – in a small sitting room. The fire has not been lit, and it's chilly.

I hold out the sling, 'Can you . . . ?'

'Of course.' She strides over and efficiently applies the sling. The relief is instant. I pass her my hoodie and she drapes it over my shoulders. 'There's a light breakfast laid out in the dining room,' she tells me.

I hesitate, wondering whether to ask what's going on. But I don't want to skip breakfast and I figure I'll have a couple of minutes alone with her in the car on our way to The Mount.

I check on Mouse on my way to the dining room. He is still fast asleep, but I've already decided I'm not going to leave him behind when Mimi and I head out; I'll have to find some food and water for him now. There's no one in the dining room, so I walk along the corridor until I come to the kitchen, where I find Jordan seated on a stool, reading the *Telegraph*. He holds it up as I approach. 'Not my first choice of broadsheet,' he says, pulling a face, 'but the household has it delivered. How are you doing today?'

'The sling helps.'

He nods. 'It can be useful having an orthopaedic surgeon on call.'

'It certainly can.'

He smiles and I smile back, trying not to be distracted by the dimples that appear in his cheeks. Pulling myself together, I say, 'I was wondering if you might be able to find Mouse something to eat and drink before we head off this morning?'

He stands up. 'Of course. I'll take him something now. Should I wake him if he's still sleeping?'

'Oh, he'll wake the minute you take in food. Mouse has never been known to sleep through a meal.'

He laughs. 'Fair enough. Have you got everything you need? There's coffee in the big pot on the sideboard.'

'Music to my ears.'

We smile at one another some more before I head to the dining room for breakfast. The coffee is dark and strong and I feel its effect like a jolt to my brain, bringing me round. I rapidly consume a cup of fresh fruit salad, a bowl of muesli and a still-warm croissant, then head back up to my room where I clean my teeth and face before going back down to find Mouse. He's not in the utility room and I have a moment's panic before Jordan sticks his head around the door to inform me that, 'Mouse is ready in the hall.'

'Oh, right! Thank you.'

'Good luck!'

'Wait! Do I need luck?' But he's already gone.

When I reach the entrance hall, I find Mouse sitting obediently at Mimi's feet, his lead already clipped to his collar.

'Mimi, what's going on? Am I in more trouble or something?'

'It's nothing like that,' she says briskly. 'Let's get going or we'll be late.'

I follow her out to the old Defender with Mouse. I'm heartened to see that he is already starting to put a little weight on his injured paw. Mimi helps him into the back of the vehicle, then I gingerly climb into the front passenger seat, clenching my teeth as my shoulder screams at the tearing pain.

'Be careful with that shoulder,' says Mimi, a little too late.

I try to interrogate her as she drives down the steep driveway and turns right on to the lane, but she simply responds, 'It will all become clear shortly,' putting a stop to my questions.

I gaze out of the window as The Mount's gates come into view, already propped open for the meeting.

My shoulder aches at the angle of the steep drive uphill. At the top of the driveway, Mimi pulls in alongside Annabelle Qureshi's gleaming Range Rover. She comes round to help me down, and then she fetches Mouse from the back and hands me his lead. He clearly realises there's something serious going on; he looks from Mimi to me with a quizzical expression.

I suppress a shudder when we reach the black wooden hut where I so recently came under scrutiny. Mouse glances up at me again, and I murmur, 'It's all right, boy,' as much to reassure myself as him.

Mimi's seat is empty, but she turns to Bubby, who is removing her coat, and says, 'Could you take that position, please?'

Bubby looks surprised, but nods and walks over to the head of the table. Mimi pulls up a chair from the side and places herself in front of the committee, in the position where they placed me last time – what I think of as the firing line. She gestures for me to take Bubby's vacated chair, and I walk over and sit down, with Mouse under the table at my feet.

'Who are we missing?' she asks.

'Just Rupert and Fiona,' says Bubby. 'Ah! Here they are.' The door opens and the remaining couple enters. Fiona catches my eye with a concerned nod towards my sling, but now is not the time to explain.

As soon as the Penwarrens are seated, Mimi clears her throat. 'First of all, thank you all for coming at such short notice. I appreciate that some of you have offices to get to, and I am delaying you.' There's a long pause, which Bubby breaks:

'What's going on, Mimi?'

'It was me,' says Mimi.

'What was you?' asks Annabelle.

'The blackmailing.' She lifts her head defiantly and looks along the row of committee members, all of whom look sceptical.

'I don't think anyone here will believe that,' says Bubby calmly, and the others murmur in agreement.

'I have proof.' Mimi draws a small plastic bag from one of the pouch pockets of her Barbour jacket and takes something from it. I gasp.

'What is that?' says Bubby, leaning closer.

'It's my notebook,' I say. 'It's where I made all my notes trying to trace the blackmailer. It was stolen yesterday from the cottage, by someone who also knocked me to the ground and stamped on my shoulder.'

Rupert Penwarren leans forward, addressing Mimi, 'How did you come by the notebook?'

'I . . . I paid someone to break into the cottage. I'm so very sorry,' she tells me, her eyes on the floor. 'I never meant for you to get hurt.'

I rub my forehead. I can't make sense of this. It can't be Mimi. As soon as I acknowledge this fact, I understand: she's protecting someone. But who? There are only two people for whom she seems to care enough to take the fall: Sherry Patel and Lucy. So which one is she protecting? Lucy or Sherry; Sherry or Lucy . . . ?' As I'm musing, the committee are continuing their questioning of Mimi.

'But . . . why?' says Fiona. 'What did you hope to gain?'

'I just felt like causing trouble,' says Mimi. 'I don't really know why. I'm sorry.'

'This doesn't make sense,' says Annabelle Qureshi. 'I'm sorry but I don't believe you, Mimi.'

'She's protecting someone,' I say. All eyes turn to me. 'It's the only explanation. My guess is, it's Lucy.'

Mimi stands up; her cheeks are flaming red. 'How dare you? Accusing my daughter of something so sordid . . .'

'Of course,' says Bubby quietly, 'Lucy.'

'That does make sense,' agrees Fiona.

Mimi looks set to object some more, but in the face of so much opposition, she deflates visibly. She sits back down, all fight gone. 'You can't prosecute her,' she says miserably. 'She didn't understand what she was doing. She's only eighteen.'

'Old enough to know right from wrong,' says Bubby firmly.

'Agreed,' says her husband.

'What was her motive?' asks Zakariya. He seems genuinely interested, rather than angry. I remember how protective he is of his own family, and I wonder if he feels the same towards Lucy.

'She surely can't be in need of money?' says Jockey.

'No, of course not,' says Mimi. 'Connell and I make sure she always has what she needs. But I think – and I know this sounds awful – maybe she was bored. She is a very bright girl, and perhaps she wasn't being suitably stimulated . . . I blame myself for that. Perhaps I haven't been giving her enough attention.'

Bubby laughs and everyone turns to look at her. 'I'm pretty sure the term "helicopter parent" was invented for you, Mimi,' she says. 'You're a very . . . shall we say *involved* parent.'

'We're going off topic,' breaks in Zakariya. 'I need to get the seven-thirty train, and I'm pretty sure you do too, Jockey?' Jockey nods. 'So, what are we going to do about all this?'

'Please don't report her to the police,' says Mimi. 'It would be the end of her, just as she's starting out in life.' Her voice sounds low and uncertain: very un-Mimi-like.

'Mimi, you know full well we've no intention of involving the police in any of this,' says Bubby.

Mimi puts a hand to her forehead. 'Of course; I wasn't thinking.'

'How about community service?' suggests Fiona. 'She could help Steph out with the gardens – that would be karma.'

I groan inwardly at this prospect: I can't imagine Lucy being a biddable assistant.

'I think we need to get Lucy over here,' says Bubby. 'Mimi, can you call a member of staff to bring her over?'

'That isn't the best idea,' says Rupert. 'Remember, she knows all our secrets. We don't want her spilling them in front of the whole committee . . .'

'Good point,' says Jockey.

'Right,' says Bubby. 'Well, in that case, I vote we all ruminate on things, and try to decide on a suitable penalty for Lucy. Shall we reconvene in a few days, to see where we're up to?'

Chairs start to scrape back but Mimi speaks up:

'I can't wait that long!' Everyone turns to stare at her. 'Well, I'm sorry, but imagine if this was one of you – finding out your own child was guilty of planned extortion . . .'

'What do you want us to do, Mimi?' asks Fiona quietly.

'I don't know! I just know that Connell's and my discipline has somehow failed her. Oh my god: Connell! He's going to be distraught when he finds out.' She puts her face in her hands.

'Can't you ground her?' suggests Bubby.

Mimi shakes her head. 'She just climbs out of the window.'

'So lock the windows,' says Jockey. He checks his watch. 'We need to be off, Zak.'

I notice that nobody thinks to mention their wrongful accusation of me. Nonetheless, as we file out, I realise there's something else bothering me: I'd been so sure Adam was up to no good, and there is still the fact that he hurt both Apple and Lucy. Are Adam and Lucy in this together, and did they argue over the blackmailing? Perhaps Apple threatened to turn them both in. I need to speak to her.

When we reach the Land Rover, I ask Mimi, 'Would you mind dropping me at La Jolla? I want to talk to Apple about something.'

Mimi looks surprised, but is too wrapped up in her own problems to ask any questions. 'All right. Give me a call when you need a lift back.'

'Thank you.'

When we reach the top of the La Jolla driveway, Mimi pulls up beside the garages, switches off the engine and turns to look at me. 'I'm so sorry for all of this. I had no idea.'

'I know you didn't. It's not your fault.'

'That's very generous of you. Is there any chance . . . Would you consider staying on here?'

I nod. 'I love it at Beaulieu, and now this ridiculous scenario is pretty much resolved, I can't wait to get stuck back into what I'm here for: the gardening.'

'Good. That's good.'

She helps me and Mouse down, and he and I make our painful way around to the back of the house – I don't want to risk running into Jockey, so the back door seems safer. I ring the bell and the door is answered by a friendly young man who introduces himself as Joe. When I tell him my name, he says, 'You're the gardener. I hear you've been accused of sending threatening messages?' There's no malice in his tone – if anything, he seems almost apologetic. His accent is East Anglian, a burr of soft vowels and missing consonants. 'So, who are you here to see,' he continues, 'the Mr and Mrs?'

I shake my head. 'Is Apple about?'

He frowns in consideration. 'I think she's up. Let me take a look. Are you OK to wait here?' I nod, and he says, 'Be right back.'

While I'm standing outside the door, Apple comes wandering by, dressed in denim cut-offs and a long-sleeved top which looks too warm for the weather.

'Steph!' She grins and throws her arms round me. I scream with pain and she jumps back, mortified, only then spotting the sling. 'You're hurt! I'm sorry!'

'It's not your fault. I got knocked over yesterday.'

'By a car?' She looks horrified.

'No, by a person. They were in my house when I got home from Peterborough, and they rammed into me before they ran away.'

'Oh my god! That's awful! Is it broken?'

'No; Mimi said it's just badly bruised.' She nods, her face showing sweet concern. 'Is there somewhere we can talk in private?' I ask her.

'You can come up to my room. Bring Mouse.'

I glance around, checking for lurking Jockeys. 'Is your dad in?'

'He headed straight to London after some emergency committee meeting. Did you need to see him?'

'No, that's fine,' I say, following her into the house.

I have never seen a bedroom as big as Apple's. It even has a mezzanine level, which appears to contain rack after rack of clothes. The pink carpet has the kind of thick pile I've only previously seen on TV dramas featuring rich people.

'We can sit on my bed,' she says, gesturing to the huge four-poster in white iron with pink velvet curtains.

We perch on the bed with Mouse stretched on the floor at our feet, and she says, 'Mummy messaged just now to say that you've been cleared?'

'Yes, that's right.'

'That's great. Mummy didn't say who did it, though.'

I hesitate, then decide to go for it: 'It was Lucy.'

She thinks for a moment, then her eyes widen. 'Of course – why didn't we think of that?'

'Who's "we" – you and Nicola?'

'Nicola?' she laughs. 'No – me and Adam.'

'You're still seeing him, even after he hurt you?'

She looks confused. 'Adam never hurt me.'

'But I saw him that day, remember? He was grabbing your wrists and you were arguing.'

'He wasn't hurting me; he was just trying to persuade me to tell Mummy and Daddy about . . . something.'

'What something?' I ask. She doesn't meet my eye. I wait for a moment, but she says nothing. 'So, if Adam hasn't hurt you, why are you wearing a thick sweater? It's unseasonably warm this morning.'

She looks at me for a moment, before standing up. She pushes her sleeves all the way up, to expose bracelets of bruises around the tops of both arms. The range of colours shows they date from more than one occasion.

'Oh my god! Who did this to you?'

She isn't looking at me as she says, 'Lucy.'

'Lucy? But why?'

'She said it was to stop me from telling anyone about her and . . . her boyfriend.'

'Her boyfriend?' I say. 'Who is he? Please tell me, Apple: I think it might be important.'

'It's the old gardener, Simon,' she says. 'They've been sleeping together since she was fifteen; that's why Ms Purdue had him fired.'

29

At my request for a lift, Apple asks her sister to take me back to The Chimneys while she looks after Mouse for me. As I leave the bedroom, I look back and see Apple helping Mouse on to the bed; he's going to have a lovely time.

Nicola steers her sporty blue BMW Z Roadster quickly and smoothly, like a racing driver. When the BMW takes the uphill drive almost as easily as if it were on the flat, I can't help but think of my poor old van's struggles.

As we near the top of the long driveway, we see Lucy getting into a taxi, with Mimi standing beside her. Nicola stops at once to let me out. I lever myself out from the low seat with a groan, and walk over to where Lucy is standing with the taxi door open.

Mimi comes to meet me. 'Hi, Steph. I see you got a lift. You go on inside. I'm just seeing Lucy off; she's going to her dad's for a little while.'

'Actually, it's Lucy I want to speak to.'

Mimi frowns. 'We discussed this at the meeting – the committee wants some time to reflect on next steps.'

'I know. This isn't about the blackmailing.'

'Then what . . . ?'

But I turn away from Mimi and look straight at Lucy.

She rolls her eyes. 'What do you want now? Dad's waiting for me.'

'Apple,' I say.

She sighs. 'What about her?'

'She showed me the bruises.'

Lucy shuts the taxi door and says, 'Mum, can you give us a minute?'

Mimi is looking from one of us to the other. She says, 'What bruises? What is she talking about, Lucy?'

'It's all right; you can leave us to talk.'

'I think I'll stay,' says Mimi.

Lucy turns to her mother and fixes her with a look that suggests Mimi rates somewhere between an insignificant ant and a mildly irritating fly. 'I don't need you here.'

Mimi folds her arms. 'Nevertheless, I am staying.'

Lucy shrugs and turns back to me. 'What did Apple say?'

'That you've been hurting her for months – possibly longer, if the bruises are anything to go by.'

'Lucy wouldn't hurt a fly!' protests her mother.

Without turning towards Mimi, Lucy says calmly, 'She's a liar; you must have worked that out by now.'

'I don't think she's lying.'

Mimi butts in: 'How dare you come over here – where I've taken you in and given you food and shelter – and start accusing my daughter?' I don't point out that I wouldn't have needed the food and shelter if it weren't for her daughter.

I keep my gaze on Lucy. 'You can't just hurt people when they get in your way.'

'You've met Apple; didn't you find her annoying?' asks Lucy.

'Please tell me you didn't do it,' Mimi says quietly.

Lucy shrugs. 'She kept threatening to tell . . . a secret.'

'About you and Simon,' I say. It may be shallow of me, but I get a small sense of satisfaction from witnessing Lucy's eyes widen in surprise.

'How did you . . . ?' she hisses.

'Apple told me, of course.'

'I take it you're talking about the former gardener?' Mimi says to her daughter.

Lucy ignores her. Her eyes are narrowed and her face is a mask of hatred. 'That little bitch . . . When I see her, I'll—'

'No, you won't,' interrupts Mimi coldly. 'You won't be going near Apple Singer-Pryce again. And please tell me you haven't been seeing Simon Drake.'

Lucy shoots her a dismissive look. 'Yeah, I've been seeing him. So what? You can't stop us. He loves me.'

Mimi laughs. 'Oh, Lucy, you little fool. He just wants to get his own back on me, for having him dismissed.'

'He thinks I'm beautiful,' says Lucy.

'Of course you're beautiful,' says Mimi. 'But he's a grown man.'

'I'm eighteen,' she says defiantly.

'Exactly: barely more than a child. That despicable man took advantage of you, and I won't have him doing it any more.'

'You mean you knew?' Lucy is facing her mother now.

'Why do you think I had him fired?' says Mimi. 'I'm just ashamed it took me so long to realise what was going on.'

'Why didn't you say anything?'

'I know I should have talked to you,' says Mimi, her voice breaking. 'But after losing one child, I couldn't face the possibility of losing you, as well.'

I break in, 'Why didn't you turn him in to the police? If Lucy was underage, it was against the law.'

Mimi looks at me. 'Underage? What are you talking about?'

'I thought . . . Didn't it start when you were fifteen?' I ask Lucy.

'None of your fucking business.'

'Fifteen . . . ?' says Mimi. Her voice lacks all of its usual strident self-possession.

Lucy just glowers.

With a sigh, I bring the conversation back to the present. 'Was Simon behind the blackmail?' I ask Lucy.

She rolls her eyes again. 'Simon? He's hot, but he's not especially bright. No, it was my idea.'

I press my point: 'But he was in on it?'

'If you count typing up the notes and printing them off, and doing a bit of the muscle work . . .' she says.

'I do.'

'And so do I,' says Mimi. 'Was it Simon who hurt Steph?'

Lucy nods and looks at me. 'We didn't expect you to come back so soon,' she says in an accusing tone.

'Well, haven't you got anything to say to Steph?' says Mimi, as if Lucy and I are six and she has accidentally broken my skipping rope.

'Not really,' says Lucy. 'It's her own fault for getting involved.'

'Narcissist,' I say. I'd been thinking it, and hadn't actually meant to say it aloud. I did Psychology for A level, and tend to diagnose people in an instinctive fashion that I'm pretty sure would horrify most professionals in the field.

Mimi tuts. 'If you mean Lucy, I have looked into it, and discovered that narcissists can't feel love for another person,' she says briskly. 'So obviously Lucy doesn't fit the profile.' I wonder if she's trying to convince me or herself.

'You've been checking to see if I'm a narcissist?' Lucy laughs. 'God, Mum, get a grip. I'm your child – I'm only what you made me.'

'Yes, and sadly that would appear to be a spoilt, unfeeling little brat,' says Mimi. Neither of us is prepared for Lucy's hand, which jerks up and slaps her mother hard in the face.

While Mimi reels, another thought occurs to me.

'I have to say, you really had me fooled on one thing,' I say.

Lucy is turning as if to leave; with a sigh she turns back. 'Is this going to take all night? Only Dad's booked The Ivy for dinner.'

'Just a minute or two. It's only that I really thought Adam Qureshi had slapped you that day.'

She frowns. 'Of course he slapped me. You saw my face – you even gave me that cream for it.'

'Yes. And it's only after something that happened with my niece that I realised the truth.' She narrows her eyes: I have her full attention. 'You slapped yourself.'

'Don't be stupid. Why would I do that?'

'Let's see: to draw attention away from yourself as the blackmailer and throw suspicion on to Adam. After all, a man who could smack a woman might be capable of anything.'

'No comment,' says Lucy.

Another thought occurs to me. I turn to Mimi, 'Tell me, do you have a smokehouse – for smoking food, I mean?'

'What . . . ?' She looks confused. 'Yes, we have one over near the wildflower area – it's an old brick building, which we had adapted.'

'Does it have an earth floor?' I ask.

'Yes, I think so.'

'That's where Simon locked Mouse up,' I say. 'After he was stolen, he came home smelling of wood smoke, but I couldn't work out where it was from. He must have dug his way out.'

'Good lord,' says Mimi.

'What was going to happen next in the blackmail scheme?' I ask Lucy.

'Simon will probably still want to go ahead,' she says. 'I mean, Mum can't really stop him, can she? He knows all the dirt on everyone.'

'Oh, Lucy!' says Mimi in horror, but her daughter ignores her, continuing:

'The residents are going to get one more note, and it's one they definitely won't want anyone else to see. It'll include a demand for money. When they pay up, Simon and I are going to move to London, so I can go to LAMDA or the Central School for my acting.' I don't point out that she'd have to pass some tough auditions to go to either of those schools.

Mimi looks astonished. 'But . . . you can do that from here – you don't need to live in central London.'

'Don't you get it? I don't want to live with you anymore. I'm tired of playing happy families. I'm not that keen on Simon, but at least he's easy to manipulate.'

Mimi recoils, as if her daughter has slapped her a second time.

'I'm going to Dad's now,' says Lucy.

There's one more thing I need to ask. 'Before you go . . .' I hesitate, but I have to find out the truth. 'Why did you kill your brother?'

I hear Mimi gasp, but Lucy responds immediately, blank-faced: 'I didn't kill him.'

Strangely, it's her lack of expression that convinces me otherwise.

'I don't believe you,' I say. 'I don't think a boy who could swim would have drowned in that pond unless someone had held him under the water.'

'I didn't hold him there; I only pushed him in. He was being really annoying. It's not my fault he caught his shirt on something and couldn't get out.'

Mimi has been listening, and she cries out, 'No . . . Lucy, you wouldn't have hurt Alfie. You loved him. He was your little brother.'

I keep my gaze on Lucy. 'He was a living person, just a child,' I say, 'and, because of you, he drowned. Don't you feel anything?'

Her expression is scornful. 'He was never my brother. He didn't even look like me.'

'It can't be true . . .' says Mimi. Her voice is tight and she's bent forward with grief, as if the new knowledge is a literal weight for her to bear. I feel awful for her, but I am only the conduit, not the cause of her pain.

And then, without a word or look towards her mother, Lucy starts walking towards the waiting taxi. Instinctively, I reach out to stop her. But I have forgotten about her martial arts training: without glancing back, she rams her elbow into my gut. Doubled over with pain and panting for breath, I can only listen as the car door slams and the vehicle drives away. Somewhere outside my field of vision, I can hear Mimi's wrenching sobs.

30

'Do you have any proof of Simon Drake's involvement?' asks Bubby.

The residents' committee is in session again, with Bubby Singer-Pryce at the head of the table in Mimi's place, and me in Bubby's seat. Mimi has been excluded from this meeting.

I've told them everything Lucy revealed to me – bar her brother's murder.

'No, I don't have proof,' I admit. 'But it makes sense: Lucy has been supplying Simon with information, and he's behind the notes. He wants the money, and it sounds like he believes he was unfairly dismissed.'

Fiona snorts at this, but doesn't say anything.

Bubby taps her pen on the table. 'Well, if Simon is involved, we need to find a way to stop him.'

'I have something,' says Jockey. All eyes turn towards him. He coughs and leans back in his chair, his hands folded on his stomach. 'It's a little awkward, but . . . well, Bubby and I host these parties occasionally . . .'

'Jockey, what are you doing?' says his wife in a warning tone. He holds up a hand to her and continues.

'It's just, I have a camera in my house and . . .'

'Are you saying you have footage of our former gardener engaged in potentially compromising activities?' asks Annabelle briskly.

Jockey nods. 'There is definitely some film that might make it . . . shall we say difficult for him to work again . . . ?'

Zakariya leans forward. 'So we let him go, with the threat that if he ever tries to blackmail us again – or we hear of him trying the same trick elsewhere – we will release the film to his new employer?'

'Exactly,' says Jockey, beaming.

The committee members start to smile. However, Fiona sighs loudly, and everyone looks at her.

'Well, it's just . . . the man is a scumbag,' she says, 'and he'll walk free. This can't be our only option.'

'I'm afraid it probably is,' says Bubby. 'Unless several members of this committee want to go to prison when their secrets are exposed to the police.' No one looks thrilled at that prospect. 'Now, who wants to talk to Simon?' she asks.

'I'll do it,' says Jockey. 'After all, I am the one with the ammunition.'

'Great, so that's decided; well done, Jockey. In that case, I think we're done here.'

The residents start to push back their chairs, but Fiona speaks up: 'Before we go . . .' She glances along the table, catching each person's eye. 'I think we owe Steph a big apology, don't you?'

There's an embarrassed mumbling, then Bubby says, 'You're quite right.' She turns to me. 'It seems we've done you a great injustice, Steph. I'm sure I speak for all of us when I say how sorry we are for falsely accusing you, and I hope we can persuade you to stay, in spite of how fraught things became for a while.'

'I'll stay,' I say. 'I'd like to see the results of the work I've done so far, and follow through with my plans for Mimi's garden in particular. But I don't want any more of these accusations.'

'We still don't know who's behind the thefts,' says Zakariya, earning him a sharp look from his wife. 'Not that I was suggesting . . .'

I smile brightly. 'As I said, I don't want to be accused of any more crimes or misdemeanours. I've noticed security is lax across Beaulieu. You all need to have words with your families and staff about not buzzing anyone in, without first making sure of their identity.'

'That is very sound advice,' says Bubby. 'Now, if we're finished here . . . ?'

'Actually,' I continue, addressing the committee, 'I'd like to hire an undergardener. It's too much work for a single person.'

Bubby glances around at the other residents, who all nod their assent.

'Agreed,' she says. 'Do you have someone in mind?'

'Would you consider letting Simone come to me for training, if she'd like to?' I ask Annabelle and Zakariya.

'Simone from our staff?' says Annabelle in surprise. She glances at her husband, who shrugs. 'I guess so,' she says. 'We can get someone else from the agency. She probably is a bit too bright to be stuck polishing the silver.'

'And I'd like it written into Simone's contract that even if I leave down the line, her job will be protected and her gardener training will continue,' I say.

'Well, if those are all your demands . . .' says Bubby wryly, stacking her notes.

'Actually, there is one more thing,' I say. 'I'd like a few days off before I start back. I'm going to bring my niece here for a short break while it's still the Easter holidays.'

'That sounds reasonable,' says Rupert. 'With all the things Steph's been through, I think a few days off are essential for her recuperation.'

I shoot him a smile and mouth, 'Thank you.'

Bubby nods then pushes back her chair and stands up. This is the signal for everyone to rise to their feet, pull on their coats and head towards the door.

Fiona comes to my side as I'm on my way out, and links her arm through my good one. 'I'm so glad you're staying,' she says, smiling at me.

I smile back. 'I'm not the one who wanted me to leave,' I say. 'Thanks so much for standing by me.'

'Of course. The whole thing was ridiculous.' She lowers her voice. 'Pompous arseholes the lot of them.' I burst out laughing – it's such an un-Fiona-like thing to say.

31

Alice is wildly excited to be staying with her Auntie Lou for the last few days of the Easter holidays. She doesn't seem to mind that she has to sleep on a blow-up mattress in my bedroom, nor that Mouse likes to share it with her, stretching out so much that she often ends up on the floor.

Apple pretty much adopts Alice by day, and my niece follows her around in besotted fashion. Her new big sister treats her to make-up sessions in her impressive bedroom, with that covetable four-poster bed. I spend a lot of time with make-up remover, wiping off glitter eyeshadow and wet-look lip gloss.

One afternoon, I have the chance to talk to Apple, while Alice is playing on the mezzanine level, trying on different outfits in front of the mirror.

'How are you and Nicola getting on these days?' I ask her.

Apple thinks for a moment. 'A lot better, actually. She's spending quite a bit more time with me. I think she was really shocked about what happened with Lucy.' There's a long pause, and I guess she's remembering Lucy's controlling behaviour, and how the girl hurt her to keep her quiet.

'You know you must always tell someone in future, if anything like that happens?'

'I know.' She gives me a hug, which barely hurts – my shoulder is healing well. 'Thank you, Auntie Lou.' We both laugh. She's been calling me 'Auntie Lou' since she heard Alice call me by that name. 'Hey! Did you hear about Simon?'

I shake my head. 'What about him?'

'Only that he hasn't contacted Lucy once since all this blew up. Apparently, she's devastated.'

'I bet she is. And are her parents doing anything about restricting her freedom?'

'They've made her stop her performing arts course. She's gutted – she thought she was the next Jodie Comer or something. I think Mummy said her dad's taking her to see a psychiatrist, but she didn't say what for.'

'Apple, come and see!' We glance up to see Alice peering over the railing of the mezzanine level. 'I've made a really cool outfit.'

'I'll be right there,' calls Apple, standing up and heading for the stairs.

One night, I call at La Jolla quite late to collect Alice, having been delayed by a phone call from Mum, who has gone back to calling on a weekly basis, like in the old days. Neither of us has yet brought up the subject of tracing my birth parents, but I'm happy she's speaking to me again.

As I reach the top of the driveway at La Jolla, my headlights pick out another van, pulled in at the garage. The back is open, and two figures are loading something large and obviously heavy into the cargo space.

I stop, blocking the exit with my vehicle, and get down, carrying a torch and leaving Mouse in the van. I have my mobile out, ready to dial 999.

'What's going on?' I call, wary of getting too close. But then I recognise one of the figures: 'James?' The Qureshis' house manager flinches at the sound of his name. I move the beam across to his companion. It takes me a moment to recognise Adam, who's wearing a dark woollen hat to cover his blond hair.

'Are you two stealing something from here?'

'No, of course not,' says Adam. 'It's just something we were asked to collect for a charity auction.'

'If that's true, you won't mind if I knock on the front door to check . . .' I say, starting to stride towards the house. My heart is beating hard.

'Wait!' Adam has caught up. He places a hand on my shoulder and I shake it off. 'Please,' he says. 'Just hear me out.'

His voice is soft and pleading, and not at all threatening. 'OK, but you have to take three steps away from me.'

He backs away. 'Sorry. I didn't mean to freak you out. I haven't really got permission to take this stuff.'

'Did you take the other things – the urns, the goldfish fountain and the sculpture?'

'Yeah . . . It's complicated.'

'Go on – I'm listening.'

'If we could move back towards the garage, where we can't be seen from the house . . .'

'No. I'm happier here, where we can be seen.'

'OK. Well, I have been stealing from the neighbours. But it's not for me. I've been selling everything to help pay for a new shelter for rough sleepers that's being built in North London.'

'Seriously?'

'Yeah. I mean, Ma and Pa have been great, really – they've given tonnes of money. But a building like that, with all the stuff we want to provide, well it costs a fortune.'

'I can imagine. But you can't keep stealing from your neighbours, Adam, you must see that?'

'It's just, everyone here has so much. And they all have insurance. If you could see the kids at the charity, how little they have. And they don't even complain. It makes me so angry.'

'So, complete your degree and go into politics, to make a real difference. Don't end up in prison, where you'll be no help to anyone.'

'Are you going to turn me in?'

'I don't know. Have you still got the pieces you stole?'

'No. I passed them all on and got the money for them.'

'So you can't return them . . .' I think for a moment. 'You need to tell your parents, and give them the chance to pay your neighbours back for what you've taken.'

'Tell Ma and Pa?' he sounds horrified. 'They think I'm this perfect son.'

'Well, that's not the healthiest basis for a relationship, is it? You can't live up to that all your life. Anyway, from what I've seen of your dad, he'll support you whatever you've done.'

'And if I do this – talk to my parents – you won't turn me in to the police? And please keep James out of this; he had nothing to do with it.'

'You give your parents a chance to put things right and I won't go to the police,' I agree. 'Of course, I can't guarantee your neighbours will feel as forgiving.'

'Sure, sure,' he says. He's quiet for a moment, then he holds out his hand. 'You have a deal,' he says. 'Thank you so much.'

I shake his hand. 'That's all right.'

Epilogue

As summer arrives, the gardens grow into the best version of themselves, and Simone and I are richly rewarded for our hard work. The walled garden at The Towers becomes filled with the delicate scent and petals of the tea roses, with a backdrop of mature clematis running along the old brick walls. We visit a couple of times a week, deadheading the roses to ensure continuous blooming. After Adam's confession, the Qureshis were able to track down the Hepworth and buy it back, and it stands again on its plinth, providing the promised angular silhouette to temper the romantic frills of the roses.

The white garden is equally lovely, with dense yew hedging offsetting white roses, clematis, lychnis and geraniums. The grounds were so well planned that our main work here has been weeding and pruning to maintain them. There is one big difference though: the gate to the secret lab is no longer locked, and Simone and I have taken advantage of the self-seeded plants in that area to introduce a miniature wildflower meadow, filled with the likes of oxeye daisies, lesser knapweed, evening primrose and cowslips.

La Jolla's tropical garden has also come into its own, the giant leaves of gunnera and delicate fronds of palms spotlit by the white flowers of zantedeschia (arum lilies). The shrub and flower borders elsewhere in the grounds are packed with colour, and abuzz with the hum of insects, from hoverflies to honey bees.

The pond at Villa Splendida is now clear, and the many fish are visible, hopefully appreciating their improved environment. I never got around to moving the kitchen garden to a more convenient spot, and the house is currently standing empty bar a couple of staff, including Francis. They are awaiting the arrival of new owners, who are due to move in later in the year. Sherry has gone abroad, and Mimi tells me she's been reunited with her husband; I'm glad they're back together, but I can only hope he has learnt his lesson about cheating people out of their hard-earned savings. Francis, Simone and I regularly take coffee together on the bench at the front, overlooking the amazing view. He tells us about his partner Jean-Louis, and how they will soon have enough money saved to buy a little cottage of their own.

The Mount's garden has only needed maintaining. I visit there as much to take coffee with Fiona as to weed the borders. Her relationship with Rupert seems to have strengthened since she discovered his secret, and he often works from home these days. Simone and I see them at lunchtime, strolling past the topiary animals or sitting on a bench in the front garden, watching the koi carp plough through the water.

'That's what I want,' says Simone one day, as we spot them walking in the woodland.

'What? A wood?'

She laughs. 'No – that kind of relationship. They seem really happy just hanging out together, don't they?'

'They really do,' I agree.

My greatest pleasure at Beaulieu comes from visiting The Chimneys, where Simone and I brought in extra help in late spring to clear the brambles and ivy from some of the trickier areas. As a result, the previously smothered and stunted trees and shrubs are now pushing their branches towards the sky, as if stretching after a long sleep. The faded, low, redbrick walls have all now been revealed; they run alongside pretty herringbone pathways that meander beneath mature trees. The shade here is dappled and enticing. It's impossible to visit The Chimneys and not feel tempted to explore. I can't deny that there is another attraction for me, too: Jordan and I have become close. I'm not sure if it constitutes a relationship yet – Ben burnt me too badly for me to be ready to trust someone else – but I love Jordan's company: he's fascinating and witty, and has me enthralled with his tales about the guests in the upmarket hotel he used to manage. He's also great with Mouse.

Of course, Mouse's favourite place is The Towers, where he can play with Fritz and Mitzi and get delicious home-cooked food, so sometimes I drop him off there on my way to work.

One evening in late October, an email comes through as Mouse and I are sitting on the sofa. It's from the owner of a small stately home in Derbyshire. Apparently, Lady Clara Fanshawe has been following my website, where I've been posting regular updates on the progress at The Chimneys. She declares herself 'quite impressed at your approach to renovating the grounds in such a way as to retain their connection to their setting,' and wonders 'whether you might consider taking on the grounds at Ashford Manor, which I have recently inherited from my mother?' She explains that she and her husband have come across some old garden plans, and need someone who can reinstate those designs. As a further enticement, she instructs me to 'let us know your fees and other requirements. We can offer you a charming set of rooms in the Round Wing, should you be happy to stay on site.'

The email chimes perfectly with a growing sense of restlessness I've been experiencing since finishing the renovation at The Chimneys. Beaulieu is gorgeous, but I no longer feel *needed* in the way I did when I first arrived. The position at Ashford Manor would allow me to reinvent myself as a gardening consultant for shorter-term jobs, which definitely appeals. I love the idea of moving from one challenge to another.

I look at Mouse, who is sitting very upright in front of the television, rumbling as he watches a school of sharks.

'What do you think, boy? Are we ready for a new challenge?'

He turns away from the screen and barks once before turning back to his programme.

'I'll take that as a yes,' I tell him. 'Hopefully, there will be far less drama at the new place. Although I should warn you: it rains a lot more in Derbyshire than it does here.' He doesn't respond, so I turn back to my laptop, click on 'Reply' and begin to thank her ladyship for her kind enquiry, expressing my keen interest in holding a video or telephone call soon, in order to discuss her project in more detail.

And then my email pings again – this time with a communication from the General Register Office, which manages the Adoption

Contact Register. Apparently, one of my birth parents has added their own details to the Register, hoping to make contact with me.

It's happening. And all of a sudden I don't feel ready. I close my laptop as the sharks programme ends and Mouse comes over.

We stroll out into the garden. It's a bright night, thanks to a glorious, orange-tinged full moon, and I stand outside while Mouse makes his way around the night scents. As I listen to the birds that make their strange calls in the dark, I can't help thinking how lucky I am that, of all the diverse industry placements I could have been offered when I applied for my apprenticeship at eighteen, it was a local gardener who agreed to train me.

Acknowledgements

My thanks are due to the many wonderful people who have supported me in my various writing projects. I hope I haven't missed anyone . . .

First of all, my fabulous agent, Jenny Todd: thank you so much for all your hard work, encouragement, cheerleading and support. You're a star.

My wonderful publisher, Embla Books, especially Jane Snelgrove for her exceptional, incisive and thoughtful editing; Mel Hayes for her energetic support, motivation and ideas, plus Anna Perkins and Hannah Deuce for their industry knowledge and kindness – and, of course, the rest of the team for their support and enthusiasm.

Thomas, Andrew and Robert: you're the best. Helen Sandler for her publishing knowledge and for being the best sister.

Sophie Hannah for generous mentoring and editorial input via her 'Dream Author' mentoring scheme.

Christina Erskine at The Urban Hedgerow (urbanhedgerow. co.uk) for horticultural expertise. Susan Erskine for arboreal advice. All mistakes in this area are my own.

Kevin Conroy Scott and the rest of the team at Tibor Jones for giving me the opportunity to cut my teeth on the *Agatha Oddly* detective books for HarperCollins. Authors Emma Pass and Jane Linfoot for their wonderful kindness, generosity and advice surrounding elevator pitches and more. Amanda Preston for being lovely.

My copy editor, Laura Gerrard, and proofreaders, Kay Coleman and Emily Thomas, for their eagle-eyed attention to detail. And, of course, Lisa Brewster, for her lovely cover and illustration.

My team of wonderful beta readers and friends, who have given me ongoing editorial advice and support over the years: Kathy Adamson, Deborah Carden, Clare Chapple, Sue Fleming, Carolyn Hall, Nick Houston (for advice on vans and tailgates!), Sigrid Houston, Sally Marks, Louise Sankey, Jane Scott-Simons, Julie Standen.

Want to find out what gardening-related murder mystery Steph Williams must solve next?

Then don't miss the second book in the series, coming soon!

MURDER TAKES ROOT

Rosie Sandler

Rosie Sandler lives in Essex, UK, where she writes novels, poetry and short stories, and is an editor and creative writing tutor. She loves dressmaking and wearing colourful outfits, which often leads to joyful encounters with strangers. Although she enjoys visiting beautifully tended gardens, Rosie's own garden is a bit on the wild side (her excuse is that this encourages hedgehogs and other wildlife). She dreams that she and her husband will one day live beside a lake. Or at least a big puddle. Rosie is co-author of the Agatha Oddly trilogy of children's detective novels.

About Embla Books

Embla Books is a digital-first publisher of standout commercial adult fiction. Passionate about storytelling, the team at Embla publish books that will make you 'laugh, love, look over your shoulder and lose sleep'. Launched by Bonnier Books UK in 2021, the imprint is named after the first woman from the creation myth in Norse mythology, who was carved by the gods from a tree trunk found on the seashore – an image of the kind of creative work and crafting that writers do, and a symbol of how stories shape our lives.

Find out about some of our other books and stay in touch:

Twitter, Facebook, Instagram: @emblabooks
Newsletter: https://bit.ly/emblanewsletter